The Many Worlds of Mickie Dalton

The First Volume in the Mickie Dalton Trilogy

Michael Davies

The Many Worlds of Mickie Dalton

First Printing June 2008
Second Printing October 2008

ISBN: 978-0-9818087-0-3

First Printing In the USA
Second printing in Australia
Third Printing in the USA

Published by The Mickie Dalton Foundation
Kempsey, NSW
Australia

Acknowledgements

The project to develop this trilogy took place at St Joseph's Catholic High School in Albion Park, NSW. It could not have happened without the consent and support of the Principal, Mr Peter McGovern and the Head of English, Mr Andrew Rout. To both of you, my huge gratitude. Classes were enthusiastic, exciting and often noisy events and my thanks to Leanne Whittall who controlled us all with consummate ease! Thanks also to Jennifer Rush for setting up the contact with Andrew Rout.

And to that extraordinary group of intelligent, creative, analytical and funny young people who made this project such a profound experience, my eternal thanks. I will never forget you.

James Arblaster
Paul Foster
James Goddard
Evan Hayes
Vincent Muller
Alicia Quinn
Samuel Troutman
Sebastian Wattam

Catherine Fitzpatrick
Melissa Foye
Michael Guinery
Gabrielle McCann
Adam Piovarchy
Michael Robson
Tarryn (TJ) Viney

To Callum Mackay, for a long time the only person besides myself who saw this book under development. Callum was the source of perspective from the target age group and his enthusiasm, intelligence and advice drove the story with great momentum.

To Linda Carlson who read the manuscripts of this and the following books in the trilogy and provided insights and support that greatly enhanced the story.

Also by Michael Davies

The Nightmares of God
The Janus Conspiracy
Accounts of a Killing
A Friendly Killing
Dreamkill
Ready, Steady, KILL!

For the Young Adults (12-18)
The Many Galaxies of Mickie Dalton
The Many Universes of Mickie Dalton

For the 8-12 age group
The Julie Malloy Gang and the Smugglers
The Quest for the Locket
The Secret of Yuri Kirilenko
The United Nations and the Extra-Terrestrial
The Secret of Charlotte's Cello
The Star of the Yshan Kings
The War of the Yshan Empire
The Red Fog of Time
The Mysterious Recorder and The Door to Elsewhere
Prisoners of the Picture

For the Little Ones (3-5)
Mary's World

And in non-fiction
The Business School Approach to Writing Your Novel

To John and Lesley Read

For the many decades of friendship

Chapter 1 – A Miserable Home

Twelve-year old Mickie Dalton looked round the dining table and knew he had to leave home.

His father was crouched over the newspaper like a vulture examining a corpse, slurping his soup and intermittently erupting with a snort like a diesel engine threatening to draw the oxygen from the room. When he reached for a slice of bread, he bit into it then jammed the remainder into his mouth as if the bread might struggle and slip away. The smacking sound of his eating was even noisier than the soup-slurping. Mickie's mother had put down her spoon and was surreptitiously eyeing her packet of Player's Extra Mild cigarettes, parked with its box of matches dangerously close to her right hand. The ashtray, a handbreadth farther away, already contained two lipstick-tipped stubs of earlier satisfaction. Mickie prayed that she wouldn't succumb to the temptation, for, if she did, smoke and ash would float over the table again, settling on his food and giving it an acrid, bitter taste. His father would follow the example, making the air even worse, while his mother's hacking cough would blast through the room before she spat phlegm into her handkerchief. Sometimes, Mickie gagged and nearly threw up when she did that, which invariably got his father's attention, which was always a dangerous thing.

"Please, God, don't let her take a cigarette," pleaded Mickie silently but with little hope. "Please don't let her start coughing and spitting. Please don't make him take one, as well. Please, God."

Apparently immune to the noisy proceedings and his desperate communion with the Supreme Deity, Mickie's older sister, an incomprehensibly alien creature separated from him by exactly two years, stared blankly at the centre of the table. Mickie had no idea where her mind was. She picked her nose idly, a crime tolerated in her, but punishable by a furious thrashing if committed by him.

Mickie disliked them all intensely. He knew he could leave home at sixteen. He knew that, because he had asked his teacher at school what was the earliest time he could go off and start work. She seemed upset by the question, for reasons that Mickie could not understand, but told him the answer gently. Once again in an endless series of times, he tried to comprehend the idea of four more years of this terrifying, damaging and miserable place called his home. *Four more years!* That was about a third as long again as he had lived already! It was a time-scale by which to measure the lives of stars and galaxies. He had no idea how to survive it.

His father sniffed again, and the ugly noise gave his mother permission for her urgent want and need to be satisfied. She reached hungrily for the cigarette packet, almost tearing the cardboard as she opened it. Mickie knew that the second course would be delayed by another fifteen minutes and would taste awful when it came.

The smoke hit him, and he coughed. He struggled for breath and coughed again. His father lowered the paper and glared at him.

"What's the matter with you?" he snapped.

Mickie felt panic wash over his body like slimy water. His throat constricted, his cheeks flamed. To the side, he saw his sister return to the world, and stare at him in the same furious way as his father as if trying to share the rage and enjoy it more. Anticipation grew in her eyes. Mickie stared down at his plate, paralysed by the familiar, awful events unfolding.

"Nothing," he mumbled.

"What do you mean, nothing?" shouted his father. He crushed the paper under his arms, warming up for action. Paralysing terror overtook Mickie. He could only shake his head.

"I said, what do you *MEAN?* Eh? What do you mean?" The shout had become a roar. The man stood up, threw the paper to one side and grabbed Mickie by the shoulder.

"Look!" he bellowed, bending over the boy. "I'm totally fed up with you, you stupid little pig!" His right hand landed flat and hard on Mickie's cheek, and Mickie fell backward against his chair. Familiar terror ran through him mixed with shame and anger that he had to put up with this senseless and undeserved violence once more.

"Oh, Jack, he didn't mean anything!" At last, his mother spoke. She didn't seem all that worried. Her cigarette was lit and in its place in the corner of her mouth, and all was right with her world. Her husband ignored her. Another open-handed slap landed on Mickie's cheek, rocking him sideways. He could barely

3

breathe and could look nowhere but down at the floor as the violence flared around him. His cheeks stung and the heat of his shame made the tears feel cold as they ran.

"Now get upstairs to your room!" said his father in cold contempt, his anger for the moment sated by the short burst of violence.

Struggling to keep the tears away and losing, Mickie ran out of the room, up the stairs and into his tiny bedroom. He resisted the urge to slam the door behind, because nothing was more certain to bring his father roaring into his room to administer another beating. He sat on his bed, the tears falling freely down his face. He was hungry, but he knew he would not see anything of the meal tonight. His mother had more important things to concern her than bringing him dinner.

Apart from his single bed the bare, stark room contained nothing but, a simple kitchen chair and a small table where he did his homework. There was a book lying on the table. He stood, picked up the book and pushed the chair to the open window. There would be enough light to read for another hour or two on this English summer night. Then he would have to retreat into imagination of a different sort, for electric light was not permitted in his room. He still had bruises from the last time his father had seen the dim glow of the small bulb, thundered into his room and kicked him out of bed shouting, "Who the hell pays the electricity bill around here?" Mickie wondered why both parents and his sister were able to read in their rooms without that unanswerable query being raised. It was merely another element of the great mystery of why his father hated him so much.

Downstairs, both parents erupted into coughing fits

that inexorably followed the lighting of a new cigarette. Mickie rubbed his eyes, wiped his nose, and opened the book. Within minutes, he was lost in the thunderous, bloody story of *Beowulf*.

When it became too dark to read any further, he crawled into bed. In the friendly gloom he imagined scenes of great excitement and action with himself as the hero. He flew jet fighters, defeated vicious killers with breathtaking displays of swordsmanship then stared with contempt at his father whom he had just rescued from painful death. Murderous beasts roared into the streets of the Manchester suburb and were destroyed by the astounding weapons he'd invented, leaving him to bask in the adoring gaze of the girls from his classroom. He developed brilliant conversations with his sister, defeated her every argument she could raise against him, killed her every statement with intellect and brilliance until she was left downcast, crest-fallen and embarrassed, acknowledging her brother's superiority with a bad grace.

At one point, he heard his father erupt into a monstrous coughing fit. A wave of anger swept over him. How *dare* that man spend so much on cigarettes while leaving his son with threadbare clothes? The rage seemed to rise to a peak and he felt an odd sensation as if he had sneezed within his head but not through his nose. The coughing fit downstairs changed into a cry of pain and fear. He heard his mother shriek, "Jack! What's the matter?" The bangs of furniture being knocked about echoed through the house and then the racket subsided.

Puzzled, but unable to avoid feeling a sense of satisfaction at the man's distress, Mickie relaxed again.

As he drifted into that limbo state between wakefulness and sleep, his imagination ran riot. He heard a strange, powerful, yet immensely distant and invisible voice that seemed to be shouting something familiar. He saw images of tiny, beautiful people who led him by the hand through pathways in dense cities of trees and laughed with limitless joy at the wonders of their world. An imposing being with a head like a wild boar stood before him and bellowed in friendly welcome, one impossibly huge right arm draped under a cloak, while on the left, two smaller arms looked delicate in comparison. A child stood by his parents and they smiled at Mickie, and they had blue faces, reddish hair and no nose at all, but he felt a wave of friendship from them. And just as he fell asleep, a wonderfully warm, gentle voice, he was sure it was a woman, spoke to him with love and comfort. Despite the awful evening in a series of awful evenings, for those few moments Mickie felt happier than he had ever been before.

When he woke up, both parents were coughing in desperation, having just lit the first cigarettes of the day.

Mickie didn't know it, but he wouldn't have to wait four years before leaving home. He had only two days left on Earth.

Chapter 2 – Close Encounters of a Strange Kind

The day was a Sunday, so there was no school to provide a complication. Mickie woke with a powerful sense of anticipation, but little remained of his weird dream, and he didn't connect it with the sense of excitement he was feeling, nor with an oddly strong urge to go to the park. After all, the familiar park was his usual refuge on weekends.

The house smelled of stale cigarettes when he came out the bathroom. But that was normal and he had learned to live with the stench until he could get outside. Ignoring the unwashed dishes sitting on the kitchen table and the traces of ash on the stove, he pulled two slices of bread from the breadbin, pushed down the toaster button and waited impatiently for the bread to cook, concentrating on the warm glow of the heating coils. When he was done, he stood in the kitchen to eat, not wishing to share his meal with the overflowing ashtrays on the dining table.

By eight, he was thankfully out of the house and into the clean fresh air of a mild and sunny June morning. He set off on his usual path to the park, knowing his friends down the road would not be out and about for a while yet. He felt a sudden pang of loneliness, wondering what it would be like to have meals with a family that loved each other, where a kid felt at home, and could talk to his parents. He crossed the busy street and entered the park, as always feeling the pleasure of being surrounded by the grass and trees, reached his favourite spot by the lake, sat down on his regular bench by the water and watched the ducks float around.

At that point, the pleasant summer morning turned horribly ugly.

Mickie heard the noise from across the pond by the site of a café where he had frequently watched diners enjoying their breakfasts in the outdoors. Turning his head, he saw a gang of youths milling around, but as he watched, some of them threw bricks at the small structure that housed the office and kitchen, smashing the glass of the windows. Several others stamped into the dining area, overturned tables and spilled food onto the ground, as terrified customers tried to escape the rampage. The mob suddenly turned away and began racing round the pond straight at Mickie, most of them laughing and bellowing their triumph at the damage caused. Suddenly frightened, Mickie saw that the mob wasn't going to run past him, but had stopped and gathered round him where he sat, frozen on the bench.

"Well, look at what we've got here!" sneered one, a large overweight young man dressed in blue jeans and a tartan shirt. His hair was short to the point almost of baldness and his face was large, fleshy with a thick lips. "A cute little boy! How about we throw him in the pond, eh guys?"

A roar of approval greeted the suggestion, and as Mickie tried to stand up and run, numerous hands grabbed him by the arms and neck and lifted him bodily from the bench. His breath was frozen, he couldn't shout, and he winced as several blows landed on his head. A bigger blow slammed into his ear, and he began to feel the same, despairing rage and terror of a beating from his father as his vision faded and sounds diminished.

But inexplicably, the hands let him go and he was dropped onto the hard surface of the pathway, scraping his knees and he lay fully stretched out, hardly able to breathe, seeing little but shoes around him starting to run. Dimly, he heard screams of fear such as he could not have imagined and as he tried to lift his head, he caught a glimpse of some impossible, huge black shape that he could not identify but caused a wave of panic through his system.

"You'd better come with us," said a man's voice from outside his range of vision, and strong, capable hands lifted him to his feet and slung him over a pair of shoulders before the rescuer started to move smoothly in the direction of the small woodland to one side of the lake.

Then Mickie blacked out completely.

He had no idea how long it was before he opened his eyes. He was lying on something incredibly comfortable. It almost seemed to have moulded itself to fit every shape of his body. He lifted his head and realised he was in a room. There were no windows and no direct lights that he could see, but the room was bright with a friendly glow. It was not a large space, perhaps the size of his living room at home but quite circular. Six comfortable armchairs were placed round a coffee table, and underfoot was a deep carpet in a light blue shade. All round the walls there was nothing but a band of black panelling starting about hip height from the floor and extending to the level of Mickie's head. The rest of the wall's surface was a light grey colour, and instead of rising vertically to a ceiling, the walls curved into a dome over his head. He sat up with a gasp of fear.

"Nothing to be frightened of, Mickie."

Across from him a woman was sitting, looking at him with a friendly expression. She was pretty, Mickie thought, dark hair falling to her shoulders, framing a face with a wide, generous mouth. On another seat to her right, a man sat in a relaxed pose, his eyes closed as if asleep. He seemed tall and thin, and Mickie could see that he had a crooked nose and ears that stuck out from his head almost at right angles. His hair was a deep shade of red. Mickie stared, unable to speak.

"Remember your dreams last night?" the woman continued. For some reason, her voice seemed familiar.

Mickie swallowed, nervously. "How could you know what I dreamed last night?"

She smiled. "You saw some tiny people who lived in trees. You saw a very large being with three arms and a head like a wild boar. You saw three people with blue faces. And you heard my voice. I told you to come to the park today."

With those words, Mickie remembered. It was the voice of the woman who had spoken to him with love and comfort as he had fallen asleep the night before. Something incomprehensible was happening, he knew, but his fear diminished.

"They weren't dreams, Mickie. We were sending you those images and talking to you so that today you'd believe what we have to tell you."

Somehow, Mickie believed her.

"My name is Allie," the woman continued. "That's my husband, Grant. He's busy right now, talking to some other people."

"Talking?" Mickie found his voice, though it sounded scratchy and harsh in his ears. "How can be talking to somebody?"

"That will take some explaining," Allie replied, nodding in understanding of his bewilderment. "And we'll get to it. But for now, you're safe."

The memories of the riot and the attack on him flooded back into Mickie's mind. "What happened?" he asked, feeling a shiver of remembered fear rush through him.

"To be honest, we're not exactly sure." It was the man who spoke, his eyes open and looking at Mickie with friendly warmth. "Something caused those hooligans to race away, but the only thing we've been able to think of is just so impossible, we can't believe it."

"I don't understand."

"Don't try to," replied the man, whose name was Grant, Mickie remembered. "I'm sure there's a lot more that you need to understand first."

"And something to settle your nerves." Allie spoke softly, her attention on a panel that was lifting from the table. It slid silently upward while another panel slid away in the side of it and a jug of what looked like orange juice was lightly set onto the table's surface. Mickie realised then how dry his throat was and watched as Allie poured a glass from the jug and handed it to him. He gulped the liquid down, almost fainting at the exquisite taste. It was all the wonderful drinks he had ever had with a sparkle added to it that bubbled on his tongue. He drained the glass, conscious of Allie's amused look. She refilled it as soon as he'd finished. . More carefully this time, Mickie drank, but the wonder of the taste did not diminish. The headache from the blows he had received from the mob had vanished.

"It's called *Sle'Ach*," said Allie. "Good, huh?"

"Fantastic!" Mickie felt alive in a way he had never done before, as if a coat of sludge had been removed from his insides.

Allie chuckled. "It's a fruit from a planet an awful long way from here."

The comment brought Mickie back to reality. The astounding things around him had yet to be explained. He hung onto his glass as something familiar in a completely strange world.

"A planet? Another planet?"

"Indeed. Another planet. And one so far away you could hardly believe." Grant seemed amused as he spoke.

Mickie looked around him, his vision clearing as his fear diminished under the calming influence of the golden drink. "This is a spaceship, isn't it?" He felt a rush of boldness that gave him back control of his voice. Something quite astounding was happening and he began to sense a wave of excitement.

"More of a shuttle," replied Grant. "The main ship is parked a little distance away."

"Where?"

"In orbit round Venus."

Mickie sat back in the luxurious seat that he vaguely noticed was adjusting itself as he moved. "Round Venus?" he echoed weakly.

"Round Venus," agreed Grant. "No chance of anyone seeing it there. Not that they could, even if they happened to be around."

"It's cloaked, isn't it?" said Mickie. "Just like in Star Trek." The idea came to him as he recalled the concept from one of his books and from the science fiction series he watched on television.

"It's invisible, yes. Just like this shuttle. That's why nobody could see us, even if they walked this far into the woods. And even if they came close, the shuttle is radiating a very shallow wave that causes fear. They'd walk away without knowing why." He stretched his legs out, closed his eyes and seemed to retreat from the conversation.

"He's talking to somebody again?" Mickie asked.

Allie laughed. "Quite right. To our friends on the main ship."

"How's he doing that? He's not saying anything!"

"He is, but not that you can hear. Mickie, listen to me." Allie said with an urgent force. "There are many intelligent races in the universe. Some are more advanced than the people of this planet, some are about the same, a few are still behind and most of those we leave totally alone for a while longer."

Calmness eased its way through Mickie's body, as if the wonderful drink had given him some strength he didn't know he had.

"Why are you telling me all this?"

Allie chuckled. "Mickie, do you think it's just a coincidence that a space-ship would land in the woods round a city in England? Or that two aliens would suddenly appear and make friends with you?"

The questions hit Mickie like a stone. "You're aliens? But... what...?" he asked helplessly.

"We were looking for you, Mickie." Allie looked serious as she spoke.

"Looking for me? But why?"

"Because we heard you calling for help," replied Allie.

"What?" The answer was so unexpected that Mickie felt as if he'd been kicked by a horse, despite the calming influence of his drink.

"We heard you."

"But I don't understand. How did you hear me and how could I be calling without knowing it?"

"That's part of the story, Mickie. I know that this is very strange for you, but I assure you, you did call, just with your mind, and your call was heard."

"You can read minds?"

"No, *we* can't," said Grant, returning from his trance-like state. "It's a form of communication we use for very long distances, but we ourselves can't read minds. Others can, and they can also transmit the details to us. That's how I've been communicating with the ship. And that's how we sent you those images last night."

Mickie didn't feel he quite understood that, but decided to ignore it for now, given the more pressing urgency of what they were telling him. "So who heard me?"

Grant smiled. "A being of a very special race about thirty million light years away. We know him as Speaker 356."

"But how....?"

"It's his job. That's what he does. He listens around the universe and passes on messages.   Telepathic impulses are not bound by time and distance. It's how we communicate around the whole cosmic area in which we travel. And that's how we talked to you last night."

Mickie looked at his glass and took another sip of the yellow juice. It still tasted magical and he concentrated on that sensation and let the power of the drink work on him again.

"There's a point to all this, Mickie," Grant said. "As you've learned, we're not from Earth. But here's the thing."

Mickie looked at him and understood something was to be said that was even more shattering than everything he'd heard so far.

"Nor are you," said Grant.

Chapter 3 – The End of a World

"Wh... what?"

"You're not a human being, Mickie," Grant repeated. "And we have no idea who or what you are or how you came to be on this little planet. But we do know that you're not one of any of the species we know in our universe and once we knew you were here, we had to come and find you."

Mickie could do nothing but stare at the two adults. Nothing could have prepared him for this conversation and he had absolutely no idea what to say next. Allie saw his obvious confusion and poured another glass of the astonishing golden drink, handing it to him and gently urging him to drink. The magical sparkle eased his vocal cords.

"I don't understand any of this," he whispered.

"It's pretty overwhelming, I know!" Allie said. "Let's try and explain a little. We've been studying Earth and its people for a long time. So when we heard about you, we had to come looking for you, because like I said, you are not one of any of the species we know. And yet you seem identical to humans, as well as to us. The mystery is great, Mickie and we all want to solve it. I bet you do, too. So do you want to come with us and find out who you are and where you came from?"

Mickie sat still and let the words sink into his mind. The whole day had been beyond his capacity to absorb and understand everything, and yet, under the whirls of confusion and excesses of information, he began to sense something... he *knew* all this was true. Somehow he realised that he had always known. Two astounding facts stood out from everything that had happened.

He was not part of the awful Dalton family. He wasn't even the same species. What he was, who his real parents were and why they had abandoned him were not known, and it was equally mysterious how they'd persuaded the Daltons to adopt him. But the mystery was solved. His family hated him because they had somehow sensed his alien quality and were terrified of it.

And the second fact was cause for pure happiness. He could leave and go with Allie and Grant if he wished. He knew he would do so, despite the concerns of his new friends.

"If you come with us, life will certainly be exciting and eventful," Allie said. "And I think the most important thing of all, you will be with a family. Grant and I will always be with you and we will be your guardians until you discover who exactly you are, if you ever do. But all the other people on the ship will also be your family, because we spend our lives travelling like this."

"I want to come with you," said Mickie. He was completely certain. Even with some regrets at leaving friends behind and even though the chance of getting away from his awful family would have been reason enough, he had realised a few moments ago that Earth was not his home. He didn't belong here. Leaving with Allie and Grant was the only path he had.

"I know that," said Allie warmly. "And we want you to come with us. But it is the biggest step any person could ever take. We don't know when we will come back to Earth again, maybe never, until Earthlings mature enough to join us, and that will be a long time."

"There's nothing for me on Earth. I want to find out where I came from."

"Of course you do," Grant said, "I suggest you go home, think a little more, then if you decide to join us, pack just a small bag with the things you most treasure and write a note to your parents. Tell them you've gone away and won't be back. They will have to tell the police, and they will eventually give up on finding you."

"My parents won't care." To Mickie, even the word "parents" had become a misnomer. They weren't his parents, they never had been and they didn't want to be, any more than he wanted them to be.

"Probably," replied Grant. "But they have raised you, they have fed you and clothed you even if it was all without any love for you. They did satisfy some of the responsibilities they had undertaken. You owe them a letter of goodbye. Then when you are ready, come back here in the morning. We will see you even though you won't see us until we set up the doorway."

"Set up...?"

"Come with me," said Grant and rose to his feet. Mickie did the same and followed Grant to one part of the circular wall that seemed no different from any other part. But without any sound, a section slid aside to reveal a gap about the size of an ordinary door, though surrounded by a green glow. Cautiously, Mickie peered out and saw the trees of the woodland by the lake.

"The green glow is part of the cloaking mechanism," Grant said. "Just walk through."

Mickie walked out of the mysterious doorway and looked back as the doorway closed again over Grant's friendly wave. As soon as it closed, the green glow vanished, leaving no sign that a space-going vehicle was sitting there. Mickie was alone in the forest clearing. It was dusk, so he realised he must have been in the shuttle most of the day before he woke up.

Something very peculiar was happening in the park. As he walked out of the darkness of the small woodland, he saw an area brilliantly lit by floodlights and several police cars were parked on the pathways round the lake, their strobe lights flashing. Groups of people were bent over several shapeless masses on the ground. Confused, Mickie crept round the side of the woods until he was safely away from the scene then ran for the exit and home.

His parents were furious when he walked in. Dinner was already over and the three of them were sitting blank faced before the television watching some game show. His father lurched to his feet as Mickie walked in, the anticipation already in his face. He crushed his cigarette into the nearest ashtray with an angry thrust, smoke billowing from his mouth.

"Where the bloody hell have you been?" he roared. The huge hand rose and slammed against the side of Mickie's head. Mickie fell backward against the wall, pain roaring through him. Dimly he saw his sister watching without a hint of emotion a scene she had witnessed many times before.

His mother took another draw on her cigarette, coughed, caught her breath and spoke in the coarse, grating tone that was her habitual voice. "Oh, Jack, let him be. If he doesn't want to eat after I've worked so hard preparing a good meal for him, why should I care, the ungrateful little brat."

His father ignored her. He bent down over Mickie, hauled him upright and towered over him, the hand raised ready to strike again.

"I said where the hell have you been? What do mean by staying out so late, eh? I asked you, what do you mean?"

The hand fell again and rocked Mickie backward. But astoundingly, the torrent of fear and despair that usually flooded over him didn't materialise. He looked up at the furious face above him.

"Did you enjoy that?" he asked, astonished at his self-control. "You seemed to. So do you want to do it again?"

"*WHAT?*" His father stood upright, baffled, furious and yet too astonished to hit Mickie again. In fact, Mickie decided there was an expression of fear in the man's face. Carefully, he turned to the door out of the room, his back crawling with the expectation that he would be grabbed and thrashed severely, but the silence in the room was undisturbed. He walked upstairs, into his room and locked the door. When he sat at his little table, he allowed a smile to cross his face.

"Wow!" he said and pulled his school bag to him, pulled out an exercise book, tore out a page and started to write. There was no salutation.

"I know you never wanted me. I know that I'm adopted. So I'm leaving. There's no point in looking for me, I promise you. You will never find me. Enjoy your new life."

He folded the paper into three parts, looked around for an envelope without any success and decided it wasn't worth it. He left the folded sheet where it was, stood up, found a small suitcase he had used when his family had still gone on holidays together when Mickie was about five, and opened it, looking at the few things he had in the room. Eventually he folded away his favourite sweater, a Rugby Union football jersey in the colours of the Australian International team he had been given at a friend's Christmas party, all his underwear and socks, his only other pair of slacks. Finally he packed away his paperback copies of James Blish's *Cities in Flight* series and Isaac Asimov's *Foundation Trilogy*. He thought he'd enjoy personally checking out the writers' visions of other worlds and see how accurate they had been. He spent the long summer evening sitting quietly by the window, staring at the sky, wondering what he would see beyond it and imagining the joys of being with the two most wonderful people he had ever met.

Mickie dreamed his last night on Earth in a peaceful, deep sleep of utter contentment.

* * *

In the morning, he dressed in his usual pants, shirt, tie and blazer as if to go to school. He joined the others at the breakfast table, conscious of the tense silence but not afraid. If anything, he sensed his own amusement at the fear that hovered around the table like a fog over a lake. His parents didn't look at him at all, merely concentrated on lighting their third or fourth cigarettes of the morning and coughing their way to wakefulness. His sister stared at him with open hostility, but when he returned her glare with a small smile, she ducked away and concentrated on eating.

His father left for work without a word. His sister collected her bicycle, hitched her satchel over her back and rode off. Carefully, Mickie waited till his mother was in the kitchen, darted upstairs to collect his small suitcase and left as quickly as he could by the front door. The last he heard of his mother was a helpless attack of coughing as she washed up the breakfast things.

He set off for the park, trying not to run, but with his heart pounding with excitement. As he reached a rubbish bin at the gates to the park, he grinned, took off the school tie and blazer and threw them into the bin with a cheerful sense of abandonment. There was no anxiety. He knew he was doing the right thing. Home was not on Earth at all. He had no idea where it could be or if he would ever find it, but the adventure ahead of him was greater than any Odysseus could have dreamed.

The morning was cool and bright with the freshness of a shower during the night. He could smell the newly-cut grass from the nearby cricket field and the fragrance of the flowers along the path. The trees in the little forest glowed with the early sunlight as he walked the narrowing path to the point at which it ended. There was no sign of the floodlit, strange scene of the previous night. He found the clearing, put down his case and waited. It was hard to believe that a small spaceship was somewhere near to him. He saw the first glow of the welcome green light and walked firmly through the doorway and into the circular room.

They were standing, waiting for him. Their smiles of welcome and pleasure warmed him like a bonfire on a cold Guy Fawkes Night.

"Glad you decided to come," said Allie. "Not that we had any doubts about it."

Grant surprised him. He picked up Mickie in a giant bear hug and swung him around. "Okay, young man, let's make a space traveller of you."

Mickie chuckled, staggered back onto his feet and looked around him. The circular room was much like it had been the previous day. Nothing resembling any sort of flight controls could be seen in the small space.

"How do we get going?" he asked.

"I'll show you. Take a seat." Grant pointed at the comfortable chairs. "Any of them will do."

Mickie did as instructed and was surprised when the other two also sat round the coffee table. They simply sat still and did nothing, though Grant seemed to stretch out and retreated from any conversation. After a few seconds Allie smiled and broke the silence. "Look," she said and nodded at the black panels.

Mickie stared. The panels held images. And he could see the Earth! It was like the famous pictures taken by the Apollo astronauts in the sixties and seventies, a green and blue sphere with cloud patterns. He felt his jaw drop and struggled to control himself. "But.... *How?*" he stammered.

"Gravitational engines," replied Grant, his eyes still closed in concentration. "They affect every atom in the field around them, so there's no surge of acceleration and you don't need seat belts."

"But you didn't do anything!"

"Well, I did, but nothing you could see, and I'm still doing them. I have a little control device implanted in my body and it transmits my commands to the engines and navigation equipment. We lifted off before you had even sat down and we're past the Moon's orbit already."

"I think you need some *Sle'Ach*," said Allie with a chuckle. "It clears the mind as you have probably worked out, apart from tasting delicious." The panel on the table did its mysterious shifting and the jug and glasses appeared. Mickie accepted a glassful from her and took a deep gulp of the starlight and fragrance of the amazing drink. He looked again at the image of Earth and it had become a lot smaller. He wondered if he should feel some regret, but he didn't. He felt more like he was leaving a place where he'd been made to stay for a time and now he was returning.... *home.*

"We're heading to the main ship?" he asked.

Grant seemed wrapped in thought, and it was Allie who answered. "Yes, we are. Grant is right now communicating with them advising of our arrival. We'll be there in about forty minutes."

"Forty minutes! To *Venus?*" The idea of such speed was fantastic, but Mickie thought back to the reading on space travel and the planets he had absorbed since his very early days. "But that's less than the speed of light. How can we travel around the galaxy at that speed?"

"Good question." Still with his eyes closed, Grant smiled. "These shuttles can't exceed light speed. Actually, they only get to about ten percent of light speed. Even then, we could do the trip in about twenty minutes, because Venus is relatively close to Earth right now. But if we went at that speed, we would cause some gravitational waves that might confuse any telescope pointed in this direction, and we don't want to attract attention. So we're moving at half speed."

"But the main ship?"

"Oh yes!" Grant returned from his mysterious reverie of communication, opened his eyes and looked at him. "The ship gets up to the speed of light, actually just a bit more than that, despite the laws of physics that say it can't. But it's not travel at superlight speeds that covers such distances. It's the entry to hyperspacial dimensions."

Mickie knew that word. It was a common idea in the science fiction books he had. "Hyperspace? I've read about that. So it really exists?"

Grant laughed loudly. "Allie, how many twelve-year-olds would know about hyperspace?" he said.

"Not that many," she replied with a smile. "I think we've got a bright young man with us!"

"Yes, Mickie, hyperspace exists," Grant said, returning to Mickie's question. "We have to reach slightly above light speed to enter it, but once in, distances become pretty well irrelevant."

"But what *is* it? And how do you get into it?"

Grant stretched as if fatigued. "Explaining hyperspace needs maths of an order well above both our heads. It's almost a sort of dream space, where normal rules don't apply. Think of it as an alternate universe with different laws of physics. And we get into it by a sort of sideways kick that shoves us just above the speed of light. A very old race, the Kaloti developed the technology, but very few people are able to understand it. When you've grown a bit and learned more about our science, you'll be able to comprehend it better."

"So how far can you go?" Mickie was enthralled by the idea of limitless distances that could be crossed with ease. Just for a second he wondered how he was able to discuss these astounding matters so calmly, but decided it must be the effect of the drink.

Grant shrugged. "As far as there is," he replied. "But in practice we travel mostly within the Local Group and a few extra long trips to specific worlds."

"What's the Local Group?" Mickie hadn't heard the term before.

"The ten or eleven galaxies nearest the Milky Way," replied Grant. There was a small smile on his lips as if he knew the astonishment this could cause. He was quite right. Mickie felt as if he had been hit in the guts.

"You can travel between *galaxies?*" This was far more mind-boggling than anything he had heard so far.

"Sure!" Grant was enjoying himself imparting this information. "Once you're in hyperspace, distance becomes almost unimportant."

"So how long can a trip take?" Mickie was so enthralled he had forgotten to look at the fast-vanishing Earth.

"We can go end to end of the Milky Way, that's this home galaxy for Earth in nine days and it stretches about a hundred thousand light years along the long axis," replied Grant. "For a number of reasons involving some rather complex cosmology, we can traverse the distance between any galaxies in about the same time, regardless of the real distance between them."

Mickie's mind was in a whirl, even with the effects of the drink to help him. Allie broke into his confused thoughts. "You may want to take your last look at Earth," she murmured.

Mickie looked at the black panel. He could just make out the blue colour of the little spot in the middle of the screen then it merged with the white gleam of the galaxy.

Again, he felt no sense of regret. There was too much excitement ahead of him.

"What happens when we reach Venus?" he asked. "Will the ship find us, or do we find it?"

"The computers will handle the rendezvous," replied Grant. "The ship is in orbit, but it will start to move out to meet us soon."

"How big is it?" Mickie had some idea of a Starship Enterprise with a crew of a few hundred.

"Massive!" Grant seemed amused. "So big you won't believe! But all it takes is about fifty people to run it, and there are another three hundred or so on the ship for all our business needs."

A new idea struck Mickie. "Are there people from lots of other planets on board?"

"Only four species in the crew." Allie joined the discussion. "But hardly representative of all the races that we know. Many species are not space travellers at all. And as you might imagine, trying to establish crew quarters for beings of very different physical types or environmental needs would be impossible."

Mickie was so happy he could hardly breathe. He tried to look inward to see what the source of the happiness was, and he could really think of only one thing. Two adults were talking to him as friends, taking an interest in him, treating him like an intelligent, useful person. Already he was starting to think of them as his parents and the memories of the ugly, smelly people he had left behind were receding as fast as planet Earth was. And after all that, he was embarking on the greatest adventure anyone could ever dream.

"Do they look like humans? Like you?" Another wild thought hit him. "Where are you from, anyway?"

"Mostly. Mostly. Kalamos." Allie seemed amused as she tried to answer all his excited questions.

"Huh?"

"Mostly they look like humans. Therefore they mostly look like us. And Kalamos is the planet that is our home world."

Mickie simply didn't know where to start working through the astounding things she was saying.

"Mostly? How mostly? And what does Kalamos mean? And where is it?" Questions bubbled from him like a stream in flood.

"Hey, slow down!" Allie laughed, a light, pleasant sound. "There is just too much for one small boy to learn before we get to the ship. But we'll tell you some of what you will be seeing soon. When we dock, you will see other people on the ship. They will all look a lot like us, and the reason for that is obvious. We must all be able to breathe the same air, live in the same light and generally co-exist in the same environment. So the crew of this ship will all be from a very small number of intelligent species around the universe. The only one that will surprise you a lot will be the captain and his immediate crew who run the ship. They are known to us as the Kaloti and it was their species that first developed space flight."

"What do these... Kaloti look like?" Mickie stumbled on the new and strange word, but his excitement made him press on.

Allie laughed, and looked at Grant. "I think our newly-acquired crew-member has a very active curiosity!"

"Good to see," replied Grant. "But Mickie, there's so much to learn, telling you about it now will be wasted.

Wait till you're on the ship and we can explain things as you find them."

"But what about language? Can everyone speak the same language? Will I have to learn another one? How will I talk to other people on the ship?" Mickie felt exhilarated by all the new ideas and concepts that were erupting in his mind.

"Not a problem, Mickie!" Allie seemed to understand the worry he was feeling. "It's just about impossible for one species to learn the language of another, if only because vocal cords are different, or because the concepts of the language are so different. But we have developed a little device that will translate all the languages of the ship into English for you and the same device everyone else has does the same for them. We will implant one in your shoulder fairly soon, and until then one of us will always be with you to show you round the ship and speak with other crew members."

Mickie was impressed and relieved. The idea of having to learn several new languages was scary. "So what about your species?" he asked. "Where is Kalamos? Are you exactly the same as human people?"

"Our solar system is about two hundred light years from this one, in the same Milky Way Galaxy," Grant said. "And yes, physically, Kalamosians and Human are almost identical, enough so that any medical test in Earth's current technology would show no difference. Some scientists think we're actually the same species that somehow got to two different planets. Anyway, you'll get a lot of new information when you're settled in."

He rose to his feet and walked to the line of panels on the wall, gesturing to Mickie to join him. "Mickie, how about you do something nobody from Earth has done before, and watch the scene as we fly to Venus?"

Mickie followed him and looked out. Soon he was lost in the sight of the stars, glowing in a way he had never seen before.

"Notice anything odd about the stars?" Grant asked after a few minutes.

Mickie switched from an almost trance state to a careful study of the view. He saw it after a few seconds.

"They're blue!"

"Well done! That's right! It's called the Doppler Effect. We're travelling at such a high percentage of light speed that the light waves are being shortened and that makes the light seem blue. You'll see that again when we're on the main Ship."

As Mickie revelled in this new experience, he occasionally thought about the Earth he had left behind, probably forever. He knew he had some regrets about not seeing his friends again. But as for never seeing the Dalton family again, he had nothing but warm, happy feelings about that.

Chapter 4 – The Voyage Begins

He was almost in a hypnotic state when Allie softly called his name.

"We're approaching Venus," she said.

With a start he realised that the scene in the panels round the cabin had changed. They were now glowing, some with a curtain of stars, others with what looked like random ribbons of assorted colours waving in a light breeze, and one... one was ablaze with a furious sea of dense, multi-coloured clouds, boiling like a huge cauldron of strange liquids.

He looked over at Grant who had taken his seat again. Allie smiled but gestured for silence. Grant seemed far away, lost in deep thought, and Allie resumed a similar pose as she and Mickie quietly took seats. He watched Grant, realising he was again using the internal controls to pilot the shuttle and occasionally looked across at the panels to try and comprehend what was happening. Quite soon, he decided the rolling fury of dense clouds was the top of the atmosphere of Venus. He had read enough of his library books to know that the planet was covered with thick, hot clouds, an atmosphere of violent storms and baking heat that would probably prevent man from ever visiting. He recalled that a satellite probe had once been dropped into that fury and had transmitted details of the hellish environment until it had died in the maelstrom.

Another panel showed the same storms but from a much greater distance, because Mickie could see the curvature of the planet, probably about a quarter of the whole. Behind the mass of brilliant white and assorted strands of colours, space was deep black, no other stars visible.

A third panel caught his eye. It was one of those with a curtain of stars, but what had caught his attention was a tiny black spot that seemed to be moving across the silvery haze. He got up and moved nearer the screen. As he did, it flickered and moved to a far closer view. The little black spot became an ovoid-shaped object with no obvious features on it at all. It resembled nothing more than an egg, slightly bigger at one end than the other.

"Yes, it's the ship," Allie's voice said from behind him. "Grant is bringing us into the launch bay. We'll be there in another few minutes."

"It looks awfully small," he said doubtfully.

She chuckled. "Mickie, the ship is just over a kilometre long and half a kilometre wide."

He stared at her in disbelief.

She nodded. "It's over a hundred thousand kilometres away at the moment."

He turned back to the view of the ship, and even in the few seconds he had looked away, it had grown dramatically, almost filling the screen.

"Somehow it's not what I thought a spaceship would look like," he said.

Behind him, Grant laughed. "No weapons, no massive engines, none of those interesting bits?"

Despite the almost-disappointment, Mickie chuckled. "Something like that," he agreed.

"Mickie, the engine that powers this shuttle is only about the size of a book. You'll see the ship's engines soon, they're huge, but they can easily be contained inside a vessel that size, and they don't need any sort of rocket exhaust. As for weapons, we don't need them. There are very few space-going races, and a fight between two ships would be impossible, given the speeds at which we move."

He pointed at the huge ship. "But if you look at the centre... see that ring of pale blue surrounding it?"

Mickie studied the egg shape. Though very faint, he realised that a ring did surround the middle of the ship, about as far from the hull as the ship was wide.

"What is it?"

"The gravitational field at very, very low levels," Grant replied. "If you could be outside the ship as it accelerated at full power, that blue ring would be brighter than the sun. Anyway, look at the near end – there's a docking port opening up."

Mickie stared, and saw a hole open up in the side near the smaller end. It had spread out from a central point, just like a camera lens did. As he watched, that gap filled the screen and suddenly vanished into total blackness. But a glow of lights appeared and Mickie realised they were inside the ship. Just a little distance away was what looked like a pure white donut resting on the surface, and Mickie saw immediately that it must be another shuttle, just like the one in which he had arrived.

"Time to look around your new home," said Allie from behind him. "Follow me out of the doorway and be careful when you step out. Remember what we told you, the gravity on the ship is a lot less than you're used to."

With no apparent movement from either Grant or Allie, the doorway opened, though this time without any weird green light.

"No cloaking required," said Grant, noting Mickie's reaction. "Come on, let's see what home looks like."

He walked straight out into the brightly lit space outside the shuttle, and with a wave of enormous excitement, Mickie followed him. He stood and looked around him. He was in a massive, vault-like space like the biggest hall he had ever seen, but many times larger. Five of the shuttle ships stood silently in a single row, and the one in which he had arrived was the nearest to the wall, but even that wall was probably over a hundred metres away. Looking around, Mickie felt a little dizzy. Then he moved a step or two and realised why. He felt as if he was in a lift that was dropping fast. The dizziness vanished immediately, he jumped as hard as he could and yelled with delight as he soared upward till his feet were at least at the level of Allie's waist next to him. He floated gently down to the floor, without the jolt that jumping from such a height would have given him on Earth. Then he ran into the endless open spaces ahead of him, screaming with wonder and exhilaration as he leaped three or four metres with each pace, feeling like he was in the middle of a fantastic dream. He stopped and turned around, saw that the two adults were a long way away, and set off in the same blood-racing, exhilarating way back in their direction. He misjudged his pace and would have dashed past them had not Grant reached out and flung an arm round Mickie's waist, pulling him back to stand on the deck again.

"Fun, eh kid?" he said. His reaction hit Mickie hard. Instinctively, he'd expected, Grant to react like his father and yell angrily at him. The gentle amusement and understanding from Grant washed over him like a flood. He couldn't stop himself and hugged Grant hard, clinging almost with desperation with the sudden fear of waking up and finding the whole wonderful experience was just a dream. Grant's arm was round his shoulder and his voice rumbled in Mickie's ear where it was planted firmly against Grant's midriff.

"You can come here and play just about any time you want, Mickie. In fact, you'll find out about a game that the kids play here. It's okay, we know how it feels. But come along now, let's find your own room, meet the captain, and then you can watch as we leave the system."

Grant started to move toward the wall with Allie walking on Mickie's other side. As they reached the huge, metal barrier, a door opened silently and they walked into a corridor. For the first time, Mickie met aliens other than Grant and Allie. Two men walked towards them. They looked perfectly ordinary to Mickie's slight disappointment. No weird heads, no tentacles, just two standard human men as far as he could see. Their clothing was a one-piece tunic of what looked like ordinary cotton. They gestured at Grant and Allie, looked briefly at Mickie and smiled. They spoke, but the words were completely unintelligible to Mickie. It sounded like nothing he had ever heard before. The sound was continuous with no obvious breaks for words or sentences. But Grant and Allie nodded, smiled and Allie spoke in English.

"Thank you," she said. "We had a great trip and as you see, we found the boy. He seems delighted to be here."

The men smiled again and walked on.

"The translation device," said Allie. "Once we get yours fitted, you'll be able to speak with anyone on the ship. Let's go up to the flight deck. I think you'll find it fascinating."

"How many people are there on the ship?" asked Mickie.

"Three hundred and sixty," replied Allie. "Fifty of those are the Kaloti flight crew, the rest are specialists in a variety of disciplines."

"Just fifty? For a ship this big?"

"That's all it takes," replied Allie. "It's nearly all automatic, and most of it is controlled the same way we flew the shuttle, with tiny devices implanted in the crewmen's bodies that react to their mental orders and then affect the ship's controls."

"Wow!" said Mickie, wildly impressed.

"Wow indeed," agreed Allie. "This way, into the transport shaft."

They had stopped by a doorway that opened at their presence. Inside it was just like an elevator car. They entered, the door closed, but no motion was detectible.

"Control Deck," Grant said. Mickie could still feel no motion.

"You could speak and state the destination if you wanted," said Grant, seeing Mickie's puzzlement. "And you can do that for yourself if you want, before the communicator is placed in your shoulder and once you know your way round the ship, because the ship's computer is already programmed with English, as well as quite a few other human languages. But we're actually moving very fast, just like the shuttle, with a gravity field round the transporter so that you can't feel any acceleration or deceleration."

In another few seconds, the door opened again. The bright lights of the corridors and the arrival vault were not here. Instead, the room was lit by a soft, golden glow as if dusk had descended on a tropical island. The same screens that had been on the walls of the shuttlecraft were all round the deck and the scene was much like the shuttlecraft, just a great deal larger. As he walked in, Mickie felt the gravity reduce even further, and he fought the small wave of dizziness for a second or two before adjusting. A circle of huge seats covered much of the centre of the space.

And Mickie met his first truly obvious alien.

At first, he hadn't seen the hugely tall shape standing motionless near one of the screens. But then it turned and moved towards them. Mickie felt his insides turn to water. The shape was at least three metres tall and less than half Mickie's width. It seemed to have two legs and two arms and was covered in the same one-piece garment worn by the two crewmen he had met before. The arms were immensely long, reaching down from tiny, narrow shoulders to well below what Mickie assumed were knees, and the hands were similar, lengthy, with fingers that were as long as Mickie's forearm. The head was almost featureless except for two enormous eyes that were ovals of pure blackness. Mickie could see no ears, nose or mouth until a slit opened where a mouth might have been expected. The sound that came out was unexpected. It was also beautiful, a long, low, melodious note like a cello played by a master.

"Yes, captain," said Allie. "Very successful. The boy seems very happy to be with us, and I'm not surprised, given the miserable life he was leading."

The beautiful cello note was repeated and Allie turned to Mickie. "The captain makes you most welcome and expresses his happiness that we were able to respond to your call for help," she said.

Mickie felt his self-control returning. The sense of friendliness he felt from the astonishing creature before him relaxed him totally. "I wish I knew how I'd called," he said.

The Kaloti's eyes opened wide, almost doubling in size and the cello note hummed with a slight tremor.

"The captain is amused," said Allie. "The eyes opening wide like that is their equivalent of laughter. He says he also wishes he knew how you called, but he hopes we will all understand one day. So, take a seat and watch how we take the ship on its travels."

The three of them sat in adjoining seats as the captain moved quietly to stand in front of one of the screens. All of the multiple black panels had come alive with a variety of different views. One showed the boiling clouds of Venus with about a quarter of the planet's curvature visible. Others showed different patterns of stars. Three of them showed what seemed to Mickie to be variable patches of coloured lights with strands waving like a patch of sea anemones in tidal flows. Mickie watched, but all he could detect happening was that some of the star patterns in the panels changed slightly and the curvature of Venus slowly increased until the whole planet could be seen. Obviously the ship was moving away from the planet.

One of the screens changed and showed the sun glowing with a bright yellow glare, then that too started to shrink and Mickie began to grasp just how enormously fast the ship was moving.

"We're moving upward relative to the plane of the solar system," said Allie in a whisper. "So instead of moving out past each of the planets in turn, we're heading at ninety degrees to that direction. That gets us away from the gravitational effects of the planets much more quickly and we need to be a few light-minutes away before we can apply full power."

She saw the query in Mickie's face and elaborated before he could ask. "That's the distance light travels in one minute, or about eighteen million kilometres. We're not travelling at light speed yet, so we'll be flying for a few minutes before we can enter hyperspace."

Those minutes passed in almost complete silence, the Captain standing motionless while the screens before him filled with alternate pictures of the planets around, oceans of stars, and on occasions, lines of numbers and symbols, none of which meant anything at all to Mickie.

"Is he doing it all by himself?" Mickie whispered. "Where are all the others in the crew?"

"They're either at the navigation stations taking the sightings or in the engine room managing the power," Grant replied in an equally low voice. "The Captain and all the crew have control devices in their body, just like I do, so while they don't seem to be doing anything, they're actually pretty busy. The Captain is getting huge amounts of data from a lot of sources right now."

Mickie nodded and resumed his study of the panels.

"We're lining up the Ship for its acceleration to light speed," Allie whispered at one moment. "The entire trip depends on these very precise positions being set up, and once they are, then we start accelerating, just like an airliner starts its take-off run. Watch the main screen in front of the captain."

Mickie did as she said and saw a screen filled almost entirely with a canopy of startlingly coloured stars on a background of silver mist that was the Galaxy. On either side, equally huge screens showed a similar view. The stars rotated and swung for a few moments more then stabilized. For the first time, Mickie felt some vibration under his feet and assumed that the engines were operating at increased power. The gentle rumble swelled and became a thunder that vibrated through the padding of the seats. In front of them, little seemed to alter at first in the observation screen, though the colours of the stars seemed to be slowly changing to a deep, beautiful shade of blue. After a few minutes, Mickie suddenly sensed a change in the views and swung his head to one side to look at the screen on the right of the main one.

At the far right edge of the screen, a deep black line had appeared. Mickie couldn't say just what it was that he was seeing. It seemed almost like a jet black curtain being drawn from behind the ship and blanketing the stars from sight. Then he saw that the black margin was growing on the left screen also, and getting wider, developing a curvature as it grew. In a few minutes, the curtain covered both the side screens and began to move over the sides of the main screen. As the curtain advanced, the stars ahead drew closer together, until no individual point of light could be seen in the gleaming mass of the Galaxy. The curtain closed more and more towards the middle of the screen then was joined by a similar margin extending upward and downward from the bottom and top of the windows.

"We're getting close to the speed of light," said Allie in a low murmur. "As we do, all the light in the universe begins to concentrate in front of us. It's exactly what the scientists on Earth thought would happen."

Adjusting his perceptions, Mickie realized there were no curtains. The Galaxy ahead was drawing in upon itself, compressing itself so that all the stars of the entire Universe appeared to be in a circle ahead of him. The acceleration of the ship must have been incredible to have reached this speed so soon, he thought, though there was no sense of thrust, just the growing rumble and vibration of the engines. The circle in front of him grew smaller and more dense and the light grew brighter until he could no longer look at it. Just as he turned his face away, the window adjusted to screen out the glare, and he resumed his fascinated stare at the entire Universe collapsing into a little ball ahead.

The ball shrank more and more. When it was a tiny point of light in the remote distance, Mickie heard a small murmur from Grant to his right.

"Hyperspace," whispered Grant.

"We're into it?" Mickie could hardly breathe.

"Watch," said Grant, and nodded at the speck of light that was the only object in the black screen. "There'll be one more surge from the engines, then that speck will vanish and we'll be in hyperspace."

Hypnotized by the light, Mickie watched it, and it faded to a minute glow and almost vanished. The rumble of the engines rose another few notches, and this time, there was a high-pitched whine that could just be heard above the rumble. Mickie felt a tiny sense of dizziness, his eyes lost focus for just a fraction of a second, but before he could comment, everything returned to normal. Silence ruled where the engines' roar had prevailed. There was nothing but darkness outside the ship.

"How do we know where we're going?" asked Mickie. Despite his fascination and excitement, his voice was small and reflected some fear of the impenetrable wall of night.

"It's really quite simple," Grant answered. "It's worked for a few hundred thousand years like this. They take a whole series of sightings on a number of specific stars before starting the acceleration run. That gives them the exact direction to fly then they aim in that direction as they enter hyperspace at just above the speed of light. The ship's computer times the precise duration, and flicks the ship back into normal space when they get there."

"So we won't see anything now until we get to where we're going?" asked Mickie.

"That's it till then," replied Grant. He rose to his feet and Allie did the same.

The captain finally moved from his pose of utter stillness. In his slow-motion style of movement that his enormous height and low gravity caused, he returned to the circle of chairs and hummed a short cello note.

"Good idea, captain," said Grant. He turned to Mickie. "The captain suggests we take you to your quarters and get you settled in."

"Let's go," said Allie. "Come on, young man, let's see if you like the room we've allocated you." She stood up and led them out of the flight deck, and Mickie blinked as the lights in the transporter returned to normal levels from the deep and attractive yellow glow in which they had been.

"You try it," said Allie. "We're heading to the residential decks, so say "Deck 37, region 12," and the transporter will obey you."

Feeling intrigued by the idea, Mickie spoke clearly and loudly. "Deck 37, region 12," he said. Nothing seemed to happen, but Mickie assumed they were in motion. Less than a minute later, the door opened onto another corridor, and this time the area seemed full of people. Mickie walked out of the car and stopped, astonished. It was like being in a concourse or a supermarket, people walked by, some talking, others walking deliberately as if on business, others relaxed, sociably chatting, while some simply stood in groups and conversed. Not everyone was in the plain cotton overalls he had seen so far. Clothing varied from drab browns and greys to brilliant hues of all colours. But nothing was obvious to make the people anything but human.... Then Mickie saw how that was no longer true. Two men and a woman were standing by a branch of another corridor. All had pale blue faces, and seemed to have no noses. Fascinated, Mickie stared and saw that where noses might have been, just two small, oval openings could be seen. As he stared, the three seemed to feel his attention and looked at him. With a shock Mickie saw that they had bright red eyes, looking demonic in the stare they gave him. Mickie couldn't help but flinch.

"Cassoleans," murmured Grant, touching his shoulder. "Not as evil as they look, I assure you. Come, let's introduce you." He led the way to the trio, waved at them and then bowed slightly, his hands folded loosely together in front of his nose. Allie made the same gesture

43

and received a similar bow in return. Feeling stronger and braver, Mickie imitated them and was delighted to receive a bow back.

"Well done," said Allie. "This is our new associate," she said to the three. One of the men in the group spoke. As with the earlier meeting with the two in the corridor, Mickie could detect nothing of any human-sounding language. It was more like a continuous growl with an occasional clicking sound.

"No, we had no trouble finding him," said Allie in what was obviously a response. "His distress was quite loud and I think he is quite happy to be with us now."

"Yes, I really am," said Mickie, feeling easier by the second. To his astonishment, the alien woman bent over him and lightly touched her face to his. She smelled of something like apples, but with an extra tinge of flavour that Mickie could not identify. He couldn't help grinning with delight and both the men touched his shoulders and spoke again.

"They add their welcome to the ship," said Allie. "Everybody aboard knows that we entered the system in search of you and they are all happy that you have come with us."

With a parting wave, she moved on and led Mickie down the corridor until they came to another branch, down that just a short distance and stopped outside a doorway.

"Speak your name," she said. As Mickie did so, the door opened soundlessly.

"You first, Mickie," said Grant. "Have a look at your new quarters."

Mickie slowly walked inside and stopped, enthralled.

The room was bigger than the entire living room and downstairs area of his old house. The carpet was light blue and luxuriously deep. Around the walls were a series of couches and two coffee tables. One wall had a bookcase and the shelves seemed full. Curiously Mickie advanced on the case and was astonished to see a whole collection of his favourite books, a line of Asimov, Heinlein, Pohl and Blish, Zelazny and all the other well-read books from home. There were other books too, an Atlas and what looked like a series of reference books. A smaller room off one side was obviously his bedroom, and it contained a comfortable-looking bed with a desk and chair as well. Coming back into the main room, he saw a television and even a stereo set.

"You can listen to any music you want, even see any television programs you want," Allie said. "We thought you'd be more comfortable at first if they looked like the equipment at home, and the computer has a complete collection of Earth programs and music. You'll learn how to ask for whatever you want. But you may have seen the books there, apart from your old favourites. There's a complete text on each world we'll be visiting and you'll need to do some reading up beforehand, though you can get most of the information from the computer's teaching functions."

"This is my room? All just for me?" Mickie could hardly breathe.

"Yes it is," responded Allie, amused at his wonder. "Grant and I have another room like this next door and you can always speak to us on the intercom set. Later, you'll be able to order meals here too, but I think we'll set a rule for now that you have to eat in the main dining room with us or other people as you get to know them.

We don't want you feeling isolated. The first shock of dealing with aliens can be acute, even if you feel happy now, so we need to watch you."

"I'm sure I'll be okay," said Mickie, and felt certain of it. He had absolutely no sense of loss at leaving Earth, quite the reverse. As he had realised earlier, sitting in the shuttle, abandoning his parents and sister had left him with a feeling of astonishing liberation, more than enough to compensate for the sadness of knowing there were some friends he might never see again.

"Probably," replied Allie. "But you have already undergone extraordinary stress and new experiences for a small boy. There will be some price to pay at some point, so we'll keep a very careful eye on you. Anyway, let's go and have dinner. It's been hours since you ate anything."

Realising how true that was, Mickie was happy to follow them to the transporter again and this time to what looked like a large dining hall, not unlike the one at his old school. Ordinary round tables, each seating about eight people filled the space, and along each wall was a huge serving area from which people were taking a variety of substances.

"Just like a buffet on Earth," said Grant with a laugh. "But some of the flavours will be a bit different."

He was right. Mickie stared at the selection of offerings on the large plates at the serving table then decided to throw caution to the winds. He took a slice of what looked like roast beef, various odd-looking vegetables and two objects he would have sworn were simple roast potatoes.

"The meat is from an animal on home world," said Allie, watching his deliberate selection. "It will taste a lot like beef but with an extra zing I think you will like. The vegetables are perfectly normal products grown on Earth, as are the potatoes. We've grown a lot of those in our tanks. We've found that human taste buds and our own are almost identical."

"So if you like something, that means I will?"

"Absolutely certain," said Allie, having filled her plate and leading the way to a table at the edge of the dining area. Grant and Mickie followed and they sat down, Mickie very much aware that many of the diners were looking at him with interest.

"Don't worry about the attention, it will soon pass," said Grant. "Everybody on the ship knows that we diverted from our regular route to look for you, so their interest is natural."

Mickie nodded and turned his attention to the plate in front of him. He had a perfectly ordinary knife and fork that Allie had picked up for him and he almost laughed at the idea that he was eating a meal he could be having in the school canteen but instead was in an alien space ship millions of kilometres from Earth.

Allie was right about the meat. Mickie had never tasted anything quite like it. It certainly resembled beef, but the similarity with the tasteless, tough substance that his mother occasionally served ended with the appearance. The meat was so delicate it almost melted in his mouth, and the flavour reminded him a little of the astonishing drink he had first had on the shuttle. It sparkled on his tongue and seemed to glow with a delicious warmth that made his whole mouth come alive.

"I think I'm going to like it here," he said. "This is *fantastic!*"

"We thought you'd appreciate our cuisine," said Grant. "It's one of the biggest advantages of living aboard."

Mickie spent the next twenty minutes giving full attention to the varied tastes then sat back with a happy sigh. "That was just the best meal ever!" he exclaimed.

"Good!" said Allie. "We were pretty sure about your tastes, though there might have been a few problems. As you said, you're not human, though you've lived as one all your life. Maybe some of the foods you ate on Earth were not to your liking as much as others would have found them."

"Or perhaps because my mother was a lousy cook," replied Mickie.

Allie laughed. "Possibly! I think you can forget that awful cuisine from now on!"

Quite happily, still with a sense of awe that he had felt seeing the ship's transition to an incomprehensible form of travel, Mickie walked along with them to the transporter, back to the residential deck and to the door next to his own. The room they entered was much like his own, but larger.

"We have more space, being two of us," said Allie, seeing his examination of the room. "And as each of us has a professional capacity on the ship, we need a study room each as well." She saw the question growing on Mickie's face and laughed. "Yes, that's part of what we need to tell you all about," she said. "Have a seat, I'll get you a drink of that lovely yellow stuff, and we'll talk for a while."

Mickie took a wondrously comfortable couch, feeling no surprise as it adjusted to his body contours, put his feet up and leaned back. "I suppose I was wondering just what this ship does," he said, feeling a repeated sense of great pleasure at his comfort in addressing them this way. He had never held any sort of companionable conversation with his parents. The memory of them was already becoming fainter in his mind, he realised.

Allie busied herself at a console against one wall and came to the seat with a tray containing a glass of the delicious yellow drink, plus two other glasses with a different colour liquid in them. "Scotch," she said with a grin. "Grant and I developed a great taste for it during our times on Earth."

She took a spot on the couch next to Mickie, placing the tray in front of him. She reached one glass of scotch over to Grant, handed Mickie his yellow drink and sat back with her own.

Feeling very warm and happy, Mickie took his drink and relaxed.

"Most of the people on the ship are from Kalamos, like us," continued Allie in her gentle voice. "The exceptions are the Kaloti who are the primary crew and the Cassoleans you saw earlier, plus a third, smaller group called X'Kasxi. They are rather strange and you'll learn more about them later. There's a good reason for this arrangement. Our three planets, Kalamos, Cassolea and X'Katcxo are quite similar, with almost identical gravity and atmospheres that each of us can breathe. The Kaloti have a different environment, but they can live with reasonable ease in ours, though their own crew quarters have Kaloti gravity and lighting levels and they spend most of their time there. But they are the real masters of inter-galactic space flight and they run the ship."

Her voice was gentle and soothing and Mickie was beginning to feel the effects of the last couple of days' stresses.

"So are there intelligent races all over all the galaxies?"

"Not all," she replied. "Some of the galaxies we visit don't have any that we have found so far, and there are rarely more than a dozen or so in each. Most of them we leave alone, because they're still primitive."

"And who owns the ship?" Mickie began to feel his eyelids getting heavy.

"The ship belongs to the Kaloti, but we of Kalamos have it on permanent hire." Grant took up the narrative. "And our mission is largely trading, with a big element of diplomacy."

"Trading in what?" asked Mickie drowsily.

"Ooh, lots of stuff," replied Grant. "Our first call will be to a very weird planet where we can pick up some astonishing plants that can be made into pharmaceutical products that work against several illnesses on a number of planets among quite a few different species. It's a rather scary place, with *very* scary inhabitants, as you will see in a couple of weeks. Then there's a planet from which we get some textiles with beautiful qualities that any number of species use to make wonderful clothing. And we get gemstones from a place where the locals have three arms. It's all a wondrous Universe."

Mickie was struggling to stay awake, despite the fascination with what they were telling him. "So what do you do in all this?" he asked, his face partly pressed against Allie's side.

"Grant is what you could call an account executive," replied Allie. "He deals directly with the various species we encounter and negotiates the buying and selling of the things we get. And I'm an anthropologist. I study the cultures of different races, and their languages. My job is to learn as much as we can about each of the species we meet and develop the ways in which we deal with other, trying to understand the values and the motivations behind them all. Then we try and enhance the language comprehension, because we can never really be sure that we are talking about the same thing with some species. Despite all the years of dealing with each other, there's an awful long way to go before we all start to understand each other with any real depth."

"So what will I be doing while all this is going on?"

"You have two major projects, Mickie," Grant said. "You have to work hard at school to learn how to be a citizen of this astonishing Universe of ours. And then there's the other one."

"What's that?" Mickie was struggling to stay awake, almost as if he'd taken a sleeping pill.

"We have to find out who and what you are, and how come you were on Earth."

But Mickie was sound asleep.

Chapter 5 – The Learning Continues

When he awoke, he was in his own bed in his own quarters. He climbed out of the bed and started to walk to the bathroom. His right shoulder felt sore and he rubbed it, looking in the mirror to see a tiny mark like a small rash somewhere near his collarbone.

"Ah, you're awake," said a small voice, apparently a few inches away from his right ear. Startled, he jumped and looked around. There was nobody in the room.

"It's okay." He realised it was Allie's voice. "We're still in our own room, but what you're hearing is the translation and communications device. It was put in your shoulder while you were asleep. The reason you fell asleep so quickly was because we'd put something in your drink so we could do the operation immediately."

"My shoulder's sore," he said.

"Don't worry. It will wear off in an hour or two. But you'll find you'll understand anyone on the ship now, so it's a useful thing to have." Even through the weird device, he could hear the warm smile in her voice and his anxiety eased immediately. "When you're ready, come and see us. Just announce your name at our door and it will open. Oh, and you'll find some clothing near the bed. You might as well dress like a crewmember."

Still feeling a little sleepy, he made his way to the bathroom and explored the equipment. It was no problem identifying the toilet and the shower and there was an ample supply of toothpaste and soap. Everything was quite familiar, but much, much more luxurious than he was used to in his old home.

Back at the bed, he saw the tunic hanging from a hook on the wall. He touched the fabric and it felt smoother than it looked, like fine silk, and nothing like the simple cotton he had first thought. He found some underwear in a small cupboard, quickly put it on and climbed into the tunic. It was a perfect fit, and more comfortable than anything he'd ever worn. A pair of shoes like sneakers were sitting on the floor and these, too, fitted perfectly. Feeling like he was better dressed and smarter than he had ever been in his life, he jauntily walked to the door, which opened for him as he approached, walked the short distance to the adjoining cabin and announced himself.

That door opened soundlessly and he walked in to see Allie and Grant sitting comfortably around the coffee table in the middle of the spacious room. They were also wearing the Ship's standard tunic. Allie's was dark red and Grant's was simple black with a white line down each side.

"So, how is the newest spaceman of our crew?" asked Grant with a cheerful grin. "Come and have some breakfast. What would you like?"

"Could I have pancakes?"

"Coming right up in just a moment," replied Grant. Mickie sat down between them, wondering if he could ever have felt so happy before. In a few seconds, the delicious smell of pancakes filled the room.

"Right there," said Grant, pointing to a table against one wall. Several plates and eating utensils were visible, and a glass-fronted device like a small toaster oven.

Mickie went to the table, opened the glass front and found a platter of hot pancakes. There was a jug of syrup, everything he needed. Carrying them back to the coffee table, Mickie felt his mouth watering.

"But how...."

"You can do it, too," said Allie with a smile. "You can give instructions to the ship's computer, just as we can. Obviously, the range of instructions you can give is more limited than ours, but you will learn all that over the next few days. What we need to talk about is what you'll be doing while you're aboard. But finish your breakfast first!"

Happy to comply, Mickie fell upon the pancakes and utterly demolished them.

"You'll need lots of exercise if you're going to eat like that," commented Allie. "Fortunately, you'll be getting more than you need."

"What about washing up?"

"Not a problem," said Grant. "Just put the plates and things back on the table. The computer will take care of it."

After returning to the seats, Mickie sat back, expectantly.

"Lots of things to learn," started Allie. "The easiest is finding out how to get around the ship. Any time you're lost or need directions, just ask the computer."

"But how do I do that?" Mickie was baffled.

"Easy. Just think the question and address the computer by its name, which is 'Albert'."

"Albert? *Albert?*" Mickie almost choked with laughter. "Whoever called a computer *Albert?*"

"Well, you will, for a start," said Grant with a chuckle. "But you're the only one who will, though Allie and I will be able to as well until you're more experienced. We decided to give it a name unique to you, as we can be quite certain there's nobody else on the ship called Albert. So, coupled with your unique brainwave, the computer will recognise an instruction or a query from you and answer through the device in your shoulder. Until you get more used to thinking your orders or questions, you can speak aloud. Try it."

Mickie thought a few moments then spoke. "Albert, how far is the ship from Earth?"

"It's not possible to give you that as a distance, Mickie," said a cool voice in his ear. "We are now in hyperspace, and distance is not a valid indicator. However, we left the Earth's Solar System fourteen hours ago."

"Wow!" said Mickie. He looked at the two adults. "Did you hear that?"

Allie shook her head. "The computer spoke directly into your communication device, Mickie, and that transmits directly to your hearing system so that you hear the words even though nobody else can. You automatically interpreted the sound to be like somebody talking near to you, but in time, you'll learn how to hear the communication within your head."

Mickie tried again, fascinated. "Albert, if the ship dropped out of hyperspace right now, then how far would we be from Earth?"

The cool voice spoke again. "That is still an impossible question, Mickie. At any given millisecond, the distance would be dramatically different. Sometimes it would be greater than a later time because the relationship between hyperspace and normal space is non-existent. However, in fifteen seconds, I will sound a small chime. At that point, I will give you the distance as if the ship had returned to normal space at that precise millisecond."

Breathless, Mickie waited the few remaining seconds until he heard a tiny, melodious chime and the cool voice returned. "At that point, the ship would have been three hundred and seventy-two thousand light years from Earth."

"Awesome, isn't it?" said Allie. "I can imagine how the computer answered your question."

"Where are we going? And when will we get there?" Mickie hung on the answer.

"That makes me feel like the computer," said Allie, laughing. "Any detailed answer I could give you would be meaningless, because you will need a thorough knowledge of intergalactic geography. But, here are the main facts. The planet is not in the Milky Way, the galaxy that contains Earth. It's not even in your nearest neighbour, the Greater Magellanic Cloud, but over thirty million light years away. We'll be travelling for about two weeks and the planet we're heading for has no name that we can discern from the inhabitants, because we have been completely unable to establish communications with those inhabitants."

"Why not? Aren't they an intelligent species?"

"We don't know. They may be, possibly more than we are. But they're completely alien in the strictest sense of the word. Not a single common bond has ever been discovered."

"So what do they look like?" Mickie was fascinated. He saw the serious expression on the adults' faces and felt an expectant shiver.

"They're spiders," replied Allie. "Absolutely <u>huge</u> spiders, twice the size of a man."

"Yech!" said Mickie loudly. He had always hated spiders.

"Yech is about right. But there's no risk if we stay together. They will not attack a group, and we carry weapons, anyway. The danger is in being alone, because then you'd be hunted and caught, and that's not anything one would wish on *anyone*."

"Will I come out with you when we get there?" Mickie was both terrified and fascinated by the idea.

"Yes, I think you should," said Grant. "If you are to be a citizen of this Universe, and if we are to find out just who and what you are, you should experience everything we do."

"I understand."

"Anyway," said Allie, "we have other things to think about, and your education is one of them."

"My education?"

"Sure," said Allie. "Grant told you this last night, but I think you were already asleep. You would have needed an Earth-type education if you'd stayed behind, because you'd want to grow up and become someone useful as well as earn a good living. Now you're part of a civilization thousands of times more complex and widespread than on Earth. Whatever it turns out that you are, or wherever we find you come from, you will need to learn about your new environment and how to live in it."

"I suppose so." Mickie wasn't too worried by the

news. He'd enjoyed school and he knew he was highly intelligent, judging by the grades he'd got. "I think I do remember last night. How are we going to find out who I am?"

"We have absolutely no idea right now," Grant said with a grin. "But we've started by finding out what we *do* know. It's quite clear you are not human, nor are you Kalamosian like us. The Ship's medical crew gave you a complete examination while they were putting in the communication chip, and you are something very similar, but not from either race. It wasn't anything physical, just some minor variations in brain scans, but enough to show the difference. As we travel, we'll probably start to pick up clues around the Universe. Somebody has to know something."

Mickie thought about it and decided the idea of being an unknown species was quite exciting. But first things first, he thought.

"Will I do the school stuff in a classroom with other kids?"

"Some of it," replied Allie. "There are quite a lot of other people of your equivalent age on the ship, and you'll meet them all in the next few days. But you'll also spend some time with Albert as your teacher and I think you'll find that's really good fun."

* * *

She was right, using Albert as a teacher was great fun. He didn't have to go to a classroom, because the computer had all the facilities for all locations. Nor was there was anything to see at first, as Albert appeared to hear Mickie anytime he spoke, and the computer's voice came from all points of his cabin.

"When will we reach Kalamos, Albert?" Mickie asked as his first efforts at using the facility. He was excited about having a whole new home planet and was eager to see it.

"The ship's schedule is that arrival at Kalamos will occur one hundred and ninety two days from now," replied Albert. Mickie decided that six months was not too long.

"Will you give me information about it before we get there?"

"Of course. But first, you should learn something about our next port of call. As you know, our first visit, scheduled for twelve days from now, is to the planet of Spiders. We have no local name for it, because no communication has ever been established with the dominant species. But common usage refers to it simply as Spiderworld and all the intelligent species in our Universe refer to it as such."

As Albert spoke, a three-dimensional image of a planet appeared before Mickie. It seemed to hang in the air in the middle of the room, slowly rotating. Mickie gasped with the shock of the sudden appearance.

"Albert! What's that?"

"This is an image of the planet we'll be visiting," the computer replied. "I will show you many worlds this way as we proceed with your education."

Mickie stared at the glowing image. The world was largely water. Ice caps at both poles were huge, even larger than he could recall of the Arctic regions of Earth, but the landmasses were a series of large islands concentrated around the equatorial regions.

"The planet has three hundred and eleven separate islands, all within a distance of about one thousand kilometres of the equator," said Albert. "There is no land under the icecaps. The planet is fifteen percent less than Earth in size, but over twenty-five percent less in mass, so gravity is quite low. Because of their position, the landmasses are all very tropical in climate, with high average temperatures and humidity. This is the dominant species."

The picture before Mickie changed sharply and he sat back with a surge of dismay. It looked nothing less than a monstrous Tarantula spider. Next to it was a picture of a man. The spider towered over the man and the image was every nightmare that anyone on Earth might have had.

Mickie watched in horrified fascination as the picture changed. The image of the man vanished and now only the vague shape of the spider could be seen, mostly hidden behind a curtain of plants. These seemed to be lush, well-flowered vegetation with enormous stems that wove around the scene like massive, coloured hosepipes. Across one section, a beautiful web could be seen, much like any spider's web on Earth. As Mickie watched, a small animal wandered into the scene. It looked something like a small deer, grazing peacefully on the ground vegetation. Suddenly, making Mickie start with a frightened jerk, another spider jumped out before the deer, which leaped in terror right into the web. Its struggles had no effect, and within a second or two, the spider hiding in the vegetation had moved out, onto the web and Mickie saw two hideous fangs bite into the neck of the deer, which froze almost immediately. The spider lifted the creature off the web and scuttled away into the vegetation. The camera seemed to follow it and Mickie saw the spider hang the deer onto a branch. The camera closed in on the deer's head and the eyes revealed that the animal was still alive. The look of horror and hopelessness caused a wave of fear in Mickie.

"The prey will live several weeks," said the dispassionate voice of Albert. "If it is to serve as food, it will be lucky, because it will be dead relatively quickly. However, if it is to serve as an incubator for the spider's young, it will live for as long as ten weeks until the eggs have hatched and begun to feed on the living flesh."

Mickie was shivering with what he had seen. "Please, Albert, can we move on?" he begged. But Albert was immune to the plea.

"Not just yet. First, you should know that we will harvest several plants from this world. They will be used to make drugs that cure serious illness in a number of the species of our Universe. These drugs cannot be synthesised, so we must return frequently to Spiderworld. However, as signatories to a convention agreed to by most intelligent races, we will only take a limited amount each trip, and each time from a different area. So far, we have not revisited any particular area, so any damage is quite temporary and repairs itself within days in the tropical climate."

"Now can we move on?" Mickie asked again.

"No, not now," said Albert. "You need to meet some other young travellers on this ship. Return to the transporter and request location 'Deck thirty, Education Centre'."

Cheerfully, Mickie moved to the door. He stopped as he thought he saw something strange. A small pool of black seemed to be settled on the carpet just to one side of the doorway. Mickie stared, and the black changed, becoming a small whirlpool of smoke that shrank abruptly and vanished. A small shiver ran down his back as he cautiously approached where the black smoke had been, but there was nothing remaining. Deciding that it was something about the Ship that he had yet to learn, he resolved to ask Allie or Grant about it later and resumed his way to the Education Centre.

Chapter 6 – Making New Friends

A few minutes later, the transporter door opened in a large, open area that seemed full of children. All eyes turned on Mickie as the door slid aside and he froze in embarrassment. He was saved from the awful moment by an adult of the red-eyed Cassolean people who walked up to him.

"Mickie," said the individual. "Welcome to our school."

Mickie's initial reaction was fear. The red eyes looked evil to him and at first glance, the face was so different from anything familiar that he froze. The man's face was smooth, almost like satin, a deep blue that seemed the same shade all over. The nose consisted of just two small holes, though the mouth was as human as anyone from Earth and Mickie saw a tongue like any other. The hair had a red tinge to it, but was arranged over the head much like a human's would be. Mickie relaxed a little as he realised that he understood the person's speech and the words were welcoming. The last time he had heard it was when he met one of this species on his arrival. Then, the speech had been incomprehensible noise, now he understood perfectly. The device implanted in his shoulder worked.

"Pretty scary, huh?" The words were astonishingly familiar and thus reassuring. Mickie felt most of the remaining fear leave him. He nodded, not yet trusting his voice.

"Don't worry, first contact with alien races is usually a time for panic, fear and general wetting of pants."

Astonished, Mickie looked fully into the red eyes. The creature was joking, and he hadn't considered that an alien could crack jokes. The face above him remained immobile, but somehow the red eyes were sparkling and seemed less terrifying.

"My name is Faldor," said the alien and touched him on the shoulder. "I'll be one of your teachers here and our job is just to make you feel at home and teach you how to get around and become familiar with the astonishing new life you're leading."

At last, Mickie relaxed fully. It was just going to be like school. "Thank you," he said simply. "I'll enjoy that."

"I'm sure you will," said Faldor. "Now, one thing before we join some others. Everybody on this ship knows that you're from Earth, and you are the very first Earthling to join a crew. They know that we altered course to pick you up, but they don't know that you are not originally from that planet. So as far as anyone else will know, you're an Earthling, human child and our trip to your planet was not just to pick up our agents there but also to collect a child in distress. You asked to come along with them and we agreed. So that's the way we will keep it. No point in having too much mystery about you. Is that okay?"

Mickie nodded. "That's okay."

"Good. Then let's join some of the others. This is a free time period, so everybody is just doing what interests them. I know just the group for you."

Mickie looked round the room. This time, instead of the sensation of a sea of strange faces, he saw that most of the children were gathered into groups of anything from three to six or seven. Some were just talking, others were gathered round odd devices or even reading perfectly ordinary looking books.

Faldor left his hand on Mickie's shoulder and guided him to where three other young people were sitting on the floor, studying a board that was multi-coloured and held several different coloured objects much like chess pieces. Working hard to keep his nerve, Mickie allowed himself to be steered to the group. The seated trio looked up as Mickie arrived.

"This is Mickie," said Faldor. "He's from Earth, our last port of call. Why don't you help him get adjusted?" With that, Faldor left.

Mickie looked at the others. One of them was another Cassolean, a young male. His red eyes had looked briefly up as Mickie was introduced, then he returned to intense study of the board game. The other two looked as human as Mickie, one a boy who seemed a little younger than Mickie and the other was a girl. She studied him seriously.

"You're from Earth?" she asked.

He nodded.

"You look exactly like me."

Mickie couldn't suppress a grin. "Not exactly," he said, and the girl's face lost its gravity as she chuckled. The other two emitted cackles of humour also, and Mickie relaxed completely at last.

"You know what I mean," she said, and the friendliness in her face was warm. She had a straight nose and dark eyes, her hair was jet black and hung in a ponytail down her back. Mickie thought she was very pretty and felt a wave of shyness.

"We could be from the same species," she continued. "Do all Earthlings look like you?"

"Pretty well. You must be from Kalamos like my guardians."

"I'm from Kalamos," she agreed. "But how could....?"

"They're called Allie and Grant."

"Oh!" The girl's face beamed. "They're great friends of my parents. I've known them since I was very little. But their names are really Alliandra and Grantorel. They used their operational Earth names for you. My name is Melkana."

"And I'm Drellion," said the other boy. "I'm her brother, unfortunately." Mickie could see the resemblance in the straight nose and dark eyes. Melkana smacked him lightly on the head.

"Insolent brat!" she said, but Mickie could see her tiny smile and the grin on Drellion's face indicated great affection between the two.

The Cassolean finally looked up from the board and smiled. "Sorry, I wasn't being rude, but this problem is tricky. My name's Fencris. Sit down and see what you think." He resumed his study of the board. His face was a paler blue than the teacher's, but the red eyes were no less startling. His hair was a sort of russet brown and worn as short as Mickie's.

Mickie sat down on the other side of the board and crossed his legs. "What's the game?" he asked.

The other two copied him and sat down on the other two sides of the board. "It's called "Sheekmetter," said Drellion. "It's really tough. Fencris is the school champion."

Mickie studied the board. His first impression had been about right. The board was broken into small squares of alternating black and white. The two sets of pieces were of various colours, and Mickie counted six different ones of various shapes.

Fencris briefly looked up at Mickie, saw that he was studying the pieces, and resumed his own careful inspection. "The idea is to surround the Emperor piece here," - he pointed at a black piece that was bigger than the rest excepting a red piece of the same shape – "with your own troops. You move one or two pieces at a time, but if you move two, they must be identical moves except that one must advance or retreat one square less than the other. There's a different move for each piece."

"It sounds like chess back on Earth," said Mickie.

Melkana chuckled. "It's almost bound to be the same game! When I heard that we were coming to Earth's solar system, I asked the computer a few questions. We probably introduced it hundreds of years ago when our first scouts came to your planet to check you out, but some changes have probably happened."

"Check mate!" Mickie suddenly remembered. "That's what you say when you win! I think it means 'The King is Dead' or something. But I think we can only move one piece at a time."

Fencris clenched both fists and shook them over his head. "Got it!" he said. "Watch! I move the two Huntsmen up here..." He moved two yellow pieces forward; one went three spaces, the other two. "Then you'd have to move the Emperor here..." The black object moved sideways two places. "Then I'd bring just one Horseman here..." A blue piece went three spots at an angle. "And I win!" He sat back, looking satisfied. The other three stared hard. Mickie hadn't followed it at all, but the two young Kalamosians nodded.

"Very good," said Melkana. "Okay, who wants to play Loopies?"

"Yes!!!" The other two boys shot to their feet, followed by the girl.

"Come on, Mickie, this is just the best!" shouted Fencris and they set off at a run to the transporter door. Mickie was happy to follow them, feeling delighted with his new friends.

A few moments of silent, smooth travel and the door opened onto the huge hangar where Mickie had first entered the ship. He followed them in a mad dash to the centre of the cavernous space, his excitement growing in response to the obvious enthusiasm of the others. Around the edge, several of the donut-shaped shuttles sat silently.

"Ten per cent, ten per cent!" shrieked Melkana as she led the foursome into the emptiness.

"Medron, set gravity at ten per cent in the Loopies arena." Fencris spoke clearly, and Mickie realised he was instructing the computer, using a personal name in just the same way as Albert was Mickie's own. As they reached the middle of the shuttle bay, Mickie felt himself becoming lighter and lighter, and he stumbled in the sense of falling and sprawled all over the metal floor in a weird slow-motion but intriguing way. The others laughed without malice and Mickie couldn't help joining in as he slowly regained control of his limbs.

"Sorry!" shouted Fencris. "I keep forgetting you're new aboard. Okay, everyone, to your sides! Mickie, watch what we do."

Each of the other three jumped in a huge, soaring loop and landed neatly, one on each of the other three sides of a massive square that Mickie now saw was painted on the floor, leaving Mickie alone on one side. Each side was perhaps twenty metres long. The four of them now faced each other, Fencris opposite Mickie, Drellion on Mickie's left, Melkana on his right.

"I'm the first catcher!" shouted Melkana. "Fencris, go!"

Fencris launched himself in a beautiful arc in Mickie's direction. He flew at least twenty metres into the air, tucked his arms and legs close to his body and turned a neat somersault at the peak of the curve. But just as he jumped, Melkana did the same, turned a similar head-over-heels manoeuvre, straightened as she reached the peak of the arc and neatly caught Fencris round the waist. Both of the children changed direction as the collision occurred and the combined forces and directions had them flying together into the corner of the square on Mickie's left.

"Six points to me!" shouted Melkana, and launched herself at Mickie, landing without a mis-step right by his side. "I got five points for catching him, and you score one point for each somersault you do before the catch. If I'd missed him, he'd have scored five points for evading me and one point for his somersault. Okay, you try it with Drellion. Just jump with enough strength to get as high as you can over the middle of the square and land on the other side. Don't try a loop yet."

She looked over at her brother. "Ready? Okay, go!"

She looked at Mickie. "Go!" she snapped.

Mickie tried. He jumped at what seemed a reasonable level of power and completely messed up. In a breathless, startling shock, he swooped straight up at only a slight angle from the vertical and soared nearly ten metres into the air. Quite unable to control his body, he spun several times, lost his orientation and panicked, letting out a shriek of terror. But a pair of arms wrapped themselves round his shoulders and the helpless tumbling slowed as he began his descent to the ground.

"Bit tricky until you've had practice," said Fencris calmly, dropping together with him, and cleverly arranging himself so that his legs reached the ground first and absorbed the momentum, leaving Mickie quite unhurt but utterly embarrassed.

"Oh Mickie, I'm so sorry!" Melkana came over to him and hugged him. "I made you go far too quickly, you should have had a couple of practice leaps first."

Rather enjoying the attention from the girl, Mickie tried to act cool. "Not a problem," he said, controlling his breathing, which was still a bit ragged. "Let me try one first."

He worked his way back to the side of the square, concentrated hard then launched himself at an angle of forty-five degrees at the opposite side. He almost got it right. With a most exhilarating sensation of flight he reached a height of some ten metres over the middle of the square and landed on his feet just a metre or two past the line of the other side. Applause from the other three greeted him as he kept his feet.

"*WHOOOOOEEEEEE!*" he shouted and made the return jump. But in the excitement he misjudged again and flew straight into the three standing together. All of them caught him and giggled loud and long as they kept him from flying past them to the wall of the hangar in a tangle of arms and legs falling everywhere.

"You'll get the hang of it," laughed Melkana. "It takes a lot of practice."

"Okay, one more," said Drellion. "Me to catch Fencris."

Mickie watched as this time, Fencris did a complete triple somersault as he reached the top. Drellion missed him by a small distance without trying a somersault at all, but landed very neatly right on the line of the opposite side.

"Eight points to me!" shouted Fencris. "Alright, Mickie, one more try. Drellion, you jump, Mickie is catcher."

Mickie watched carefully as Drellion jumped, tried to judge the arc of his flight and leaped off the floor. Keeping an eye on his target, he saw the smaller child do a single somersault and then realised he was going to miss by at least a couple of metres. Drellion flew by above Mickie, giggling with delight.

"Six points, six points!" he shouted as he flew by. Mickie was so absorbed in trying to make the catch that he forgot about setting up for the landing and fell in tangle of his own arms and legs, slowly bouncing a couple of times though quite unhurt in the low gravity.

"Wow!" he said, breathlessly. "This is hard! But it's great fun. Will you guys teach me how to do it properly?"

"It's our favourite game," said Melkana. "And the grown-ups encourage it because it's great practice for space walking when you have to work in zero-gravity."

"And wait until you see the grown-up's version," Fencris added. "It's called Gravity-Ball and it's pretty wild. Loopies is training for that when we get a bit bigger."

They spent another half hour of play, and Mickie began to feel he might learn to handle himself at this startling and exhilarating game that was like so many of his dreams of flying. But the game was interrupted by a voice that seemed to come from nowhere, though Mickie realised it must have come through his communication device in his shoulder.

"Okay, kids," said the voice of Faldor, the teacher. "Time to clean up and report to the main classroom for Galactic Geography."

Mickie walked with the others to the transporter, gave his directions and was back in his room within minutes. After showering and putting on a new tunic, he found his way back to the education centre where he had first met his new friends. He decided that school was a lot more fun than in Manchester, back on Planet Earth. But Galactic Geography? This should be interesting.

The room that had previously been a large, flat area now had become an auditorium, with three rows of seats in a semi-circle around an empty area about five metres wide. Faldor, the teacher who had first met Mickie was standing in the middle of that area, talking to two children, one a Cassolean like himself, the other was Drellion. The conversation seemed animated.

Mickie took a seat in the rear of the room, still feeling shy about being too much in the public gaze, but he saw Melkana and Fencris sitting in the front row waving at him. More relaxed, he went down to join them.

"One of my favourite classes," Fencris said. "I think you'll like it."

"*Every* class is his favourite," Melkana said with a smile. "This blue-faced twit here, your new buddy, is supposed to be a total genius. If he ever goes back to Cassolea, he has his pick of Universities."

"I sort of got that impression," Mickie said. "Have you always been this way, Fencris?"

"Mostly." Fencris was neither embarrassed nor boastful about discussing the topic. "I've been lucky. Both my parents are University professors and this travelling is for their research. So I had a good start anyway, and the education they gave me was brilliant. I just seem to suck up anything I want."

"Unlike the rest of us who have to actually *work*," Melkana said.

Fencris chortled. "Listen to her! Wait till you see what she gets up to!"

Amused and pleased at the closeness that seemed to surround his new friends, Mickie looked around as the class settled down. The class seemed to have about as many blue-faced children as any another. Drellion joined the three with a wide grin on his face.

"Recovered from the bruising of Loopies, Mickie?"

"Just about. Hey, all I see are Cassoleans and Kalamosians. Aren't there any other races in the class?"

"Not often," Melkana replied. "There are no Kaloti children aboard and very few X'Kasxi, only three or four, I think. I think X'Kasxi kids aren't normally allowed to travel, for some reason, but honestly, we know so little about them. Anyway, they always have their lessons alone, though they do appear in free time sessions."

"I haven't even *seen* an X'Kasxi," Mickie said. "What do they look like?"

Before Melkana could reply, the lights dimmed in the auditorium and brightened over the teacher's area.

"Inter-Galactic travel has been around for just over three hundred thousand years," Faldor began without any opening introduction. "As you know, the Kaloti were the first and greatest pioneers into the technology of hyperspace and gravity control, both of which were essential for crossing distances of millions of light years. However, in that time, we have only begun to explore the Universe and our travels take us to just twenty-four galaxies, leaving millions still untouched. However, our local neighbours represent the range of galaxy structures, as far as we know. There are Spiral Arm galaxies....."

With a soundless flicker, a three-dimensional image appeared between the teacher and the class. Mickie's first impulse was to laugh with delight at how beautiful it was. The image of the galaxy glowed with its own light, looking like a stupendous Catherine Wheel, brightest at the centre while multiple arms trailed off from the rotating middle, fading from thick roots down to fine ends where individual stars could be seen.

"This is the most interesting galaxy for us, because it holds the home worlds of all but one of the species on this Ship," Faldor continued. "We will look at the Kaloti home galaxy in another session, but the rest of us come from various solar systems here.

"*This,*" – a small spot on the edge of the main body of the galaxy glowed red – "is the home system of the X'Kasxi. They call the galaxy the Silver Sea. We will look at their home system later."

Another spot lit up. It was way across the main body of the galaxy and lay in the thicker part of one arm that was trailing from it.

"This is the Cassolean home system. We of Cassolea named the galaxy the White Ocean, an interestingly similar name to the X'Kasxi. That distance across the main body between these two systems is 80,000 light years. And over here," – another red spot lit up – "is the Kalamosian System."

The red spot was in an adjoining arm to that containing Cassolea, but a little further outward from the centre, in a thinner part of the limb.

"The distance between the Cassolean system and the Kalamosian is about 5,000 light years. The people of that planet named the galaxy Glowing Sky, a name common to all areas of their world for many thousands of years, since they were primates. Now, here is an interesting development."

Faldor paused for a moment. "Now we have a new region to interest us. For here, very close to the Kalamosian system is the home system of our newest colleague, Mickie Dalton."

Yet another red spot glowed, this time looking just a finger-width distance from Kalamos.

"Mickie, stand up, will you, just so everybody can recognise you?"

Fighting embarrassment, Mickie rose briefly to his feet, looked round the room and sat down again.

"As you see," continued Faldor. "The two systems are unusually close, a mere two hundred light years. This proximity is far less than any two populated systems encountered in the history of inter-galactic travel. And as you have just seen, the physical resemblance between Humans and Kalamosians is almost absolute, defying anything but advanced scanning equipment to identify the differences. This has been the subject of considerable study at a number of universities in the ten years since our agents have been examining Mickie's home planet, Earth, and most experts believe that there is a common ancestry between the two species."

Mickie remembered that Allie had said something like that during the trip to meet up the Ship and it pleased him to think he was perhaps the same species as she and Grant were.

"However," the teacher continued, "that implies events in history so far back that nobody has any knowledge of, but will be of crucial importance if we are ever able to learn of them. Meanwhile, back to Galactic Geography. And by the way, Humans call the galaxy the Milky Way, again quite similar in style to the other names our species have given it."

The image of the galaxy began to expand, though the edges disappeared as it grew, as if a camera were homing in on the red area that had been named as the Cassolean home system. In a few seconds, there was nothing but a single glowing sun hanging over the teacher's area.

"Balgos," said the teacher. "That's the Cassolean sun. As seems a common pattern in most species, the name was once the word for light or fire in one of our ancient languages. Similarly, the name of our planet is also an ancient word meaning earth. Now, here is a model representation of our system, showing the planets and their distances from the sun. Note that is not accurate, this is just a model."

The glowing sun vanished, and in its place was just a white ball about two metres in diameter. Several models of planets hovered at increasing distances from the sun. The nearest was tiny, just the size of a pea, the second was much larger, the size of a cricket ball, the third about the same size, then a smaller one was fourth, followed by six more of gradually increasing size. The third one suddenly lit up as if a bulb had gone on inside it.

"That is Cassolea," said Faldor. "It is about nine light minutes from the sun."

Something about the model tugged at Mickie's memories, but he stopped puzzling about it as a second image appeared in the air alongside the first one.

"This is the Kalamosian System. The two models are to scale. What do you see about it that is noteworthy?"

As with the Cassolean model, planets lined up from the sun. The third one out was lit up also, so Mickie assumed that was Kalamos. It looked to be about the same distance from the sun as was Cassolea. There was a tiny one nearest the sun, a planet of similar size to Kalamos was second, a smaller one was fourth, then six more much larger planets at increasing distances, with one tiny one at the end.

"And here's the system of Mickie's Earth."

A third model appeared. One difference struck Mickie. Where there had been a fifth planet out from the sun in the other two models, now there was a line of asteroids in a complete ring round the sun. Otherwise, the three models looked very similar, with Earth lying about the same distance from the sun as the other two populated planets were from their suns.

Finally, a Kalamosian girl behind Mickie spoke up. "They all look alike," she said. "Apart from that asteroid ring in the last model."

"Good," said Faldor. "And that asteroid ring is the wreckage of a planet that was once there. What about the populated planets?"

"They look about the same distance from the sun," the young girl said.

"In fact, *exactly* the same, nine light minutes," Faldor said. "Which tells us something about the conditions required for the life forms we represent, all very similar. The differences are that Cassolea's sun has a different radiation pattern that has caused the blue faces, though the degree of blue varies by region. On Mickie's planet Earth, another variation has arisen, in that Earth wobbles on its axis of rotation more than our other planets. Can anyone tell us what that could do?"

This time a Cassolean boy raised his hand. "That would cause more extremes of climate between equator and pole," he said.

"Excellent, Jarrol!" Faldor was delighted. "And what would that do to the inhabitants?"

"More extremes of physical type," Jarrol replied.

"Exactly. And on Earth, they vary from very tall, slender, black-skinned people in the hot regions, to short, stocky, white-skinned people in the very cold climates and numerous shades in between. Physical types mostly result from the body's efforts to manage its environment."

The models vanished from the air and the lights in the room returned to normal.

"That's it for now," Faldor said. "Tomorrow, we'll learn about other galactic structures and look at the ones nearest our own. Please do some study ahead of that and come prepared."

"So how was that, Mickie?" Drellion turned in his seat to look at him.

"A bit overwhelming," Mickie admitted. "I've read a bit about these things, but it was always so *theoretical.*

Suddenly, I'm seeing whole galaxies as places we'll actually visit!"

"I think you're going to have a wonderful time," Fencris said. The other two grinned in support.

"I think so, too," Mickie said.

"Dinner time," said Melkana. "Come on, horrible little brother, let's go and see our parents."

Drellion blew a loud raspberry at her, but cheerfully followed her out of the school room. Realising with pleasure that meals with his family were no longer awful, dangerous affairs, Mickie waved at all of them and set off to join Grant and Allie.

After a couple of days of adjustment, Mickie was able to get closer to his new friends and talk individually to them. He had to pinch himself sometimes as he realised that he was talking to aliens from other worlds, but acceptance came quickly and they turned out to be just the same as he was, kids enjoying a colourful, exciting life. One afternoon, he spent some time with Fencris, seeing what the young Cassolean was doing in his studies into physics and mathematics. He came away from the first session almost frightened by the technology Fencris used with casual ease. The Cassolean had built a miniature gravity-control unit the size of his thumbnail and installed it into his armchair, floating the thing in graceful arcs around his cabin, laughing loudly at Mickie's expression of amazement.

"But... how did you *do* that?" Mickie gasped.

"Actually, it's quite simple. You shouldn't be too worried Mickie, it's pretty standard technology, really. I just played around and built my own."

"It makes me feel like a real dummy when I see what you're all so used to," Mickie said.

"You'll learn fast." Fencris brought the chair down to the cabin floor. "Let me show you what I'm working on in maths."

He tried, but Mickie, who had never found mathematics all that easy, was totally lost within seconds as Fencris projected a series of formulae from his computer terminal onto the wall and tried to explain the process he was exploring.

"Hey, Mickie, I grew up with this stuff and I'm supposed to be a genius, anyway," Fencris said with his sparkling red eyes aflame with amusement. "You'll get to learn more as time goes on."

"It scares me, I must say. I wonder if I'll ever be useful in this society."

"Useful? Mickie, we wouldn't have diverted this huge ship from its travels just to pick up some useless twit from a backward planet if a lot of people hadn't seen a lot of value in you, now would we?"

"I suppose not." Mickie felt a little more sure of himself after that and decided Fencris was a good guy to have around. "Will you tell me about Cassolea?" he asked. "What's life like there?"

"Not now," Fencris said. "Later, we'll have more time, and anyway, you could learn the first bits from the computer. Once you have that, I'll fill in the details!"

"It's a deal," Mickie said, deciding that he had made a special friend in this blue-faced boy with the demonic red eyes.

"But there was something else I was wondering about," he continued.

"What's that?"

"Everybody seems to get on so well on this ship," Mickie said. "I suppose I would think that with several different races all in a confined space, even though it's so huge, there'd be some sort of conflict, some of the time."

"Good thought, young Earthling," Fencris said with a grin that reflected appreciation of Mickie's insight. "Normally, that's exactly what would happen. But when you join a crew like this one, you get some very direct training in tolerance, because at some point, our lives, the whole Ship might depend on just one person, or several people doing their job right. You might get some of that training in school."

"Okay, I see," Mickie said thoughtfully. "But what if two people simply hate each other? Sometimes it happens and neither of them knows why."

"It does," Fencris agreed. "And the computer handles it. First thing is that two such people wouldn't be allowed aboard if they worked in the same field and had to have regular contact. But if they wouldn't meet professionally, then the computer watches them both if they are getting near each other and warns both of them. We're all trained enough to accept that limitation. You wouldn't be accepted for the position if you were too immature to handle that."

"That's clever! And I suppose you'd never be allowed to join up if you were the type that just hated aliens?"

"Hey, why would anyone like that want to do this job? Come on, let's go and meet the others."

Sometimes he found himself alone with Melkana, sitting and talking about some of the adventures she and the crew of the ship had experienced in the last few months and about their possible futures. Something about her serene face and easy smile made it easy for him to express his worries, his excitement and his mystification about his past, present and future. It had not taken long before he felt comfortable enough with his new friends to let down his guard.

"This is humungously exciting," he said to her one day as they sat in the coffee lounge. "But I wish I knew what I really was."

She looked at him curiously and Mickie realized he had let slip something he wasn't intending.

"Why?" she asked. "I thought you were from Earth."

"Well...." He hesitated, realising he was about to enter new territory that might affect his friendship.

"I wasn't planning on telling anyone, but you're my friend." With a small start, he realized how much that was true. All three of them had become the closest friends he had ever known. "It seems I'm not really a Human. I must have been born somewhere else and placed on Earth, but Allie said they don't know what I really am."

"How amazingly cool!" she said. "A man of mystery! But don't you know anything at all?"

Feeling buoyed by her enthusiasm and interest, he decided he'd made the right decision in telling her. "Not a thing," he said. "I've got no memories of anything other than being miserable with those awful people."

"Were they that bad?"

"They were." Without embarrassment, he told her the whole story of his life on Earth. Her gentle empathy made it easy for the words to flow out.

"Don't worry about it," she said. "You have lots of time to find out who you are, and now you have two wonderful people to look after you instead of those silly people back on Earth."

"But what if I turn out to be some sort of monster? Or something so retarded I'll never be able to learn the stuff you need?"

"You won't Mickie, I won't let you. One day, you'll find out the truth and I just know it will be something fantastic and you'll help the whole universe."

"I hope so! What are you going to do when you grow up?"

"I don't really know yet. I love playing music and I can play several instruments. I may become a teacher. I can paint, too."

"Wow! I could never do any of those things. Can I see some of your paintings?"

"Not yet." Melkana seemed a little shy. "When I've done some better stuff. I'll play some of my instruments for you, though."

"I'd like that. What have you got?"

"My favourite is my flute," she said. "And I like the piano, which is a lot like the ones you'd have known."

"You're amazing. You can do so many things."

"Well, I'm pretty sure you'll find out that you can do some pretty cool stuff too, Mickie. It's just that you've been cooped up on Earth with those horrible people in that stinky house!"

"You'll stay on the ship, won't you?" Mickie was suddenly anxious. In just a few days, all his friends had become hugely important to him, but Melkana had developed a special place in his mind and travelling without her would be a lot less enjoyable.

"Oh yes," she said to his great relief. "Our parents are having too much fun to give this up for ages yet!

Anyway, I wouldn't miss seeing what we're all going to get up to on the next trip!"

In their laughter they had another drink, just as Drellion and Fencris appeared and demanded to know what all the cackling was about. Mickie decided he had never been happier.

Chapter 7 – The World of The Spiders

Days followed days with dizzying speed. Mickie spent half his time consulting Albert about the various species of the known Universe, and much of the rest of it with his friends in the school. He didn't see much of Faldor, the teacher, but eventually guessed that it was deliberate, allowing him to become familiar with other races at a fairly slow rate, using the friendship with the others as a tool. Mealtimes he usually spent with Allie and Grant and it never became any less of a delight that he could sit with them and tell them about his school experiences and know that they were genuinely interested and pleased with his progress.

"We get to Spiderworld in two days," said Grant one evening. "We plan on taking you out with us, if that's okay with you. Are you still ready to join us?"

Mickie felt a tremor of fear, remembering the monstrous images from his first learning machine session. "What will we be doing?" he asked, trying to swallow his fear.

But Allie must have seen it. "Don't be frightened," she said. "Stick close to us and you'll be fine. Grant will be the one examining the vegetation to ensure that it's the right type and he'll define exactly how much we take to minimise damage. I'll be looking around for any signs

I can see of intelligence, such as spider nests, any indicators, any sort of design that shows meaning. I'll also be trying to communicate again, but so far it's been hopeless."

"How do you do that?" Mickie was fascinated, despite the worry.

"We use the Speakers. Remember what I told you about them. They communicate telepathically, and that mode of speech is instantaneous over all distances, though we have no idea how. So I'll ask the Speaker who will work with us to try various ideas, questions, concepts and so on with any Spider we meet, and he will try and transmit to the Spider. If anything happens at all, the Speaker will let me know."

"Can I listen in too?"

"Of course! So what I suggest is that you do some more study in the morning session with Albert and ask about the Speakers and that will help you understand when the time comes."

"You bet!" Mickie was proud that she would let him in on the process of her work and some of the fear went away. The rest of the evening passed in a relaxed, happy manner as the three talked about Mickie's learning, about the wonderful game of Loopies, about some other species that his guardians had encountered, and Mickie finally decided to walk back to his own cabin, feeling the wave of delight he felt each time he entered, at the thought that this was all his own, so different from the bleak, miserable room on Earth.

The door opened at his bidding and he walked in, humming cheerfully to himself.

And stopped.

The small pool of darkness was there again. It was

larger than before and resembled a whirlpool of dense black smoke. Mickie shivered, sensing a wave of cold and hatred from the thing on the carpet.

"Allie? Grant? There's something in my cabin," he managed to say. He heard the indrawn breath of Grant and both of them appeared within seconds.

But the blackness had gone. Mickie found he was trembling. The emanations of pure cold and anger left him with a sick feeling of fear in his gut.

"Mickie, what is it?"

Grant's comforting hand was on his shoulder. Allie stood on his other side.

"There was something there," he pointed at the spot on the cabin floor. "It was black, like smoke and it spun..." His voice trailed off, realising how silly he sounded.

"Nothing there now," Grant said. "You're quite sure?"

"I've seen it before," Mickie said, his voice shaky. "Just before I first went to the school."

"Speaker 356, can you detect any sort of presence near Mickie's cabin?" Allie spoke softly.

"There's .... something," a new voice sounded in Mickie's head as if coming from someone standing a few feet away, though there was nobody else around. "I don't believe I have ever sensed anything like it before. An energy force certainly, but not like any form of life I have encountered. It's gone, however."

"Will you set a watch on this area, Speaker? If you sense anything like that again, advise us and the Captain immediately."

"It's done, Alliandra."

"I think you can sleep in our cabin tonight, Mickie," Grant said. "We'll have Security run a full scan of this area before you come back."

"Was that the Speaker?" Mickie asked, curiosity overcoming the cold fear in his mind.

"That was Speaker 356," Allie said. "He'll look after you."

Still with a cold fear in his mind, Mickie returned to the other cabin where they made up a bed on the couch. It took him a while to get to sleep, the memory of the cold hatred forcing shivers up his back several times, but after a warm drink and a sedative pill, he was finally asleep.

* * *

"Shuttle Bay Fifteen."

The order came from a new Cassolean whom Mickie had not met. He was larger than any others of that species so far, and like many others in the group he was carrying what Mickie assumed was a weapon resembling a light machine gun. Rather nervously he had followed them into the transporter that was now very cramped with dozens of individuals, many carrying weapons or large bags.

Together with the Kalamosians and red-eyed Cassoleans was a group of five individuals of a species new to Mickie and which he assumed were the X'Kasxi. Allie had said the name translated as "The Kindred." They were thinner than humans and a little taller on average. Mickie found their faces difficult to like, as they were reptilian in appearance. The lower half of the face protruded forward, the mouths being quite a long way forward of the nose, and briefly Mickie saw a snake-like tongue flicker out from one of the four X'Kasxi in the transporter with them. Over their eyes, they had a distinct ridge of bone that gave them a menacing air, though the size of the ridge varied, some of them being barely detectible.

One of the X'Kasxi realised Mickie was studying him. He turned his reptilian eyes to him and seemed to freeze. Some form of communication must have passed between the others of that species because all five turned hard stares on him then looked away, appearing to have a quick conversation that Mickie didn't catch. He tried to hide the unease, telling himself that they had also heard about the Ship going to find him and were obviously interested in him. But not all the discomfort disappeared.

"The X'Kasxi seemed interested in me," he whispered to Grant as they made their way from the transporter to the shuttle.

"Hardly surprising," Grant replied. "They'd heard about the kid from Earth."

"But they stared *really* hard, almost as if they knew something."

"Let me check with the X'Kasxi troop commander later," Grant said.

Mickie nodded and resolved to ask Albert about these beings when he got back to his room.

Shuttle Bay Fifteen was different from the one in which he had first arrived and later played Loopies. Although the bay was about the same size, the shuttles were much larger, at least half as big again than the one in which he had travelled from Earth. There were six of these enormous craft on the floor of the bay and three lines of people were standing by one of them. Instead of the simple donut shape of Mickie's first trip, these had a second level, like a smaller donut on top. The upper level had windows, the first time Mickie had seen them on a shuttle. As Mickie's party arrived, three doors opened at intervals round the shuttle and the lines of people began to file in. The interior was also different from his previous shuttle. Instead of a small circle of armchairs, several rows of more functional seats lined the floor. Mickie counted quickly and saw that the shuttle could take a hundred people and almost all the seats were filled. He sat down between his parents. Almost nobody was talking.

"Why is everyone so quiet?" he asked.

"Nerves," replied Allie. "Even though we are quite safe, nobody likes to visit here. It's an uncomfortable experience for all of us."

"And who's flying the ship?" he whispered.

"There's a separate flight deck above our heads," replied Grant. "There are three pilots in there, one to control the movements, the other two to search and select the best area to farm."

Sensing the atmosphere, Mickie remained silent. It was about twenty minutes before a buzzer sounded and everyone began to shift and stand up. Although a few conversations could be heard, they were subdued and Mickie could make out nothing from anyone's words. The door opened to the outside and Mickie got his first view of Spiderworld.

The light was dimmer than he was accustomed too and the shadows amid the exotic vegetation seemed full of menace. Mickie shivered a little, even though the heat of the atmosphere was striking, then determined to show no fear, steeled himself, following Grant and Allie away from the shuttle. For a moment he felt a wave of excitement, realising this was his first step on a world other than Earth. Now he was truly a space traveller. They stood in a large clearing of soft grass, while all round the edge was dense foliage, huge dark bushes with bright-coloured flowers in great quantities. Behind those, enormous trees towered, looking perfectly normal, like any woodland on Earth. Mickie took a breath, sensing odours he had never experienced before. There seemed to be a hint of cinnamon, possibly a smell of oranges, but the rest were new and delightful to the senses. The air was heavy and damp, and with the heat, sweat broke out on his arms and neck immediately.

"Now, you must stay with us," said Allie. "If either of us has to separate, stay with whichever of us is in the bigger party."

"Okay," said Mickie, feeling subdued and nervous, despite his determination. Several teams of people began to fan out from the shuttle.

"They will be looking for suitable patches of the vegetation we need," explained Grant. "Any likely patch, they'll ask me to come and confirm it's suitable for harvesting. Meanwhile, let's stay with Allie as she looks for signs of intelligence."

Needing no persuasion, Mickie stayed close as Allie walked a pattern of squares in the vegetation, examining each metre with care. The rest of the party stayed in a block of about ten people, all carrying weapons.

"Look," she said suddenly and pointed. "A web."

Mickie followed the direction of her finger. At first he could hardly believe it. The web was massive, stretching between two tall growths of yellow fronds that were at least fifty metres apart, and rising to some thirty metres above the ground. The pattern looked like any web he had seen on Earth, but the size terrified him.

"That means the spider is somewhere near the base," Allie continued. "They hunt in pairs so both are very close to us. This is the time to try communication."

She stood up straight and looked directly at the web. "Speaker 356, are you in contact?"

"Hello, Alliandra!" said a voice, the same voice Mickie had heard in his cabin a few nights before. "How nice to talk to you again." The speech sounded to Mickie perfectly normal, a man's voice with no accent that he could identify.

"Always my pleasure, Speaker 356," said Allie. "As you can see, my husband and Mickie are here."

"Grantorel, a delight as ever," said the very ordinary voice.

"Mine too," said Grant.

"And Mickie, welcome to our universe!" With a start, Mickie realised he was being addressed.

"Thank you!" he stammered. He was trying hard to understand that this pleasant, educated voice from nowhere originated many millions of light years away.

"I'm delighted you are with us," continued the Speaker. "I hope you have recovered from the experience of the other evening?"

"Yes! Thank you!"

"You may not know it," continued the Speaker. "But I was the one who first heard you on Earth."

"How did you do that?" asked Mickie. The whole idea seemed extraordinary.

"I suppose you could say I was just mind-surfing!" replied the Speaker. The amusement was obvious in his voice. "But the distress you were emitting was quite powerful and the mental band you were using was so unusual that I investigated further."

"What did you do?" Mickie was intrigued.

"I took up residence in your mind," said the Speaker. "I watched everything you saw, but I also studied your mental patterns and that's when I realised you were not human and I contacted Alliandra who asked the ship's captain to divert to your world to look for you."

Mickie was shaken and felt unable to speak. That such luck would come to him!

"Speaker, we believe there are at least two spiders close to us," said Allie. "Can you detect them?"

"There are several sources of mental waves in your area," came the reply. "But I can only differentiate them from your party's, not read any coherent message."

"Okay, I will try," said Allie. "I am Alliandra of Kalamos," she said firmly. "And I would like to establish communication with the natives of this planet. Will anyone talk to me?"

The silence lasted several minutes.

"Nothing," said the Speaker. "I have transmitted on several bands near to the one I think I saw from the waves around you, but I felt no contact."

"Just as always," sighed Allie. "Keep trying, Speaker, we will keep searching."

"Of course. Good luck."

Grant suddenly turned his head. "I got a call from one of the harvesting parties," he said. "I need to examine a likely patch." He moved away, taking two of the armed contingent with him. Mickie stayed and watched Allie return to examining the scenery with disciplined care. There were still a half dozen armed guards with them. But after a few minutes, he began to feel bored and started looking around the area for something more interesting. A flash of colour caught his eye and he turned to see more clearly. To his delight, he saw a small deer-like animal studying him from the edge of the clearing. The little creature was the most glorious gold and red colour and it posed in the same dainty way that deer have on Earth. Mickie was charmed and began to walk slowly toward it, hoping he could get near enough to touch. The little animal looked curious but unworried as Mickie moved closer, but as he reached within a few metres, it moved away cautiously and Mickie followed. This small dance continued for a few more repeats until Mickie was quite a long away from where he had begun.

But it ended when the little animal suddenly started, turned away and shot off. Mickie sighed in frustration then sensed the movement behind him. He turned and his whole body turned to icy fear as he saw the enormous spider standing just a few metres away from him. The sight was infinitely more horrible than the brief pictures Albert had shown him. It loomed over him like a monstrous truck and he could see the awful jaws just a short distance above him. With a terrified gasp he turned and ran. He managed to move only five metres before he came up short and in utter horror he realised he was caught in the spider's web and knew that he was about to bitten and paralysed by the dreadful creature and would spend several pain-filled, horrific days as a food source before he would die.

Already he was paralysed, but with terror, not venom and he could not speak, forgetting entirely about the communicator in his shoulder. Tears rose in his eyes and could think of nothing but how he would feel the bite and the venom start to paralyse him.

But nothing happened. After several moments of his breath sobbing in his own ears, the spider had not attacked. He tried to move his arms and legs but could not. He was facing in the direction he had been running and his face was against one strand of the web. From the corner of his eye he saw an immense black shape move into view. The spider had travelled round the web and was now on the other side. It appeared to be studying him, possibly as a totally new form of captured prey. It moved directly in front of him, close enough so that Mickie could see the hairs on its legs and several sets of eyes looking fixedly on him.

The voice that entered his mind was cold, merciless, quite without tone or pitch.

"Why are you here, Pfafth?"

Mickie was still sobbing with fear and the iciness in the voice that slid into his mind like a cold knife only increased the terror. He said nothing, unable to comprehend what had been said to him. He sensed the tremor in the web as something moved heavily, and a second massive shape appeared next to the first. The two spiders studied him further.

"Why are you here, Pfafth?" repeated the cold voice.

Mickie realised that the two dreadful shapes before him were not going to attack him. Why that was so, and why he understood it was not something he could comprehend, but he drew deep into himself and tried to extend the moment a little longer. Surely Allie would have seen he was missing by now and be searching for him. Thinking about Allie triggered a question to his mind, despite the awful fear. He took a deep breath and forced it out.

"Why... why haven't you communicated with us before?"

"It is not yet time," said the icy voice into his mind.

"So why me? Why now?"

"Because you are Pfafth."

"What is Pfafth?"

There was only silence from the monstrous shapes before him.

The most magical, beautiful thing in the world happened. Allie's voice rang out firmly behind him. "It's okay, Mickie, we'll have you out of there in a few seconds."

Beams of energy flickered around him and the web melted. One of the beams flashed past him, hit one of the spiders and it shook violently a second or two before collapsing motionless with its legs folded beneath it in an oddly dignified manner. The other spider seemed to watch with a cold study for a second or two then simply vanished. Mickie fell to the floor of the clearing and lost consciousness.

"We told you not to move away from us."

Mickie was unsure which terrified him most, the memory of the spiders or the realisation that Grant and Allie were angry with him. It was the first time they had spoken to him in anything but tones of affection and it hurt him terribly to hear the edge in Allie's voice. He was lying in his bed. His tunic had been removed and there was no sign of the sticky cable that had been part of the web still sticking to him.

"I..." he started then burst into tears. Allie moved closer and put her arms round him.

"Mickie, we're only upset because we could have lost you," she said firmly. "You disobeyed us and look what happened. Being on alien worlds is always dangerous, never mind when you already know how terribly dangerous the local life is. Do you understand how frightened we were when we heard your terrified sobs in the communicator, but you had vanished?"

He nodded, the movement restricted by his head being so firmly hugged into her shoulder.

"So never again, okay?" Grant was sitting in the chair next to the bed. Mickie tried to shake his head with the same difficulty, but his tears started to slow down. Allie released her tight hug and looked down at him and Mickie saw tears in her eyes also. He sniffed and wiped his face with his hand.

"It spoke to me," he said.

The shock on the faces of the adults was massive.

"It *what?*" said Allie.

"It spoke to me," he repeated.

"What did it say?" The urgency in Allie's voice was like a police siren.

"I...." Mickie tried, but the words were lost in the overwhelming terror of the few minutes he was imprisoned in the web.

Grant spoke clearly and firmly, but not to Mickie. "Computer," he said. "Play back the recording of the transmissions received by Mickie's communicator while he was on the planet. Give only the last ten minutes."

The computer's response was immediate. Allie's voice rang out clearly, just as it had when Mickie heard it and realised he was saved.

"Computer, play the two minutes preceding that extract," ordered Grant.

"There is nothing recorded," said Albert.

"Mickie, are you absolutely certain the spider communicated with you?" asked Allie, looking deeply into Mickie's eyes.

"Yes, I really am, honest!"

"Okay, we believe you, Mickie." Allie's voice was warm and loving again. "Speaker 356, are you with us?"

"Yes, Alliandra, I have been listening with great interest," came the voice of the Speaker.

"Can you find the memory in Mickie's mind of what he heard?"

"I will try. Please wait. Mickie, may I have access to your mind for a few moments?"

Astonished, Mickie could only nod his head.

"Thank you," said the Speaker. "As you see, you do not need to vocalise communications with me. Give me a little while."

Mickie felt nothing at all, and the silence in the room lasted just a few seconds.

"This is very strange," said the Speaker. "Mickie is quite correct, there is a memory of one sentence, spoken twice to him, then a few words after that. As there was no recording in the computer, it means the spider communicated by telepathic means. Very few races have developed that capacity."

"And what did it say?" Allie's face reflected strain and worry, but also considerable excitement.

"It said, '*What are you doing here, Pfafth?*' and Mickie recalls the tone as being cold and menacing," said the Speaker.

"*Pfafth?* What in all the multiple galaxies is *Pfafth?*" Allie was shaken. "Have you heard that word before, Speaker?"

"No, Alliandra, I have not."

"You said a few more words were spoken. What were they?"

"Mickie also addressed the spiders by telepathic means," said the Speaker. Allie and Grant looked sharply at Mickie who shook his head in bewilderment. He was starting to recall the moments with the spiders, but he was certain that he had spoken aloud to them.

"Mickie asked the spiders why they had not communicated before. One replied that it was not yet time. Mickie then asked 'Why me? Why now?' They simply replied *'Because you are Pfafth.'* That's when you arrived."

Allie was silent a moment, seemingly lost in thought. Then she and Grant looked at each other and seemed to come to some agreement.

"Then we were right," she said. "Back on Earth, when that bunch of thugs attacked you then ran away screaming, we thought we saw a giant spider. But the idea was so far-fetched, so insane, we decided it wasn't possible. But something killed three of the attackers."

"A Spider arrived and saved me?"

"It appears so," said Grant. "And that gives us two appalling questions. Apart from the question of how it transported itself across a few hundred million light years, there's the quite insane issue of just why it would do so to save you."

"I've just spoken with the Captain," Allie said. "He wants to see us all in his cabin."

Chapter 8 – A Question of Ancestry

The captain's cabin was lit in the same dim, warm yellow glow as the flight deck had been. The captain was sitting in a huge chair as they entered, and he rose to his feet, towering over the group.

"Please be seated," he said. Mickie heard the translation as if spoken aloud, but he could just hear the lovely cello tones of the Captain's actual utterance. Allie and Grant took seats that were obviously there for human-sized bodies while the Captain resumed his huge seat across from them. Sitting down, he still towered over the others. Before Mickie found a seat, he saw something in the corner and turned to look more closely. It was apparently a sculpture, about a metre high, roughly a cylinder about half a metre wide, but as he looked at it, he felt his mind twist as if he had shifted gravity fields, much like when he ran into the shuttle bay as Fencris reduced the gravity strength. He caught himself and stared at the object. He could not tell what it was, but as he looked, waves of emotion ran through him. He felt happy, then ecstatic then the shape seemed to melt and run away in small rivulets of fire before reforming as a bust of an extremely beautiful woman.

"Mickie's found his first work of Maragos," said Grant with a chuckle. Mickie tore his eyes away from the astounding object and looked at Grant.

"What is it?" he asked, his breathing heavy as if he had been running.

"It is beautiful, is it not?" said the Captain. "There are few of them around the Universe and they are priceless."

"But what is it?" Mickie turned back to the shape and let his eyes roam free. It seemed to change shape as he looked, but he saw that the effect was from the extraordinary curves and interwoven patterns that distracted the mind. But the most astonishing thing was the waves of different emotions that travelled through him. Again he felt happiness, then a rush of sheer awe, followed by a deep sense of excitement.

"Mickie, come here, you'll lose yourself for hours if you stay there!" The command from Grant was firm and Mickie tore himself away to take a seat with the rest.

"Maragos was a sculptor. We think he was male, but the records are not clear," said the Captain. "He was one of the very last of a race of beings from a planet they called Shuramee. That planet is in a galaxy in the Local Group. We visit it frequently in our normal trips and it is deserted. The last of that race died out over thirty thousand years ago, and there is little of the civilisation left. We'll be going there on this trip, and while the major point is archaeology to learn everything we can, we always search for more of these sculptures."

"Were they an advanced race, and do you know why they died?" Mickie was awed by the experience of looking at the sculpture and saddened by the fact of a whole species dying out.

"Very advanced," said the Captain, his eyes widening greatly, which Mickie remembered as signifying laughter. "They had immense mental powers, they could alter the molecular structure of objects, and they could move huge structures by thought alone. In fact, the geological studies indicate that at some point, they moved their entire planet to a wider orbit when their sun entered a period of increased heat output."

"Then how could they just die out?" Mickie was startled by the idea of a race that could shift a whole planet and yet not prevent its own death.

"It was simply their time," said the Captain, and Mickie understood the topic was to change. "Mickie, I have heard the tale of your misadventure on the planet," continued the hugely tall shape. "I think I believe your guardians that you will never be that silly again."

"Yes, sir," Mickie said, feeling subdued.

"Good. Then let us move to the events themselves. The spider spoke to you?"

"Yes, sir."

"And that is the astonishing thing, because nobody, not even the Speakers have ever been able to communicate with these beings. Did you say anything back?"

"Yes sir, I asked it why they hadn't communicated before. It said it wasn't yet time."

"A commendable presence of mind. Anything else?"

"I asked why they had communicated now and with me. It said because I was *Pfafth*."

"The Speaker reported that Mickie spoke telepathically to the spiders," said Allie. "That's why we didn't hear the exchange on our communicators."

"Telepathically? But neither humans nor your species have so far demonstrated telepathic skills other than when using primaries like the Speakers."

"Exactly, Captain. This is very strange."

"But it is the word it used to address you that is fascinating. The word 'Pfafth' is quite new to everyone."

Silence reigned in the yellow-lit room for a few seconds until broken by the disembodied voice of Speaker 356.

"I think I have discovered it," said the Speaker. Even in the distant, cool tones, Mickie could hear the shock that the telepathic being was experiencing. "I have travelled into many thousands of minds in the Universe in the last few minutes, and I asked all my colleagues on our home world to do the same. As you know, while you do not travel beyond a certain area of the Universe, there are other races in remote regions with whom you have made only rare contact. In the memories of one of the very oldest such species, we found reference to *'Pfafth.'* It is believed to be the species name of the very first intelligent race. But the Pfafth vanished over a million years ago and their existence is mostly the stuff of legend, with no facts to support the stories. There has been no trace of any such beings since and we do not have any record of where their home world was located, not even in which Galaxy."

All three of the others in the room sat back and stared at Mickie.

"This cannot be," said Allie. "The Spiders must have been confused, though why they would come up with that name escapes me."

And into Mickie's mind came the same cold, merciless voice that he had heard before. *"We were not wrong. You are Pfafth."*

Mickie cried out in terror and curled up tightly.

It was a few moments before Allie's gentle voice could get through the fear in his mind.

"The Spider spoke to you again?"

Mickie nodded, fighting the cold fear that the Spider's mental touch caused.

"Can you tell us what it said?"

He swallowed hard and gained control of his voice. "It said they weren't wrong. I'm Pfafth."

Allie was lost in thought for a few seconds. "I think we must consider this whole episode as very useful," she said at last. "We have made progress with our major project of finding out the origins of this young man. We have the name of his species and we know some things about it, including the fact they seem to have vanished a million years ago. We know that the Pfafth have telepathic powers and for some reason, the Spiders recognised him, though how or why they did that is a complete mystery. Then there's the whole issue of a spider somehow arriving on Earth when Mickie's life is threatened. And they didn't harm him when he was caught in the web. Just as critical, those Spiders have shown that they can communicate, also telepathically, as well as teleport across light years, something we have never experienced before. We have learned a great deal today. It's quite astonishing, given that this was Mickie's first planet-fall."

Realising that he had contributed a lot, Mickie felt some comfort and was able to put the stark terror he had felt from the Spider's communication behind him.

"So how can Mickie be the sole survivor of a race that vanished a million years ago?" the Captain asked.

"That is certainly an interesting problem," Allie said. "As much as is the question of how he ended up on Earth. We have a long way to go to find out the answers."

"And another issue," Grant said. "I asked the X'Kasxi troop commander why his men had seemed so interested in Mickie. He completely froze up on me. It's impossible to read expressions in their faces, but I got the strongest sense he was holding back something."

A short silence hung in the air.

"You have brought a fascinating project of learning aboard my Ship," the Captain said. His wide eyes indicated amusement, but Mickie felt there was concern as well as great interest in the tall being.

* * *

"Good morning, Mickie." Albert's well-modulated voice woke Mickie from a painful reverie of his old life on Earth. For some reasons, the memories of that ugly, foul-smelling home and the constant fear he felt whenever he was there had returned to haunt him and he couldn't shake off the depression. So Albert's interruption was welcome.

"Hi, Albert, what is it?"

"Grant wants to know if you would like to see the engine room."

"The engine room? You bet!" Mickie found the idea of seeing the power that drove the ship to superlight speeds quite fascinating.

"In that case, he asks that you meet him on the engineering deck. He will be waiting for you outside the transporter doors."

"I'm on my way!" Mickie leaped to his feet and ran to the door. A few moments later, the transporter doors opened and Grant was standing there, chatting to a Cassolean crewman. He grinned a welcome as Mickie arrived.

"Hi, kid!" he said. "With you in a few seconds."

A short sentence or two occurred and the Cassolean departed. Grant lightly punched Mickie's shoulder. "It took a while to get permission for this, but everyone gets to see the engine room sometime, so today's the day."

"Fantastic!" Mickie was delighted to spend some time alone with Grant, an experience that rarely happened during the working day. They walked down the corridor a few metres and stopped by an unusually heavy double door.

"Grantorel," Grant said. "Mickie, speak your name. The sensors know there are two people here, and it's a high-security area. They must validate both of us."

Mickie dutifully complied and the doors slid apart.

Mickie was expecting a loud racket and intensive activity, but that was not the case as he entered the huge space inside. The wall on his left was covered with the black slabs that served as observation screens and instrument panels, and some half-dozen Kaloti moved languidly up and down that wall. The floor space held a number of the enormous chairs built for the elongated shapes of the crewmen. But the wall on Mickie's right... that grabbed his attention.

The entire wall, some thirty metres high and at least a hundred metres long was transparent. On the other side was a room the size of a hangar that could have held a dozen Boeing 747s. But instead, it held a series of black boxes, each nearly the height of the room, about twenty metres wide and he estimated about fifty metres long. He stood by the transparent wall and counted them, finally getting a total of twenty-four units.

"The wall is crystal," said Grant's voice behind him. "It's been treated with some highly specialised processes and on the other side is enough radiation to kill a whole world."

Mickie shivered at the tone of Grant's words.

"Just for comparison," Grant continued, "the engines that power the little shuttle that we rode from Earth to Venus are about the size of a book. Even with that, there's a solid floor of that crystal between it and the cabin."

"This is incredible," Mickie whispered, sensing the incredible power behind that wall. "How do they work?"

"Mickie, I could not even begin to tell you," Grant replied. "Gravity control is perhaps the most complex technology ever devised and only the Kaloti, of all the species we have so far encountered, have ever mastered it."

Mickie stared at the silent black mountains. Movement caught his eye and he saw a small machine moving down the street between two rows of engines.

"What's that?" he asked.

"Service module," Grant answered. "Mainly it sweeps up the dust and grime that gathers in any space. And it sweeps off the dust that sticks to the sides of the engines from the static that develops. Occasionally, those robots will disconnect one engine from the series to allow minor maintenance, but any serious repair work gets done back at the Kaloti home world. There's a lot of work being done on several planets as other species learn how to build and maintain those engines."

"What would happen if someone walked in there?" Mickie couldn't resist asking and Grant gave a small laugh.

"They'd be dead before they could take a step," he said.

"So not a place for us to go and play Loopies?" Mickie asked with a straight face.

"It would be the shortest game on record," Grant said. "C'mon, youngster, let's go and see some more of the ship."

Cheerfully, enjoying this time with Grant, Mickie followed him out of the engine room and down another corridor.

"What are we going to see?" he asked.

"Plant pathology," Grant replied. "That's where I started my career when I was just a baby botanist."

"A botanist? So how did you end up being an executive type?"

"Probably because of Allie," Grant said with a laugh. "She said I had to get out more! So I started studying management and accounting and stuff like that, and I discovered I was a pretty good negotiator. It wasn't too long before I moved into that side of the business and I have to admit, I find it pretty exciting! But as you saw on Spiderworld, I still have some botanical duties."

He opened another door and let Mickie walk in ahead. Mickie's first reaction was that he'd entered a jungle. All he could see was solid greenery with what looked like vines and trees, brilliant colours and mysterious scents. The air was moist and heavy and Mickie felt his skin start to sweat almost at once.

"It's another world, isn't it?" Grant said. "Like a rain forest, and it's here we grow most of our fresh fruit and vegetables."

"It's beautiful," Mickie said with enthusiasm. "But doesn't it take a lot of water?"

"It does, and you might think water would be a problem on a spaceship, I agree. But it's not. With a ship this enormous, we can carry thousands of tons of minerals we dig up on the surface of asteroids or moons, and we break up the minerals, extract hydrogen and oxygen, and create water, lots of it! That's why we don't have any restrictions on showers or bathing. We'll pop into that area when we're done here."

He stopped as a tall young man, about Grant's age walked out from behind a huge bush of unidentifiable type.

"Hey, young Grantorel!" the man said loudly with a big grin. "Our most famous escapee from Plant Pathology!"

"Mendor!" Grant replied with obvious pleasure. "So you still hide from real work in this jungle?"

"Of course! If they find me, they may make me into a boring account executive like you, and who'd want that?"

Grant laughed and put his hand on Mickie's shoulder. "This is our newest crew-member, Mickie Dalton," he said and Mendor took Mickie's hand and shook it enthusiastically.

"I heard all about you," he said. "Welcome aboard and I hope this reprobate doesn't mess you up too much."

"No chance!" Mickie felt at ease with this friendliness and was happy to spend half an hour wondering through the exotic plants and colours of this ship-borne rain forest.

"Time to move on and let you pretend to do some work," Grant said at one stage.

"Okay, you go on," Mendor said. "I do have actual work to do. I'll see you on the gravity-ball court next week?"

"You will, and we'll beat you senseless!"

"Hah! No fat, dumb and happy mob of executives is going to beat the athletic brilliance of the Botanists!" Mendor snorted with derision. "The cup is ours!"

Grant smiled and waved a cheerful farewell.

"My friends have mentioned gravity-ball," Mickie said. "You're on the team?"

"One of them. We have a league of twelve teams aboard, mostly departmental groups, but some are just groups of friends. We play a championship table, then a final every six months. It's great exercise, so we encourage people to play."

"They said Loopies is a sort of practice for it," Mickie said as they returned to the transporter.

"Quite right. You need to develop really good skills in low gravity before you can play the adult game, because it's pretty violent, very fast and takes exceptional low-gravity handling skills."

"But what is it?"

"I'll tell you about over lunch. Wait till we've seen the mineral processing plant."

A few moments later, Grant opened a door and led Mickie inside. He found himself behind a glass partition gazing out onto a scene of what looked like utter devastation. The area was at least the size of the engine room, but instead of neat rows of massive, silent engines, huge mounds of rocks, rubble and plain dirt were piled up to the ceiling.

"These are just some of the mineral ores we pick up when we can," Grant said. "Sometimes we mine on a planet when we get permission, or on isolated moons. Other times we take in a complete chunk of an asteroid in deep space. Then we break it all up here."

"How?" Mickie asked. "I can't see anything happening."

"Look over there, at that pile over on the right."

Mickie followed Grant's pointing finger and saw a pile of blue-grey rocks. As he watched, the top of the pile seemed to melt, rivers of fine sand pouring down the sides of the small mountain. From the other sound of the partition, a musical warbling could be heard.

"What's happening?" he asked.

"Laser vibrators," Grant replied. "You can't see them, but several beams of lasers are focused on the rocks, and they vary in pitch and frequency at millions of times per second. That warbling sound, that's just a tiny fraction of the frequency range as it passes through the human hearing range. The beams act like a jackhammer and the rock gets shaken into such small grains it's almost down to the molecule level. Then it gets sucked into tubes that take it to the next stage for further reduction. We extract oxygen and hydrogen where it occurs, and we also suck in huge amounts of hydrogen from free space as we move, because there's lots of it. After that, it's simple chemistry, two molecules of hydrogen to one molecule of oxygen and we get water!"

For a few minutes, Mickie watched as the mountain of rubble melted away like a snowman on a hot day then they set off to the restaurant.

Grant waited until they had selected their choice of lunch and found an empty table. Around them, the area was bustling with cheerful noise and clatter as tables filled with groups of varying sizes. The smells of different dishes reached Mickie's nostrils. At one point, he was sure he smelled custard and wondered if that was a common dish on an intergalactic spaceship and resolved to seek it out next time. Maybe he could even find apple crumble, his favourite dessert.

"Gravity-Ball," Grant said as they sat down. "Think of a mixture of lacrosse, ice-hockey and rugby, but played in three dimensions in a very low-gravity area." He cut up and took a slice of the same delicious beef that Mickie had eaten on his first visit to the dining room.

"That's not easy!" Mickie said with a laugh. "I can't begin to think of such a mix!"

"And we play in seven percent gravity, not ten percent as you play Loopies," Grant replied with a small grin. "But the only way to understand it is to see it. Wait till the match, then you'll get the picture."

"When is it?"

"In a few days, just before we land on Mayoowani."

"Could I play Gravity-Ball?"

Grant shook his head. "Not for a while. You need to get really good at Loopies first, and you're still a beginner at that. Then you can play some junior games starting when you're fifteen, but you'll need two or three years at that level before you can play in the major league."

"I'll look forward to it. Loopies is difficult enough, so I'll see how I go with that." Becoming more and more relaxed in Grant's easy-going company, he decided to open up a little. "Hey, how did you and Allie meet, anyway?"

"At University, in my second year, Allie was in her first. I was doing Botany, she was doing Galactic History and Exo-Philology."

"Exo-*what?*"

"Exo-Philology. The study of alien languages. She's got a real gift for it, and quite a lot of the alien tongues that our computer can handle were studied by Allie and then programmed into the computer."

"That's pretty cool! So how did you meet?"

"The company that runs this Ship, they were recruiting at the University and we both went to the meetings, because both of us wanted to see other worlds for our respective professional reasons. I managed to spill a cup of coffee over her new white dress and she nearly attacked me!"

"Not the most romantic meeting!"

Grant laughed out loud. "That's an understatement. She was with her boyfriend as well!"

"Bummer!" Despite the friendly conversation, Mickie as tensing up as he realised he needed to ask Grant a most serious question.

"Yes! Baldorest was quite hostile to me over that, but I offered to pay for the dress to be cleaned, and when I took it back to her, somehow we started getting on just fine and Baldorest became a good friend, even though I started dating Allie. Actually, you'll meet Baldorest in a few weeks when we land on Merrison."

"Okay." Mickie paused then found the courage to start a conversation he had wanted to have for some days. "Grant?"

"What is it, kid?" Seeming to sense that something serious was happening Grant put down his fork and sat forward, leaning his elbows on the surface.

"When we met, you and Allie said you'd be my guardians."

"We did."

"Would it be possible for you to be my parents, instead?" Mickie felt breathless, having finally got the question out.

"Funny thing, that," Grant replied, his face serious. "Allie and I were talking about that issue last night. We were thinking of asking you the same question. We thought it would be better for you to be part of a real family and get over that horrible mess back on Earth."

"You mean... you could?"

"We could, and we'd like to. Would you?"

"*Would* I? Of course I would!"

"Then it's done!" Grant finally let a smile reach his face. "We'll set up the adoption procedures and send the details to Kalamos for registration." He picked up his fork again. "Finish your lunch, kid, then let's go and see your mother and tell her face to face!"

Feeling as if the sun were shining on him, Mickie walked out with his new father and decided the universe was a pretty good place to be.

* * *

"Tell me about the Speakers, Albert," commanded Mickie when he got back to his cabin. Immediately the centre of the room lit up with a huge image of a planet. The globe rotated several times then the camera began to close in and focus on scenes from just a few hundred metres up. The world had six continents equally spaced out in grey-looking seas, and what looked like hundreds of smaller islands. But the land all looked much the same, empty, wind-driven, sparse vegetation and no signs of civilisation at all. Not a single city or even collection of buildings broke the monotony of the harsh scenery.

"We have no name for the world," said Albert, "because the Speakers have given it no name that we can comprehend, just as their names for each other are far too complex for us to understand. They appear to identify each other by a total sensory image of the entire person, their thought patterns, their work history, everything. It would take pages to try and put the name into words, almost like identifying someone by their life story and everything they have ever said and done."

The camera came lower and focused on a plain hillock that looked like a termite mound. A computerised image of a man appeared by the base of the mound, which Mickie judged to be about three times higher than the man, so perhaps five or six metres in height. It was featureless, covered with dark green vegetation like ivy.

"This is a Speaker," announced Albert. "Speakers live to about eight hundred Earth years."

Mickie could hardly believe it. "That doesn't look like an intelligent life form at all," he complained. "It doesn't even have any arms or legs!"

"Correct," agreed Albert. "Nor eyes, nose or mouth, and no need for such things for a creature that never moves once it has taken root."

"Root?" Mickie was baffled. This was quite unlike anything he had imagined.

"Speakers are asexual," said Albert, falling into the smooth lecturing tone that he adopted when teaching. "That is, there are no males or females. They produce offspring like flowers do, with seeds growing and maturing in the vegetation you see covering them. At one point, the seeds develop long strands of fibre and float off in the high winds that are common. Thousands will float away, some will eventually land and take root, but only a tiny number will survive to become mature Speakers. It takes about sixty years before the new plant develops awareness and consciousness, and another twenty after that before its telepathic skills grow. At that point, older Speakers take over the teaching of the young one and nurture the skills until the young one learns to control its extraordinarily powerful sense."

"But how does it eat?" asked Mickie.

"The air is always full of seeds, pollens and small insects that land on the mound and become stuck in the vegetation. They become absorbed into the Speaker's system, as do small mammals, nothing bigger than a small rabbit-like animal, that get caught after being attracted by the smell of the flowers. And the roots draw sustenance from the minerals in the ground. Speakers need very little intake, given their motionless life."

"And is that what they do, act as telepathic links with the rest of intelligent people?"

"Not entirely," said Albert. "In all the continents, there are only about seven million adult Speakers. Perhaps a few hundred thousand spend their time doing that, while others search the Universe for new intelligent life. Many simply study whole worlds by taking up mental residence in the mind of a single individual, usually with that person's consent, and then move to another for a new perspective on the world. A few hundred are dedicated to developing the very primitive intelligences that are encountered from time to time."

"Will we visit their world?"

"That would be fatal," replied Albert. "The average

temperature of the place is just over freezing point, though the atmosphere is breathable to humans, a little high in carbon dioxide and lower in oxygen. But the power of their telepathic signals would do serious damage to a human brain or any similar species that got within two light years of the planet."

"So if nobody can go close to the planet, how did you get these pictures?"

"It took some organisation," the computer replied. "One of the Kaloti ships took a drone with cameras to about two light years' distance. The drone was very slow, only about twenty percent of light speed, so even that took some years to reach the planet, and the ship returned to its regular business. Some years later, another ship came to retrieve the drone."

Mickie was impressed. "And do humans have some telepathic skills?" he asked.

"Very primitive, but yes, they do. In time, we believe they could be enhanced. But it is enough to be able to communicate with a Speaker if a minimally telepathic individual tried and knew how to go about it."

"So can I talk to a Speaker any time?" Mickie was excited by the idea.

"Most certainly. Of course, you already have, when Speaker 356 picked up your cry for help during a standard search of the area in a routine hunt for intelligent life. And then again, you have established communication in recent days."

"So can I do it again?"

"Any time you wish. Speaker 356 has pretty well adopted this ship and its crew as his personal project, so he is always on hand for communications."

Mickie decided he was prepared to put up with giant spiders if he could talk frequently with a Speaker.

* * *

"Mickie, come to the Medical Centre. I think you should see this." Allie's voice sounded in his head as Mickie was deep into a study session with Albert about the history of his adopted home world, Kalamos.

"I'm on my way," he replied, realising that he had become quite adjusted to communicating without any obvious electronic means. A few moments later, the transporter opened in the Medical Centre. Mickie had spent some hours here in his first days on the ship, undergoing intensive examinations by the ships' doctors.

A young Cassolean female was waiting for him, holding a medical gown. She smiled.

"You'll need to wear this," she said, and draped the gown over him, placing a close-fitting cap over his head and finally handing him a visor that held a complete screen over his eyes. "It's an autopsy," she said as she led him to a door a few metres down the corridor.

"Yuck!" he said, flinching. "I'm not sure I want to see somebody cut up."

"This isn't a somebody," she replied. "It's a some *thing.*"

The door opened, and Mickie almost turned and ran. In the middle of the brightly-lit room was a Spider. Only when he realised that his parents and several other crewmembers were standing around the monster did he understand. It must be the corpse of the Spider that died when the guards released him from the web. Taking a breath and fighting to control his nervousness, he walked into the group of people and stood by Allie and Grant.

"This is the first time we've had the chance to dissect one," Grant said. "I expect this will answer a lot of questions."

A very tall Kalamosian looked briefly at Mickie then continued with what he had been doing. Mickie decided he must be the lead surgeon on this project.

"So," the Kalamosian said, "we have removed all the hairs from the skin and these have been taken for further analysis. Now we will remove the eyes. There are eight of them."

Without any obvious gesture from him, a large mechanical device lowered itself from the ceiling. It seemed to have several arms folded against its sides, and one of these spread out like a bird's wing unfolding. A yellow beam flashed and like a laser, hummed softly as it moved over the monstrous body, cutting out each of the eight eyes in turn and placing them in receptacles on a small trolley that appeared from the side of the room.

"And now the skin," said the surgeon.

Again, the laser hummed, cutting a square of skin, about a metre on each side. Small plumes of smoke drifted from the point where the leaser beam met the Spider's skin, and Mickie smelled an acrid, unpleasant odour. He pulled the collar of the protective gown over his nose and waited for the smell to subside. A mechanical claw reached down, gently picked up the skin sample and lowered it down to the surgeon. He briefly examined it, nodded, and the claw placed the flap onto another small trolley that moved away silently.

"X-Rays," commanded the surgeon. For a second, Mickie wondered how the term had become the standard in an alien culture and language, then realised it must be the translation he was being given by the device in his shoulder. A large screen against one wall flickered alive and strange shadows and shapes appeared, obviously the X-ray scan of the Spider. A sigh of astonishment ran through the group and Mickie looked up at Allie for an explanation.

"See that large block of darker matter at the top of the screen?" she said. "That's a brain. A *huge* brain. As we always thought, these things are highly intelligent. That brain is several times larger than ours, relative to the body size."

The image changed as the X-ray scanner moved further along the enormous corpse. The surgeon made a comment that was not translated for Mickie. But his astonishment was still obvious.

"Better revise your opinion even further upward, Alliandra," the surgeon said. His eyes were fixed intently on the image and Mickie heard Allie draw in her breath sharply.

"That's a second brain?" she said. Astonishment made her voice higher than normal.

"It certainly is," agreed the surgeon. "And just as big as the first. And the structure looks quite similar to Kalamosian or Human brain structures. And look there..." He took a small device like a pen from his pocket, but it was a light pointer such as any lecturer on Earth might use. A small spot of red light traced the patterns of lines in the image. "These are connections of brain matter and nerve cords. They are linking the two brains the way two computers are linked. Alliandra, we're seeing something we've never seen before."

"Yes," she agreed softly. "It looks like the Spiders are by far the most intelligent species we have ever encountered in the whole Universe. And that includes ourselves."

Chapter 9 – The Tree People of Harliya

Two days later, they left orbit around Spiderworld and Mickie was able to watch again as the Universe contracted into a spot of light before him then faded into the blackness of hyperspace as the world and his insides seemed to jump and blur. With a return to the pleasant routines he was developing on the ship and with the closeness of the friendships with the other three, Mickie soon forgot the terrors of Spiderworld. He worked hard at the difficult and wonderful game of Loopies and the most wonderful celebration was called for when he scored seven points with a double somersault and a successful catch of Drellion one day. His education into the mysteries, wonders, terrors and dangers of the Universe continued also, some at the hands of Albert and some in conversation with his parents.

"The Captain seemed to cut me off when I asked him how the people of Shuramee could all die out," said Mickie one day.

"He did," replied Grant. "It intrigued me also, and I wondered how much it had to do with the fact that the Kaloti are also declining at a dramatic rate and will soon disappear."

"The Kaloti are vanishing, also?" Mickie felt distress at the thought that this beautiful, intelligent species might die out.

"Their population has declined by over ninety percent in the last hundred years," Allie replied. "Every prediction is that the last of the species will vanish in the next twenty to thirty, as there has not been a single new Kaloti birth in fifty years."

"But that's terrible! Isn't anyone doing anything about it?"

"Help has been offered, but the Kaloti have always declined. The strange thing is that the Kaloti themselves seem unconcerned, almost as if they welcome the process."

"Does the Captain ever talk about it?" Mickie felt intense curiosity mixed with his sadness.

"I've tried to discuss it," said Allie. "But the only time the topic is discussed is when the plans for teaching other races to pilot the Kaloti ships are raised."

"What are these plans like?" asked Mickie.

"Very intensive. Several thousand people of the three main humanoid races, ourselves, the Cassoleans and the X'Kasxi are being taught the technologies and many ships are already piloted and crewed by these races. But we are quite unable to get any hint of why the birth rate of the Kaloti has reached zero. There is no panic on their home world, it's almost as if the process is natural and expected."

"Could it be the same with the people of Shuramee?" Mickie sensed an awful, catastrophic story.

"We have no idea," replied Allie. "Many races around the Universe have addressed this issue, we have asked the Speakers to help, but they report that they cannot find traces of thought on the topic in any Kaloti, almost as if they were being blocked out. I even took the liberty once of asking the Captain directly what was happening. He simply said it was the time for the Kaloti."

"That's almost the same thing he said to me about Shuramee when we were in his cabin," said Mickie thoughtfully. "Sounds like he knows more than he's telling."

"We are all quite certain of that," laughed Allie. "However, you need to go and study up on our next port of call. Ask Albert about the planet of Harliya. Make sure you ask about the Long Feeders."

"The Long Feeders? What are they?"

"Very nasty, very hungry, very lethal to the Harliyans and no danger to us at all," replied Allie.

"Why are they no danger to us?"

"On our very first visit here, over a hundred years ago, a Long Feeder killed one of the crewmen on the ship," Allie replied. "But it spat him out again immediately. Since then, no attack has ever taken place, which indicates the creatures have some form of communication that interests me enormously. The Harliyans assure us that nobody will be taken. How they know that is a mystery, but it's been true."

"I really hope you're right," Mickie replied, feeling very unsure about the whole trip.

* * *

"It is good to see you both again, Alliandra and Grantorel," said the small being standing before them. "I am Seefumaraboldin."

The creature was no more than a metre and a half high and quite humanoid, but its skin was a blotchy green, varying from light to dark in random patterns. The small group of crewmembers stood in a leafy cavern that Mickie knew to be at least a hundred metres above the ground. But the floor seemed solid, though made up of leaves and branches.

"We have not met you in this incarnation," replied Allie. "When was our last meeting?"

"Three years before. I was then Jalurandifindas."

"This we remember," said Allie, bowing slightly.

A ghostly voice spoke into Mickie's ears. He recognised Albert speaking directly to his communications device. "The naming conventions on Harliya are complex and we have not yet interpreted them. However, Allie has found a common thread that suggests the name involves some form of continuity with the previous incarnations of the soul now reincarnated in a new body."

"Incarnations? What's that all about?" Mickie had learned how to formulate speech in his mind so that the device in his shoulder could communicate with Albert.

"It's an interesting feature of this race. They tell us that they reincarnate many times, possibly more than a hundred, and that they communicate with their dead as easily as ordinary people talk to each other."

"Is that really true?" Mickie asked.

"We have no real way of telling. Several theories have been put forward that the entire species suffers from a form of mass hallucination. Others have suggested that they are just having us on for their own entertainment. But things happen that we find inexplicable. For example, just as Allie has experienced here, our people will meet a Harliyan that they have never met, and that Harliyan greets them as if they had worked together before, reciting events and segments of the conversation that our people had with someone who died years ago. So we don't argue or debate the beliefs unless one of them wishes to discuss it with us. We are here for trade."

Allie was still discussing matters with the Harliyan.

"The last time we spoke we determined the region from which you would be permitted to take fifteen trees," said the Harliyan. "And I had to redirect you from the area you had selected to another one because of the imbalance that your selection would cause."

"I remember," said Allie. "And do you now have the region selected for this harvest?"

"Yes. We have examined the growths and determined that you can take twelve trees from the region you have named Area 32AS. We have already marked the ones you may take."

"We are grateful," said Allie. "May I direct our cutters to those trees immediately?"

"Not yet," replied the Harliyan. "There are two Long Feeders passing that area now and to start cutting would cause some panic and an imbalance. In one hour and twenty three minutes, your cutters may start."

"Our thanks, Seefumaraboldin," said Allie. Mickie wondered how she remembered the names, but thought that her intensive training in cross-species studies must have helped. Or perhaps Albert prompted her, he thought, recalling the silent communication that the computer could use as it had with him. He realised the small creature was looking at him.

"A new crewmember?" asked the Harliyan.

"Our son. He is a child by our growth cycles," replied Allie. "His name is Mickie."

The Harliyan moved closer. He stood about chest high to Mickie, and the two examined each other.

Seefumaraboldin looked much like the image Mickie had seen in his training session, but the eyes looking deeply into his reflected a quite human sparkle of interest and amusement.

"Perhaps the young Mickie would like to be shown around?"

Before Mickie could reply and express his worries about moving through a tree world that was a hundred metres or more above the ground, Allie spoke for him.

"Our son would be deeply honoured," she said. "If you would like to arrange that, we will offload the tools and supplies of brandy we have brought for you."

Seefumaraboldin let out a cackle that might have come from any human being. "Then we shall have a gathering of our people and celebrate."

Mickie saw no movement or signal from him, but a number of the Harliyans appeared from out of the green walls that surrounded the place where they had met. He looked at Allie, feeling nervous that she had so easily let him be taken away from her and Grant, but she smiled at him.

"You are perfectly safe, young man. The gravity belt you wore to bring us to this level will keep you from falling. Go and learn about this world from its inhabitants."

"But what about the Long Feeders?"

"They will not touch you. Remember what I told you before. But it's highly likely that you'll see an attack and some of your hosts taken. If so, you must try and show no shock, no fear. Remember, it is the common lot of every one of them and they accept it as such. However hard it is for us to comprehend it, we must allow them to live that way."

Feeling reassured by her confidence, Mickie turned to the waiting group of tiny beings. His young enthusiasm for adventure took over and wiped out his earlier fears. "Let's go!" he shouted and ran with the group of about a dozen individuals who laughed like any group of children and surrounded him.

"Let me advise you of something, Mickie," said Albert into his hearing centre. "The average Harliyan life span is only about eight Earth years. The group with you may look like children, but by their cycles, they are all mature adults. In fact, they are fully mature at eighteen months and can breed at that time. A Harliyan female will breed continuously from that age until she is only weeks from death, if she is allowed to live her full life capability."

Mickie hid the astonishment and decided to behave as if he was with just another group of kids his own age, for that is certainly how they appeared.

"This way!" called one and led the group along a branch that must have been two metres in diameter and showed no signs of bending under the weight. As he ran along the wooden highway, Mickie looked down but could see nothing but solid greenery in a never-ending carpet. Allie had explained the workings of the gravity belt that he wore. It had lifted him with the others of the group to the designated area where they had met the Harliyan delegation, and then it had reset itself so that in the event of any sudden drop, he would be lifted back to the level from which he had fallen.

The group swerved right, under the leadership of the one in front, and jumped a small gap onto another huge branch. Confidently, Mickie followed and the line moved swiftly until it came to a massive, empty space that resembled a cathedral, so huge and so peaceful was it.

"This is our gathering space," said one of the group. Mickie looked closer and realised it was a female, with feminine curves and a pretty face, despite the uneven green shades of her skin. "When the tribe needs to be together to say farewell, or when the elders need to talk to us, we gather here. And here is where we meet when any great danger faces us."

Mickie saw that the entire group had gathered around him. The last statement puzzled him.

"But aren't you always in danger from the Long Feeders?" he asked.

There was laughter in the crowd. "That's just the law of balance," said one. "The Long Feeders keep our numbers where they should be and we keep theirs where they should be. Everything is in balance."

"So what dangers do you fear?" Mickie still could not believe the casual way in which his friends dismissed the certainty of bloody death in the jaws of a monster.

"Imbalance!" The chorus was loud and cheerful.

"What is imbalance?" Mickie was baffled.

The female who had first spoken seemed to have become the chief instructor. "Imbalance is when things aren't working properly," she said. "So if we get a disease in the trees, which sometimes happens, then our food supplies decline. So the numbers of our people decline and the Long Feeders start to move away. Then things clear up in the trees, but then our numbers get too high for the food, so things go wrong again. Or if the prairie hunters kill too many Long Feeders' young, the same starts to get out of balance again. It's very important that everything works together."

"So that's why you only let us take a few trees each time?"

"That's right!" The girl laughed and looked like any other kid on any planet. "If you take too many, the Long Feeders lose their homeland, so do we, the food supplies dry up for both of us and we get imbalance again."

The subject of food suddenly made Mickie realise he hadn't eaten for some hours. "So what do you eat up here in the trees?"

"We'll show you!" The girl leaped away, followed by the whole crowd and Mickie joined the fast-moving line racing along another huge branch. As they left the cathedral-sized meeting place, they entered a corridor in which the trees alongside grew so close there were only about two metres of width in which to move. But at the end of a few hundred metres of this, the corridor opened up into another hall-like area. Here, the solid green was mixed with bright flowers of amazing patterns and colours.

Mickie let out a gasp of pleasure. "It's beautiful," he said.

Several of the crowd moved among the flowers and groped around behind them, coming back with what looked like mushrooms. The group sat down on the ground and the food was passed around and Mickie received a mass of the broken items. He smelled it cautiously, aware of the amused glances around him. The odour was delicious, something like fresh bread with spices and other aromas he had never met. He took a mouthful and nearly fainted with delight. The taste was astounding, much as the smell had forecast, but with a texture that made his whole mouth come alive. His whole body reacted with pleasure.

"WOW!" he said and took another bite. It seemed even better than the first.

But the party was shattered by the whole wall of the area to his right being torn apart as a massive, evil, lizard-like head broke through, reached up the ceiling at the end of a serpentine neck and came crashing down on the girl who had been Mickie's guide. She was sitting just an arm's length away and Mickie smelled the breath of the Long Feeder as it descended wide open, revealing lines of dreadful teeth. The jaws smashed together over the shoulder and chest of the victim who emitted just a tiny cry of pain as Mickie heard bones crack. A gush of green blood spurted out, some of it hitting Mickie who screamed in shock. At his left, just a metre away, a second massive head had burst through the forest wall. To Mickie's utter horror and panic, the appalling teeth opened wide only a small distance above him and began to descend. Mickie's heart nearly seized up. But the head stopped just above him. Almost too frightened to move, Mickie looked up. The creature was motionless, the great red eyes staring down at him. There was almost an expression of puzzlement on the face. A breath of foul air rolled down on him and the animal's head sharply swung away and the jaws crunched on another victim. As quickly as it had happened, the two creatures vanished again leaving dead silence. Mickie felt trembles of awful shock running through his body. He looked around the depleted group. All had their heads bowed as if in prayer.

One of them looked up and saw Mickie's expression of fear and horror.

"Do not grieve," he said. "We'll be able to talk to them again within a few hours. And they'll be back among us again within a few weeks."

"Talk to them?" Mickie tried to control the tremble in his voice. "But they're *dead!*"

"Yes, of course they are!" The new speaker was a male and he seemed amused. "We usually are when a Long Feeder has eaten us! But it takes a few hours to adjust to being dead, and then we'll be talking to each other again."

"But... how?"

"Don't your people talk with your dead?" asked another in the group. They had all gathered round Mickie as if to comfort him, and Mickie sensed the weirdness of that. They had lost their friends and they were comforting *him!* "Not that I can think of," he replied, his voice still shaky. "Once somebody's dead, they're gone."

"And they don't come back?"

"Not that I know of. Talking about coming back, shouldn't we move from here? What if the Long Feeders come back?"

"They won't," replied another female. "They always hunt in pairs and they only take one each every few hours. There's no other hunting pair within an hour of here."

Mickie's shock was replaced by curiosity as he remembered his parents cautioning him that the event he had witnessed was quite likely to happen. "You really mean that you can talk to somebody who has died?"

"Of course! Why not?"

"But where are they?"

"It's just another plane of existence," replied another of the circle. "The next one up from us. We think there are other, higher planes, but we don't know how to see those."

"And do you remember being on that plane?" Mickie was fascinated now. "When you're dead, I mean?"

"Oh yes! It's rather fun!"

"Being dead is fun?" Mickie almost laughed.

"Sure." Each of the group was talking in turn now, obviously happy to have a new face in the crowd. To Mickie, it seemed he was chatting to a crowd of kids, but he remembered Albert's words that the Harliyans were fully grown adults after only eighteen months and so many of the people in the group around him were possibly quite elderly in Harliyan terms.

"When you're there, you can do so much more," chimed in another. "You leave the physical world behind, everything is controlled by thought, so you can create anything you want."

"I don't understand," said Mickie. "How can you create anything just by thinking?"

The other gave a human-like shrug. "Hard to describe when you're incarnate like this. But I like to create a lovely room with all the best plants to eat, and that's where I do my review."

"Your review? What's that?"

"It's when I talk over with other souls how I lived the last life and what I want to achieve in the next one."

Mickie felt that his mind was spinning. "And you can remember being dead like this? And you can talk to people who are still alive?"

"Oh yes! I've been dead at least fifty times!"

"Ten for me!"

"Thirty!"

The giggling faces around him could have been kids talking about how many presents they had got for Christmas.

"So how many times can this happen?" Mickie asked. "Do you just keep coming back again and again?"

"Oh no! There'd be no point in that at all! After about a hundred lives, we move on."

"Move on? To where?"

"Another level." The speaker was a girl with wide, alert eyes. "But we don't know anything about it and we can't communicate with it."

"Falhuminoparta will probably be going there next time," said another female sitting a few places away from Mickie. She's already lived ninety eight lives, so this cycle is probably about over."

"Yes, I think so," agreed the girl named Falhuminoparta. "I'm really looking forward to it."

Mickie was aware that he was dealing with something totally outside of his experience or even his thinking. What little religious instruction he had received in school had provided no basis for dealing with the information he was getting here.

"But how do you know about the next level if you can't communicate with it?" he asked.

"It's just that we know we keep meeting the same people between both the levels," said Falhuminoparta. "But after about a hundred lives, they just stop coming back and we can't find them on either one. But in the last few times I've died I've begun to sense a new direction. I just know that there's another level, maybe even more. But we have no idea what happens after this."

"But I don't understand," said Mickie, still struggling to get his head round the new and rather frightening concepts he was meeting. "What's the point? You live such very short lives, you aren't a technological race, so you don't change very much. When you said you review a life after you've died and plan the next one, what is there to do?"

"We talk to the Speakers," replied the one called Falhuminoparta. "And through them we talk to other species round the Universe. So while we are not a technological species, we do understand about technology and its role and we learn a great deal about other planets and other species. But our main task is to learn to understand."

"Understand what?" asked Mickie.

"The Universe. Our role in it. How to help others understand their roles."

"But... *why?*"

"Because that is our mission."

Mickie could get no further than that and eventually gave up. A few hours later the shuttles returned to the ship with a cargo of rare wood and the leaves that could be woven into empathic clothing.

Chapter 10 – Mayoowani

"I tried visiting Harliya last trip," said Fencris. "But I caused some difficulties with them because our red eyes remind them of the Long Feeders, and it's disturbing for them to see so many, so none of us from Cassolea can visit any more."

"We've been there," said Melkana. "Our parents are on the scientific team that checks the trees and leaves before cutting. It's very beautiful, but a lot scary too." She was wearing something different from the standard ship's uniform, almost a pants suit. When she had come into Mickie's cabin with the others, the suit had been light blue, but as they had settled down, Mickie had watched with fascination as the suit had changed to a deep, warm yellow. She saw his stare and chuckled.

"I just had it made up from the stuff we picked up on Harliya. It's empathic clothing."

"But how does it work?" Mickie was unsure which was more interesting, the graceful elegance of Melkana or the way her suit was now changing into a bright pink.

"The leaves have this tiny telepathic ability," she said. "It picks up on the wearer's mood and changes colour."

"So what does bright pink say?" Mickie asked.

Drellion chortled loudly. "I think it means she knows you've got the hots for her!" He jumped up and fled round the cabin, angrily pursued without success by his sister until she haughtily gave up and sat down again. Mickie tried to hide his own confusion.

"That place is certainly scary," he said with great feeling. "I thought I was dead when that horrible Long Feeder head starting to descend on me. Then it stopped and took one of the others."

"Do you believe all that stuff about being killed all those times and coming back again?" Fencris spoke with a superior smile. "I've heard it from lots of people who visit, but I think it's all rubbish."

"I'm not so sure," replied Mickie. "They seemed very sincere. And I must say, I like the idea of living on another plane for a time when you can create any environment you want."

That started a fun debate about what sort of environment each of them would create if they had that sort of ability and it became a competition, with points awarded to the best.

Drellion, the youngest jumped in first. "I'd have summer all the time," he said with a big grin. "And I'd live by this beautiful big lake and I'd have my own motorboat and I'd go fishing every day. And my house would be huge, with a swimming pool, and food stores in every room so I could get all my favourite foods any place where I was."

"You'd get awfully bored," said his sister. "And fat as a pig."

"No I wouldn't!" Drellion was indignant. "I'd have my computer so I could talk to all my friends and they'd visit any time they wanted, or I could fly my own aeroplane and go and visit them."

Mickie was rather astounded at how similar the world of Drellion seemed to Earth and how much like his own dream that could have sounded.

"I'd have an aeroplane, too," said Fencris. "I love flying. I'd do the wildest aerobatics, and my plane would be an atmosphere-skimmer, so I could fly right out into space and stay in orbit looking down at the world. But my house would be deep in the woods and I'd go hunting with my two holvairs and fight broxies."

"What are holvairs and broxies?" Mickie was fascinated at the wildness that appeared in Fencris' face as he described his perfect world.

"Holvairs are sort of like your dogs on Earth," Melkana replied. "But they are really hunting animals, not like any of your pets. And broxies are very wild and fierce animals, something like wild boars. They can kill an adult and it takes real skill and bravery to hunt them. The Cassoleans do it on foot and armed only with spears and knives. Honestly, you've no idea what a primitive brute this friend of ours really is!"

"That's right, I am!" Fencris said enthusiastically. "Guns are forbidden on a broxies hunt, you have to make the kill on foot and close. I've been on two hunts so far. Next time I get to go in for the kill myself."

"Wow!" said Mickie, impressed. "What about you, Melkana?"

"No, I don't want to," she said, suddenly looking shy. "Why don't you tell us your perfect world, Mickie?"

Mickie thought deeply for a few moments, then realised his answer. "It's all this," he said, waving about him. "I couldn't have anything better than this ship, my parents, all this travel to new planets. And you guys."

His response was met with a short silence. Then Melkana broke it with a pleased laugh. "I like that," she said, and jumped to her feet. "Hey! The Gravity-Ball match is about to start," she shouted and dashed for the door. The others followed with yells of excitement.

"Mickie, this is going to blow your mind!" Drellion said as they raced along the corridors.

"I still don't think I believe the game!" Mickie said with a breathless laugh. "But it sure sounds wild!"

"Wild doesn't begin to describe it," Drellion said. "I can't wait until I'm big enough to play."

Mickie decided almost the entire Ship's complement was in Hangar Ten. The large square they had used for their own Loopies games had been cleaned off, and a new oblong shape, fifty metres long and about forty metres wide painted in bright white lines. The eight shuttles had all been moved against the wall. On one long side of the oblong, starting about two or three metres from the line, tiers of seating had been set up and they were nearly full. There were six individual seats at each end area also. It was the first time Mickie had seen the entire crew together. He noticed that the X'Kasxi had all gathered in one group at the ends of the back three rows and quickly counted them, reaching 25 before Melkana pulled him to the second row and they found four seats together. Even the Kaloti were there, all wearing eye shields against the bright lights of the hangar and Mickie realised that the gravity setting in the hangar was much lower than normal, obviously for the sake of these tall, fragile-looking creatures. Pleased, Mickie realised that Allie was sitting behind him, and he was even more pleased that Melkana sat on his left, while Drellion was on the other side, with Fencris at the end.

The oblong arena had been augmented by walls, he saw. They were transparent, nearly invisible, almost like the crystal barriers in the engine room, but he saw a series of loops that seemed to be arranged at random locations around the walls. They looked like the straps for standing passengers on a bus. On the opposite end walls, he saw that there was a black ring, some three-quarters of the way up and about half a metre in diameter. The excitement in the Hangar was enormous. Mickie could almost touch the tension in the air.

"It doesn't feel like seven percent gravity," he said to Drellion.

"Not out here, it isn't," the youngest replied. "But inside the box, it is."

"They can control it that well?"

Fencris leaned over from his seat the other side of Drellion. "To within a metre," he said. "That's why the seats are spaced a bit away from the walls."

Impressed, Mickie studied the area again, this time seeing that there was a ceiling over the area, about thirty metres high, so that the entire playing arena was enclosed. The ceiling was equally transparent, but it held a small black dome in the very centre. As he looked around, the lights in the spectator area of the hangar began to dim, while those inside the playing area brightened. Then a group of eight men appeared at one end and began to approach the far wall of the arena. Cheers rang out from the crowd, particularly from one group in the middle.

"The Botanists," Melkana said into his ear. "They won the championship last time and they're the favourites this time."

One of the men touched the wall and a door opened in the transparent crystal. Five of the team entered, while the remaining three took the seats just behind the opening. As the group walked to the centre of the arena, Mickie recognised Meldon, the botanist who had showed him round the plant pathology area. The group was dressed in tight tunics, coloured a bright red, much like the shorts and shirts worn by racing cyclists. They wore helmets that held a screen in front of the faces, and they had thick gloves on their left hands, though Mickie saw that one of the team sitting outside wore his on his right hand. All of them carried what looked like long squash racquets, as long as themselves, though instead of tightly-strung surfaces, they had small nets at the heads

Meanwhile, another group made a similar appearance at the opposite end of the arena, and Mickie saw Grant among them. This group was dressed in identical manner, except that their tunics were black. Again, five of them, including Grant walked in through an invisible door, while three took seats outside. More cheers greeted the group and this time, the kids rose to their feet and yelled lustily. Turning round, he saw that Allie was grinning widely and applauding like the rest. He decided to join in and cheered for his father's team.

"What are they called?" he shouted above the racket.

"The Executives!" Fencris bellowed back and Mickie laughed loudly.

Silence slowly descended on the Hangar. Four more men stood up from the front row of seats and took position, each of them in the middle of one side. They were dressed in ordinary Ship's tunics with nothing to distinguish them except for a whistle hanging round their necks. Mickie chuckled at how a referee could always be identified, even on an intergalactic space ship flying in hyperspace.

"Can they hear those whistles inside the box?" he asked.

"No problem," Drellion replied. "The walls are actually fine mesh, they're not solid."

Meanwhile, the ten players had leaped slowly off the floor and each of them took hold of a strap attached to the walls. One man from each team was stationed on the end walls that held the black rings, while the others clung to the side walls. Mickie could see no pattern to their positions; they seemed only to choose a preferred location, ranging from only a metre or so above the ground, to almost touching the ceiling. They had leaped in slow, graceful arcs that made Mickie's flights in Loopies look clumsy.

One of the referees blew a shrill note and from the little dome above the ceiling, a ball appeared and slowly dropped. It was about twice the size of a cricket ball or baseball and it glowed a bright yellow.

All the players used their feet to kick away from their positions, but there seemed no pattern to their directions. Only one from each team made a direct leap at the dropping sphere and it was a red-clad Botanist who reached it, neatly netting the ball in his racquet. As he caught it, he tucked his arms and legs and turned two complete loops, making the Executive player miss completely, the move causing a yell of appreciation from the Botanist's supporters and a groan of dismay from the others.

But there had been a pattern to the seemingly random movements of the other players. The Botanists fell into a moving line that stretched from high up near to where the first player had caught the ball to near the floor. All of them were moving towards the far wall, slowly drifting downward, but maintaining their relative positions. The ball catcher flicked his racquet and the ball shot toward the nearest player who caught it in his net and just as quickly flicked it along the line. But the third player couldn't catch it. One of the black-clad Executives intercepted him and wrapped his arms round the Botanist's, forcing him out of position. But Mickie saw that there was more to the move than just an interception. The Executive had timed the angle so perfectly that the Botanist was stopped dead and began a slow drift downward, while the interceptor carried on to the wall, turned so that his feet met the wall first and then leaped sharply away again.

"A stop! A great stop!" Drellion shouted, applauding loudly, as were many others in the crowd.

Melkana smiled at Mickie's confusion. "It means the interceptor is still active and can move on. But when a player is stopped like that, he can't do anything but wait till he reaches the floor, which means he's out of the game for a few seconds and the other team has a man advantage."

Mickie began to realise the game was extraordinarily complex and required extremely fine timing and athleticism as well as an ability to think in three dimensions.

Meanwhile, another Executive had followed the interception and swept up the ball. He carried on to the wall, turned, used his footing to sling a bullet-fast pass right across the arena. The ball bounced off the wall, up to the ceiling and down, right into the net of another player almost at the far end. He turned, cleverly missed a tackle by a Botanist who crashed into the wall, and passed the ball to a team-mate who was flying in a fast arc across the arena. In a single movement, the catcher caught the ball in his net and threw it at the black ring. The ball hit just inside the black circle and a buzzer sounded, causing half the crowd to rise to their feet and yell enthusiastically.

Above the black ring, a glowing digit "1" lit up.

There was no stoppage in action. A Botanist netted the rebounding ball, flung it forward to another of his team and this time, the five players began a complex passing movement that had the ball flickering between all of them in a series of short passes, too fast for any of the Executives to tackle a man with the ball in his possession. As they did, the five moved as a group, advancing on the Executive end of the arena. But their positions did not remain constant. As one reached floor level, he kicked himself back almost to ceiling level, or to a mid-level on the wall, and then across the arena, each time maintaining the weaving passes that had the Executives helpless.

"That's what they're good at," Fencris said in admiration. "They do this better than any of the teams."

Mickie had to agree, the process was enthralling.

Suddenly the weaving passes ended. One man who had been hanging on a strap midway along the arena launched himself directly at the Executive goal. As he shot through the confused defenders, the ball was catapulted to a point midway between him and the goal. Man and ball met about ten metres from the black ring, the ball was caught in the net and launched forward, slamming into the dead centre of the ring.

Half the crowd erupted in delight, and even the other half applauded enthusiastically at the demonstration of high-speed ballistics that the players had demonstrated.

Just as at the other end earlier, a glowing "1" appeared above the ring.

An Executive player caught the rebound out of the black circle and paused.

Melkana touched Mickie's arm. "After a goal is scored, a defender has to be first one to touch it and nobody else can be within ten metres of him or they get penalised."

Mickie nodded his thanks, his eyes still on the game. While the Executive defender paused, the remaining four Executives positioned themselves with leaping arcs in different directions and heights. The ball was launched towards the middle of the ceiling, bounced down and was neatly caught by another Executive who had leaped in a fast arc to meet the rebound. Immediately he flicked the ball in a direction that seemed aimless to Mickie, but he didn't see Grant launching himself from midway up the right-hand wall just before the ball was thrown and he caught it in a well-planned move and again passed it behind him in a slow arc that seemed to leave it helpless, had there been any Botanist players around. But again, another black-clad player had launched himself in a pre-planned jump from the floor and caught the ball.

Mickie realised he was watching a beautifully choreographed set of movements and rose to his feet with the crowd to applaud the action. But it hadn't ended. Three more such passes were made, all of them with such precision that none of the defenders could anticipate the flight of the ball. It culminated in one more move when Grant caught the ball as he rose vertically from the floor, spinning around his own axis, spun once more and released the ball like a bullet at the target, the crowd again applauding the athleticism of the scoring play.

The action fell into a scoreless stalemate for a while, each side initiating beautifully planned moves that involved both teams flying back and forth along the arena like flights of swallows, but shots at the black circle either missed or were intercepted by defenders, sometimes in their nets and sometimes with their gloved hands. Collisions were frequent and violent and many times, players spun off each other and drifted helplessly to the ground before being able to connect to a hard surface again and push off back into play. Several times, a referee blew his whistle and play stopped briefly, though Mickie couldn't see what rule had been broken. The only one he could identify was when one Botanist got accidentally hit in the face by a racquet, and play stopped for a second while all the Executives moved back to allow him to pass the ball without interference. Another time, a Botanist tackled Grant at high speed, but Grant had already passed the ball. The tackle was less scientific than most and both players crashed hard into the wall, causing anxiety to Mickie as he saw Grant collide hard. But there seemed no damage done, and the two players touched hands briefly in acknowledgement of an accident without malicious intent.

"He was lucky," Drellion said as play resumed. "If the referee had thought it was deliberate, that guy would have been grounded in one corner for two minutes as a penalty."

The lights over the arena flickered sharply for a few seconds and this seemed to indicate a break in the play with the Executives leading two to one. The teams drifted to their exits and then walked out as they met higher gravity, each team gathering around a drinks supply.

Grant walked up to the group with a wide grin on his face, breathing hard, and sweat running down his face.

"Hooooo-*weeee!*" he said, leaning over a chair and panting. "It's rough in there! How are you finding it, Mickie?"

"It's astounding!" Mickie said with a laugh. "Now I see why we have to get good at Loopies first!"

"That's for sure!" Grant smiled as Allie handed him a bottle of cold water and he drained it in one go. "Okay, back to the front lines!"

As he slowly gained understanding of the game, Mickie wondered if he would ever really grasp the complexities of the strategies involved. The athleticism, the ballistics, the speed of movement all enthralled him and when the final lights flickered and the Botanists managed to scrape a win with a last-second fling at the goal, he applauded wildly with the entire crowd, not caring at all that his father's side had lost. It had obviously been a phenomenal match and everybody seemed happy at the exhibition.

Chapter 11 – The Gelkka

"The planet of Mayoowani is really two stories," said Albert the computer as the three-dimensional image of a new world formed in the middle of Mickie's room. He had already looked down on the planet from orbit a few hours ago when the Ship had arrived. "The story of the planet and the Mayoowi people takes place over a million years while the people evolved from forest-dwelling simian hominids into a peaceful civilisation of some two billion people and then becomes the story of a people as a subject race under the military domination of the Gelkka."

Mickie watched as the world of Mayoowani revolved before him. It had four continents, two that spanned almost from pole to pole and looked roughly equal in size, and two other land masses that were almost rectangular, one about twice the size of the other, both in the southern hemisphere.

"These are the Mayoowi," continued Albert. The planet vanished and two holographic images replaced it. Both were slender in build, somewhat delicate in appearance. One was a little smaller than the other.

"However, for now, we shall look at the planetary invasion that occurred about a hundred years ago when the Gelkka arrived."

The two Mayoowi images were replaced by something that made Mickie draw back with a gasp.

The being standing in the middle of Mickie's room was monstrous. It stood at least two and a half metres tall, with a massive chest and shoulders that made the creature look extraordinarily top-heavy. The face was frightening; the skin was a dark green, huge eyes glared at Mickie over the top of a beak of extreme cruelty, like the face of an angry eagle. It wore what looked like metallic leggings under a hip-length green cloak swung to one side.

"The Gelkka evolved from a creature not that dissimilar to the dinosaurs on Earth," said Albert. "And like Earth, one branch of the primitive animal became a raptor very similar to Earth's Pterodactyl, while the intelligent, sentient branch became the dominant animal on the planet."

"The Gelkka were a highly competitive and warlike species, nearly destroying themselves and the home planet of Gelokk in a series of inter-tribal wars that ended about five hundred years ago. They must be treated with extreme caution or you may risk a lot of lives on this crew. One final thing, then. There are legends running round the planet about some mysterious Saviour who will free the people from the Gelkka tyranny. You must not mention this to anyone at all. I hope you understand me clearly?"

"Er... yes. I do." Mickie was a little taken aback at the sudden note of command in the computer's voice.

"Good. Then report to Shuttle Bay Fifteen to meet your parents and transport down to Mayoowani."

Feeling a little subdued, Mickie followed instructions.

* * *

All three of Mickie's friends accompanied him on this trip.

"We're getting crazy being cooped up in the ship," said Melkana. "Drellion and I told my parents and we said the same to Fencris' parents. They said the same as ours, that there was no danger on this planet if we behave ourselves."

"I'm glad," Mickie said with feeling. "I could have used you on the last two planet-falls."

"Yeah, you need us to keep you out of trouble," replied Fencris with a grin, his red eyes flashing like small fire beacons. "Anyway, we were pretty fed up with you getting all the trips. Your parents seem to want to give you a lot of experience pretty fast."

"That's because I'm so new to all this," Mickie tried to explain. "So, have you been here before?"

"We visited on the last trip," Drellion piped up. "It's a bit grim the way the Mayoowi creep around, but those Gelkka, wow! They're awesome!"

The conversation was interrupted by the voice of the shuttle pilot.

"Planet-fall in one minute. Ground party, prepare to disembark. The reception committee of Gelkka is waiting."

Allie moved over from where she was sitting with Grant and took a seat next to Mickie. "Okay, kids," she said with a smile. "You're free to go anywhere, but remember this is a subject world of a very ruthless occupying army. Remember the rules. You have some local currency. You can get a meal at any café and buy small souvenirs. It's okay to talk to Mayoowi, but the very, *very* strict rule applies here. Do not talk about liberation, do not mention a Redeemer or a Saviour. And do *not,* under any circumstances talk to a Gelkka unless one addresses you. If that happens, obey any instructions and return to the shuttle if that seems appropriate or the safest thing. Okay?"

There was a firm note in Allie's voice that demanded obedience, and all four nodded gravely.

The doors opened to bright sunlight. Mickie had not felt any bump on landing, but the gravity motors were always smooth. As instructed earlier, the four children waited for the adults to leave and when the ship was empty they moved to the door.

They had landed in the centre of a town. The ship was in a large square surrounded by attractive buildings, none more than three storeys tall. It reminded Mickie of pictures he had seen of old European towns, with ancient stone walls and neat, white-rimmed windows. The sun was extremely bright and seemed to have a vaguely blue tint to it. Gravity was a little higher than was standard in the ship and Mickie felt a slight tremble in his knees from the unexpected weight. It was another reason Allie and Grant had wanted him to make these planetary visits, so that he could maintain full muscular efficiency. Like everybody on the Ship, Mickie was very fit, but there was nothing like extra gravity to make the heart work harder, the muscles to tone up and lungs draw oxygen deeply. He looked across at where the adults were meeting the Gelkka and, despite his preparation, felt a wave of fear. They were so huge, towering over the crewmembers who looked tiny in comparison and the Gelkka seemed to have an air of menace about them.

"Come on, let's get out of here," said Fencris from behind him. Pleased to have the momentary fear banished, Mickie set off at a run across the square, enjoying the feeling of working his leg muscles again. The four ran headlong across the square and into one of the streets that led off. Mickie realised what was feeling so wrong.

"Where is everyone?" he asked. All four looked around them curiously.

"You're right," Melkana said. "This is weird."

But as she spoke, the scene changed. A double line of Gelkka appeared, seemingly in uniform for all were dressed in the same leggings and green cloak that the hologram figure had worn in Mickie's cabin. At the front of the line, a solitary figure rode on a strange vehicle. It was nothing but a platform with a massive seat on it and it floated about a metre above the ground, obviously powered by some form of gravity engine. The troops moved down the street where the four youngsters stood watching nervously. As it passed, the figure on the platform looked straight at Mickie. Huge, angry eyes stared at him over a cruel raptor's beak and seemed to stare right down into his soul. Mickie shivered and went cold as the platform stopped a short distance from the small group. Some form of silent order must have been passed, because four of the troops detached themselves from the double line and walked straight to the children.

One of them emitted a harsh growl and the device in Mickie's shoulder immediately produced comprehensible words.

"You! Come!" said the towering creature, staring down at them with the same furious eagle eyes of the creature in the chair.

"Whoops!" muttered Fencris, but walked with Mickie, Drellion and Melkana to the floating platform.

His whole body trembling, Mickie stood silently and looked back as calmly as he could at the terrifying image before him.

The figure that Mickie assumed to be the officer in charge pointed a talon at Mickie. "Come here," he commanded. As he spoke, the platform settled gently on the ground.

Forcing his legs to comply, Mickie advanced to the edge of the machine. Even seated, the officer's massive head was still more than a metre above Mickie's.

"You are from the visiting Kaloti ship?" The words were snapped out contemptuously.

"Yes," he managed to reply.

"Have you talked to any cattle?"

"Cattle?" Mickie was bemused.

"Cattle," the officer repeated. "Those that serve us."

Did he mean the Mayoowi people? Mickie was appalled. "No," he replied.

The officer continued to examine Mickie as if he were a specimen of some ugly insect. "You are different," he said suddenly. "Why?"

"I'm from Earth," Mickie stammered.

The officer seemed not to hear. For a few more awful moments, he glared at Mickie. "Have no dealings with cattle," he commanded, and the platform rose silently and moved away followed by the two lines of troops.

Mickie found he was holding his breath and slowly released it in a long sigh.

"What the hell was all that about?" said Fencris. His red eyes were flashing dangerously.

"He seemed puzzled by you, Mickie," added Melkana. "That was horrible, I've never talked to a Gelkka before."

Mickie was about to answer, but a small sob from Drellion interrupted him. The youngest of the four was looking absolutely terrified and tears were rolling down his face. In sudden concern, his sister put her arms round him. "Hey, it's okay," she murmured. "They've gone now and they won't hurt us. They wouldn't dare, they know the weapons we have on the ship."

It took a few minutes to soothe the frightened little boy, but eventually he seemed calm again.

"I think we need something to eat," said Mickie, remembering how Allie had first eased his sadness at their first meeting. "Does that look like a café or something over there?"

They stared across the street and certainly the building they looked at resembled a restaurant. The windows were wide and tables were visible within. There were even some figures seated at two of the tables.

"Let's go," said Melkana. "We visited one last trip with my dad. They do really great hot cakes and coffee."

The four strolled across the road and entered the door of the shop. The most wonderful smell of bakery and coffee greeted them as they walked in, and Drellion immediately cheered up. Mickie looked around him and studied his first Mayoowi. They looked exactly like the holograms Albert had shown him, just as small, just as delicate in appearance. There were five seated at one table and two more at another. All of them looked curiously at the visitors.

"Hello!" said Melkana brightly, but all seven faces immediately turned away.

"Let's take that table by the window," suggested Mickie and they sat down, immediately finding that the chairs and table were built for their size, rather than adults. Mickie chuckled. "It's kids' world," he laughed. "It's nice to be the right size for a change."

He carefully looked at the Mayoowi at the other table, trying not to be obvious about it. They looked almost human, he decided. Their faces were delicate in structure, but the forward chin and receding forehead definitely suggested the simian ancestry of which Albert had spoken. Another figure appeared at the far side of the room and advanced cautiously to them. It was smaller than the others at the table and more slender in build, a female, it seemed. Her nervousness was obvious. Melkana took the lead, having been there before.

"Can we have hot cakes and coffee?" she asked. The female Mayoowi made no gesture, but turned and walked to what Mickie assumed was the kitchen. Through the window, the street had produced a few pedestrians or – a few pedestrians were appearing. Mickie wondered if they had been inside until the Gelkka patrol had passed and now felt confident enough to walk outside again. He pondered for a few moments on the idea of living that way, in fear of an occupying and technologically superior force and decided it was a horrible concept.

"What'll we do after we've had this?" asked Drellion. He seemed to have recovered his spirits.

"Just look around the town, I guess," Melkana answered. "I'd like to look at any shops they have and get a couple of souvenirs."

All four stopped talking as the waitress appeared with a tray. The smell of the hotcakes almost overwhelmed Mickie. It was even better than the first breakfast he had eaten with Allie when the odours of bacon, eggs and pancakes had made his senses swim. The smell seemed to be a mix of pastry, cinnamon and honey with the extra flavour of coffee. And when he took his first bite of the cake, he decided he had never tasted anything so delicious, not even the food of Harliya.

All four emitted the same sigh of delight.

"Just like I remembered," said Melkana. "Only better!"

"Definitely better," agreed her little brother.

Mickie was ecstatic. "There's good stuff, even on occupied planets."

"Shhhhhh!" Melkana jumped on his comment. "Remember what our parents said."

Mickie hid his annoyance at himself and took a sip of the coffee. It tasted like the very best coffee he had ever drunk back in Earth, but with the added flavours of mint, cinnamon and others that he couldn't identify. "This is incredible," he said. "Can we buy some this to take back with us, do you think?"

"If we find any sort of shop, I suppose so," Fencris said. "And I certainly want some also. It's just too good."

For the next twenty minutes they busied themselves in the magical flavours till they sat back with a contented sigh, the food completely gone. As he did so, Mickie realised that the other Mayoowi in the café had been watching them. But as he looked around, they all immediately ducked their gazes down to the table. The group of five at the one table stood up and silently walked out of the café.

The waitress returned and placed a piece of paper on the table. Mickie picked it up and studied it. The symbols written there were completely unintelligible to him and for a moment he panicked. "How do we know how much to pay?" he whispered.

"It's okay," replied Melkana, reaching into her bag and extracting a small notepad. "My dad gave me the translation table. He said they use a duodecimal system here, and he said it's very convenient, 'cos everything divides by two, four, six and twelve. Let's see now..." She studied her notepad and the bill together. "That looks like the symbol for forty-eight, and that's the one for a six." She took some of the local currency notes and again studied them, extracting three from her small wad. "That should do it, two twenty-fours and a six," she declared and waved at the waitress. "Is that right?" she asked. The woman nodded without comment and took the notes, watching the four get up and leave with what seemed to Mickie an expression of relief in her face.

Back on the street, they looked around.

"Let's keep walking in the same direction," Mickie suggested. "We know the main square is back that way, so let's keep walking away from it."

Nodding agreement, the four children ambled along the street. There were more of the locals moving around now, and they seemed to be walking in the general direction Mickie's group had taken. As they passed a small side street, they could see that a small crowd had gathered at the far end.

"A market!" Melkana cried with pleasure. "That's what we want!"

Cheerfully, the group joined in the throng in a smaller version of the main square in which they had first arrived. Like any other village market, the area was lined with tables, all of which seemed full of products. Although conscious of the stares from the Mayoowi people, Mickie and his friends moved around and studied the various offerings. After a while, he forgot the sense of horror and despair he had felt in the café at the thought of living under an army of occupation and began to feel at ease, enjoying the colour and general cheerfulness that seemed to fill the town square.

At last he found what he was looking for, a large stall selling foodstuffs. He stood and examined the array of items, aware that the little Mayoowi standing on the other side was regarding him with interest. Mickie saw the pile of beans in a bowl and pointed to them. "Is that coffee?" he asked the stall keeper who nodded.

"The very best," he replied and took a small handful of the beans and dropped them into a grinder. After just a few moments of manually grinding the beans, he lifted the cap and placed the device under Mickie's nose. The same wonderful aroma he had experienced in the café seemed to envelope his head and Mickie laughed with pleasure.

"Oh yes!" he exclaimed. "How much?"

"Thirty-six a blex," replied the Mayoowi, leaving Mickie bemused. His puzzlement caused a smile in the merchant. "A blex will fill this," he said, lifting a small tin from under the table. It looked about a kilo, Mickie thought, and recalled that they had paid fifty-four of the local currency units for the meal. He decided that seemed fair and reached for his wallet, then realised he had no idea of how to read the unit values on the notes.

"I'll have to trust you to take the right amount," he said to the merchant.

The Mayoowi gave a shrug and what seemed to be an expression of resignation. "You can trust us," he replied. "In our world, any cheating will cause my death."

Feeling shock at the words and what they implied, Mickie let the man take two notes from his hand and fill the tin with the coffee beans. Tucking the tin into the backpack he had taken for the day's outing, Mickie smiled at the man and continued looking around. He saw the other three chatting at another table at the very end of the line, and moved to join them. The stall sold textiles and Melkana was obviously enjoying herself examining several bolts of brightly coloured cloths.

Mickie stood silently, observing the market place, relishing the experience and reminding himself with some amusement that only a few weeks before he had been a miserable child living on Earth with absolutely no comprehension of the numbers of advanced civilisations in the star systems so far away.

He felt a small tug on the bottom of his jacket and looked down to see a Mayoowi tucked under the stall table. He couldn't tell if it was child or adult, male or female. He crouched down and looked at the small person eye to eye.

"Hello," he said.

The other looked hard at him. "We want to talk to you."

"Who's we?"

"My friends and I."

"And where are your friends?" Mickie felt a twinge of worry, remembering the angry eyes of the Gelkka troop leader and his order to "have no dealings with cattle."

At that moment, he was joined on the ground by the others who looked with interest at the Mayoowi.

"Hello, what are we doing down here?" asked Drellion.

"This... er... what is your name, anyway?" asked Mickie. "We can't talk without knowing names. I'm Mickie."

"Viliamondini," said the Mayoowi. "Can we go and talk in that room over there?" The words were accompanied by a finger pointed at an open door just a few metres away from the stall.

"Mickie, I don't think we should," Melkana said hesitantly. "Remember what that Gelkka said."

"I agree," chimed in Fencris. "That guy scared the living daylights out of me, never mind just little Drellion here."

"I know." Mickie's nervousness was high as he remembered not just the threat of the Gelkka, but also the orders of his parents.

But their conversation stopped as they all sensed the frightened silence that descended on the town square. They stood up and looked around. The scene was frozen except for movement at the far side where the Gelkka squad led by the officer on the anti-gravity platform was moving into the market.

The line of troops moved steadily into the centre of the square. The line stopped and two of the Gelkka soldiers advanced on the merchant standing behind a table. Grimly, Mickie realised it was the stall at which he had bought the coffee. The soldiers seized hold of the man and dragged him to the officer seated on his platform. Mickie could not hear what the conversation was about, but he saw the frantic denials of the man. But the scene changed to one of utter horror. The soldiers dragged the man some metres to the nearest wall, threw him hard against the stone, backed away just a metre or two and drew weapons from under their green cloaks.

"No, they can't," begged Mickie. "Oh please, no, they can't....."

But they did. A line of pure white light jumped from the soldiers' hands to the tiny Mayoowi against the wall and he vanished in a blaze of fire.

Screams started rising from points in the square. The Mayoowi under the table jumped out, grabbed Mickie's hand and pulled him fast to the doorway he had pointed out. "All of you, quickly, come with me!"

No longer thinking straight, Mickie let himself be led into the doorway and the other three followed him. Inside the room, Mickie almost collapsed against the wall, his whole body trembling.

"Why? Why did they do that? He'd done nothing wrong!" Tears flooded down his face and he choked, gasping for breath.

"The Gelkka don't need excuses for killing us," replied the Mayoowi. Mickie looked up and realised there were several other Mayoowi in the room. Judging by the height and build of the one who had pulled them into this room, Mickie decided that Viliamondini was a male.

"What is this place?" demanded Melkana. "And who are you all?" She looked nervous and shaken, much as Mickie felt.

"We are your friends," replied Viliamondini. "But we also need to ask for your help."

"Help? How can we help? We're just kids from off-world. And you're getting us into serious trouble." Fencris was looking angry, his red eyes glowing dangerously. Viliamondini looked frightened and turned to Mickie.

"All we want is for you to take our need for help and tell the rest of the inhabited worlds," he said.

"I think they already know," replied Mickie. "Our telling them again won't change things."

"They already know?" Viliamondini looked angry. "If they know, how come they won't help us get rid of these scum Gelkka?"

"My teacher said it won't work unless you do it yourself," said Mickie. "If we tried to help a rebellion, it could make things much worse."

The entire group of Mayoowi seemed to slump in despair at Mickie's words. Even with the different body types and facial structures, their despair was obvious. For a moment, Mickie wondered if some body language expressions were universal in species of different planets.

"That's what the Redeemer has said," one of them commented from the back of the room. Slimmer and smaller than Viliamondini, Mickie decided she was female.

"The Redeemer?" he asked. "You know about the Redeemer?"

"Of *course* we know," she snapped in some anger. "But how come *you* know?"

"Er..." Mickie felt helpless, unsure if he should let these people know that their mythological Redeemer was already known to the outside worlds.

"We heard about him on a previous trip," Melkana interjected smoothly. "But we don't know if he really exists."

The anger and dejection in the room seemed to lift. "He exists, all right," said Viliamondini. "Some of us in this room have even seen him and heard him speak."

"What does he say?" Mickie's curiosity had driven the fear of the Gelkka from his mind. The idea that one person could lead the whole Mayoowi race out of its slavery was fascinating. Like any other child on Earth, he had heard the biblical tales of Moses and Jesus and the idea that a similar Messiah could be present here and in his own time was enthralling.

"He says that all of us dreaming with him, dreaming together, could drive the Gelkka away from Mayoowani," said the girl at the back of the room. There was a hum of agreement from her companions. "He says that the power of all minds working together is irresistible, invincible," she continued. "And the time for ridding the world of the Overlords is coming."

"Wow!" said Fencris under his breath. "That's crazy! They believe that they can just *think* those monsters away?"

"Yes, we do," replied the girl. She was at least five metres away, Mickie decided and developed a healthy respect for the power of Mayoowi ears. "And if you came with us this evening, you could hear him say it again."

"He's here? In this town?" Mickie felt stunned, excited and frightened all at the same time.

"Yes, he's here." Viliamondini seemed calm. "And if you came and heard him speak, then maybe you could tell the rest of your people that he really exists and now is the time for them to help us."

"Where will he speak?" asked Melkana. "How can you avoid the Gelkka with a crowd like that?"

"We go out of town. Not many of us, because that would warn the Overlords. And we don't stand in a crowd for the same reason. The Redeemer sits in shadow and we all hide in nearby caves, or in ditches or under bushes and listen to him. Then we take his words back to our people. If you join us, you'll be safe like that."

"When does this happen?" Mickie asked.

"Very soon. It all has to be done before the evening curfew. The market will start again soon and that's our cover for just a few of us to slip away out to the stone quarry where he'll speak. I can guide you and get you back here before dark."

"My dad said we'd be here till after dark loading up the shuttle," said Melkana. "I think we should do this."

"You're nuts!" said Fencris. "Mickie, she's crazy! Don't do it."

"You don't have to come with us," replied Mickie. "You and Drellion can go back to the shuttle."

Fencris looked disgusted. "No, you need me to keep you two idiots out of trouble. Drellion, you go back to the ship."

"Not a chance!" snapped the smallest of them with more determination and fierceness than Mickie had seen before. "I want to see this Redeemer too."

Viliamondini looked out of the window. "It looks clear," he said. "The Gelkka do that quite often, just come into a group, cause trouble, kill one two people then leave. I think they see it as light entertainment." The bitterness in his tone came through despite the translation device.

He opened the door and led the four out of the building, through the market, which had resumed its business and along a street until an abrupt division marked the town from the countryside. As the street ended, fields began. Viliamondini followed a line of huge trees then into a deep ditch that led to a stone quarry. They were only about fifteen minutes from the town and

Mickie felt anxious that they would be obvious to the Gelkka.

"There!" Viliamondini pointed to a small cave about two metres above them. All five scrambled up and into the little alcove, and took positions behind a chunk of rock that hid them from the outside.

"The Redeemer will sit over there," said Viliamondini pointing at an overhanging curtain of stone about twenty metres away. "We'll hear him quite easily. Now, stay quiet until he arrives."

Sitting somewhat uncomfortably on the hard and rough stone, the five were silent, not moving except for when Viliamondini occasionally peeped out to check the situation. Then suddenly, "He's here!" he whispered. His excitement was obvious and Mickie felt a responsive surge of energy.

Carefully, they stood up and arranged themselves to see the figure that had appeared under the overhang. There seemed nothing extraordinary about him, thought Mickie who had been half-expecting some shining, god-like creature. But it was just another Mayoowi, no larger, no more impressive than anyone else they had seen today. He carried no notes, he didn't do anything of the usual things speakers did, such as clearing his throat or looking around his audience. He just sat down on a rock and placed his hands on his knees.

"The power of a sentient mind is extraordinary," said the man without any introduction. "A single mind can cure itself of disease, can lift its owner over huge problems, create a solution to problems in seconds that a thousand computers will take days to confirm. A thousand minds together can create medicines, lift a nation to greatness, can dissolve worries that have haunted its citizens. A billion minds dreaming together can collapse mountains, crash down walls, drive the invaders from our land and close the gates behind them.

"Dream along with me, all of Mayoowani, and we will do this thing. Decide now that the time of the Gelkka is over, and soon they will leave, but not know why. All two billion of us on this one small planet will make the Overlords tuck their tails between their legs, call for the Kaloti ships and fly home to Gelokk. They will go home in disgrace, for no Gelkka army of occupation has yet been driven from its serfs, but this one will. We will drive them off, just by our dreams and our thoughts and by our refusal to be serfs any longer.

"That is all I ask of you for now. Dream along with me. Let us all say together that their time is done, and soon it will be."

The speaker rose to his feet and somehow vanished. Mickie assumed he had moved into the cave behind him. He felt his heart pounding and could not understand why. The words had been simple enough, the message had almost been silly. How could two billion minds thinking together drive a technologically superior occupying army off a planet? But there was *something*.... There was power in the short message and Mickie sensed it. So did the others, it seemed, for they were all silent and withdrawn into their own thoughts.

"We have to go." Viliamondini's words broke into their private worlds and they filed out of the little cave and back down to the ditch that led away from the quarry. The sun was starting to get low and Mickie was increasingly feeling nervous about getting back to the shuttle and the safety of the crew. The ditch came to an end and the line of trees was now their guide back to town. Staying close to the cover, they walked as softly and as smoothly as they could until they could see the buildings a little way ahead, the first street lights rising from the dusk.

But the walk became a deadly nightmare. A sudden swish of silent flying shapes raced across the fields, their shadows immense on the empty fields.

"Gelkka!" gasped Viliamondini in obvious terror. "Get down at the bottom of the trees, under any shrub you can and don't move."

His breath sobbing in his throat, Mickie and his friends dived at the base of a huge tree close to them. There was heavy undergrowth there, and they frantically crawled under the greenery and tried to attach themselves to the tree, freezing into immobility.

He sent a desperate message to Albert, but nothing happened. He got no response and the silence was as terrifying as the events around him. What had the Gelkka done to the Ship?

In the distance he heard the shouts of orders and acknowledgements from the Gelkka troops and he prayed for their safety. He wondered if his parents had heard anything of his movements through his communication device, having completely forgotten about it till then. But now it was too late to call for help, for these terrifying monsters with the faces of angry eagles would probably hear any sound. He felt trembles in his body.

The troops were coming closer. He heard the swish of grass and bushes being swept aside and once he heard the hiss of the weird weapons the Gelkka carried in their claws. He knew that it was quite possible he could die in the next few minutes.

A huge arm swept away the protecting shrubs and a roar of triumph thundered from the monstrous figure that filled the sky above them. Mickie felt every muscle in his body turn to water and he heard a little whimper of terror from Drellion.

Three other Gelkka appeared. They seized the five small shapes and carried them without evidence of any effort to the floating platform. Mickie had no idea if it was the same officer who had warned them before, but the first words confirmed that it was.

"You were ordered to have no dealings with cattle," the officer said, his massive, furious eyes glaring into Mickie's soul. "Now you will pay for that disobedience."

The eagle eyes turned to one of the troopers and pointed at Viliamondini. "Destroy that one," the officer ordered. Mickie didn't even have time to shout or plead. The unearthly beam of light hit the small body of the Mayoowi and there was just a small shout of pain as he shrivelled and burned rapidly. A small scattering of dust fell slowly through the air where he had been.

For a moment, the only sounds were the suppressed sobs of the four children. Mickie couldn't think, his whole body was just overwhelmed with terror and grief at what his actions had caused, not just to himself but to the two Mayoowi who had died and his three friends who would soon die as well.

"Bring them," commanded the officer. Four troopers each seized one of the children and mounted the platform, holding them firmly with their awful claws. The squad moved the last kilometre into the town and stopped outside a large stone building that stood alone, several metres from the next nearest structure. Helplessly they were carried inside and dropped onto the hard floor of a large room. The four troopers who had carried them took stations along one wall and the officer followed, closing the door behind him.

"What did you see?" The officer spoke softly, but the fury under the words was obvious. Desperately, Mickie tried to think. He decided that the words he had heard could not mean anything significant. He forced himself to speak.

"Just... just... just a man, alone," he said.

The raging raptor's eyes glared at him. "What did that cattle beast say?" the officer demanded.

Mickie struggled to force words through his tight throat. "He said that if everyone dreamed along with him and thought the same thoughts, they could drive the Gelkka off the planet."

The officer's sharp beak opened and emitted a screech, just like a bird of prey. Mickie could not tell if the sound was laughter or rage.

"Did the talking cattle-beast give a name?" The officer returned his furious eyes to Mickie.

"N.. n.. no," he stammered.

The huge being moved to stand over Mickie. He was like a massive statue and Mickie could not look up to him. He was so near that he detected the smell, a mixture of acid, sweat and a curious musty odour he could not identify. "You were ordered not to deal with the cattle," said the huge voice from far above him. "Those who disobey us pay the price."

With a swirl of the green cloak that caused a wave of musty air to cross the room, the officer moved to the door and turned back to face the four children. The strange weapon was clutched in his claw and it pointed directly at Mickie's head. In one awful, horror-filled second, Mickie knew that all four of them were about to die. He heard a small sob of fear from Melkana and felt a wave of dreadful sadness that he had let down his new parents by his insane impulsiveness.

But instead of the murderous beam of light from the weapon, the officer's hand dropped to his side. A strangled, gasping sound struggled out of the wide-open beak and the massive eyes looked confused and frightened. Behind Mickie, similar sounds began to issue from the four guards and all five Gelkka dropped to their knees, the sounds of pain growing louder by the second until they were more like the appalling screech that the officer had emitted earlier.

Mickie dragged himself to his feet, bent down and helped the smallest child, Drellion out of his curled up, terrified posture in the corner. "Quick, let's get out of here!" he snapped to the other two who seemed to shake themselves out of a stupefied trance.

Holding up Drellion who could hardly walk, they opened the door of the cell. The five Gelkka had now fallen flat out to the floor and were no longer moving. Mickie peered out into the corridor and saw nothing. They scrambled along to the entrance to the building and at the lobby area found more Gelkka fallen into death-like postures. Two had blocked the doorway and with a sense of huge revulsion, they climbed over the bodies and raced into the open. It was dark and for a terrible moment Mickie had no sense of direction.

Fencris was turning round, examining the view. "That way!" he snapped. "I can see the market square we were in before."

"I can't see..." Mickie began, but Melkana joined him to help pull her little brother along.

"Trust him," she said with an astonishing grin. "Cassoleans can see perfectly at night."

They ran as fast as they could, and it got easier as Drellion shook himself out of his terror and began to move of his own accord.

"Mickie, are you hearing us?" Allie's voice slammed into his head and Mickie nearly stumbled and fell. The communications device in his shoulder was at last working.

"Allie! Oh thank god, Allie, we're just near the small square in the town! Please come and get us."

"Mickie, we're on our way. The computer has you pin-pointed. Where have you been? We've been trying to contact you for hours."

"I'll tell you later..." He broke off, because ahead of him he saw a massive black shape just visible against the sky, with two brilliant beams covering the ground between them. The shuttle had lifted off and was coming for them. A few seconds later, it was on the ground metres away and the door at the side opened up to show what was to Mickie the most beautiful sight in the universe, his parents coming for him. All of the remaining resilience left him then, and he collapsed into Allie's arms weeping just like the terrified little boy that he was.

* * *

"There are two big things here to work on Mickie." Grant was sitting across from Mickie in his quarters. Allie sat next to him. Both looked very sad and very severe. Mickie felt terrible, knowing what was coming and how much he deserved it. He had let them down again, disobeyed their instructions and nearly killed his three friends and himself as a result.

"You know how terribly disappointed we are that you deliberately disobeyed us, Mickie. This must never happen again. If it does, we will have to take you to our home world and leave you with guardians, because we cannot risk such events in a ship like this. You risked the lives of four of you, next time you might risk the whole ship and its crew by doing something just as stupid. The Captain is too angry to talk to you, but he would choose to let you off at the next port of call if he could."

Mickie's heart nearly stopped at the idea that they would abandon him. He felt tears begin to squeeze out from his closed eyes. "I won't do it again," he whispered.

"Good. And we believe you." Grant's voice was calm. "So let's turn to the next issue and that is most intriguing. How you got away from the Gelkka prison sounds impossible. Are you sure you have told us exactly what happened?"

"Yes, I'm certain." Mickie began to relax as he sensed that the worst was over. "The Gelkka officer was about to shoot us, I'm sure, but he seemed to get a terrible pain of some sort and collapsed, just as the other soldiers in the cell did. And as we walked out, there were Gelkka bodies all over the place."

"It sounds utterly impossible," Allie said gently. "There is no sane, logical explanation for why twenty or so Gelkka would collapse in great pain and into unconsciousness just at that moment."

"They're not dead?" Mickie was astonished. "They seemed to be."

"No, not dead," said Grant with a small smile. "As we were getting ready to leave, several of them came hurtling out to the shuttle on those gravity platforms and were very, *very* angry with us. They accused us of setting off a sonic bomb or something. But they backed off when we just as loudly accused them of setting up a communications jammer to stop us contacting you, which indeed they had. And they didn't want to admit to having been about to kill you kids, so we parted in a sort of hostile truce."

"Will they take it out on the other people in the town?" Some of Mickie's sense of horror returned at that idea.

Allie looked grave. "Almost certainly. But that is not your fault, Mickie. That will be because they have been given further proof that the Redeemer does exist and they will be furious that they have missed him again. But that is one aspect of your misadventure that has been valuable and will pay off in the long run. Now that we have definite proof that someone is filling that role, we can start sending agents to Mayoowani to bolster the message that is being given. Even if it turns out that the man you heard is not the eventual true Redeemer, we can help the growth of morale throughout the world."

"But is it possible?" Mickie was fascinated with the idea that the Redeemer had preached. "He said that just everyone dreaming the same idea could drive the Gelkka away. How could that be?"

"Wait until you learn about Shuramee," said Grant. "That will tell you something about the power of pure thought and the amazing things that can be done. And even back on your Earth, there are many examples that could be proof of this. Some of the great psychologists and other thinkers have suggested something like this power. But Shuramee will be the most astounding example for you to learn about."

Mickie suddenly thought of something else. "My backpack!" he said. "I've lost it."

Allie shook her head. "No, it was still on you. It's in your cabin."

"Good! I bought some of that fantastic coffee. I want to have it for breakfast."

The two adults roared with laughter. "Mickie, why do you think we come to Mayoowani? There's fifty thousand kilos of the stuff in our holds right now!"

Feeling silly, Mickie sat back. "I still can't understand how ...."

An icy silence clamped down on his mind. He felt that Allie and Grant had fallen behind some cold, dangerous curtain as terror filled him. The voice that entered his head was horribly familiar, still as terrifying as the first time he had heard it.

"Now you can believe us, Pfafth," said the cold, quiet, menacing voice of the Spiders. *"We saved you again. One day, we will perhaps both understand why we had to."*

Mickie gasped with the shock and fear of the cold contact that didn't ease until his parents had their arms round him and slowly he stopped shaking and trembling.

"I heard the Spiders again," he said, his face resting on Grant's arm.

Allie was the first to take action. "Speaker 356, did you hear that conversation?"

The response from millions of light years away was immediate.

"No, Alliandra, I did not. We have been continually trying to communicate with the Spiders since Mickie's first experience. But I have read the memory in Mickie's mind and the Spider's words indicate that they were the ones to cause the Gelkka to collapse, but they do not understand their own motivation in keeping watch on him nor in saving him. We are completely unable to comprehend what is happening or how the Spiders are communicating."

"This is quite extraordinary," Allie said. "There has never been any record in history of the Speakers being unable to communicate with any other sentient species. And to have a species communicate in a manner that the Speakers cannot detect is almost impossible to comprehend. The Spiders are becoming a very great mystery."

"And one closely connected with Mickie's identity," added Grant.

"They called me Pfafth again," mumbled Mickie.

"That is confirmed," said Speaker 356. "And we have found no further records anywhere in the Universe of what Pfafth means."

Mickie sat upright and wiped the tears from his cheeks. "I suppose I'd better get used to the idea that the Spiders are actually our friends," he said.

"Indeed," Allie agreed. "It's an interesting lesson that any space-going people need to learn, that the outward appearance doesn't always reflect reality."

"I suggest, kid, that you overcome your fears as much as you can and try and establish communications with the Spiders." Grant was thoughtful. "At some point they must open up a little more and tell you how they communicate and how they recognise you as a Pfafth, and what that means."

Mickie nodded, aware of the mixture of fear and excitement the idea caused him.

"Meanwhile," Grant continued, "you're grounded. All four of you are going to spend the next few weeks till planet fall at Shuramee working hard at school. You all have a lot to learn about the essential disciplines of living on a spaceship. Your teachers are setting up a tight schedule of lessons and rather more physical working out than you've been doing."

"But we can still play Loopies?" Mickie asked anxiously. He'd fallen in love with the athleticism of the game and was fast becoming adept at it.

Grant nodded. "It's an essential conditioning for free-fall, so it's on your schedules, but it will be when your teachers dictate, not on your impulses."

Mickie felt he'd been let off lightly.

"Plus," Allie joined in. "You will have regular sessions with Speaker 356. That will achieve many things. One is for you to learn more about the Universe out there. But it will give the Speaker an opportunity to explore some of your hidden memories of your origins and maybe find some indications of how the Spiders are communicating with you."

That did not feel like any punishment at all to Mickie.

Chapter 12 – Speaking with a Speaker

He sat in the middle of his room, seated on a huge cushion. He knew that he didn't need any sort of meditation techniques to communicate with the Speaker, but for some reason he felt that he could concentrate better if he did.

"Speaker 356, are you there?" He spoke aloud, as he had not yet been able to focus his thoughts as accurately as he needed for telepathic speech.

The response was instantaneous. "Of course, Mickie, I keep a constant link operating with you." Mickie knew the words were only within his head but it sounded like a regular voice spoken aloud.

"Why? What's so important about me?"

"You represent a complete missing group of knowledge about the Universe, Mickie. Whatever the Pfafth were, or perhaps are, we know absolutely nothing about them. But the Spiders seem to, and the fact that they communicate only with you and by a means we do not understand, represents another aspect of this knowledge."

"So you just concentrate on me? That seems an awful waste when there's a whole universe needing you."

"Ah!" The Speaker seemed amused. "No Mickie, I don't communicate with just one entity at a time. Right now, I'm having conversations with two different Kaloti Ship Captains at massively different locations. I'm also talking with the head of an archaeological expedition on an abandoned world once occupied by the citizens of Shuramee and another one with a government official on your parents' world of Kalamos. I can keep a link open to you that activates when you try to speak to me."

"I had no idea you could do that," Mickie said, his mind whirling at the idea that someone could carry on multiple conversations across the Universe.

"It takes a lot of training." Mickie could still hear the amusement in Speaker 356's tone.

"Tell me about that. That will be okay, won't it?"

"Certainly. Part of my task with you is to teach you about the Universe in areas that you won't experience in your travels. And you will not travel to my home world, ever. It would kill you."

"Yes, my parents said that. They said your mental waves are powerful enough to burn out a brain within a couple of light years."

"It depends on the species. But certainly there is no species we have encountered yet that could live near to my world. So let me tell you about our training."

"Yes, please!" Mickie leaned back and reclined full length on his cushion.

"My species reaches self-awareness after about sixty years of your time," continued the Speaker. "We have little or no sentience before that, and none of us have any memories of that growing period. We need another twenty years for the telepathic skills to develop, but every one of us that survives to that age is then assigned two or three teachers who gradually nurture our minds to full communication capability. That whole process takes about a century, and we spend the time speaking to known representatives of different species around the universe until we are familiar with the mental structures of each of them and can communicate freely with them. Then we move to multiple conversations and it takes at least another century before we can do what I am doing now."

Mickie was startled. "So how old are you?" he asked.

"Roughly four hundred and fifty of your years." This time, the amusement in the Speaker's tone was stronger. "And I'm quite a youngster."

"Wow!" Mickie was highly impressed. "So how old can you get?"

"Most of us last till we are over eight hundred, many of us live to a thousand years old. There's no disease on the planet and no predators, so it's a risk-free environment."

"But don't you wish you could travel around the Universe and see it in person?"

"But we do, Mickie. We are able to transfer part of our consciousness into the mind of a willing host and we see and experience everything the host does. It's exactly the same as physical travel, but the experience is as deep as the actual living entity can have. So I have been on a thousand worlds, Mickie, many so far away that even the Kaloti ships have not yet been there."

Mickie spent some time trying to absorb the concepts the Speaker had been describing and eventually decided it was beyond him for now.

"What else are we supposed to do?" he finally asked.

"The biggest issue we all have is the relationship you have established with the Spiders," said Speaker 356. "All of us are very excited that communications have at last been established with that species, though we are very envious that only you have been selected to talk with them. We are also utterly baffled by the means they are using, because it is quite beyond our experience or ability to identify. There are many bands of telepathic speech, just as there are many bands of radio communication, but the Spiders are using something else. You can imagine how we feel about this, because this is the only profession my race practices."

"I suppose so," Mickie said uncertainly.

"Let me try and give you an example. Imagine an airline pilot of your time on earth. He flies the latest and greatest airliner, uses the newest and most advanced technologies and takes perhaps 400 people over a huge ocean to a safe landing after a twelve-hour flight. Pretty impressive, huh?"

"Pretty impressive," agreed Mickie.

"Now that pilot is suddenly shown the space ship on which you are now travelling through hyperspace and is taken to the Captain's flight deck where that one being appears to do nothing but look at huge screens, seems to give no orders to anyone, but somehow the ship travels a hundred million light years in a few days. What will our Earth pilot think?"

"It would blow his mind completely," said Mickie, seeing something of the crisis affecting the Speakers.

"Indeed it would." This time, there was note of sadness in the Speaker's voice. "So perhaps you can see what we are experiencing, discovering an entirely new mode of communication that we cannot even detect, never mind understand."

"Yes, I can see the problem. So how can I help?"

"Two things you have to do." The Speaker's tone was all business now. "One, is to allow me to transfer some of my consciousness into your mind, the way I described before. That way I will see and hear and experience everything you do. Second, you must try to establish communication with the Spiders. Once you are talking with one of them, maybe I'll be able to work out how your mind is processing the data and then perhaps I'll understand the mechanism."

Mickie hesitated. The idea of having a permanent resident in his mind seeing and experiencing his entire life was a little uncomfortable.

"It won't be a problem." The Speaker seemed to have anticipated the issue. "I will only activate the link when you start communicating with a Spider. All the rest of the time, the part of me will be quite dormant, but contact with a Spider will trigger it."

"Okay then, go ahead." Mickie tried to relax and see how it felt to have another intelligence enter his mind. But nothing happened. "I said, that's okay, Speaker. You can go ahead."

"It's all done, Mickie. You will be quite unable to detect my presence, whether the link is activated or not."

"Oh! Okay, so what do I do now?"

"Now, later, whenever you feel like it, try and establish connections with a Spider. Concentrate on the image of the individuals you encountered on their world, keep addressing words to them. If they respond, it's up to you what you talk about, but you may want to ask them how they know you are Pfafth, why they talk only to you and not to anyone else and what their mission is regarding you."

"Okay, I'll try that. But I still get scared when I try to talk to them."

"I know that. For your species and many others, the Spiders are the stuff of nightmares. But it does seem that they are protecting you, possibly without even understanding why. And for now, they are the only clue we have as to your origins, and probably to one of the great mysteries in the history of the Universe, who or what are the Pfafth, and do they still exist. If you are the last remaining survivor, then it is still a massive problem of why?"

Mickie felt awed by the Speaker's words. "Can I talk to you again about some other species in the Universe?" he asked, trying to shake himself from the frightening possibilities of the task ahead of him.

"Of course. Any time. And I will also set up some conversations with some of those races, if you like."

"Oh cool!"

Mickie Dalton was still a twelve-year old kid, despite his experiences of the last few weeks.

"Mickie, we have news from Earth if you'd like to see it," the Speaker continued.

"From Earth? How can you have news from Earth?"

"I kept a watch open for anything relevant after you had left. I downloaded several news programs on television into the Ship's computer. You might like to see them."

"About me? Cool! I'd love to see them. Albert? Can you play them?"

Immediately, the wall on one side became a huge television screen. To his astonishment, the familiar images and introductory music of the BBC news appeared.

"This is the six o'clock news for Wednesday, July the sixteenth," said the familiar image of the BBC's newsreader before Mickie's eyes. "Police have now charged twelve youths in connection with the riot in a Manchester Park last Sunday. None has been charged over the deaths of three of the gang, which remains a major mystery. The police have revealed the fact that the three bodies had sustained damage from a sharp object, though this has not been identified. Meanwhile, all the youths remain in deep shock, several of them muttering about "Giant Spiders" appearing. A government spokesman discounts this as simply a mass hallucination, probably resulting from illegal drug use."

Mickie let out his breath. "So that confirms it. It *was* a spider that came."

"Meanwhile, in other news, a police manhunt is on throughout the Northwest for twelve year old Michael Dalton who was reported missing on Monday after failing to appear at school and did not return home. Police say there is no reason to believe there is any connection with the fact that Michael had been in the same park where the riot occurred the previous day."

A picture of Mickie appeared on the screen and he felt an enormous shock run through his system. The picture had been taken from a class photograph taken just a year ago. From the shoulders of the kid next to him, the child in the picture was obviously quite short and rather skinny. The face before him seemed like some scruffy, very young boy, so much so that he could barely recognize himself. The features were thin and pale, the light brown hair untidy. He realized that the last few months must have changed him beyond description.

"Michael's parents reported that he had left for school that morning, but the school principal said he had not reported at attendance or at any class since. Anyone who has seen any sign of this boy should call their local police station."

The screen went blank, but remained bright.

"That was the first news," said the computer. "A few nights later, this is what happened."

The face of the newsreader appeared again. "The police hunt for the missing twelve-year old Michael Dalton has stepped up, following reports that he was seen in the local park after the riot occurred, being carried away by a young couple."

With a shock, Mickie's father and mother appeared on the screen.

"He must be dead," said the ugly tones of his father. "He was such a happy kid and we loved him so much, he'd never run away." Next to his father, his mother nodded. Mickie felt utterly repelled.

"What about the note I left you?" he demanded of the screen. "You know damn well I ran away, you lying old bugger!"

The next installment pleased Mickie intensely. After a brief summary of the police investigation so far, the newsreader passed the story to a local reporter who was interviewing more people in Mickie's old haunts. To his delight, the first was with his friend from school, Paul who lived down the road.

"Do you have any ideas why Mickie would have gone off on his own?" the reporter asked.

Paul looked very composed, not at all disturbed by being on the news. "Well, I know he hated it at home," he replied. "It sounded horrible."

"Are you sure? His parents said he was very happy and they loved him a lot."

"That's a load of bullshit," said Paul with determination. "He's been at my house plenty of times just about crying with the treatment those parents gave him. We gave him food sometimes, because they'd thrown him out without dinner."

The camera focused full face on the reporter. "Those comments were endorsed by Paul's teachers," said the reporter. "As a result, police investigations are returning to Michael's home and to his parents. And as it turns out, police have found that Michael was actually adopted, and under unusual circumstances."

Mickie was riveted to the screen.

"It seems that Michael was left outside the doors of the local orphanage near his adoptive parents' home in Whalley Range when he was just six weeks old. In the carry-cot in which he was found was a document that would lead to any parents who adopted the child becoming the beneficiaries of a trust account set up at a nearby bank. That account paid Michael's parents over a thousand pounds a month. Investigations at the bank have not been able to identify those who set up the account. So far, the names have resulted in dead ends, though the trust account still contains a sizeable amount."

Mickie was having trouble breathing. At last, a tiny, probably useless pointer, but a pointer nonetheless to his origins. But at least it gave some reasons for why the Daltons would have adopted a child for whom they could have no affection.

"Police attention has now shifted from searching for the young couple seen with Mickie the day before he vanished and on to the parents who have apparently lied about the relationship between themselves and the boy, which were extremely hostile, quite unlike the loving affectionate family that they claimed. While the question of murder has not arisen, it is clear that the parents have not been entirely truthful. We have been told by the police that the parents have now revealed a note written by their son, in which he states his intention to run away."

The reporter signed off and the screen went blank. Mickie's mind was in turmoil, wrestling with the information that he had received about his origins and the glee he was feeling about the horrible discomfort his one-time parents must be facing.

"Albert, are there any other reports?"

The screen came alive again with the same reporter.

"Police investigations into the disappearance of twelve-year old Michael Dalton are continuing. The local pond has been dragged without result and tracker dogs are searching the woods. Meanwhile, attention remains focused on the boy's adoptive parents as a pattern of constant abuse emerges from interviews with school friends, teachers and neighbours. Michael's History teacher has revealed that Michael once asked her when was the earliest age he could leave home, and she says he often arrived at school displaying considerable distress. The parents have refused interviews with us. However, we have learned that under the terms of the agreement of the trust account, payments to the parents have ceased. The principle sum which is quite substantial has now been paid to the orphanage, under the original terms of the trust."

"Haha!" shouted Mickie. "That'll teach 'em!"

"No charges are being brought on anyone at this stage," the reporter continued. "Given the miserable home life the boy faced, it is still possible he has run away as he said in his note and the search has been extended to cover the whole country. If anyone sees this boy..." Mickie's photo appeared again on the screen. "They are urged to contact their nearest police station."

"Fantastic!" Mickie shouted to the room. "Albert, is there any more?"

"No, Mickie. The Speaker has indicated that he will maintain a watch for more broadcasts but has not yet downloaded any to me. I will advise when he has done so."

"Do my parents know about this?"

"I have just advised them a few seconds ago. They echo your amusement and pleasure at the Daltons' discomfort."

"Just incredible," Mickie said, feeling pleased at the news of the evening, sat in his armchair for an hour musing on it, asked Albert to replay the broadcasts again, and went to bed in great satisfaction.

* * *

It took him a few days to work up the courage to try establishing communications with the Spiders. He spent as much time with his friends as he could, using their support and warmth to help him get to the point where he could face hearing that awful, cold voice in his head.

They spent most of their time reliving the adventure on Mayoowani, particularly the escape from the Gelkka. Mickie didn't feel he could tell them yet about the words from the Spiders and the fact that their rescue had come from such a frightening source.

"I reckon they just panicked when they saw Fencris' evil face," Mickie joked. "Perhaps he reminded them of some devil or something on their home world!"

"Actually, it's funny you should say that," replied Fencris without offence. "We Cassoleans do have to be careful. There've been a couple of times when we've caused problems on other worlds."

"No, it was Melkana!" Drellion chimed in. "I mean, just look at how ugly she is!"

Melkana lightly smacked her brother on his head. "Not a chance," she said. "I think it was Mickie. It was the first time they'd met an Earthling, so they probably got all confused."

"I suppose I do look pretty weird," agreed Mickie, pleased by the friendly ribbing they were all doing.

"You can't be that weird!" Drellion was laughing. "You look just like us and there's nothing unusual in your body or anything, not that anyone has found out, anyway."

"That's true." Mickie thought back to the extensive medical examinations he'd had in the first few days aboard the ship. The doctors had stated he was completely normal, both for Earth and for Kalamos where almost identical physical characteristics existed. The tiny differences they had found in him would not be detected by the medical technology of Earth.

The discussion was terminated by a call from their teacher for an extended and very rigorous session of Loopies. It was not as much fun playing with the teacher dictating every move, but all four still had a great time and there was much applause when little Drellion completed a triple loop and caught Mickie perfectly at the top of his arc. The smallest of the friends was rapidly becoming the best athlete of all of them as his body filled out and his muscles developed. Melkana tried to hide her huge pride in him, but even her condescending criticisms of Drellion's technique did not cover the grins she displayed during her brother's flights over the hangar floor.

But after showering in his cabin and delaying the moment as long as he could, Mickie finally forced himself to sit down and try to contact the Spiders.

Nothing worked.

He concentrated hard, created visions in his mind of the lush growths and the enormous webs of the Spiders' home world. He thought of the terrifying moment when he first was caught in the steel-like threads of the web and how the two spiders examined him before speaking to him. He tried speaking aloud, trying to address the last individual that had spoken to him, unsure if it was the same one who had contacted him each time.

But no echo of the cold, merciless tones thrust into his mind as he had experienced before. In fact, Mickie sensed a dullness in the room, as if a blanket had somehow been spread across the cabin, cancelling any communication to anyone or anywhere at all. Thinking he must be fatigued, he stood up to make himself a hot drink, and stopped in horror.

The whirling pool of darkness lay on the carpet between him and the food-dispensing outlet. It rotated, like black smoke from a fire, but without any heat. It seemed to suck the light from the room as it drew the warmth from the cabin and the courage from his body.

"Allie," he stammered. "Grant, this thing is back in my cabin."

But no friendly, reassuring voice responded.

"They cannot hear you," said a voice like a snake's hiss. Mickie's insides turned to water. This was far worse, far more terrifying than the first contact with the Spider.

The black, smoky whirlpool rotated faster and rose up higher, becoming a pillar of darkness reaching to the ceiling, draining even more light and warmth from the room. Mickie began to shiver, both from cold and from fear. This thing before him represented great evil, that much he could understand.

"You cannot know how much joy it gives me to discover you, little Pfafth," hissed the black entity. *"I have long hungered to eat the souls of your kind as I did before."*

Mickie couldn't speak. He felt his own death fast approaching, but even in his dread, realised that this terrifying entity knew something fundamental about the Pfafth.

"The fact that you are here tells me that there are many Pfafth somewhere in the Universe. I will find them and destroy them as I did before. All of life will be mine."

The pillar of absence of light rotated faster, there was a sudden flicker of a white face, huge dark eyes, a mouth open in triumph, then it vanished again. Mickie began to feel his life being sucked from him, he grew weaker and sank to his knees, knowing these were his last moments.

A tiny click sounded in the cabin and music began to pour into the icy, fear-bound atmosphere. Dimly, Mickie realised that the automatic setting he had made with his music system to give him some soothing music each evening before falling asleep had come on.

There was a sound of pain and the blackness before him almost exploded, wisps of smoke blasting out into the room, the pillar seeming to bend like a man hit in the stomach. The smoke drew in upon itself, was sucked back into the flat whirlpool on the floor, a single shriek of pain and fury filled the room and the blackness vanished.

Mickie found his voice, though it was terribly weak and the trembles that shook his whole body made his words barely audible.

"Allie? Grant? Can you hear me?"

"Mickie! What's wrong?" Grant's alarm filled his ears.

But Mickie couldn't answer. He had collapsed onto the floor, still shaking violently and only dimly heard the sound of the door opening and his parents rushing into the cabin.

It was an hour before he recovered enough to describe what had happened.

"We didn't hear you the first time," Grant said. "It sounds like some sort of communications suppressor was in effect, but the computers didn't register anything."

"Yes, it felt like there was a whole blanket over my cabin," Mickie agreed. The trembles still shook him every now and again, but a strong sedative in his drink had calmed him enough to talk. The dark fear in his mind refused to go away, though.

"That thing obviously knows a lot about the Pfafth and hates them," Allie added. "But if the Pfafth vanished a million years ago, that's very hard to comprehend. There's absolutely no record of such an entity or life-form like it anywhere in the Universe."

"Odd how it vanished," Grant continued. "Almost as if music is somehow painful to it."

"That's a thought," Allie agreed. "Mickie, set the computer to maintain a continuous music thread at all times you're alone in the cabin. That may well be enough to insulate you."

"Do you think it's still on the Ship?" Mickie asked, fearing to hear the answer.

"The Captain ordered a thorough sweep, and the Speaker did a complete scan of the Ship, so it's unlikely," Allie replied. "Though it leaves us with the problem that if it's gone, it left while the Ship was in hyperspace and we've always thought that must be impossible."

"Strange things are happening around you, Mickie," Grant said. "Obviously this Pfafth thing is critical, and we'll be finding out more as time goes on. But you'll be safe from that whatever-it-was from now. The cabin's sensors will detect any drop in temperature, the music in the room should help, and we'll keep the door open between your cabin and ours."

Feeling comforted and with the help of the sedative, Mickie was finally able to get to sleep.

Chapter 13 – Shuramee

"Shuramee represents one of the great mysteries in the Universe," intoned Albert. The image of the world hung before Mickie's face in another of his education sessions with the computer. As it rotated, Mickie counted several continents, one being an oddity in that it covered almost half the northern hemisphere and about a third of it extended down to the equator at which point it cut off, leaving an almost perfectly straight equatorial coastline of several thousand kilometres in length.

"You will have noticed the abrupt end at the southern boundaries of the major continent," Albert continued. "Originally, that continent extended considerably further south, but continental drift on the tectonic plates was abruptly increased during a feat that ranks as the greatest engineering project in the whole Universe, when the inhabitants of Shuramee moved the planet into a new orbit, a few percent further away from their sun as the star increased its heat output."

Mickie had heard this astounding fact from the Captain, but it was still impossible to believe. "They *moved* their planet to a new orbit? How could anyone do that?"

"They thought it there," replied Albert. Mickie could have sworn that the computer's voice held a dry note of amusement. "You have already heard several examples of where mental powers are considered able to cause change."

"But how? How can someone affect matter or events just with their minds?"

"We'll come to it. First, let us look at the long-vanished race of Shurameens."

The slowly turning globe vanished soundlessly and two figures stood before Mickie, together with the outline shape of a human male that Albert always displayed to show relative sizes. The Shurameens looked like images of Neanderthals that Mickie had learned about in his school days on earth. They were big, standing a good head taller than the image of a human male, even the female looked to be over six feet tall and enormously muscular. Both were dressed in what looked almost like a military uniform of Earth, though more loosely fitting. They did not stand erect, being rather stooped and the huge heads tilted back a little on the necks to allow for forward vision. There seemed little attractive in these beings, Mickie decided.

"Where the Shurameens differed from any other known intelligent species is in their ability to control matter," Albert continued. "Even as children, they learned simple exercises in telekinetics, the ability to move objects just with their minds. By their early adult stage, which they reached at the age of approximately forty years, they could manipulate matter at the atomic level, and so could change the nature of matter, being able, for example, to erect a structure in steel and stone, or restructure common materials such as wood or silicone into food materials or anything else they needed or wanted."

"That's brilliant!" Mickie exclaimed. "It means you could have anything at all you wanted and never have to work for it!"

"That's exactly right," Albert agreed. "And that led to an interesting social order in which crime was almost unknown. Certainly the crimes of material need were unknown, for why would one steal anything when they could create it for themselves without effort

"So what do we do there?" Mickie asked curiously.

"Our trips to Shuramee and the colonised planets are for two purposes. One is to drop off archaeological teams to work through the remains of their cities, and the other is to search for the art works, which are extraordinary. The most famous and the most valuable are the sculptures of the man known as Maragos, and you have seen one of those in the Captain's quarters. Finding even one like that would more than cover the costs of this expedition."

"So do we know why they just died out when they did?"

"No, Mickie, we do not. Records we have located show that birth rates began to plummet on all seven of their worlds and reached zero about thirty thousand years ago. What is strange is that all the texts we have unearthed and been able to translate show no panic or grief at the event. It seems as if the whole tragedy was expected, planned for and no cause for concern. Much the same is happening now on the world of the Kaloti."

"So what will we find on Shuramee?"

"Mainly ruins. Plant life is plentiful, as is insect life, some small birds, but there are no mammals or any other life form, except in the oceans where enough fish exist to maintain themselves."

"So will I be allowed down to explore?"

"Yes, the Captain and your parents have said your grounding is complete when we reach orbit and all your friends will come down with the exploration teams. It's a heavy gravity world, so the experience will be arduous, fatiguing and a good work-out for all of you."

"Okay," said Mickie.

*   *   *

He felt the extra weight on his body as soon as the shuttle settled and the engines were turned off. It felt like being at the bottom of the swing as he rushed from the top of the arc at one end to the top of the arc at the other. For a moment he felt his vision swim a little and standing up from his seat was a major effort. His weight was now nearly double what it had been on the ship.

"Use the gravity belt whenever you get tired, or in an emergency," Allie said as she walked by him to join her group of researchers. "But try and leave it off as much as possible. This is great exercise and a much-needed workout for all of us. You're young enough to adapt quite fast."

With a small wave to all four of the kids, she walked out, her face already showing the excitement of possible new discoveries about the long-vanished and extraordinary race of Shurameens.

"Wow, this is hard!" Melkana complained. "I'm not going to go too far under this load."

"Nor me!" her brother added. "Can't we just stay here?"

"I'm okay," Fencris said. "My world is higher gravity than yours, anyway, so this is just a bit tougher, but not too bad. How are you feeling, Mickie?"

"It was a bit grim at first," Mickie said. "But I seem to be adjusting. I'd like to go exploring. It's a whole new world and at least we can't get into trouble here! Adjust your belts, you two, let's go and explore!"

With some exaggerated sighs from the other two, they all left the shuttle and looked around. The ship had landed in a valley just on the outskirts of a ruined city. The sense of tragedy hit Mickie immediately. The city had obviously been a large one. Lines of streets stretched into the distance, but there was no remnant of a building higher than his head anywhere he looked. The desolation was awful. He could see the research teams fanning out into the remains of the structures and decided he would not want to be part of that task. He felt the heat of the large sun and decided that being under that was not a good idea, either.

"Let's go up into those woods," he said, pointing up into the hills where a line of extremely dark green trees suggested a sizeable forest.

"Climb *up*, in this gravity? You have to be joking!" Melkana looked outraged. "The climb will kill me!"

"Use your belts! C'mon, bet there's tons of stuff up there to find." Mickie set off at a good walk, no longer conscious of the extra pull on his body. Fencris joined him, grinning widely.

"Those babies! This'll teach 'em! I must say, Mickie, you've adjusted amazingly. It's the first time I've seen a difference between you and the Kalamosians. They could never have got used to this gravity the way you have."

"I think it's just that I haven't lived on the ship as long as they have." Mickie was pleased at the comment, but didn't put too much importance on the situation. He was enjoying the hard work his legs and heart were doing and he looked up to the forest.

From behind him, he suddenly saw Melkana and Drellion floating past him, cackling loudly. They had set their belts to zero gravity and were floating a metre above the ground, flapping their arms like crazed birds.

"Hey, the only way to travel!" laughed Melkana, swooping round in a circle behind the two boys and passing them again.

"Idiots!" called Mickie, trying not to laugh at the sight. "Remember what they said, we need the exercise."

"Okay," agreed Melkana, and both of them touched down next to him and adjusted their gravity belts. "But it seems to be harder on us than on you two, so I'm giving myself just a little help here. I promise I'll reduce it to zero when I get more used to it."

"Hey, I'm not your dad," said Mickie, though he felt pleased that the siblings were doing as they had been asked. He was still horribly aware of how much trouble he had got himself into by ignoring his parents' orders.

They reached the tree line and the temperature immediately dropped to a more comfortable level. The harsh sunlight became a soothing shadow through which occasional shafts of sunlight sparkled. It reminded Mickie of the woods near his home where Allie and Grant had kept their shuttlecraft, and for a moment experienced an odd sense of homesickness. It passed as he thought about the astonishing adventures he'd had in the last few weeks and of the misery of the Dalton home.

"Hey, look up there!" He pointed a little further up the hill where it looked like the highest point. "There may be a valley up there. Let's have a look." Without any sense of extra weight he raced up the hill, followed closely by Fencris, aware of the half-amused grumbling from Drellion and Melkana as they followed some distance behind, obviously breathing hard.

Mickie and Fencris reached the skyline and indeed had arrived at the entrance to another valley. It stretched to the horizon, a solid blanket of dark green. Mickie stared, entranced at the openness after the confines of the spaceship. With much gasping and heavy-footed tramping, the other two joined them and stopped, equally impressed. The scenery was magnificent.

Mickie saw a flash of colour to his right and turned to see a small bird about the size of a wren alight in the tree a few yards away. It seemed to be displaying the same interest in the four children as they did in it, and Melkana let out a laugh. "It's pretty," she said.

Several more similar birds arrived and watched the visitors.

"They don't see many people, I suppose," Fencris said. "The only visitors to Shuramee come to look for sculptures and paintings and stuff like that, and they concentrate on the towns."

"I prefer this," said Drellion, his breathing back to normal and a pleased smile on his face. "We can have a picnic here."

That met with general approval, and they spent some time looking for a suitable picnic spot, settling down eventually in a beautiful clearing where the ground was covered with a soft moss, unhitching their backpacks and tucking into the small feast they had prepared and packed before leaving the ship.

After an hour of lazing around and talking idly about their lives on their home planets, some strategies for

Loopies and other small-talk, their restless energy demanded some action. Drellion and Melkana seemed to have adjusted to the extra gravity and were amenable to a game of hide and seek and that occupied another hour before becoming just a crazy game of running around madly and catching each other.

Mickie found himself racing down a curved, leafy corridor in hot pursuit of Fencris. Unable to gain ground, his breathing starting to come hard, he tried taking a short cut through the trees to cut off his target. To his right, a leafy bank rose up above his head and he was galloping along the side of it when he tripped and stumbled into the side. It hurt, badly. Winded, he collapsed against the bank, astonished at the hardness after all the soft ground they had been running on. He sat down, leaning on the incline, rubbing his bruised knee and the side of his ribs that had collided with the surprisingly hard wall.

"Are you okay?" Fencris had seen his pursuer fall and heard the small cry of pain and come back to see what had happened.

"Yes, I think so, just a bit bruised. This hill is awfully hard, not at all like the rest of the place."

Fencris bent down over the green side of the bank and hammered his fist against it.

"Ouch!" he said. "You're right. This is weird." He searched around and eventually located a stone about the size of his foot. He brought it to the hill and banged it hard against the wall. There was no softness whatever, no give in the contact.

"Even weirder," said Fencris thoughtfully and began scratching away at the surface with the stone.

"What's up with you guys?" Melkana appeared out of the trees just as Drellion arrived and saw the other two boys intent on examining the small hill.

"This hill," muttered Fencris. "I think it's made of metal." He had scraped a small patch bare of the green moss and the smooth shine of a metal surface was quite obvious.

"You're right, it's weird." Forgetting his bruises, Mickie examined the metal patch then looked for a tool to join Fencris in his work. Finding a similar stone with a sharp edge, the two boys enlarged the metal patch until it was about half a metre square.

"Definitely metal," said Melkana. "This whole hill looks like a building of some sort."

"Let's walk around and see if we can see a door or something," Fencris suggested, and they began a slow, careful study of the hill. After shoving a few bushes aside, they walked round the complete hill and decided it was actually a dome about ten metres across and about two metres high.

"What on earth is a metal dome doing out here?" Mickie asked nobody in particular.

"I suppose the real question is what is this dome covering up?" Melkana suggested and Mickie looked at her with respect.

"You're right," he said. "I'd say there's a lot of space under it, probably going down quite a bit."

"I bet there's all sorts of treasure down there!" Drellion was looking very excited and his words caused a similar reaction in the others.

"We've *got* to find a door," Fencris said with new energy. "Let's each take a quarter of it and really, *really* look hard."

"Good thinking," Mickie agreed, and they separated, each taking a quarter of the dome's surface, finding more stones and scraping away to make bare metal patches every few centimetres. But after an hour, each had scraped away large patches of their sections and found nothing.

"Okay, let's try new bits and try again," Fencris suggested. Without comment, each of the children moved round a section and tried again. But another hour passed without a sign of any break in the smooth metal dome. Just as they were about to move on again, Melkana let out a squeal of excitement.

"Come here!" she yelled. "There's a line in the surface."

With delighted whoops, the four of them congregated where Melkana was bent over, closely examining the surface. She was right, there was a fine line extending vertically across the small patch of metal she had scraped clean.

"Let's try scraping away along that line," Mickie suggested. Melkana made no comment but began doing exactly that, scraping upward, a centimetre at a time. Being smaller, Drellion began tackling the bottom of the patch, working downward on the line. Mickie looked at his stone tool and decided it was worn too far, so set about searching for a replacement. It took about five minutes before he returned with a suitable sharp-edged stone. Melkana and Drellion had stopped their work, clearly tired and Fencris had taken over. The line had become an oval shape, about half exposed.

"Can you start work on the bottom section?" Fencris asked. "We can get this finished in about twenty minutes or so."

"Sure," said Mickie and bent down to continue where Drellion had left off, touching the line to see if he could detect any ridge. But he didn't have to do any scraping. As soon as his fingers touched the line, a sharp beep rang out. Startled, the four children jumped back.

A crackling sound came from the oval shape. On the still-covered side, the moss broke away as the complete oval shape appeared. The shape moved backwards a few centimetres then seemed to snap away and vanish. The opening was about a meter high, a little less in width. But the most startling thing was that a pale light glowed from within the dome.

"It opened as soon as you touched it, Mickie," gasped Fencris, his red eyes flashing like fire beacons. "We've been scraping for hours, but as soon as you touched it..."

Mickie could hardly breathe. He had no idea why the door had opened. He stood rigidly and stared at the glowing opening to the dome. He worked hard to control his thumping heart and slowly calmed himself. He looked at his friends and all of them were doing as he had done, staring with fascinated fear at the opening.

"We'd better have a look in there," he said, just a small tremble in his voice. Forcing his legs to move, he walked back to the oval entrance and looked inside. He could see no source of light, but the pale shine illuminated a flight of stairs descending steeply a few metres, ending at a flat surface. He could see no further than that, but assumed there was some sort of corridor.

He stepped back and looked at his friends. They were staring at him expectantly. Mickie could see mixed fear and excitement, sharing his own conflict of wanting to go down that passageway while being frightened of the dangers he might face.

"I have to go down there," he said. "It's obviously important."

"I'll come with you," Fencris said. "I was the one who realised it was a dome."

"But what if the door closes again?" Drellion looked distressed.

"On the other hand, I say we all stay here," said Fencris, nodding at Drellion's words. "And we'd better call the crew. I bet this is the sort of thing they're looking for."

Mickie had to laugh. Fencris' dry understatement revealed a sense of humour that appealed to him. "Yes," he said. He spoke aloud, thinking of Allie as he did. He knew that the communications device would read his brain wave and transmit his words. "Allie, are you busy?" he asked. The reply was immediate.

"Hi, kid! What are you up to? Yes, we're busy, we're digging into a ruined building that has some promise."

"I think we've found something you'll find has even more promise. Can you pinpoint us?"

The sharp tone was obvious in Allie's voice. "We already have, and we'll be there in a few minutes. What is it?"

"It's a doorway into something underground."

"Stay there. Do not go in, okay?"

"Okay." With a mix of regret and relief, Mickie stood away from the door. He knew he had been terrified of making the trip down that strange flight of stairs but felt he would have had to if he'd been alone. Something was calling him, he knew it, but could not understand what. Why had the doorway opened at his touch but at none of the others? He saw that Fencris was showing a similar mix of emotions, having deduced the nature of the conversation between Allie and Mickie.

"We wait, huh?"

"We wait."

Melkana and Drellion looked relieved.

"Good," said Melkana. "After Mayoowani, I don't think we should do anything the least bit silly."

All of them laughed at that. "You're right," Mickie said. "Another few weeks of being grounded would be deadly."

All of them turned as the first figures of the crew came swooping over the trees, riding their gravity belts and settled in the clearing. Allie walked up, adjusting her belt, looking hard at the oval doorway, then at the children.

"You did the right thing calling us," she said. "Is everyone okay?"

"No problems at all," Mickie said.

Allie grinned at him. "Well, done, all of you. This looks astounding."

Two of the crewmembers were entering the doorway. They were displaying great caution, taking readings of every metre before moving further, but after a few minutes they had vanished from view down the stairway.

"How did you find it?" Allie asked, taking her eyes from the doorway.

"We sort of fell against it," Fencris began, and they told Allie the whole story, all four of them chiming in as they thought of new bits. But it was when they reached the point of the opening occurring at Mickie's touch that Allie broke in.

"Say that again. The door opened only when Mickie touched it? All the others had touched it at least once?"

"I'm not sure if I did," said Melkana. "I think so, though."

"I know I did," Drellion said.

"Me too," Fencris finished.

"A bit like the Sword in the Stone, Mickie?" Allie was only partially joking, Mickie could tell. There was something very serious in her tone and expression.

"What's the Sword in the Stone?" Melkana asked.

"It's the same as the Story of Alquiveer," Allie replied. "Or like Trossenare," she added to Fencris. "Almost all planets have some sort of story of a future leader who is able to do something to retrieve the sign or badge of leadership when nobody else can. On Earth, it's the story of a mythical King who pulled a sword from a stone when nobody else could, and the legends said that he who took the sword would be king."

"I don't want to be a king," said Mickie.

Allie smiled and broke the atmosphere. "I don't think that's it," she said. "It' probably a chemical in your body or a mental vibration equivalent to some old Shurameen characteristic and the doorway responded to that. We'll do more tests on you when we get back and see if we can trace anything we haven't seen before."

There was a shout from the doorway. The two men who had gone down before had returned. The grins on their faces were enormous.

"You'd better get down here," one of them shouted. "You're not going to believe it."

"Can we come?" Fencris was the first to shout the question, but all four of them could hardly restrain their excitement.

Allie smiled. "You found it. It seems safe. Come on, then."

His heart pounding, Mickie followed Allie into the doorway, the other three close behind. They were followed by several more of the crewmembers, while four men remained outside in case of the sudden closure by the porthole.

The pale glow remained as they descended the stairs, though Mickie could see no source of the light. At the bottom, as he suspected, a corridor led away from the opening. It was about twenty metres long then bent away to the right. Allie and the four children walked to the bend, silent in their excitement, but they all let out a mutual gasp of astonishment as they made the turn. Another few metres along, and the corridor ended. The huge room at the end was the size of a cathedral, again lit by that strange source-less light. As they walked in, Mickie could see that the walls were lined with pictures. There were stands and cabinets in rows along the floor and several plinths held statues of different types and shapes. One was a statue of a Shurameen, Mickie realised, the same shape and appearance as the holographic image he had seen in his room.

He turned to Allie to ask her what she thought, and stopped. She was standing before another plinth, her hands clasped before her mouth and tears flooding down her face. Slowly, he moved to her and he knew what she was seeing. The same incomprehensible shapes and curves of the Maragos sculpture he had seen in the Captain's quarters stood before him. He stared transfixed at the sculpture. He felt his mind swim, felt strange emotions run through his body, saw the curves and lines of the article seem to change shape and colour, sparkle with brilliance or fade to dull reds and browns and colours for which he had no name.

He had no idea how long he stood there until a hand on his shoulder pulled him away.

"Come and look at the paintings," Allie said softly, the tears on her cheeks still glistening like tiny diamonds. They walked to one wall. A single, massive painting dominated it, at least ten metres long and five metres high. Mickie could not tell what it represented, but the surface was a riot of colours, some with no names that Mickie could think of, a mass of curves, twists, strange shapes that did the same to his perceptions as the Maragos sculpture did. Mickie's emotions took on a life of their own. He felt waves of delight, happiness, grief and joy flood his body; his mind seemed to launch into space, he saw comets flying by, strangely coloured suns drenched him in their light.

Yet again, he returned to the present as Allie touched his shoulder and turned him away.

"They are very powerful," Allie whispered. Around the gallery, groups of the crewmembers stood and seemed lost before statues, paintings and other artefacts in the display cabinets.

"I think it's a repository of some sort," Allie continued. "The Shurameen may have put their greatest treasures here when they knew the end had come. There are at least twenty Maragos sculptures, and some pictures by the same man. We never knew before that he had painted as well. Mind you, that's probably not the right term. As a Mentalist, Maragos would never have touched a brush or a chisel. Everything was done by the mind. And there are works by others that we have never seen before."

"How do you know so much already?" Mickie asked. "We've only been down here a little while."

Allie chuckled. "While you stood lost before the Maragos, two hours passed, and another hour before the painting. We've catalogued a lot of the place in that time."

Mickie believed her. He looked round and saw the other three friends locked in place before the sculpture that had stolen his mind for two hours. "Is all this worth finding?" he asked.

Allie looked down at him seriously. "Mickie, any one of those Maragos works would have paid for this entire trip. This whole crew has just become immensely rich, and that includes you. These works will go to the greatest museums and galleries in the known universe and holographic images will be available to everyone. This is the greatest find in history and we can learn a lot more about Shuramee from what's here."

A huge yell sounded from the far corner of the gallery. One of the women in the crew, a Cassolean Mickie saw, was studying another sculpture on a plinth. Even from here, he could see it was not a Maragos work, but the woman looked very excited. He followed Allie as she moved rapidly to join the small crowd gathering round the plinth.

The woman stood up as they arrived, her eyes burning brightly, almost drowning the pale light of the gallery.

"Alliandra, look at these symbols," she said excitedly. "They are not Shurameen."

Allie bent and studied the article. It was like a big disk, about half a meter wide, as thick as a big encyclopaedia. In the centre was engraved an image Mickie could not identify, and around the edge was a series of smaller symbols. The group fell silent as Allie studied the item. She stood upright and looked around the group.

"We've seen these before," she said. "There's a huge mural on the world of Kamotar. It has no resemblance to anything else on that world, and it has three lines of similar symbols. The Kamotari do not know where it came from or the meaning of the symbols. We were able to identify a few of them but not many. Where's our language specialist?"

"We left him outside," replied the Cassolean. "We didn't think we'd need him as we've never found any non-Shurameen script here before. I'll call him down."

There was a short wait while the specialist came down the steps and entered the gallery. He was an X'Kasxi, but even the reptilian face showed astonishment as he saw the magnificence of the display. He walked up to the disk on the plinth and immediately nodded at Allie.

"Yes, Alliandra. It is Kamotar Script Four as you said. Give me a moment."

He squatted down before the disk and took a small device from his belt. It looked to Mickie like a hand-held computer, with a keyboard and a small screen. The X'Kasxi entered a few keystrokes and studied the results on his screen, tapping in a few more letters and digits at intervals. The room was silent as he worked.

"There's very little I can make of this," he finally said, standing up. "Only a few of the symbols are the same as those we found on Kamotar. That one..." he pointed at a symbol on the far left side of the disk. "That one says 'Visitor' and the one two down from it says 'Power' but in what context these are, I have no idea. But there's one group of smaller symbols that is interesting. Instead of being a single hieroglyphic, it is made up of letters and I have codes for all of them. So I know what *that* says, at least."

He pointed at a small group of symbols near the bottom of the disk.

"It says '*Pfafth.*'" He looked at Allie and shrugged his shoulders in a very human gesture. "I have no idea at all what it means."

Allie moved closer to Mickie and put her arms round his shoulders. It didn't stop him trembling, but it comforted him none the less.

Chapter 14 – The Space Dwellers

"So what does 'Pfafth' mean?"

The four were in Mickie's cabin. Melkana, who had asked the question, was squatting on a floor cushion, Drellion and Fencris on chairs, all drinking the yellow sparkle of *Sle'Ach*. Mickie sprawled at length on the couch. He was silent for a moment then sat up.

"I don't know," he said. "Nobody does, except the Spiders, but it seems to have something to do with me."

"The *Spiders?*" Fencris was shocked. "What have the Spiders got to do with it?"

All three of his friends were staring at him, expressions varying from astonishment to bafflement. Mickie finally told them the whole story of how the Spiders had rescued him on Earth and then communicated with him.

"But the Spiders have never talked to *anyone*," Melkana protested. "Not even the Speakers!"

"This is fantastic!" said Fencris, grinning from ear to ear. "Somebody who can talk to the Spiders!"

"But I *can't*," Mickie complained. "They talk to me when it suits them, and it's only been three times so far. They won't answer when I try and talk to them."

"Did they say what a Pfafth is?" Drellion asked.

"No. It's what they call me, but they don't explain it."

"Do you think it has anything to do with how you opened the door to the mound?" asked Fencris.

"I'm not sure I did that," Mickie said. "Maybe it just opened up after you'd cleared a certain amount of dirt. I may have touched it just at the right time."

"But you have to admit, Mickie, odd things have happened around you," Melkana said. "Look how the Gelkka collapsed just when they were about to shoot us."

"That wasn't me," protested Mickie. "The Spiders said they did it, but they didn't know why."

"The Spiders saved us?" Melkana's face was a study in shock. "So that's what happened! But that means they're watching you all the time!"

"And everything going around you, too," added Fencris. "Well, that's one good thing about being friends with you, Mickie."

"What's that?" Mickie was amused by the cheerful grin on Fencris' face.

"It means if we hang around you, we'll always be safe!"

"Ha!" Melkana expressed everyone's reaction. "I think it's dinner time. I'm going to the restaurant."

"Well, we can certainly afford anything we want now, thanks to our efforts," Fencris said with a smug smile. "I heard my dad say that this crew has made more on this trip than all trips combined in the past. And that includes us."

Deciding not to tell them about the terrifying pillar of blackness, Mickie took enormous comfort and pleasure in realising what good friends these three had become.

In a very good mood, the four of them headed out of Mickie's cabin and to the restaurant.

* * *

"Mickie, I think you'll want to see this." Albert's voice broke gently into Mickie's reading of a book by Isaac Asimov, his favourite science-fiction writer. Knowing that the ship's computer would not interrupt him for any trivial matter, Mickie put his book down.

"What is it, Albert?" he asked.

"The ship has left hyperspace and we are at a dead stop, relative to our nearest contact."

"Stopped? But we're days from our next planet-fall! What's happening?" Mickie felt worried for a moment, then realised Albert had not declared any sort of emergency, just interest.

"The Captain suggests all of you join him in the observation room."

That was enough for Mickie. The Captain's "suggestions" were absolute orders. He placed a page marker in his book, left it on the table and walked out to the transporter.

He had spent little time in the observation room. His first view of leaving Venusian orbit and entering hyperspace had been from the flight deck and all the times they had spent in orbit round other planets, he had been down on the surface with his parents, so he'd had little opportunity to look at a planet from the huge windows of the observation room. At all other times, there was only a featureless blackness as they traversed the unfathomable mysteries of hyperspace, so there was little point in coming.

Almost the entire ship's crew was in the room as he entered. It was the first time he had seen the sight and for a while he was transfixed by the colour and strangeness of several different humanoid life forms all in the same place.

"If only the kids at school could see this," he thought with a laugh, remembering the scorn with which several of his friends had treated his passion for science fiction. He looked out of the enormous windows and drew in his breath sharply.

Instead of the deep black of empty space with the background of stars, the windows were a riot of colour and movement. Streams of brilliant sparks twisted and flashed, raced round the ship and danced in an exhilarating, glorious blanket of lightning like the most enormous fireworks show ever let off in the whole universe. The reaction of the crowds watching was very much like that too, Mickie thought, remembering the wonderful displays that he had seen for the new Millennium and how the crowds had gasped and laughed like children.

He sensed the arrival of his friends, looked briefly at them and quickly returned his entranced stare to the brilliant display outside.

"What is it?" he asked, watching a particularly beautiful flare go off, almost overshadowing the rest of the display for a few seconds.

"It's the Family," Fencris replied. "We're lucky, hardly anyone ever gets to see them. It's the first time for me. I just never knew..." His voice tailed off as he lost himself in the wild beauty happening so close to the ship that the lights within the observation room were dimmed by contrast and the shadows of the people and the furniture leaped and danced around them like a spirit ballet in the underworld.

"What's the Family?"

"It's another species," Melkana murmured, having obvious difficulty concentrating enough on Mickie's question while absorbed in the beauty outside. "We only discovered them in the last few years and realised they were intelligent when the Speakers were able to talk to them. This is the first time Drellion and I have seen them, too."

"They're an intelligent species?" Mickie could hardly believe what he was hearing. He decided to stop asking questions when he saw the slight look of irritation that Drellion gave him and realised he was spoiling the show by talking. He switched to the ship's computer instead, realising he could let Albert talk privately to him as he watched the astonishing and wonderful dance of brilliant colours.

"Albert, tell me about the Family," he silently commanded the computer and the response began immediately.

"The Family is just one collection of individuals as you are seeing now," Albert said. "It is really more of a tribal group and there are several such groups scattered round the Universe. The entire species refers to itself as The Greater Family and exchanges of individuals between tribal groups do sometimes occur, though we have yet to understand the reasons or basis for such exchanges. Each individual makes up a discrete mass of the sparks you see and they are entirely composed of energy. There is also less illuminated energy within them, so you only see part of the individual and they are able to mingle and occupy the same space, but nonetheless, each of them has its own identity and is self aware and can communicate with others."

"But how do they live? What do they eat?"

"They live like this, free spirits in space. They feed on the energy emitted from stars, but they cannot get too close to a star because the radiation can burn and kill them. They are sexless, and breed by fission, in that the young split off from the elder when it reaches a certain level of energy within itself."

"So how do we talk to them, and why have we stopped now?"

"Communication only works through the Speakers. The language concepts are impossible to match between such entities and planet-dwellers like yourself, so the discussions are very limited. But we have stopped because the Family requested a meeting. As far as we can understand, they have curiosity about us and wish to examine us a little more. They are intensely curious about the ship and why we travel like this. Oddly enough, they also seem to express great pity for us."

"Pity? Why would they pity us?"

"As far as we can understand this, they feel that we lead terrible lives, bound by gravity and noxious atmospheres, living in dreadful dirt and squalor. Compared to their lives, I can understand why they feel this way."

"So what's going on in this meeting? And who is meeting with them?" The astounding sight outside the ship had entranced him.

"The Captain and just a small number of people are having a three-way discussion with them, facilitated by the Speakers. Your mother is in that discussion group, and they are simply exchanging information about each other's lives. The question of trade has been raised, but as you can imagine, there seems to be nothing that each can offer the other that might be useful. However, it appears that the energy released by this ship is the equivalent of a succulent feast of rare tastes to the Family and the Captain has just released a sizeable output as a gesture of good will. That explains the intensity of the display we are seeing. The Family is having one whale of a party and quite a few of them are the equivalent of being seriously drunk."

For another hour, the wonderful fireworks display continued. Then with astonishing abruptness, the entire mass of colour and flashes outside gathered into one brilliant ball that was almost like a sun, so bright was the glare, and vanished, leaving a small trace of brilliance that faded within seconds. The Family had resumed its incomprehensible existence and the crew of the giant Kaloti ship dispersed as the engines thundered their return into hyperspace.

There was one more surprise for Mickie though. As he walked back to his cabin to return to his Asimov, his mother called him on the communications link.

"That was astounding," Allie said. "It was truly one of the more extraordinary experiences I've had in trying to communicate with an alien species. We seemed to part as friends, though just what we could have in common escapes me! But as they left, just as that giant ball moved off, we got one last message."

"What was that?" Mickie was curious at the tone of fascination in Allie's voice.

"As near as the Speaker could translate it, the Family asked us to pass on their regards to the Pfafth."

"What? To me? How did they know?"

"We have absolutely no idea. And the Speaker cannot establish communication again to ask them. It looks like yet another example of a race that seems to know something most of us don't."

The news left Mickie disturbed and he was not able to get back into his book for some hours.

Chapter 15 – Some Self-Discoveries

Mickie was drowsy. The hour was getting late in the ship's artificial "day" and he'd been busy. A full day of classroom studies and further consultations with Albert back in his own quarters had left him weary. He changed to his pyjamas, finished tidying away his clothes and the book he had been reading earlier and climbed into the amazing bed that always adjusted itself to fit the precise contours of his body. The gentle music that was permanently playing in his cabin as a hopeful barrier to the black, smoky entity was a peaceful backdrop.

But he could not fall asleep. A small twinge of irritation became obvious within him and he tried to work out what was causing it. Was it the news that the space-dwelling species known as The Family had sent a message of greeting to him without telling his parents how they knew he was a Pfafth? Was it still the worry about just what a Pfafth was and how come he was one? But as he thought about trying once more to contact the Spiders, the irritation grew more obvious and he realised that it was that precise inability to get an answer from that frightening species that was causing his disturbance.

"Why don't they answer me?" he said aloud, and at that moment they did. The cold, merciless voice slid into his mind, causing him to shudder a second or two before he was able to control himself.

"Why do you want to talk to us, Pfafth?" said the cold voice in his head.

Mickie hoped the Speaker had realised the contact had occurred and was listening in. "I need to understand some things," he said, working to stop the trembling in his voice.

"It is not time for you to understand."

"Why not?" Mickie felt frustrated by the answer.

"Because you are still too young and ignorant to understand."

"Why do you call me Pfafth?"

"Because you are Pfafth."

Mickie felt his irritation growing. "And what is Pfafth?"

"We cannot tell you."

That irritated him. "Why can't you tell me? You called me a Pfafth, so you must know."

"We do not."

"You don't know? That's crazy! I don't understand how you can't know!"

"It is not time for you to understand."

Mickie felt the remorseless block in place to that line of questioning. "Why did you save me from the Gelkka?"

"Because it is our task."

"Who gave you that task?"

Silence greeted his question. Mickie felt his anger grow. "I said, who gave you that task? Answer me!"

For the first time, Mickie heard or sensed something other than the cold, flat tone in the Spider's words. It felt almost like surprise.

"The Pfafth."

"Why? And how did they give it to you? Did you meet them?"

"No."

The anger faded in Mickie, replaced again by eagerness. "Then how did you know it was your task?"

"Because we knew."

"But how did you know? Where were they when they told you this? Are there other Pfafth somewhere?"

"We do not know."

"When did they tell you this?"

"Millennia ago."

"Millennia...? What? How could they tell you to protect me thousands of years ago? I'm twelve!"

There was no reply. Mickie wrestled with the weird issue for a few moments, but was interrupted.

"There is great danger in the Universe, young Pfafth. There are forces that threaten all of life."

Mickie felt a wave of fear at the cold emotionless words. "All of life? How can that be?"

"We do not know what those dangers are, but they threaten you, we know that."

"Are they something to do with that black thing that was here the other night?"

"We have no knowledge of any such entity. Explain."

"A black pillar, something like smoke appeared in my cabin. It said it wanted to kill all the Pfafth and had been their destroyer before. It was about to kill me, but somehow the music in my room drove it away."

"That is impossible. We know that we will sense when you are in danger."

"I think it had some sort of suppression thing going."

Even in the silence, Mickie got a sense of the rage being emitted by the distant Spider, and the tension was evident when it finally spoke.

"This must not be permitted! We cannot protect you if that happens."

"Can I do anything about it?"

"Maybe. But it is our task to help until you can look after yourself."

"When will that be?"

"When it is time."

"When will it be time?" he asked.

"When it is time," said the Spider.

He tried another tack. "Will you always be watching what I do?"

"No."

That surprised him. He felt a mixture of relief and alarm at the same time. Relief that he would not always have the terrible sense of being watched by such a fearsome observer, yet some worries that perhaps there would not always be a guardian for his friends and him.

"So how will you protect me the way the Pfafth have told you?"

"In times of danger, you will call us."

"I will call you? I don't know how. You've not answered my call before until now."

"You will call the way you did when the Gelkka threatened. And we will hear. But we are worried by the news you have given us about the black entity. We must investigate."

"I don't understand. How will you investigate?"

"It is not time for you to understand."

That block again. He tried one more question that occurred to him. "And do you deal often with the Pfafth?"

This time, he sensed the withdrawal from his mind. He was alone again. Well, maybe not. "Speaker 356, did you hear that conversation?"

"What conversation, Mickie?" The response from the Speaker was immediate.

"The one I just had with the Spider. You said it would trigger your awareness and you'd listen in."

"I heard nothing. Are you sure you just spoke to the Spiders?"

"Of course I'm sure! It's not something you forget easily!"

A tiny pause occurred before the Speaker replied. "I just reviewed your memories, and there's no doubt you were speaking with some entity. But only your questions have been recorded. I find no traces of the Spider's words to you. This is baffling. It means that not only do they communicate in a way we do not understand, but the Spider was somehow able to avoid triggering me. This hasn't worked. I shall withdraw my presence from your mind."

Mickie was almost in tears. Something huge was happening around him, something to do with his own origins and his life and he was not able to get information.

"We tried talking to the Family about their reference to you, Mickie," the Speaker continued.

"Yes?" Mickie felt a surge of hope.

"They will not reveal anything. They ignore all questions about the reference to Pfafth."

The hope faded, replaced by a sense of hopelessness.

"How will I ever find out anything?" he mumbled, tears close to his eyes.

"We are all certain that everything will come clearer as time passes," replied the Speaker. "You are very young yet. Perhaps you need to grow older before you can make sense of the facts."

Somehow, the words gave him comfort. The fatigue and drowsiness returned, and he was asleep within moments.

* * *

In the morning, he felt more cheerful. The memory of the conversations he'd had with both the Speaker and the Spider remained with him, but the worries had gone. He sensed that a change had occurred within him, though he could not identify what it was. He had breakfast with his parents and told them about the previous night's events.

"The Spiders don't know what the Pfafth are? That's a bit weird," commented Allie. She had made coffee that morning with some of the stock from Mayoowani, and the wonderful aroma drifted through the cabin.

"It sounds crazy! They call me Pfafth but they don't know what it means?" Mickie was baffled.

"Somehow they recognised you, but it seems they don't know how," Allie replied.

"But it certainly is evidence that the Pfafth, whatever or whoever they are, still exist somewhere," Grant joined in. "But if so, it's weird that the Speakers have not had any contact with them."

"They haven't had any contact with the Spiders, either," said Allie. "The kid here seems to be the only one who had done that."

"And I think it's getting the Speakers a bit crabby," added Mickie with a grin. He was feeling cheerful, realising that there was something special about him and it added to the pleasure of having breakfast like this with his parents.

Something very strange happened. For a few moments, Mickie seemed to lose his perception of where he was. He got a swift blur of an image of himself sitting at the table, with Grant on his right. He felt a wash of affection for the two images he saw then he returned to his own perception of himself, feeling a little dizzy. He looked up and saw Allie watching him and realised that the view he had just seen was the one from her position. It was as if he had been looking out of her eyes for a few seconds.

"Are you alright, kid?" Grant asked. "You look like you've just seen something scary."

"Wow! It was wild!" Mickie said. "Just for a second I seemed to be looking at us two from Allie's eyes."

"Whoops!" Allie sat down quickly across the table from Mickie. "Tell us again, but take your time. What happened, exactly?"

Mickie took a deep breath and recounted the events of the last few seconds, explaining how he also felt the emotion that went with the image.

"And just then, I was looking at both of my two men, thinking how happy I was at having you here," said Allie.

"So he went into your mind for a second or two," said Grant, looking thoughtful. "That's an empathic quality that so far, only the Speakers have ever demonstrated. Could you tell what Allie was thinking, actual thoughts, not the emotion?"

"No, I don't think so," Mickie replied. The reaction to the extraordinary experience was setting in, and he was feeling a little shaky.

"We must remember," said Allie, "that Mickie sent out a telepathic call from Earth and did so a few times, according to Speaker 356. So we already know he has some unusual telepathic talents, even if he doesn't realise it."

"Mickie, this is a rare ability you seem to have," said Grant. "It looks like you have only just met it and it's very under-developed. So I think there are two things to do. First, you'd better be extremely careful when you are around people. If this happens again, best not tell them until you have developed some control. Second, we'd better have the Speaker look at you and perhaps start teaching you more of how they control that talent and try and impart it to you. Okay with that?"

Mickie nodded, still feeling shaky. "It's scary," he said.

"Yes it is," Allie agreed. "And it's just as scary for other people. That's why you had better stay discreet about it. If it does happen with someone else, it's best not to tell them, for now at least, and certainly not before you've learned to control it. You will probably find you have full telepathic powers too, judging by the way you called for help back on Earth, so all that needs training. It looks like you're going to be busier than ever now that you need this education with the Speakers."

"Speaker 356, are you with us?" Grant spoke aloud, so that the other two knew what he was doing. He paused a moment as he received a private message from the Speaker, then spoke again. "I have Alliandra and Mickie here. Please include them in this conversation."

Immediately, the cool tones of Speaker 356 sounded in Mickie's head. "Good morning, my friends. How can I help you?"

"Speaker, Mickie has just experienced a short episode of empathic connection with Alliandra. It was very vivid and suggests considerable power. Can you review the memory?"

"Yes, Grantorel, I just have. You are correct, that was a mental transfer of surprising power in a non-Speaker. I suggest that the latent talents have begun to emerge following his extended communications with both the Spiders and with me."

"Then we need some training for the boy."

"Indeed you do. Mickie, we must spend a considerable amount of time on this. This is a powerful but possibly dangerous ability."

"Dangerous? Why?" The Speaker's words caused a tremor of alarm in Mickie.

"You can enter peoples' minds, their most private self. Nobody will tolerate that willingly and so far, only Speakers have been able to do so. For people to realise that you, a non-Speaker can also do it could cause a great deal of alarm and resentment."

"I think I see that," Mickie replied.

"Alliandra, Grantorel, I will ask that you permit Mickie to experiment at certain times through you and only with you. I will warn you beforehand, and then it will only be with your permission. Is that acceptable?"

"Of course." Allie spoke for both.

"At a later stage, Mickie will need to experiment with other species," said Speaker 356. "I will advise the Captain at that time and ask that he be the other experimental partner. He will need to know and we can count on his discretion."

"Okay," said Grant. "Mickie, this is going to be hard work. But it's obviously all part of finding out who and what you are."

"I know," replied Mickie. "I'll cope with it."

"We know that, son," said Allie. "Now, have some more coffee. It's from your supply, after all!"

Chapter 16 – The World of the Three-Armed Kamotari

"They are big, they are powerful, they can look more startling than the images Albert has projected, so show self-discipline," Allie had warned the four kids during the shuttle trip down to Kamotar. Mickie had agreed with his friends that Allie was being unduly careful, because they all felt that they had grown up quite a lot during the recent trips. Surely, there was nothing the Universe could throw at seasoned space-travellers like themselves that would scare them?

That supreme self-confidence lasted as the shuttle touched down in the middle of the industrial city of Damurangan that served as the Capital of the united world of Kamotar.

"We'll extract some mineral ores from the planet," Allie had told Mickie. "Gold is quite plentiful here, and although it doesn't have the mythical value it has on Earth, it's still a highly useful metal for electrical engineering and for artistic developments. Mercury is also common and that has high value on many worlds for chemical and industrial uses. Diamonds are like common stone in some regions, and the Kamotari use them for industrial tools and decoration, but they have no value beyond that, so we pick up lots of them. In return, we give the Kamotari advanced computers, which they have never successfully developed themselves, and some of the pharmaceutical products we've developed from the plants we took from the Spider world."

The shuttle doors began to open and the light of the golden sun of Kamotar streamed into the shuttle interior.

"My dad says the Kamotari are incredible athletes," Melkana said as they sat back to allow the prospecting and diplomatic teams off the shuttle first. "They've got this powerful right arm and they're balanced by two smaller left arms which have incredibly delicate fingers that can do fine detail work."

"Albert said they've got their national game which is a lot like basketball on Earth," added Mickie. "But it's played on a huge circular field about two hundred metres in diameter, and the ball weighs about twenty kilos and they can throw it fantastic distances with those huge right arms."

"That would be worth seeing," Fencris laughed, his brilliant red eyes sparkling with interest. "Hey, everyone's gone, let's get out there and look around."

They walked down the ramp into a pleasantly mild day. Gravity was a little higher than Earth-normal, so Mickie felt the effort in his legs and knees immediately, after several weeks in transit in the Kaloti ship since their visit to Shuramee. The others obviously felt the same, as all three emitted little moans of protest. But the small pain and extra effort faded as they met their first Kamotari. So did their supreme self-confidence at their ability to stay cool whatever the Universe threw at them.

The being at the base of the shuttle ramp was huge. But more than his size – and Mickie saw that the Kamotari was a male, from the instructional review he'd had with Albert a day before – the creature's sheer presence was overwhelming. It stood at least two metres tall, with enormous, muscular shoulders that made him look like an armoured player in the American football game. But it was the head that shook the kids' composure. It resembled a wild boar, with small tusks standing out from the back teeth and slightly larger horns behind the ears. Only after seeing that and adjusting his perception of the animal as an intelligent, aware person did Mickie look at the three arms. The right arm was indeed enormous, as Melkana had said earlier, with a hand that could have folded completely over Mickie's head. The two left arms were both about half the size of the right one, so that the weight of the Kamotari was equally distributed. The upper left arm was attached to the shoulder, much as was the right arm, and the lower, about twenty five centimetres below the first, grew from the rib cage in a manner that Mickie could not see.

The Kamotari stood with those arms folded in a way that made Mickie look hard. Finally, he saw that the big right arm was folded across the chest, while the two left arms crossed it, the lower hand supporting the right one just forward of the elbow, the second clamping on the wrist, with the elbow of that upper left arm pushed backward a little. The hands appeared very human in shape, with four fingers and an opposing thumb on each.

The Kamotari wore what seemed to be leather, gleaming black in colour. Trousers came down to the knees and covered hugely muscular legs, and the top was more a tabard, leaving the sides uncovered for all three arms to move freely. However, a cloak was suspended from the right shoulder and hung down to well below waist level, covering the right hand. Down the left side of the tabard was an ornate strip of mixed red, gold and green patterns.

The total effect was enormously impressive and intimidating and Mickie understood what Allie had meant when she said that the reality was more startling than Albert's projected image. He wanted to shrink back up the ramp, but his pride refused to allow that.

"Good morning, my young friends," the huge creature said. Behind the translated words of the device in his shoulder, Mickie could hear the actual voice, sounding more like a confused growl with an odd honking sound underneath it. "My name is Zhumaton."

The unexpected friendliness emanating from the Kamotari was reassuring and Mickie relaxed, sensing the same in his friends.

"Well, hello, Zhumaton!" said Fencris brightly, being the first to reach full composure. "Have you been sent to guide us?"

"Those are my instructions. I am what you would understand to be a 'cop'."

"Understand to be?" Mickie was curious. "What does that really mean?"

The huge head turned to him and looked down from its vast height. The mouth opened wide, revealing a somewhat fearsome set of teeth. Mickie hoped it was an expression of amusement.

"Which one are you?" asked Zhumaton.

"I'm Mickie. I'm sorry I didn't introduce myself before..."

"Ah, the Earthling! You are the first of your race to visit, so let me make you extra welcome," said Zhumaton. "I see that this is Fencris, because I recognise a

Cassolean, and so you are Melkana and Drellion. Again, welcome to all of you."

Mickie relaxed completely. He found himself liking the Kamotari.

"I was briefed on all your home planets," continued Zhumaton. "Earth and Kalamos have similar systems of a paid professional police force. Cassolea has a rotating system of public service in which everyone at some point spends a portion of their time as law enforcement personnel. Here on Kamotar we have a professional, hereditary class and we are both police, as you understand it and also warriors. On Earth, you might equate it to the old Japanese Samurai."

"Then we are very honoured to have your friendship and your protection, Zhumaton," said Melkana, displaying a diplomatic skill that surprised Mickie. It obviously worked, because Zhumaton bowed in her direction.

"You certainly have been well briefed," said Mickie, trying to emulate Melkana. "Can I ask why we need your protection?"

"That's easy!" Zhumaton opened his enormous mouth widely again, and this time, Mickie was certain it was an expression of humour, much like a human's. "You are small and fragile on this world, and my people are rather boisterous in almost everything we do. Alone, you might suffer unintended injury, but with me, you'll be safe. People seeing us will give you space to move."

"This is great!" Melkana seemed delighted with the arrangement. "So what shall we do today?"

"I suggest a general tour of the city first," replied Zhumaton. "But then I think you would be interested in our national game of Prottaskorp. You are lucky, today is the final championship game for this continent and I can take you to see it if you wish."

The three boys whooped their approval. "I saw some images of the game on the ship," Fencris said with excitement. "It looks *fantastic!*"

"However," broke in Zhumaton, looking at Melkana, "if the young lady would prefer perhaps to go shopping, I could arrange for one of my colleagues to accompany you."

"Heavens, no!" Melkana said indignantly. "There's no knowing what trouble these children could get into if I'm not there. I'll come to the game, too."

Zhumaton laughed again, and Mickie decided he could really get to like this enormous creature with the frightening head and arms. "Come then," said the Kamotar. "We'll ride in my vehicle."

He led the way to what looked to Mickie like nothing else but a passenger van at home. It was just like a box on four wheels, with windows round the sides and four doors. As they approached, the doors opened just like on a regular car and the engine started, sounding exactly like an internal combustion engine on any Earth truck.

Zhumaton climbed into the right hand front seat where he sat behind a half wheel, much like that of a light aeroplane, and the four kids chose their places, Melkana exercising her right as a female to sit beside the driver, much to Mickie's amusement, remembering how his sister had always insisted on that privilege. He studied the control panel and the steering wheel and was astounded. The entire front panel looked like it was made of gold. The gentle, rich sheen was quite lovely, and even more astonishing was the end of what looked like the gear lever. Mickie had no experience in gemstones but he could have sworn that the sparkling object was a diamond that was at least the size of a chicken's egg.

"Is that a *diamond?*" gasped Melkana, beating Mickie to the question. "And is that all *gold?*"

Zhumaton glanced down at the objects of her wonder. "Oh yes," he said carelessly. "Both are very common on Kamotar, though I understand that they are extremely valuable in other places. That's what the traders on your ship come for."

"I think that diamond alone would make anyone back on Earth *unbelievably* rich!" exclaimed Mickie.

"Can't understand why!" replied Zhumaton. "Plenty of those in the hills. We use them for tools, mostly."

"And that gold panel," added Mickie. "I can't even begin to think how much that's worth!"

"Strange people, you Earthlings," said Zhumaton with his enormous grin. "I'll give you each some diamonds when you leave!"

All four children laughed loudly, feeling great friendship with the massive Kamotar, then settled down to look at the scenery. But Mickie also watched how Zhumaton drove the vehicle. He used the right arm strictly to hold the wheel, while the two left arms manipulated other controls in a way that would have been the impossible envy of a driver on Earth.

The city was much like any other city, Mickie decided. There were streets filled with similar vehicles to the one in which they were riding, pedestrians thronged the pavements and walked in and out of buildings, shop fronts lined the roads, even traffic lights controlled the vehicles, though Mickie was quite unable to work out the coding of the multi-coloured lights and the instructions they gave the drivers.

The buildings were huge and heavy in style, almost fortress-like, and several particularly massive castles stood out for their enormous doors, towers and what looked like fortified walls.

"That's the administrative centre for the whole world," said Zhumaton with pride, pointing out a complete region of such castles within the city. "The Leader works there."

Mickie had studied the political system of Kamotar with Albert, but was happy to have the lessons taught again by a resident.

"The Leader is always one of the Ten Denoted Families," continued their guide. "Those Families have led our world for over a thousand years, and they select a new Leader every five years, taking it in turns for each family in sequence. The current Leader has been in his position for four years, and he is of the House of Jarowar. Next year, the House of Gyanwert will appoint a new Leader. But there is also what you would know as a Parliament of over a thousand representatives and they are elected by all the people. They can create new laws, and they have to be signed by the Leader to become effective, but he can be over-ruled if eighty percent of the Parliament members vote that way. The Leader can only propose new laws. It all works very well."

Remembering that Kamotar had not experienced a major war or even regional uprising in over four hundred years, Mickie had to agree with him. He watched the pedestrians outside and felt grateful that he and his friends were being driven around. It looked rough out there. People moved fast and directly, and collisions seemed quite common, but he never saw any dispute or argument starting as a result. Collisions, even the really heavy ones appeared to be the norm for these powerful people.

He caught sight of one pedestrian who stood apart from the rest, dressed in pure white robes and wondered what was odd in his appearance apart from the unusual garb. Then he saw it and shouted excitedly.

"Zhumaton!" he cried. "There's a man over there, the one in the white robes. He's got a major *left* arm and two on the right! I didn't know that happened!"

"Ah!" commented Zhumaton. "He's a Gryvestra. That's like being a left-hander to you, Mickie, but it's very rare indeed. Only about one child in ten million is born with reverse physical shape, and they are always outstanding in their intelligence, their athletic abilities, and their social behaviour. If one of them opts to become a professional Prottaskorp player, every team in the world will compete for him and he can name his own price and be worth it. Many go into commerce and are valued as managers and as legal advocates. Most will become members of the parliament, and that perhaps explains why the system works so well."

The four children watched the white-robed being walk along the pavement. He was followed by a small group and was given plenty of space in which to move, nobody coming near him to threaten with the rough and tumble of ordinary pedestrian travel.

The morning passed happily for all of them. Zhumaton was a cheerful and informative guide and they all became firm friends. He took them on a walking tour of one of the parliament buildings, and that was a little nerve-racking for them as the random violence of standard pedestrian motion came close to them, but they remained unharmed. But around them, people collided with enormous frequency, seeming not to notice, only rarely acknowledging a bump, usually with a casual nod. Mickie thought that just one of those crashes would break several bones. As he studied the people, he saw that the multi-colour strip down the side of Zhumaton's tabard was unique to him and he asked about it.

"That's my badge of rank as a cop," replied the Kamotari. "It is quite informative, if one knows how to read it, and it certainly guarantees safe passage for you. We grow up with great respect for the position."

It impressed Mickie no end.

"We must take one trip before lunch," said Zhumaton at one point as he drove out of the city and into the countryside. "Mickie, your parents requested this visit and anyway, it would be strange to visit Kamotar and not see the Great Wall of The Visitors."

"The Great Wall? What's that?" asked Drellion, speaking for the first time since planet-fall. He had been quite cheerful and Melkana had quietly told Mickie that her little brother was a good tourist, always fascinated by a new planet and his silence was nothing to worry about.

"It's a massive mural," replied Zhumaton. "It's carved on the walls of a hill a short distance out of town."

Mickie realised what they were about to see. The X'Kasxi linguistics expert had referred to it, as had his mother when they were in the massive vault of art treasures on Shuramee. They said it contained hieroglyphics that had been impossible to decipher beyond a few small symbols and letters. He felt his tensions rise and sensed the thoughtful looks from his friends.

The ride was about thirty minutes when Zhumaton pulled into a small valley. Several other vehicles were parked in the space in which they stopped and a number of Kamotari were standing in a group along a fence that prevented closer movement to the side of the hill.

"It's a common tourist spot," said Zhumaton, leading his party to the fence.

The mural covered an enormous area, perhaps a hundred metres along and twenty metres high, vertically carved into the hillside. Along the middle, stretching from one end to the other was a line of big symbols, the shapes meaning nothing that Mickie could identify. Under that were three lines of smaller symbols, reminding Mickie of Egyptian hieroglyphics he had seen in museums.

"It's the great mystery of our world," said Zhumaton quietly. "We have no idea who built this, it's been here as long as our civilisation can recall. We cannot decipher the symbols, though I've been told that one of the linguistics experts on your ship has identified a few of them and we can now make out two or three distinct words, but we don't know what they mean."

Mickie stood and stared. Was this the work of the mysterious Pfafth of which he was a child? He felt awed by the size of the mural and by the mystery it represented, but he felt no sense of kinship, familiarity or belonging with the huge work. The small valley had the same sense of spiritual peace and reverence that could be felt in a cathedral, but it touched no core of memory in him.

After half an hour, the group returned to the vehicle and drove back into the city.

Lunch was at a restaurant, and Mickie was amused by how like an English restaurant it was. Lines of tables, people meeting people, waiters moving through the room bringing food and drinks to the diners. He also learned something of protocol in a race with three arms. Zhumaton sat in a normal position at the table, but the huge right arm was tucked firmly below his chest, resting on his lap. Only the two left, smaller arms were visible and used for feeding.

"The right arm is for combat, defence, sports and lifting," explained their guide. "Because it's so dominant, good manners require that the major arm is not normally displayed in any aggressive manner and certainly not at the dining table. It is not required that the arm be always covered, nor is revealing it in normal motion considered ill-mannered, but you will have noticed that normally I keep the cloak over it and common courtesy is for the major arm to be discreet."

Zhumaton ordered for the party, and the food arrived in just a few minutes. Mickie anticipated another delicious surprise, but unlike his experience on Mayoowani, the food was unexciting, rather bland in style, resembling and tasting more like ordinary meat and potatoes, and he was happy when Zhumaton said it was time to move to the Prottaskorp field for the Grand Final Match.

Zhumaton drove the vehicle through the gates of the enormous sports field and right up to the steps leading into the stands. "You've seen how boisterous we are in normal conditions," he said with his cheerful, wide-mouthed expression. "Can you imagine how long you would survive, even with me here, walking through a crowd of many thousands, all excited by the prospects of the biggest game of the year? You'd be squashed into pancake mix in two minutes!"

He led them up the stairs, quite difficult for them as the steps were built for much larger beings than themselves, and with the higher gravity they were gasping as they emerged into the stand, but that did not prevent an even greater gasp of astonishment as they saw the view.

The field was a good two hundred metres in diameter, a brilliant emerald green. Completely circling it was a block of stands with five tiers, and Mickie could not see how far back the rows of seats went. He looked round where they stood and finally counted over thirty rows. As far as he could tell, every seat was filled, and the noise was astounding.

"This place seats over 250,000 people," said Zhumaton, seeing Mickie's inspection. "And today is a sell-out."

He led them down the steps of the sloping tier and took seats at the very front. "You won't see a thing if we sit any further back," he explained. "Any time something exciting happens, everyone stands up and you'd be completely blocked. So, let me explain the rules."

He pointed at a structure below them. It consisted of four poles in a row along the edge of the field. The inner poles were about two metres apart and some ten metres high with a net hanging between them down to the ground. At the top, there was a circular net hanging vertically. The outer poles were another three metres further out and a couple of metres shorter, and a net hung from top to bottom of those also. At the other end of the huge arena, Mickie could see a similar structure.

"There are fifteen players on each team," began Zhumaton. "The object is to throw the ball into that circular net on the top of the central posts and that scores six points. If the ball misses and hits the net below, it scores two points, and if it misses the centre posts completely but hits the outer nets, it scores one point for the other team. The ball is passed from one player to another and he can run a maximum distance of ten paces before he has to pass again. A player can grab the ball, he can run into an opposing player, but he can't take hold of him in a tackle. You can see the opposite posts at the other end."

"Who's playing?" asked Fencris. "You said it was the continental championship."

"That's right. The season lasts half the year, during the summer months and there are over a hundred teams on this continent. Each week, teams play in a knockout tournament and eventually, the last two teams meet here. So our own team from Damurangan is here and they're playing the team from Jutasloven, which is on the southern tip of the continent. The winner will play another champion from another continent, and we have six of those, and the very final game to establish the world champions is in another month. That will be here, also, and we're all hoping our team will be out there in the field."

The noise level rose several notches and Mickie looked out over the field. One of the teams had filed out. They wore red shirts, none had sleeves and their right arms were raised vertically in what he assumed was a gesture of threat or defiance.

"That's the Jutasloven team," shouted Zhumaton over the racket. "Here come our players."

The noise became monstrous as what must have been the entire quarter million spectators roared their support for their teams. Another group emerged, this time wearing white shirts, with their arms raised in the same gesture of aggression as the other team had done. Abruptly the noise ceased and a deadly silence fell as the thirty players on the field took positions and seemed to be waiting for something. As Mickie looked around for what could happen, he saw a large ball soar out from one edge of the field into the centre and the whole field erupted into action. One of the Jutasloven players caught the ball, using his left arms as Mickie noted, flicked it into his major arm and threw it an astonishing distance to a team-mate some fifty meters away. The ball flew at great speed, but the receiver caught it easily, again with his left arms, ran a few steps and flicked it just a short distance to another Jutasloven player. But as he caught it, a home team player collided hard with him and both players fell to the ground, the ball rolling free. An ear-busting roar erupted as a white-shirted player grabbed the ball. Immediately, a line of Damurangan players formed, several meters apart, all moving fast toward the nearest goalposts. The ball was snapped from one to the other, being caught with the pair of left arms, flicked to the right arm and then thrown.

After four such rapid passes, Mickie saw that a home player had raced forward about fifty meters ahead of the last pass receiver and the ball was launched in a huge arc straight at him. This time, the ball was caught with the major arm, the player spun once and immediately hurled the ball at the net below Mickie's seat. He missed badly, too high, and Mickie realised with a shock that the ball was coming straight at him. He ducked, terrified, but it wasn't necessary. Above him, Zhumaton laughed with delight and picked the ball out of the air before it reached Mickie. As Mickie sat up, Zhumaton handed the ball to him.

"Try it for weight," he said.

Mickie took the ball from him and nearly dropped it, quickly doubling the effort needed to hold it up.

"Holy cow!" he said as the cop took it back from him.

With effortless ease, Zhumaton threw it back to the field and resumed his seat. "It's good luck to handle a ball from the field," he said. "Now we both have some!"

"That thing is incredibly *heavy,*" Mickie whispered to Fencris. "These people are supermen, throwing it like that!"

Play had resumed, and the Jutasloven team were working the ball rapidly to the other end. A shot at goal missed but hit the inner net, opening the scoring for the visitors and causing a huge groan from most of the crowd, with a smaller bunch, obviously supporters from the south cheering wildly. The ball was brought back to the other end in a series of long throws, but the advance was again stopped by an interception. Mickie found the game enthralling for its mix of speed and strength and violence. It reminded him of the American game of football that he had occasionally been able to see on television at home.

The home team was bringing it back to Mickie's end again, and a huge pass was thrown, the longest he had seen yet, probably over seventy meters. It looked well able to reach the Damurangan player waiting for it just a few meters from the goalposts, but a Jutasloven player appeared with startling speed, launched himself to an amazing height and intercepted the ball about four meters above the ground. Mickie realised the player was a Gryvestra, a reverse Kamotari with his left arm being the major one.

"See what I mean," said Zhumaton above the collective groan of disappointment. "Gryvestras are amazing!"

"Do we have one on our side?" asked Melkana and Zhumaton shook his head sadly.

"There are only three playing in the whole world and we don't have one."

Play had returned to the other end and the crowd moaned in dismay again as the visiting team scored a full goal, the ball flashing into the circular net from a fifty metre throw by the Gryvestra.

Again and again, the home team brought the ball back to the near goalpost, each time with a scoring attempt spoiled by the astonishing agility of the Gryvestra. But the home team developed a plan for the situation. The ball was being passed down the left side of the field, Mickie saw the Gryvestra moving to position himself for yet another intercept when there was a sharp change of direction. The ball flashed out laterally, was caught by a player on the other side and a similar flickering series of passes had the ball into the hands of a Damurangan player who lobbed a quick shot at the goal. The ball flew neatly into the centre of the net and all four children put their hands over their ears to try and block some of the noise that exploded around them.

From some hidden source, a siren sounded and play stopped, all thirty players running off the field.

"Quarter-time," announced Zhumaton. "How are you enjoying this?"

"It's fantastic," shouted Fencris and the other three nodded enthusiastic agreement.

The noise level declined to a reasonable murmur and conversation became easier. But as their guide was about to say something, a noise came from beneath his cloak. Zhumaton flicked out what appeared to be a communications device.

"Zhumaton," he announced. Mickie could not hear what was said, but the cop snapped "Coming!" and stood up. "We have to go. I'll explain on the way. Stay behind me."

Obediently, all four children tucked in behind the huge shape of the Kamotari as he moved rapidly back up the stand and to the exit. They raced down the steps and reached the vehicle, still parked where they had arrived, and climbed aboard. Zhumaton steered out of the grounds and reached the road, accelerating fast as they headed in to the city centre. As they reached a junction where traffic was slow, one of Zhumaton's minor arms hit a switch and a siren began sounding from the roof and traffic swerved out of their way.

"I should have dropped you somewhere," their guide said, concentrating hard on his driving. "But there's no time and it wouldn't be safe. You're coming with me. There's been a big explosion at a building near the parliament. About twenty killed. It was obviously a bomb and the killers have left with ten hostages."

"Why would anyone do that?" Mickie asked, clinging tight to the arm of his seat as they swerved round a line of cars. "This seems to be such a peaceful world."

"Smegandri," Zhumaton replied shortly. "They are a species from a planet in the nearest solar system to ours. Their world is deteriorating from pollution and the race was dying out. About fifty years ago, we offered sanctuary to the remaining population, which was down to less than a hundred thousand by then and it turned out to be a major mistake. They kept on fighting their tribal wars, pulling some nasty terrorist stunts like this one and demanding ever-increasing concessions from us. We kept telling them, stop the terrorism and we'll provide a secure region for you. But it never stopped and the terrorism against Kamotar got worse. This looks like another example."

None of this had appeared on Albert's instructional programs about Kamotar and Mickie resolved to update the computer when he got back. Their vehicle burst into an open square. Mickie could see the towers of some of the parliament buildings a few blocks away, but the scene before them was dreadful. A complete building had collapsed, leaving just a skeleton of some structures. Flames still flickered inside the devastation and smoke and dust rose in towering columns. What looked like ambulances and other official vehicles filled the area and Mickie could see bodies being loaded into the ambulances and driven away.

Another Kamotari approached their van, stared hard at the occupants and addressed Zhumaton.

"Definitely Smegandri," the newcomer said. "We've found a few bodies in the rubble, all armed. And some of the Kamotari dead have been killed by those weapons."

"Any more idea of how many hostages they've taken?" snapped Zhumaton.

"Eye witnesses say at least ten," replied the other. "They took off in a fleet of cars waiting for them, nobody's sure which way they went after leaving the area."

A buzzing sounded and Zhumaton reached for his communications device. "Yes!" he said sharply and listened. After a few seconds, he replaced his radio and looked at his colleague. "They have the Leader's daughter," he said.

The other's words were incomprehensible to Mickie and the translation device seemed unable to provide any clarity. But something strange was happening to him and he was not interested in the other cop's words. He seemed to be falling behind a veil of silence that was blanketing out the terrible scene of destruction in front of him. A warm, slightly unpleasant sensation was reaching through his chest, he felt sadness creeping through his veins and his vision became blurred. Almost he was moving away from the city square to somewhere else...

He became aware of a throbbing noise, of restrictions to his arms and legs and severe pain in his head, blood was running down his eyes... The noise became a *"whop, whop, whop"* like helicopter blades, he was tied to someone else, too tightly. In front of him was a nightmare shape, a huge, distorted head, a dreadfully ugly face with teeth protruding downwards over the jaw. He turned his face away in horror and looked out of the window at his side. He saw a body of water, a huge tower something like a radio transmitter and forests behind it.

"Mickie! Mickie! What's happening?" He came back to the immediate reality to feel Melkana pulling his shoulder. He turned and saw her terrified face staring at him, the other two boys looking equally worried.

Something clicked in his mind and he returned to full awareness of where he was, but astonishingly, he kept a view of the other horrible scene, almost as if he had a camera watching that story and showing the picture to a fraction of his mind.

He took a deep breath. "What does a Smegandri look like?" he asked Zhumaton. The cop was distracted from his conversation with his colleague who was giving details of the damage, and he looked curiously at Mickie.

"Smaller than us, but their heads have teeth that extend over the lower jaw, no horns. Why?"

"This is going to sound strange, but you have to believe me. They're in a helicopter. They've just flown past a huge radio tower by the side of a lake, and they're heading over forests nearby."

"How the hell do you know that?" Zhumaton's mouth was open, but it did not seem to be an expression of laughter this time.

"Zhumaton, you have to believe him! He's a Pfafth!" Melkana was pleading with the cop.

The cop hesitated just a second then snapped into action. He grabbed his radio and spoke urgently into it. "Get me a flier! Get two more loaded with armed men and follow me out. I'll explain later."

He looked down at the kids. "This had better be good. Mickie, you can see what's happening?"

Mickie nodded. The rolling film in his mind was like watching an inset on a television screen. "They're over the lake and almost over the forest. There are at least two other helicopters with the one I feel I'm in. The prisoners are bound. Can you tell where this scene is?"

"Almost certainly Lake Rakjulic," the cop replied. That's the only radio tower within the flying time they've had."

As he spoke, a flier settled down in the square a few metres away from them. At a gesture from Zhumaton, all four left the vehicle and raced across to the helicopter with their guide. A door slid open and they all piled in, strapping themselves in the seats. Mickie found a headset lying under his seat and pulled it on, but it was so large that he had to hold it against his ears.

"What are these off-planet kids doing here?" demanded a voice in his ears, presumably the pilot as the machine lifted off. "And where to?"

"Lake Rakjulic," replied Zhumaton. "Past the Radio Tower, we'll probably know more then. And the kids are helping more than you can understand. Mickie, any more?"

Mickie switched his attention to the moving image within his head. He felt the pain and terror of the captive through whose mind he was seeing this, saw the forest passing lower under the helicopter, but saw no more indicators of where they were. He shook his head.

"They're coming down," he said into the speaker of his head set. "But I can't identify where."

"Okay, keep listening in."

"Would someone tell me what the hell's going on?" demanded the pilot. "Who's listening in? And why am I playing tour-guide to a bunch of off-world kids?"

"You wouldn't believe me if I told you," replied Zhumaton. "Just shut up and fly this thing. Mickie, can you explain a bit?"

But Mickie was concentrating on the images in his head. The helicopter was landing, he could tell from the trees bending away from the rotor and through the window he could see one more similar machine. He tuned in more closely to the mind that he was following. He felt a blow on the head and the sickness within him increased and the blood flow over one eye almost blinded him. He felt himself being hauled out of his seat, stumbling as he tried to move while still tethered to another person, and he was thrust and shoved out of the helicopter to the outside. Unable to control the movement of the prisoner, he tried to see what he could as the captive's head moved around, and eventually decided that there were at least ten other Kamotari tethered in a line and five armed Smegandri guarding them. But as he was shoved around, he caught a glimpse of another group being dragged out of the second helicopter. He waited and watched and was finally rewarded by a glimpse of several cave openings. He was dragged towards one and dumped in its mouth. He withdrew his full focus from the helpless captive.

"At least twenty hostages, more than you thought," he reported. "And probably ten Smegandri. They've landed by a group of caves..."

"The Kaaren Caves!" shouted Zhumaton. "It's the only possible place. Pilot, head there, now!"

"Okay," grumbled the pilot. "But someone owes me an explanation later. I've advised the troop carriers to follow us."

Silence fell in the aircraft and Mickie looked out of window, still following the picture in his mind. The prisoners had been forced to sit inside the caves, and he could hear the loud shouting and exuberant yells of the Smegandri terrorists. The blood over the one eye had dried and all vision had gone, leaving only partial sight in the other.

He jumped as a familiar image passed before him. Below the helicopter he saw the same radio tower and dark lake that he had previously see through the eyes of one of the captives.

"That's the tower!" he called out in excitement.

Zhumaton nodded. "It had to be," he said. "But you're sure that's exactly what you saw?"

"Quite sure," Mickie replied. "We're on track."

"I'm relieved to hear it," the cop said and Mickie realised that Zhumaton was telling the truth, he'd been anxious about his decision to trust Mickie's vision with nothing concrete to support it. Mickie grinned at the cop, expressing his support and admiration then wondered if his facial expression had indicated the right thing to a member of another species.

"We're heading down," reported the pilot. "We'll have to land some distance from the caves or they'll hear us, though the heavy trees will hide the noise to some extent. There's only one usable clearing, but it will leave us with a walk."

"Acknowledged," said Zhumaton.

A few minutes later, they had touched down in a huge clearing surrounded by dense forest. They were accompanied by two more helicopters that disgorged a platoon of cops carrying weapons and the whole mass of men set off through the woods.

It was hard going. Mickie was feeling the fatigue of a busy day and it was obvious that Melkana and Fencris were in a similar state. He felt more worried about Drellion, the youngest, who was having trouble keeping up. But as soon as Zhumaton saw the little boy's distress, he bent down and swooped him up in his major arm.

"You can ride along with me," he said, and that caused a smile of delight on Drellion's face.

The hike took an hour before the commanding officer of the armed squad suddenly stopped and waved his men to a halt. Mickie switched his attention to the image in his mind, finding it increasingly easy to follow both the internal view from the captive's eyes and his own at the same time. He tried to look as far as he could through the restricted image, and he could see no signs of nervousness in the terrorists.

"I don't think they know we're here," he whispered to Zhumaton who nodded and passed the message to the commander. For a moment the officer stared at Mickie, obviously puzzled by the entire nature of this mission, but finally nodded his acceptance at Zhumaton and spoke softly to him. The cop came back and spoke in a whisper to the children, putting Drellion down with them. The youngster had fallen asleep.

"We'll attack in just a moment," Zhumaton said. "I want all of you to stay right here. Do not under any circumstances come any nearer. It will get very dangerous in a few moments and I'm supposed to be protecting you. Understand?"

They nodded at him, and he turned and walked back to stand by the officer. For a second there was silence, then the troops vanished into the woods.

Mickie waited tensely, then jerked as the sounds of gunfire and shouts rang out. He moved his attention to the internal image and saw the captors leap to their feet in panic, he saw several of them fall and then the armed troops raced into his vision. The surprise and the victory was complete, or seemed so for a moment. His attention was snapped back to his immediate location when he heard a scream from Melkana. Mickie turned in shock and saw three of the Smegandri terrorists race into the clearing. They were carrying some sort of guns and shouting in rage and fury. Mickie shuddered; they seemed even more ugly and frightening than the Spiders. The terrorists advanced on the four children. The translator could make nothing of their words, but the sounds of their speech resembled the ugly grunting of an angry pig. Mickie's heart froze as the Smegandri raised their weapons, and then felt a surge of such vicious rage as he had never felt before. It felt like heat and pressure building up in his head. He walked straight at the intruders who stopped.

"Bugger off!" he shouted. In utter astonishment, he saw the creatures stumble backward and collapse, their weapons dropping from their huge hands. Breathing hard, Mickie walked slowly backward to rejoin his friends who were staring at the collapsed bodies. He felt Fencris' hand on his shoulder and he put his arm round Melkana. Both of them were trembling at yet another awfully narrow escape. The pressure in his head seemed to have subsided.

A sudden, fleeting memory came to his mind, of the night before he left Earth, when a spasm of rage enveloped him at his father's cigarette smoking, the odd sensation in his head, almost a silent sneeze ands how his father had bellowed in pain.

The silence was broken as the troops returned. They were leading a group of Smegandri who were roped in a line, their hands firmly tied. Behind them came a subdued group of the hostages. Mickie tried to return to the internal image to identify which of them had been his conduit, but the inset view had vanished. There was no way he could now identify which of the hostages had been his unwitting ally in their rescue, and several of them had blood-stained heads in the way his mental host had. One of the hostages was smaller than the rest and was being treated with particular care by the troops. Mickie assumed that she was the Leader's daughter and he felt happy that the child had been rescued without obvious damage.

The troops looked cheerful. They had achieved total victory and obviously sustained no casualties. Zhumaton came up to them.

"Well done," he said. "I think we got them all."

"Not quite," said Melkana, looking quite composed again. "What about those three?" She pointed at the huddled shapes on the ground a few meters away.

"What the...?" snapped Zhumaton and walked over to the Smegandri. He pushed their weapons away and bent over them then stood up, staring at the children. "They're dead. How did this happen?"

His words hit Mickie like a cold wave. The creatures were dead? The idea couldn't seem real to him. He tried to remember what had taken place, but all he could think of was that somehow the Spiders had intervened again. There was no way he could explain that to the Kamotari cop. "I don't know," he replied. "They came racing in here and then they just collapsed."

For a long moment, Zhumaton looked hard at him. "Okay, back in the flier," he said. "It's time I got you back home."

In relief, they climbed back in, with Zhumaton picking up the still-sleeping Drellion and the plane lifted above the trees and set course for the city. At some point, Zhumaton broke the silence, his jaw yawing wide open in what was obviously a huge laugh.

"Not exactly what I had in mind for a day of being tourists," he said over the noise of the engines.

"Nor us!" Mickie said, exhaustion catching up with him. He was still trying to work out what had happened and resolved to try and make contact with the Spiders later. He heard the radio device buzz on Zhumaton's belt and watched as the cop listened to his message.

"Hah!" said Zhumaton in high spirits. "Guess what? Our team won!"

*　*　*

Several hours later, Mickie was alone in his cabin again. He had not yet told his parents the story of the day, excusing himself with his extreme fatigue.

"I need to talk to you," he said aloud, concentrating hard on the image of the Spiders. It took nearly an hour before he got a response.

"Why are you calling us, Pfafth?" The voice was the same icy, menacing and emotionless tone as before, but it did not cause Mickie to feel the same fear as he had on previous occasions.

"You saved me again," said Mickie. "I wanted to thank you."

"That is untrue."

"What? But the same happened as before with the Gelkka. It *had* to be you!"

"You called us, certainly," said the Spider. *"We saw the Smegandri attack. But we did nothing."*

"You did nothing? That's impossible! They fell dead!"

"That is true. But we did nothing."

"Then who.....? Mickie stopped. He already knew the answer

"That is correct, Pfafth. You did it yourself. You have progressed rapidly."

Mickie found he was trembling. "Progressed? To what?"

But there was no answer from the Spider.

Chapter 17 – Learning the Speakers' Art

"Training sessions with the Speakers have become even more critical," Grant said. They were sitting round the table in Grant and Allie's cabin and the mood was serious. "That last episode on Kamotar showed that whatever your powers are, they're becoming stronger by the minute. You really do need to learn how to control them before you hurt someone."

"It only seemed to happen when I got really angry." Mickie was worried at the seriousness of his parent's mood.

"We know, but it could also mean any other intensive emotion could trigger it," replied Allie. "That's when it could get a bit strained. After all, fear could also be a trigger, and if you got frightened by something on one of our visits, you might damage someone or something by accident."

"I suppose so." Mickie hadn't thought of that, and the idea appalled him. He was still trying to adjust to the idea that he had killed three creatures. Murderous as they had been, violent terrorists who had themselves killed many innocents, he was still tortured by the idea of killing intelligent beings. Another thought hit him.

"The night before I met you," he said. "I remember being in my room and my father started his smoker's cough. I got furious and he suddenly yelled in pain. Do you think I did that, the first sign of some of these powers starting?"

"Probably," said Allie. "Which means you need serious training to control this."

"So, until next planet-fall, lots of training sessions with the Speaker, okay?" Grant was firm.

"What *is* the next planet-fall?" Mickie was not yet ready to be bored by the series of new adventures that each planet represented. The level of excitement that filled his blood each time he boarded the shuttle to drop down to the planet that filled the ship's observation screens was as high as the very first time. This time he wanted to see what happened when the ship left hyperspace and he resolved to instruct Albert to give him plenty of warning so that he could be in the observation room.

"We'll reach X'Katcxo in four days," replied Allie. "For the first time, we'll be landing on the home world of many of our crew, and some of them will leave to be replaced by new crew members. Then there will be one more visit before we head home to Kalamos for a vacation that I think we all need."

"We go to Kalamos?" Mickie remembered with delight that Albert had told him of this some weeks ago and the idea of seeing his newly-adopted home planet and having an uninterrupted vacation with his parents was magical.

"Indeed we do, and we have a month off. And I promise you, it will be great!"

"What do we trade on.... X'Katcxo?" Mickie found the harsh, sibilant word very difficult to say.

"We supply the pharmaceutical products we

obtained from the Spiders' world, some of the plant material from Harliya that is used to make textiles, gold and diamonds from Kamotar and for all that, we buy mineral ores. Very boring, but it's a mineral-rich planet."

"It's also a very old planet, with an extraordinary and very complex culture," added Grant. "So be sure to get a full briefing from Albert, we can't have you offending anyone with an inadvertent mistake, not with the defensive powers you seem to have acquired!" The words were friendly and punctuated with a smile, but Grant was obviously giving a firm order and Mickie knew he had better do some serious homework about X'Katcxo. What with that and the training sessions with Speaker 356, he doubted there would be much time for playing Loopies in the next four weeks.

"But you said one more trip after X'Katcxo?"

"Ten days after that, we go to Merrison," Allie said. "And it will not be a standard trading call on a planet that knows about us."

"What's the problem?" Mickie was intrigued.

"This is more like our visits to Earth," Grant joined in. "Merrison is actually some decades behind Earth's culture, and like we were doing on your home planet, we've had agents there for some years, living as locals and observing them. This trip is to see how things are progressing."

"Why don't the agents just report through the Speakers?"

"The kid's not stupid, dear Husband, is he?" Allie laughed.

"Indeed not," Grant agreed. "And the answer, my bright young son, is that we like to get there ourselves now and again and get the feel of the place. The other reason, and it's the more important one, is that our agents get to the point sometimes when they desperately need contact with their own kind, can relax with friends and let their guards down and have a good talk over some fine scotch, something not available on the planet."

"And will I come down with you?"

"You will. The more inter-planetary experience you get, the better. But there are risks on this one, and you'll get a full briefing before we go down. But after that, then we go home for a holiday!"

*　*　*

"Speaker 356, are you with me?" Mickie was alone in his cabin and had settled in comfort in the armchair to take the first mental training sessions from the telepathic being such an incomprehensible distance away. He had started to study the galactic maps of the Universe and now he knew that the Speaker's planet was over sixty million light years from Earth.

"Yes, Mickie, I'm here."

"So how do we go about this?"

"First, I will run what might be termed a diagnostic review of your mind."

"What's a diagnostic review?"

"It's something very similar to what a computer engineer on your home planet would do when looking for a problem or the total capacity of a computer of Earth's level of technology. I will track down all the neural connections in your brain and try to locate the control mechanisms that provide the powers you seem to have."

"Wow!" Mickie was enthralled. He'd loved playing with the computers at school and had spent hours reading about the operating systems. It had been a source of great frustration that his parents had refused to buy one for the home, and his sister had shown no interest in the technology at all. The idea that the Speaker would do something like a software review of his brain was fascinating. "Go ahead," he said and sat back in his seat, trying to feel what might be happening inside his head but without success.

The silence lasted just a few seconds.

"Done," said the Speaker. "That's very interesting."

"What is?" Mickie held his breath in some anxiety.

"We have been reviewing human brains for a few hundred years," said the Speaker. "It's part of the process we follow with all intelligent races that are not yet aware of other species. We follow any developments, particularly looking for telepathic skills. In humans, we have found a very tiny telepathic capability in a minute portion of the population, but overall, human minds represent a large capacity for development rather than a level of maturity to cope with inter-planetary communication."

"So have you found anything different in me?" Mickie could hardly control his patience.

"A few things," replied the Speaker. "They are the same little indicators I saw when I first heard your call from Earth. They tell me you're not a human or a Kalamosian, but there's nothing to explain these immense powers that I can see."

"No?" Mickie was shattered. He was so sure his mind would prove to be something vastly superior.

"Nothing. It would seem you have an almost normal human mind and I can see nothing at all that would explain the powers you have demonstrated."

"Not even the telepathic powers?" Mickie was having trouble controlling his disappointment and loss of pride.

"That's the strangest part," replied the Speaker. "At first examination, I would have thought you displayed no telepathic skills at all."

"But I must do!"

"One would think so." Mickie could sense the intrigue in the Speaker's thoughts. "After all, you have clearly demonstrated such talents, so we must conclude that you do so by some means that we have not before detected."

"Like the Spiders?" Mickie felt worried at that thought. Surely he could not be related to the Spiders in any way?

"Yes, like the Spiders. Every Speaker on my world is fascinated by this."

"So can you still help me develop these skills and control them? My parents are very worried about it."

"Have no fears, we can certainly help. While the mechanism you are using is unknown to us, the rules of control are almost certainly similar, and the main thing we'll be doing is helping you focus and control your talents, not modify them."

"Phew!"

"I agree!" Mickie sensed the humour in the Speaker and wondered at the possibility that such totally different beings as he and the immobile mound on a distant world could share something as ordinary as a sense of humour.

What followed was an intensive two-hour session that left Mickie exhausted. The Speaker made Mickie concentrate hard on certain spots in the room, straining his mind to see an item such as a door handle or a pattern on the carpet, looking deep into the object until he felt he could almost see inside it.

"That will do for today," the Speaker said suddenly.

"But what have we done?" asked Mickie. "That didn't feel like telepathy at all!"

"It wasn't. It was all about focus. And while you were working at that, I was tracking brain waves and energy fluctuations."

"And did we get anywhere?"

"Further than you know. Perhaps on this occasion, I learned more than you did, but what we did in those two hours was the same exercise I did with my tutor when I first started my training."

The fatigue hit him at that point. He crawled out of the armchair and staggered to his bedroom, falling asleep as soon as he was horizontal on the form-fitting bed.

After a week, the Speaker suggested a new phase of training.

"Now we will ask your parents' cooperation as we suggested earlier," said the Speaker. "They have just agreed, so what you will try now is to enter your father's mind and see what he can see. I will block from your perception his own thoughts as this is to be just a trial of empathic vision. Are you ready?"

"Yes, I am. Is Grant?"

"He is. Now, concentrate. First, can you locate your father?"

Mickie closed his eyes and concentrated on expanding his awareness throughout the ship as he had been practicing in the last three sessions. He sensed the huge numbers of individuals as a single energy mass, unable to identify any one specific individual, but he maintained his concentration, picturing Grant's face in front of him. He lost all awareness of his room, felt himself detached from his body, reaching out his arms to embrace the entire ship... He saw the ship below him, seemingly immobile in the mathematical uncertainties of hyperspace, then felt himself being drawn down, back into the ship's hull, to the corridors between the locations, to the observation deck... he was looking out at the emptiness that he had just felt himself occupying... he was looking through his father's eyes, felt his body, taller, more muscular than his own, sensed the awareness of the sudden intrusion of a new mind... he was looking out through Grant's eyes.

"Excellent," said the Speaker. "Return to your own perception."

"Wow!" gasped Mickie, looking around the room as if he had physically left it and then returned.

"Grantorel, did you sense Mickie's empathic contact?"

His father's voice spoke as if Grant was in the same room. "Yes, I did. Pretty well done, young guy!"

"Thanks, dad!" Mickie was delighted with the approval.

"Okay, that shows the ability to make contact with a specified and known person," said Grant. "But Speaker, how does that explain his contact with the unknown hostage on Kamotar?"

"It doesn't." replied Speaker 356. "That will require further study. However, we have made progress. There's a long way to go."

Three days later, Mickie had another classroom test.

"This time," the Speaker said, "the object is to

determine the awareness of every individual on the ship. You will not enter the minds of anyone, because you have not been given consent and that is a prime rule among telepathic species. It can only be broken for emergencies. But I want you to try and identify the individual mental patterns emitted by each and every person on the ship and compare the variations between species."

Again Mickie concentrated and in some timeless moment found himself looking at the ship from outside, seeing the massive ovoid as a stationary object in hyperspace. He brought his consciousness closer to the ship and somehow entered through the thick hull without a thought. Initially, he sensed only a seething mass of energy from the hundreds of people aboard the vessel, but he struggled, applied the newly found powers of concentration to focusing on individuals and made the first connection. Unlike his empathic encounters, he knew he was not inside the mind of the young Kaloti officer reclining in the deep, beautiful, yellow light of the Kaloti-like environment that was standard in the crew quarters. He felt he was alongside the tall, stick-like body of the young male, but he sensed the man's brainwaves almost as if he was hearing his voice. There was a cadence, a series of waves, a pattern... Mickie broke away and concentrated on the next.

He was reading the brain patterns of his friend, Fencris... The cadence was quite different, the pattern had intriguing colours, interplays of light flickered across his awareness, he did not know how he was sensing all this...

"You're doing very well," said the reassuring voice of his teacher. "Notice how the Cassolean pattern is so different from that of the Kaloti. Look for a Kalamosian brainwave ..."

Mickie disconnected from the connection with Fencris, read the entire ship, felt that this time it was less of a seething mass but more of a huge collection of sparks, any one of which he could follow and then decide to approach.... A new pattern touched his mind, a young Kalamosian girl dining in the ship's restaurant, talking with her friend, another Kalamosian... different cadences, different patterns, different sensations...

"Oh my!" he said, pulling back, feeling fatigue hitting him.

"A good learning session," said the Speaker. "That will do for today. Your progress is excellent."

Mickie fell asleep within minutes.

He had three more such sessions the next day, and three the day after that. Each time, he felt that it was easier to reach out and embrace the ship, sense the numerous entities aboard and focus in on any one individual. By the end of two weeks, he was familiar with the mental patterns of each of the species aboard. The new skills enormously enhanced his enjoyment of being part of the crew of the amazing Kaloti ship. More and more, he took to joining his friends and walking through the common areas where the restaurants and shops were located, with several pubs and entertainment centres. His awareness had expanded so that he always knew who was about to appear in his view and he maintained a general consciousness of the location of everybody on the ship.

"I don't know of any species that can do this, other than the Speakers," Allie said with pride. "But I worry that perhaps it's more than you can handle. You're awfully young to have such abilities."

"I'm not using it for any purpose," Mickie replied with some anxiety. "I'm not sneaking in anyone's mind. You told me I mustn't."

"Yes, we did, and I'm proud of you for working so hard to follow that," Grant said. "But I can imagine the temptation is extremely high, sometimes."

Mickie thought about it. "I haven't found that. Honestly, I don't think I want to pry into someone else's mind. I'd feel... I don't know, but I don't want to."

"Then that's okay," Allie said. "Talk to us first if you find the temptation starting to grow."

Mickie remembered the conversation as he strolled through the promenade deck with Drellion, Melkana and Fencris. He had worried that these new skills would cause some difficulties between them, but the other three regarded the growing talents with interest, simply another set of characteristics of a newly-discovered race. The topic of being a Pfafth rarely arose, but when it did, the conversation was friendly, more jesting about what next he'd be able to do. Sometimes they played the game of testing him to see if he could tell who was behind him, or in a room they were about to enter.

They reached a coffee shop that had become their favourite stopping point on the promenade. Not that "shop" was an accurate description, as no purchase was necessary and the items ordered were delivered by the computer system at their table. But the social atmosphere always seemed cheerful and they regularly stopped there for a taste of the sparkling *Sle'Ach* drink, or a mug of the wonderful Mayoowani coffee.

"Alright, Mickie, who's behind you at the table two down from us?" Melkana asked.

"Er... two Kalamosian guys and a Cassolean girl," Mickie replied after just a second or two of reaching out his mind.

"Right. And the table behind them?" Drellion joined in, still slightly in awe of this talent.

"Er... an X'Kasxi, a Kalamosian man and a Kaloti crewman."

"Are you sure?" Melkana looked puzzled and stared over his shoulder at the table in question.

Mickie reached out his mind and again detected the three as he had described. "Yes," he said. "Why, what's the problem?"

"Those three are there, alright, but there's a second Kalamosian with them. Turn round and look for yourself."

Feeling baffled, Mickie did so and stared at the group at the table. There were four people sitting at it, all intent on their drinks, the X'Kasxi gesticulating as he talked. As Mickie looked at the group, he was overcome by the weirdest sensation of not being able to see one of the two Kalamosians. It was as if he was looking at a photograph from which one person had been neatly cut, leaving only the outline. He focused hard on the mysterious fourth, trying to read the mind pattern. He was quite unable to see anything.

As if aware of the study, the Kalamosian looked up, looked right into Mickie's eyes and stood up. Mickie felt a shock run through his body, knew sweat was running down his back and was short of breath for a second.

The Kalamosian walked out of the room.

"Mickie, what was that all about?" Fencris' red eyes flickering like coal embers. "How come you didn't see him?"

"I don't know." Mickie was feeling like he had just finished a training session with the Speaker, fatigued and limp. "But even when I tried direct contact, I couldn't. Who was he, does anyone know him?"

Melkana slipped from her chair and went up to the three remaining men at the table. "Do you know who that Kalamosian was?" she asked directly.

"Well, sure," one of them replied. "He's a plant specialist, name of Arageenom. He's from my town of Zhanshur on Hirospet. What's all this about?"

"I just thought I recognised him," replied Melkana. "But I don't think that's possible."

She returned to the other three with a small frown on her face. "You're really sure you couldn't read him?" she asked. "It wasn't just tiredness?"

"Definitely not." Mickie was quite firm. "There's something strange about that guy. Did you get his name?"

Melkana repeated the information she had obtained. Mickie decided to call for help.

"Albert," he said softly, but loud enough for the others to hear. "Can you identify a Kalamosian plant specialist named Arageenom on the ship? Include Drellion, Fencris and Melkana in the reply."

The reply was immediate. "Arageenom Forazhot, plant pathologist, crewmember joined the ship at the last planet-fall on Kalamos."

"Speaker 356, are you with me?" Mickie brought in more help.

"Yes Mickie."

"Include the others in your reply. Can you identify a Kalamosian on this ship, name of Arageenom Forazhot?"

A split second of silence occurred before the Speaker replied. "No, I cannot. I can find no Kalamosian with that name on the ship."

This time the silence was longer as the four looked at each other.

"Oops!" said Melkana. "I think the Captain needs to know this."

Fifteen minutes later, after telling his parents about what had happened, Mickie got a message from Allie. "We talked to the Captain," she said. "He tried to call this Arageenom but got no reply. The computer is unable to locate him anywhere. He's not on the ship."

"But that's impossible! We're in hyperspace. How can anyone leave a ship in hyperspace?"

"It's impossible. But he's gone."

"And there is no record on Kalamos, either of his residence in Zhanshur, or anywhere else," came the voice of Speaker 356. "He did not seem to exist before he joined the ship."

"He looked at me as if he recognised me," Mickie said.

The new voice that entered the conversation was familiar, frightening and unwelcome.

"He did," said the voice of the Spider. *"And it means that the Enemy is starting to make some moves. Young Pfafth, the war is starting."*

Chapter 18 – The Kindred of X'Katcxo

"The culture of the Kindred is most complex," intoned Albert. The three-dimensional holograph of the planet of X'Katcxo hung in Mickie's cabin, slowly rotating   "The term 'Kindred' is the nearest term I can find in English," Albert continued. "It means more of a single racial family, for there are no separate races on the planet and no obvious physical differences between any of that species, regardless of where on the planet they originated.   In many ways, the culture of X'Katcxo resembles that of traditional Japan on your planet. It is one of very strict rules and mores, with a strong social classification system based on a complex pattern of both birth and achievement, so that one can move upward within the system, but only by significant achievements in business, the arts or academia."

The holograph stopped rotating and a glow appeared on the upper, east quarter of the southern land mass. "This is the area known as Hrz'Ashcha. It consists of fifteen nation states that have grouped into a single political entity of which the City of Brx'Jashcha is the capital. The entire continent is also named Hrz'Ashcha, but there appears to be an emphasis on one vowel that defines whether one is referring to the continent or the region, but no language specialist has ever yet been able to pin down the pronunciation to that degree. That city is also the primary space port for the planet and we will make planet-fall there in three days."

The image switched to showing the line between day and night.

"The planet's day is twenty nine hours and eleven minutes by Earth reckoning," said Albert. "And the year is nearly one point five Earth years. Local standards divide the day into twenty periods and your translator device will refer to them as hours for your convenience. You will be fed a drug in your last meal before planet-fall that will reset your body's internal clock to match the planet's diurnal cycle, otherwise it would be very difficult for you to cope with the lengthy days and nights. On your return to the ship, you will probably sleep nearly twenty hours and an additional drug dose will reset your internal clock to ship time."

The image of the planet disappeared, to be replaced by a holograph of a strange, lizard-like creature. It stood upright, with a tail that stood out horizontally as a balance. Immediately, Mickie could see that the head was quite similar to the heads of the X'Kasxi crewmembers he had already met, but the image before him looked far more animal-like and primitive. The image expanded to show only the head.

"This is the ancestor animal of the X'Kasxi," Albert continued. "It is known as L'Akshi and you will notice that it has quite prominent bone outcroppings over the eyes. Such shields remain to this day in the modern X'Kasxi and a huge cultural aspect exists in this regard. The people believe that the degree of sophistication of the individual, actually, the maturity of the individual's *soul*, varies directly with the smallness of these shields. The smaller and less obvious they are, the more is that person deemed to be a superior soul, spiritually advanced and attractive. So a major industry exists in cosmetic surgery to reduce the bone to something similar to the human eyebrows. For those born with minimal eye shields, it is a matter of great pride to prove that point with something like a human female eyebrow liner that outlines the shield as if to show that it is so minimal, that the owner has to paint it to display it. In ceremonial situations, that make-up is of strong colours and quite artistic designs, as you will see when you walk about the city. It is wise not to stare, or to show amusement as a child might do, because it could cause great offence, so please be on your best behaviour."

"Yes, Albert," said Mickie, thinking of the X'Kasxi crewmembers he had met on the ship. Now that he understood the meaning, he could recall that some of the individuals had prominent eye shields, and one or two had almost none. But he had seen none with paint being used to highlight them. He must have been vocalising his thoughts internally, because Albert picked them up.

"In a professional environment such as a space-ship, it would be considered excess vanity to use eye-liner. No X'Kasxi in such a position would dream of so doing. However, once back on their home planet, I know of several of the crew who will return to that custom. But it must be said, for a species with whom we have dealt and worked for a hundred years or more, we know remarkably little about them."

"How come?"

"Their culture is, as I said, intensely complex and private. They mix with other crewmembers as little as possible, no more than the minimum for their duties.

One of their rules is that every Kaloti ship must carry an X'Kasxi doctor, regardless of how few X'Kasxi there are in the crew. No other doctor is allowed to treat them and the information we have on their physical structure, internal organisation and chemistry is severely limited. Now let us turn to spiritual matters, for here we have something similar to your previous experience."

Mickie's attention picked up and he stopped thinking of the oddly grotesque idea of lizards using make-up.

"I must first point out that we know very little for certain about the spiritual values and beliefs of the X'Kasxi," continued Albert. "What we do have has come from just a few conversations with X'Kasxi crewmembers, from odd comments from people picked up during visits to that world, from occasional books that touch on the topic, but it is such a closed, private society that obtaining information is extremely difficult. The X'Kasxi are almost unknown to us."

"That's weird," Mickie commented.

"However, we do know that the X'Kasxi are highly developed in their spiritual beliefs and therein lies the key factor of their culture."

Mickie sat back to listen. He found this topic engrossing.

"A few, very wise and highly trained X'Kasxi become what are known as Guides. They are the spiritual leaders of their world and they have only a few, but most critical functions. The Guides believe that they can read the soul of the new-born and define its strength. They have a term for this. They use the word *"m'rrhai"* which roughly translates as "soul-strength" but we think also means maturity of the soul, probably more than that, but we still have much to learn about this. Every newborn pup is brought before a Guide who will read the child's soul and tell the parents what must happen. This can even include the killing the pup if the Guide deems its *"m'rrhai"* inadequate for the life to come. They will dictate the pup's future, its career, the education it must have, all these things, and the parents will obey."

"That seems awfully cruel,"

"'Cruel' is a judgemental term," replied Albert. "If the Kindred are correct, if the Guides do indeed read the ability of the soul in the newborn, then the process they go through could be the most efficient and stress-free approach to raising a child, as it will be mentored and trained in the career and lifestyle that is most suitable to it."

"I suppose so," Mickie said, thinking deeply about the matter.

"That will do for now," Albert continued. "Planet-fall is in twenty hours and you have some schoolwork to do. You also asked me to remind you in time to watch the exit from hyperspace and you will need some sleep before that event which will occur in seventeen hours and thirteen minutes from...."

A musical chime rang in the cabin.

"...then." Albert completed his instruction.

The windows of the observation lounge were jet black, quite featureless. They could have been panels of basalt, so smooth and perfect were they. The four friends had the huge room almost to themselves, just a half dozen similar curious watchers scattered round the area. Almost everyone else was either too familiar with the upcoming event or were thoroughly preoccupied preparing for their jobs on the approaching planet.

"How long, Albert?" Mickie asked.

"Two minutes thirty seconds from...." The chime sounded gently in Mickie's ears.

"I've seen this twice before," Melkana said. "I still get a buzz from it."

They fell silent after that and waited.

A tiny glow appeared in the middle of the panel in front of the four youngsters. The pin-head size fireball expanded rapidly, filled the one panel and even more quickly began to fill the panels around it. In just a few seconds, the fire faded and dissolved into the glowing stars of the galaxy, the same galaxy that contained Earth's solar system, Mickie reminded himself. He realised he had been holding his breath since the first tiny glow had appeared and he slowly let it out, hearing the same from the other three.

"Wow!" said Drellion. "That was wild!"

"I'll say!" agreed Mickie. "I'm staying here till we hit orbit round X'Katcxo."

"Okay, we'll see you at the shuttle before we go down," Fencris said. "I have to see my parents before then."

"Us too," said Melkana, and they raced off, leaving Mickie to watch the stars of the far end of the Milky Way drift past the ship as it moved at sub-light speed to rendezvous with the planet of the lizard-like X'Kasxi.

He leaned up sideways against the back of the seats that lined the walls of the lounge and stared out at the stars. He thought back to the days that seemed such a lifetime ago but yet were just a few weeks ago when he had been a depressed, lonely child in a suburb of an English city, desperate to leave home and make his own way in the world away from his awful parents. He chuckled inside as he thought about what had happened, the worlds he had seen, the strange beings he had met and befriended, fought as he had fought the Smegandri, or who had terrified and nearly killed him as had the Gelkka.

He thought about his own mysterious origins and wondered if he would ever find out what he was and how he had been placed on Earth. And he thought about the strange and astonishing powers he had found within himself and was developing and learning to control with the guidance of the Speaker, a being he could never meet in person but who had become a close friend. And with all the excitement of the changes, there was a dark undercurrent of worry about what the Spider had said. Who and what was "The Enemy" and why was a war starting? Why was he seemingly at the centre of it?

He realised that he'd been watching a spot of light growing stronger and brighter. The windows of the lounge darkened to protect his eyes from the sun of X'Katcxo that was about the same size as Earth's Sol and Mickie knew the ship must be close to the home planet of the X'Kasxi. He saw it a few minutes later, first a small brown and green ball that quickly filled the windows until only a quarter of the sphere was visible. Beneath him rotated the continents, oceans and islands he had studied on the holograph in his room and he decided he could never weary of this approach to a planet, regardless of how many times he saw it.

"Time to collect your bag and meet everyone at the Shuttle," said Albert. "You are staying several days, so be sure you have enough. I am instructed to advise you to bring a swimsuit."

Mickie rose from the seat and went to meet up with the landing party.

"We've been greatly honoured," Allie said to the four of them as the shuttle floated down to the enormous city of Brx'Jashcha with its population of forty million people. "Because of the huge find of treasure on Shuramee, we've been invited to stay at the home of one of the greatest X'Kasxi Guides. His name is X'Kaa Tz'Horzash and he's a member of the same house as one of our X'Kasxi colleagues, one of those being trained as a pilot by the Kaloti. He's now very rich because of what you four did on Shurameen." She smiled down at Mickie. "So we are all honoured guests on this trip. So much so, that we will be allowed to witness something no off-worlder has ever seen, the birth of a new pup to that house and the soul-reading by the Guide. Believe me, this is an extraordinary thing to happen and we're very excited by it."

Mickie was unsure if that was a great deal at all, but politely agreed that he felt greatly honoured. The two boys seemed equally unimpressed, but Melkana seemed thrilled by the idea and Mickie had already decided that there was nothing he wouldn't do for this energetic, resourceful and intelligent girl.

"What do we need to know about staying at someone's house?" Melkana asked.

"It's more a mansion," Allie replied. "We will all have our private rooms and we will be served breakfast and lunch there. But the evening meals will be taken in the common area and it's a very formal affair. Meals will be specially prepared for individual diets, as X'Kasxi food is not always acceptable to other species. Call our host just "Guide" and the translators will take care of the precise title. I think you're all old enough to understand that he is to be treated with the utmost respect, as if you were staying at the home of a world leader back on your home planets."

"What will we do while you're working? We'll never find our way round this city!" Mickie was astounded by the incredible size of the city he had seen from orbit.

"You'll have no problem finding people happy to show you around," said Allie with a laugh. "You four are famous because you have made all the crewmembers rich! But be back each evening for the meal, it's considered rude to miss it without seriously good reasons."

The shuttle doors opened and the light of the sun filled the cabin. It seemed to Mickie to have a slightly reddish tinge, but he had no idea what the local time was, so perhaps the sun was showing a red, evening light. Then he remembered there was always help available with just a focused thought.

"Albert, what time is it here?" he asked the electronic permanent assistant on board the orbiting ship.

"Half past fourteen," came the immediate answer.

Of a twenty-hour day where every hour was much longer than an Earth-hour, Mickie remembered, so mid-afternoon of this long, long day. He hoped the drug he had taken earlier would help him adjust. He followed his parents out into the sun and realised that the reddish tinge was in the sunlight itself, with no clouds to cause it.

There was a line of what looked like buses waiting a few metres away from the shuttlecraft. One of the X'Kasxi crew approached Grant and pointed out the first vehicle in line and Grant led Allie and the four children to it, accompanied by the X'Kasxi. Before entering, Grant introduced the crewmember to the others.

"Guys, this is Kr'Horzash. It is to his home that we'll be going and staying."

Kr'Horzash bowed slightly. "It is my honour to have you. You have brought me great wealth and success from this trip and the House of Tz'Horzash makes you most welcome."

Once on the bus, the young man became less formal. "It is my sister who gives birth tomorrow and you will witness this proceeding. Then we will have the Head of the House, who is the great Guide X'Kaa Tz'Horzash read the *m'rrhai* of the new pup. We have been praying to our ancestors that the pup will be worthy of the House."

Mickie was extremely doubtful about witnessing a birth. From what little he knew of the process with humans, it was a noisy, messy and highly intimate affair and the idea of being at close hand was disturbing. He concentrated on looking out at the city as they drove through. The size was awe-inspiring. The streets were wider than anything he had ever seen before and the buildings that lined them were even greater than the castles and fortresses he had seen on Kamotar. Buildings rose like monstrous cliffs on both sides of the roads, making the scene more like a ride through a vast canyon. Sometimes, instead of vertical skyscrapers, the buildings were built in tiers, ranging back two or three hundred metres before reaching their peaks like some enormous foothills.

The vehicles in the streets all seemed to be of the gravity-powered variety, as was the bus in which they were travelling. The noise level was therefore very low, and he soon saw that the traffic was moving in four levels, each separated by perhaps twenty metres. He watched carefully and soon saw that vehicles could change levels by moving to areas marked by flickering lines of lights at each side of the road. Rising up a level required a move to the right of the road, down a level meant moving to the left, then in both cases, travelling along the marked lanes to merge into the new traffic flow. It seemed to be a smooth, unflustered process, with the slowest traffic on the lowest level and speeds increasing the higher up it went. Mickie imagined that there would be speed ranges defined for each level.

At one point, the bus moved to the highest level and its speed increased dramatically till it was travelling at what Mickie felt must have been at least two hundred kilometres an hour.

"All on auto-pilot and satellite navigation," said Fencris who had taken the seat behind him and was watching the scenery with enjoyment. "This is my third trip here, but it's the first time we get to stay at a Guide's house. I tell you, Mickie, our trip to Shuramee has paid off big-time!"

Mickie chuckled. "And all because I hurt myself on a chunk of metal!"

The city ended quite abruptly and the bus was now flying through flat, featureless farm land. Just as suddenly they stopped as a large building appeared and the bus settled smoothly to the ground.

"Again, my welcome to the House of Tz'Horzash," said their X'Kasxi companion. "Servants will show you to your rooms and your bags will be brought to you. I must first visit with the Guide, the head of our House. I ask that you be ready for dinner at seventeen hours and the servants will bring you to the dining hall."

"My, my, I could get to like this life," Melkana chuckled softly and received grins of agreement from the other three. Several X'Kasxi approached from the house, all dressed in similar style, plain black trousers and green shirts with white trimming. Mickie was not sure which were male and which female, having had little communication with the members of this species aboard the ship. There seemed little difference in height or build between any of them. One of them addressed the four younger members of the party. "May I lead you to your rooms?" it said, and began to walk into the house, followed by the children.

"How do you tell which is male and which is female?" Mickie whispered to Melkana as they entered the huge building.

"Females have ears that you can see. Males only have a small hole on each side of the head and no external flaps," Melkana whispered back. Mickie felt a twinge of shame that he had never found this out before after so many months aboard. He looked again and saw small earflaps on the head of the servant leading them. A female, then.

The building was truly enormous. It felt like one of the Stately Homes Mickie had once visited on a school outing, with a gigantic entrance lobby and hall with corridors leading off in three separate directions. The young female servant led them into the hall and then turned right along the corridor. She stopped by one large door that gleamed in polished wood with inlaid ivory or similar substance in intricate patterns in panels.

"Miss Melkana, this is your room," she said. At least, that was what the interpreter in Mickie's shoulder said, and for a few seconds Mickie wondered exactly what title she had given Melkana and what it might mean in this strange culture. His musings were cut off as the remaining trio were led to the next room.

"And you three young men will be in this one," said the servant and opened the door.

The room was as massive as he had learned to expect. They all stood in awe for a few seconds, gaping at lavish drapes, enormous windows, luxurious furnishings and three emperor-sized beds spaced around the room.

"The bathroom is through that door," the servant said, and Mickie led the way through, stopping yet again in amazement.

"It's a swimming pool!" Fencris gasped, and indeed it was, fully twenty metres long and ten metres wide.

"This we've got to try, right now!" Mickie shouted and dashed back to the bedroom. Their bags were already in the middle of the room and the servant had gone. He seized his, ran to the bed nearest the swimming pool door and started unpacking. "This one's mine," he proclaimed, extracted his swimsuit and swiftly changed, the other two boys doing the same, and a few moments later had leaped into the pool and all three were splashing about with yells of delight.

When they returned to the bedroom, they were surprised to find new clothing had been laid out for them. Each of them had been given an identical set. It consisted of black trousers and a white jacket that zipped at the front, and the edges were trimmed with gold braid. To Mickie's eyes it resembled a military officer's style for ceremonial occasions and it was undoubtedly the smartest clothing he had ever seen.

"This is pretty stunning stuff," Fencris commented as he examined his. "I wonder how they knew our sizes?"

"I'd say they asked the ship's computer," Drellion suggested.

"Hey, this kid's not stupid, is he, Mickie?" Fencris said, his eyes glowing and Drellion grinned, obviously pleased at the approval of the elder boys.

A knock on the door interrupted their inspection of the clothing and the young servant came in.

"Dinner in half an hour," she said. "I will be waiting for you outside the door to take you to the dining room."

"Is there something special about this stuff?" Mickie asked. "It looks like a uniform."

"It is the prescribed dress for an honoured guest of the House of Tz'Horzash," the girl replied. "Please be ready on time."

She left and the boys occupied themselves with putting on the magnificent garb. Mickie had never in his life worn anything so fine and he felt the glow of a very special occasion.

"Well, I'd say we all look pretty horrible," said Fencris with his red-eyed grin, obviously feeling the same sense of occasion. "Even little Drellion here looks quite cool."

In great companionship, they opened the door and walked out to find the servant waiting. She led them to Melkana's room and knocked, and immediately the door opened to reveal their friend. All three boys stood stock still as Melkana walked out.

She had on the same tunic as the others, and her hair had been released to fall freely behind her back. Her eyes and pink cheeks reflected the same excitement that the boys were feeling and it suddenly occurred to Mickie that she was really quite beautiful. He became aware that the perfectly-fitted clothing was demonstrating some lines that made his throat dry and held his eyes. The same wave of shyness he had felt when he had first met her came back and almost overwhelmed him.

As was often the case, Fencris seemed to be the one with the quickest recovery.

"I must say, Melkana, you look considerably less revolting than we do."

She smiled shyly. "Well I think you all look very handsome. Shall we go to dinner?"

They followed the silent servant down the corridor, back to the entrance hall and turned right up the middle corridor. Already Mickie could hear the sounds of conversation, and when the doors opened to the dining room, the noise swelled to a sizeable roar. There must have been a hundred people, he thought, looking round for his parents. He finally saw them in conversation with two other couples, one Kalamosian like themselves, the other Cassolean, all dressed in the same style as he was. When he looked round the banquet hall, he saw that the X'Kasxi were all dressed alike, but their tunics were green, also with the gold trim. The room was massive, even more ornate and beautifully furnished than their bedrooms. Four long tables were arranged in the shape of a letter "E."

He saw that Allie was waving at him and all of the four friends moved to join her where she was standing with Grant.

"My, what a handsome son we have," said Allie. "That's the first time we've seen each other in formal attire. I think I like it!"

"Me too," Mickie replied and indeed, both his parents looked very striking.

"Mickie, meet my parents," said Melkana and Mickie

shook hands with the couple who had warmly embraced Drellion and his sister. They too looked impressive, but privately Mickie was quite sure that his parents were the handsomest couple in the banquet hall. Finally, he met Fencris' parents, their red eyes and pale blue faces looking startling atop the white and gold tunics. They had greeted Fencris in an oddly formal manner, but Mickie assumed that was normal for that species, because Fencris seemed perfectly happy to be with them.

"My mother is Selvana," Fencris said. "My father is Devenar."

"We are all very proud of you four," said Devenar. "You have displayed the initiative and courage that we seek in our children and we are all much richer as a result."

Mickie was about to reply when three blasts from a musical instrument sounding something like a French Horn burst over the room. Everyone stopped talking and turned to where a small procession had entered the hall. Two lines of three servants walked on either side of a single male wearing pure green robes with gold trimming. The colour scheme was the same as the rest of the X'Kasxi wore, but the robes were quite formal, much like the traditional Roman Toga Mickie had seen in pictures in his history books. He looked hard at the man and decided he was very old. Grey patches round the mouth and deep wrinkles in the neck indicated considerable age, though he had no idea what was the standard life expectancy of an X'Kasxi. He focused a question to Albert, unsure if he would get a reply, but was not let down.

"About a hundred local years," said Albert, "which is about a hundred and fifty Earth years. This Guide, X'Kaa Tz'Horzash is eighty three X'Kasxi years old."

The procession reached the centre of the head table in total silence until the Guide sat down, and everyone followed the example, the conversations breaking out again all over the room. Mickie sat on Grant's right with, to his great pleasure, Melkana next to him, Fencris and Drellion sat across from them between Melkana's parents. Fencris' mother sat the other side of Grant and Fencris' father sat the other side of Melkana. It was a cheerful bunch where everyone seemed to like each other. Mickie remembered that Melkana had told him at the first meeting that their parents were old friends.

Food started to flow to the tables and Mickie was astonished to receive, not the fare that he had become used to aboard ship, but what looked and tasted exactly like English roast beef and Yorkshire pudding with gravy, sweet potatoes and horse-radish sauce.

"How did they know?" he asked Grant in amazement.

Grant chuckled. "It's traditional to serve off-world guests with the food of their home planet, so we had some questions from our host and it looks like they did pretty well."

"I'll say!" Mickie tucked into his plate with great enthusiasm and was not surprised when, a little later, his dessert was his absolute favourite from England, Sherry Trifle.

"That looks yummy!" Melkana was studying his bowl with considerable interest.

"Have some," Mickie suggested and she slid a spoon into the bowl and took a mouthful, her expression indicating utter delight at the taste. Mickie felt like a prince at the Royal Ball and decided this was just the best day ever.

After the plates had been cleared, the general mingling resumed. At one point, as the four kids chatted together, they were approached by Kr'Horzash, the X'Kasxi crewmember who had invited them to stay. He was accompanied by three others, two female and one male. He bowed to all of them and introduced the female by his side.

"My friends and colleagues, may I introduce my wife, Bj'Horzash of the House of Pr'Krujinsk?"

One of the females bowed also.

"And this is my sister, Etr'Horzash. It is her child that we will see birthed tomorrow. This is her husband, Utr'Klapthin of the House of Ftr'Klapthin.

All bowed to each other, Mickie hoping against hope that Albert had noted all the names and could prompt him when needed. But he was also feeling confused. The mother-to-be looked as slender as any other female in the room and yet would give birth the next day? He had met several pregnant women back home, mothers of his friends at school or one or two elder sisters, or friends of his mother, and they had always looked enormous if they were any time close to having their children. And how could they know that tomorrow would be the day? He felt baffled.

As polite words were exchanged, Mickie noticed the eyebrows of the four X'Kasxi. The two men had very small bone outcroppings over their eyes, so shallow that they did indeed look like human eyebrows. Their colleague and his brother-in-law (if that was the actual relationship – Mickie decided he had better ask Albert about family structures with the X'Kasxi) both had narrow, dark lines above and below the bone, which outlined and somehow pointed out how small they were. But with the two women, bright, colourful patterns had been painted all round the line of bone, making it the central feature of the faces in the way that Earth women used eyeliner and lipstick. Mickie found it very appealing and thought it was a fashion style that could really take the fancy of girls back in England.

After a few minutes of courteous conversation, the three moved on to mingle with other guests. A little later, Allie and Grant joined them.

"Probably time for you kids to be in bed," Grant said firmly. "The drugs are helping, but it's still a long day for you and tomorrow will be even longer."

"I think you're right," Melkana agreed. "I could do with flopping into that enormous bed."

"Allie, we just met the mother-to-be for tomorrow," Mickie said. "How do they know when all this is happening? And why does she show no signs of being pregnant?"

"It beats me, son," Allie replied. "I'm very excited by this, because the whole basis of birth, this Soul-Reading and everything else is all a secret to us. We don't even know how long a pregnancy lasts, in fact we know almost nothing, even though we've been partners with the X'Kasxi for over a hundred years. So we'll probably learn a great deal tomorrow and believe me, there are hundreds of thousands of people around the known worlds who are waiting for the information. We are really greatly honoured."

"Do we get to meet the Guide?" Fencris asked.

"Tomorrow," Grant replied. "At the soul-reading ceremony. Now, off to bed!"

Cheerfully enough, the friends obeyed and found their way back to their rooms. As he entered, Mickie took one more look at Melkana and decided that she really did look pretty awesome that evening.

Chapter 19 - The Reading of Souls

They were served breakfast in their room the following morning. For Mickie, this was a first-time ever experience, and coupled with the sheer luxury of their surroundings, he enjoyed it to the fullest. The menu augmented the pleasure – eggs and bacon, mushrooms and fried potatoes, exactly the breakfast he had eaten the first time he had met Allie and the memory of that meeting made him feel happier than he could recall.

After another wild bout of splashing in the pool, they donned freshly washed shipboard tunics and were ready when the servant tapped on the door again. Mickie came to earth rapidly as he remembered that he was now to witness a birthing ceremony, and he was most uncertain of how he would handle this.

His confusion and uncertainty were increased when the servant led them to the entrance hall, picking up Melkana on the way. There in the middle of the hall was the couple he had met the previous evening, the sister and brother-in-law (if those were the X'Kasxi relationships) of the crewman. The wife looked cheerful and excited, but was she not about to give birth? Mickie looked his puzzlement at his friends and all seemed to echo his confusion. To his relief, the three sets of their parents were also there and the four friends joined them.

"Allie, how can she...?" Mickie began and was rapidly silenced by a short gesture from his mother. He decided all this was very strange and tried a silent question to Albert.

"I'm sorry, Mickie, I cannot explain this," Albert replied in his mind. "We know nothing of the physical aspects of child birth with the X'Kasxi, nor of this ceremony you are about to witness. This is why so many thousands of academics and others are so excited by the honour you have been granted and are waiting eagerly for our description. I can only ask you to stay silent and follow your parents' example. They have so much more experience in cross-species cultural learning."

The expecting couple were standing together with another couple, almost in a traditional wedding group with a best man and a bridesmaid. They had their heads bowed and the silence in the hall was absolute.

A gong sounded from some distant point, and the four in the central party started to walk down the left corridor, followed by the thirty or so others in the hall. At the end, a large doorway opened as they approached, and they filed in to find a large room. In the centre of the room was an enclosed space surrounded by glass, with seats round the walls all looking inward to the glass room. The central party of four went to the far end and took seats while the rest of the group found seats at the opposite end. Mickie was quite baffled. He looked into the glass enclosure and there was nothing but a pure white, polished floor. However, he realised that the aisle around the enclosure was only on three sides and the fourth side was connected to the side of the viewing room. As he looked, a door opened on that side and a group of X'Kasxi entered, pushing a trolley. It was an ornate construction of metal, with the House colours of green and white draped round the sides and a cushion of pure white on top. But the object the trolley carried finally indicated what was happening.

It was an egg, about the size of a Rugby football, a mixture of mottled white, blue and red in colour.

As he realised what he was seeing, Albert's voice echoed in his head. "Your mother asks me to tell you that she now realises that the X'Kasxi are not mammalian. They produce eggs, not children by live birth. What we are about to see is the birth of the pup from that egg."

Mickie glanced quickly at his friends and saw that they had just received the same information. He turned his attention back to the centre of the enclosure. One of the attendants had produced a fearsome looking knife that gleamed in the lights of the room. The knife was placed at one end of the egg and a slice was made right through to the other end. The attendant then peeled back the edges of what looked like a soft shell. At the other end of the room, the young parents of the pup were sitting quietly, showing no sign of excitement or tension that Mickie could identify.

The attendant reached inside and carefully extracted the tiny shape. It looked no more than perhaps twenty centimetres long to Mickie's eyes, but he could see that it was humanoid, tiny arms and legs wriggling actively. The new pup was placed on the cushion alongside the egg, which was then removed and left on the floor. The other attendants carefully washed the newborn and wrapped it in green cloth taken from under the cart. The cart was pushed to the edge of the room to the new parents who stood and silently examined their child, still showing no obvious emotion. The attendants left the room, leaving the parents alone with their child.

The couple turned and pushed the cart with its occupant toward the transparent wall and Mickie followed the example of the rest by standing as the child was placed by the glass for inspection. It looked awfully ugly to him and he was a little startled to see that the pup seemed to have quite a large, pointed horn standing out of its forehead. After a few seconds, the parents and child left by the entrance they had used before and vanished.

"Mickie, your mother asked me to pass on her conclusion that the pup would normally release itself from the egg, using the horn you saw to cut through the soft shell." Albert's voice spoke softly inside Mickie's head. "Using a knife appears to be part of a ritual, though she is unsure what the significance is. She thinks the horn probably falls off after a few days."

Mickie sat down, still feeling quite baffled. The whole thing had been quite unemotional. But more was to come. A gong sounded again and the entire visitors' party moved to the far end, through a door that opened as they reached it and turned right, following a corridor that seemed to lead to the room to which the pup had just been taken. Mickie found that it did, and they entered that room to find lavish luxury. It was much like his bedroom, he decided, but instead of beds, there were lines of deep cushions along one side, and a small podium opposite those. The guests took seats, sitting cross-legged on the cushions while the new parents went to the podium.

A door opened just behind the podium and in walked

the Guide, X'Kaa Tz'Horzash, wearing pure white robes. He bowed to the couple and received bows in return, and the first words were spoken.

"I see you, Utr'Klarshin of the House of Ftr'Klarshin," the Guide said and bowed to the male.

"I see you, X'Kaa Tz'Horzash," replied the new father and bowed again.

"I see you, Etr'Horzash of the House of Tz'Horzash," said the Guide and bowed to the female.

"I see you, X'Kaa Tz'Horzash," she replied.

All three took seats on the podium and the door opened again to reveal one of the attendants carrying the new pup. The attendant gently placed the bundle in the arms of the Guide, who held it closely with seeming great affection and bowed his head over the child. Total silence fell in the room.

It lasted by Mickie's estimation two or three minutes, then the Guide spoke.

"The child is a fine addition to the House of Tz'Horzash," he said. "His *m'rrhai* is strong and he may go to Hr'Mong. This child is a third stage Old Soul and he will be best placed in academic studies, then to become a teacher. He will help and guide other, more junior souls. He brings us closer to The One. Now you may take your child."

He handed the bundle to the mother who took it silently, but this time it looked to Mickie that both parents showed happiness and possibly relief as they bent over their child.

The witnesses rose to their feet and filed out and returned to the hallway where they had first met. Mickie was bursting with questions but decided he had to restrain his curiosity for fear of causing unwitting offence. He stood by his mother and waited until she could talk to him. She was standing by Kr'Horzash, the crewman from the ship.

"We are deeply honoured that you have permitted us to witness this wonderful event," Allie said. "May we ask some questions?"

"Yes, but I may not be able to answer them all," he replied.

"I understand. What is at Hr'Mong?"

"It is the family school to which all our children go after their birth if accepted by the Guide. There, they will be taught how to live and behave as a member of the House and they will receive the essential education that all citizens must have as a minimum."

"And how long will they stay there?"

"Until their tenth year. At that time, they will again go before the Guide for a final reading. If they have developed as planned, they will be brought into the House as full members and begin their professional training."

"Can a child fail that second reading?"

"Rarely, but it happens. But sometimes a pup is born who it is decided at the stage you have just witnessed will not enter the House. They will be taken to the school, but at the Year Ten reading, they will be directed elsewhere."

"May I ask how long the gestation period was for the child?"

"Half a year. It can vary by ten days either side, but it is always half a year."

"How did you know that the birth would be today?"

"The breeders are highly trained medical people. From the time they receive the egg immediately after it has been produced, they tend it in ideal conditions of heat and light, monitoring it carefully. The signals of imminent birth are quite accurate and we know to within minutes, two days ahead, when the child is ready."

"Can you tell me what is the process of reading the soul?"

"No, Alliandra, I cannot. However, the Guide has invited you to meet with him in a few minutes and he may tell you, but I must warn you that he may not be able to describe the process."

"I see." Allie bowed her head slightly in acknowledgement. "Then can you tell me what the Guide meant by the term "third stage Old Soul"?

"Alliandra, I have been advised that such knowledge is not to be passed to you. That must remain within the House."

Allie seemed a little shaken by that firm refusal. "Is the term itself to be kept secret? May I discuss it with others when I leave here?"

"The Guide has advised me that it is becoming time for others to learn about such things, so there is no requirement that you do not discuss it. But it is not yet time for you to learn more."

Mickie stood silently with his father and friends and watched the discussion. He knew that something hugely important had been learned, but the door to new knowledge had been opened only a tiny fraction.

"Then we thank you most sincerely for letting us be part of today." Allie smiled warmly at the X'Kasxi. "Is it now time to visit the Guide?"

"Yes, it is. Let me instruct you in proper procedures. I will take you to the same room that we have just left and ask you to take seats as before. The podium will have gone and the meeting will be far more informal. Before the Guide enters, you will be served with cups of mint tea, but please wait until the Guide has sat down before you and greeted each of you before drinking. There is no need to stand as he enters. The mode of greeting is as you saw, but the Guide will only greet the adults in this way. He will at some stage ask to meet the children and each child should give his name without any formal words. Once the Guide has greeted the adults, you will be free to ask questions."

He turned and led the way back down the corridors to the room they had just left. As he said, the podium had gone and the cushions were scattered in far less formal arrangement than before. The six adults and four children sat down and within moments, servants appeared with small pots and tiny cups, poured mint tea into each cup and smoothly departed. They sat silently, Mickie observing his mother obviously deep in intense thought. After only a few seconds, the door opened and the Guide appeared, seating himself in front of the waiting group.

"I see you, Grantorel," he said softly.

"I see you, X'Kaa Tz'Horzash," Grant replied, and the formality went round each of the adults.

"And these are the children?" The Guide's manner became warm and friendly. "Come and sit with me, children."

He waited until the four had moved closer to him, and then took a sip of his tea, letting everyone else do the same.

"Did you learn much from this morning?" he asked, putting down his cup.

"Indeed we did, Guide, and we owe you sincere thanks for letting us witness it," Allie replied.

"But you have questions, of course?"

"Of course." Allie smiled in response to the warmth and friendliness the old Guide was showing. "First, can you tell us what exactly you do when you read the child's soul, his *m'rrhai?*"

"That is not easy. I see into the soul in a way I cannot describe, but I read the strength of his *m'rrhai* as colours. The stronger the hues, the stronger the soul-strength."

"Do those colours mean anything?"

"They tell me the nature of the child's soul."

"The nature? What is that?"

But the Guide looked downward at his cup and took another drink. Clearly, the question was out of bounds.

"And how do you tell where the child's development lies?"

The old Guide looked up from his cup as if to acknowledge the question, then lowered his gaze to the floor in deep thought. "That is perhaps experience. But I am not alone in that reading."

"Not alone?" Mickie heard the shock in Allie's tone.

"I too am guided."

"By whom?" There was an urgency in Allie's voice that had Mickie feeling on edge. Something very powerful was happening.

Again the Guide paused then briefly looked at Mickie. He felt a massive jolt of energy pass through him as their eyes met and he let out a small gasp. Allie looked curiously at him then returned her intense look to the Guide.

"You have met the Harliya," the Guide said. "You know that they live many lives, living on another plane between each life."

"They tell us that. We have no real way of knowing how true it is," replied Allie.

"It is true. But they do not yet know of a plane above that one."

"But they do!" Mickie could not hold back the words. "They told me that they know there is a plane above, because many souls do not come back after living lots of lives."

The Guide returned his eyes to Mickie and intense interest showed there.

"So the Harliya are progressing," he murmured, more to himself. "That is interesting." He returned his eyes to Allie. "Very advanced souls live on that Ascendant Plane," he said. "One of those is my guide."

"Ascendant Plane? Can you tell us more of what that means?"

"No, it is not yet time for you to know."

Mickie felt a small chill, remembering how the Spiders had used the same words to him.

Allie paused in thought for a second. "When you referred to the child as a third-stage Old Soul, what did you mean?"

"We live many lives, Alliandra. We pass through stages of growth and learning with each life."

"What are those stages?"

"That I will not tell you. It is not time for you to know."

"But do all species pass through such stages of soul growth by reincarnation?"

"We are all part of The One."

"Can you explain that?"

"I will not."

"Then I must ask, why have you told us so much and why will you not tell us more?"

"Because it is time that you started to learn. But not everything at once."

"Why is it time now?"

"The Kindred are a very old race, Alliandra, far older than any of you, even the Kaloti. Learning about The One must come to you in time. It is now time for you to start that learning."

"How do you know that, Guide?"

"My Guide tells me. I do not know from where he gets that knowledge or instruction."

The silence rang like a bell in the room.

"Guide, does this have anything to do with the vanished race of the Shurameen?" Allie asked from out of the silence.

The old man's head lifted sharply and he gave a piercing stare. "It does." Mickie thought his answer was given with reluctance.

"And with the current rapid disappearance of the Kaloti?"

"That too."

The Guide held up one hand as Allie was about to ask another question as if to block further questions on a topic that was out of bounds. "Now I must meet the children," he said. He turned and faced Drellion. "What is your name, young man?"

"Drellion, Guide."

"Take my hands, Drellion."

For a few seconds, they sat like that, the Guide smiling gently. "You have a powerful soul, Drellion," he said at last. "You will achieve greatness as a leader of your people. Your family can be proud."

He dropped the boy's hand and turned to Fencris, taking both his hands. "And your name?"

"Fencris, Guide."

A similar process was followed before the Guide spoke again. "This is another powerful soul. Your work will be in the sciences, in mathematics, in engineering. Many problems will fall before that intellect. Great honour will come to you and your family."

When he took Melkana's hand, he smiled a most human smile. "Yours is a soul of great beauty, child. There is music, art, there is great warmth in you. You will bring happiness to many people."

He turned to Mickie and took his hands.

"I am Mickie, Guide."

The Guide's eyes widened perceptibly and Mickie felt the pressure on his hands increase.

"Who are you, Mickie? These are not your parents." His tone was sharp.

"No Guide. I was found on Earth."

"But you are not of Earth. And Earth is not yet on the travel routes of any of our species."

"No, Guide. My parents and the Speakers say I am not from there, but I don't know where I'm from."

The Guide sat motionless for another few seconds, but Mickie felt the slight trembling in the hands holding his.

"There is huge power in you, Mickie. But it can be a dangerous power. I can read very little beyond that power. And you have very great dangers to face."

He released Mickie's hands and seemed lost in thought for a few moments. But when he looked up again, the warmth and friendship was evident.

"I invite you to one more ceremony," he said to the group at large. "Tomorrow we will be reading for the Tenth Year at Hr'Mong. I would like you to be there."

With that, he stood up and walked out quickly.

* * *

"There is a term I heard on Earth," said Allie into the silence. "The term is gobsmacked. I tell you now, I am gobsmacked by what we have just heard."

"I think we learned more about the X'Kasxi today than ever before," Grant agreed. "I'd like some backup here. Speaker 356 are you with us?"

"Yes, Grantorel," said the voice from millions of light years away. "I read all the people with you and will include them in my communication."

"Thank you, Speaker. Will you review my memories of what we just heard from the Guide?"

"I have reviewed all your memories. These were interesting revelations."

"In all your contacts with X'Kasxi, Speaker, did you not learn anything of this in the last few hundred years?"

"No, we have learned nothing of this. The X'Kasxi have highly disciplined minds as befits a race so old and with that culture. They have never permitted our residence in their minds. Their use of our services to communicate across light years has always been for messages only and they have never permitted other forms of contact."

Allie entered the conversation. "Have any other species made reference to the terms "Ascendant Plane" or "The One," Speaker? Particularly the Shurameen and the Kaloti."

A silence of a few seconds lasted in the room before the Speaker replied.

"I have checked with all my colleagues. Some recall both terms occurring between Kaloti clients, but no explanation or further details were ever given. No traces of such terms occurred with the Shurameen."

"This is quite stunning," Allie said. "We've been given new data about the nature of spiritual life almost as if it were to some planned schedule. But the most astonishing things is that there is some link between these data and the disappearance of two complete races from the universe."

"And I don't think the Guide was quite ready for you to make that connection," said Grant, confirming Mickie's own view of what he had seen and heard.

"I think you're right," Allie said.

"And what astonished me most," said Devenar, the first words Mickie had heard him say since the Guide had left, "is that the Guide offered direct evidence for a spiritual afterlife for all intelligent species. This will shake all of us to our roots and have profound impacts on religious practices in all the species."

"That is certainly true," Allie said. "Speaker, will you transmit the details of our experiences this morning to all those waiting for them?"

"It is done, Alliandra," the Speaker replied.

"Then there is also the issue of the Guide's reaction to Mickie," Grant said. "He was obviously shaken by something and immediately recognized Mickie as something other than Human or Kalamosian."

"Just like the X'Kasxi troopers in the shuttle," Mickie said. "They seemed disturbed by something about me."

There was silence for a few seconds as everybody thought about the implications. Finally, Allie expressed what everybody was thinking. "The X'Kasxi are becoming a more interesting species as time goes on," she said. "They seem to have some secrets to the Universe that nobody else has."

"Do you think they may know about the Pfafth and aren't telling?" Mickie asked.

"Possibly, but if they do, how could they have kept it from the Speakers all these years?" Grant said. "They use the Speakers for telepathic communication as much as anyone, and it would be impossible to keep all stray thoughts about something as critical as long-lost, powerful species locked away. The Speakers would have been bound to pick up something."

"I suppose," Mickie said sadly. "I was just hoping somebody would know something about me."

"It will happen," Allie said. "Something this big is going to take time."

"And it's time for lunch," said Grant, breaking the melancholy mood in Mickie.

* * *

The long afternoon passed casually and without excitement. Mickie was more than happy to spend time playing in the pool and Melkana joined them, though she had a similar pool attached to her room.

"Water is the basis of life to the species," Albert explained when Mickie asked him about this amazing luxury. "The X'Kasxi ancestry is reptilian as you now know, and they share the same need to spend much time in water as do crocodiles and other animals on Earth. So while the pools you have are certainly grand and large, they are considered essential for any household. There is even one on the Ship, but it is located in the X'Kasxi crew sections and not open for use by other crew members."

"But does that mean that every house has one?" Mickie asked.

"We still are not certain. Logic suggests that poorer families may have only tiny pools, perhaps only access to a public pool. Our observations do show many public pools in the city, but we are still at the early stages of learning about this species."

Dinner was as splendid an affair as the previous evening, with fresh ceremonial clothing again appearing on their beds when they had finished with the water sports and all four children were happy enough to go to bed when their parents suggested it. The drugs were certainly helping them to acclimatize to the long days and nights, but the extra activity level still left them very fatigued by the evening. And Mickie knew he had been part of an extraordinary day where new knowledge had been revealed that had great impact on the whole universe of intelligent species.

The next morning after breakfast, a bus was ready for them and the six adults and four children boarded as requested by their servants.

"It is a half-hour ride to Hr'Mong," one of them said as they climbed aboard, and the estimate was accurate. The trip was not back into the city but further out into quite featureless countryside before they reached a single level building nearly half a kilometer in length. As the bus stopped by the front entrance, they were greeted by several X'Kasxi, all dressed in the green and white robes of the House of Tz'Horzash. Some minutes were taken up by the formal greetings and bows exchanged between the adults.

"I am Ftr'Horzash," said the obvious leader, a female Mickie saw from her earflaps. "I am what you would understand as the Principal of this educational institute. I am also a Guide, but very junior as such people go, and I have many years of training ahead of me before I can accept such a huge responsibility."

She led them inside to an entry lobby of sizeable proportions.

"My instructions are to let you observe a Ten Year Reading," she said. "But as you understand, such a moment is most critical both to the student and his or her parents and very difficult to all, and to have strangers, particularly off-worlders would be both stressful and offensive to the family. So you will watch from an observation room next to the ceremonial room. You will be able to see and hear everything, but those in the room will not see you."

"We understand," said Melkana's father. "And again, we are grateful for the opportunity to observe this critical moment in a child's life."

The Principal was being very formal, thought Mickie and he sensed that she was not at all comfortable with having these strangers in her school.

"May we see the rest of the school?" Grant asked.

"My instructions are not to permit that," the Principal replied and the finality of her comment was most obvious. She led the way along the corridor to one side and opened the door to a room. It reminded Mickie of the rooms he had seen in police dramas, where the suspect was interrogated on one side of a one-way mirror while observers watched from the other side. Through the wall-to-ceiling window in front of them was a room almost identical to the one in which they had watched the soul reading of a newborn pup the previous day. A small podium sat on one side, and across from that, just four or five metres away, was a solitary cushion.

"There are two students who have reached their Tenth year today," the Principal said. "The process will start in a few minutes, so I must leave you here and attend to the ceremony."

She left without further words, and Grant smiled at the group. "I got the impression she was not at all happy to see us here," he said.

"I can understand," Melkana's mother replied. "I think we are offending some traditional values."

Short nods and grunts of agreement ran through the group, then all turned to see the room in front of them. The Principal had appeared with a smaller individual, presumably the child, who took his seat on the single cushion. She left, and a servant appeared, depositing a pot of the mint tea, Mickie assumed from yesterday's experience, by the side of the child and pouring a small amount into a cup before leaving. The child sat perfectly still and Mickie tried to imagine what he was going through, about to have his entire life decided for him in the next few moments.

The door behind the podium opened and the Guide, X'Kaa Tz'Horzash entered, again wearing white robes. He was accompanied by the Principal and by two more X'Kasxi, presumably the child's parents. All four took their seats on the podium and a servant again appeared and poured the mint tea.

"I see you, Jl Tz'Horzash," said the Guide.

"I see you, X'Kaa Tz'Horzash," the child replied.

Mickie thought he detected a slight tremble of nervousness in the voice, even through the microphones and the translator device.

The Guide took a sip of tea and the others followed suit. The silence echoed for over a minute while the Guide seemed to concentrate on an infinite distance.

"You will enter the House of Tz'Horzash this day," said the Guide, and Mickie could see a small releasing of tension in the bodies of the child and his two parents. "You have the skills and the intellect to become an engineer who will build great buildings and that is your own inclination as you have known for the last two years. Tomorrow you will move to the University in the capital city and commence your studies. The House of Tz'Horzash makes you welcome."

The child rose to his feet and advanced on the Guide who took his hands for a few seconds. The warmth and the welcome in his posture were obvious to Mickie who had seen the same reaction yesterday to his friends and himself. The child then moved and bowed formally to his parents who inclined their heads in return and he moved back to the door by which he had entered and left the room.

At the podium, the Guide and the other three also rose, bowed at each other and the Guide left first, followed by the parents and then the Principal.

Allie let out a sigh of released tension. "Imagine it," she said. "Ten years old, about fifteen in Earth years and you have spent your whole life waiting for this moment, always wondering if you will make it and be accepted into your family. The self control and discipline of these people is astonishing."

Two servants entered the ceremonial room, removed

the pots of tea and the cups and straightened out the cushions. A few minutes later, the process began again, with the Principal escorting in another child who took his place on the cushion and received a pot of tea and a cup from the servant. Mickie studied him and confirmed that he was indeed a male, but unlike the previous one, this child had quite marked bone outcroppings over his eyes. It was the first time he had seen this phenomenon, because all the X'Kasxi he had met on this visit had very fine lines over their eyes, often enhanced by the black lines and coloured designs.

The Guide returned with two more parents and the Principal and the formal greeting ceremony was repeated. This time, Mickie could see great tension in the body of the young student and he waited for the Guide to finish his concentration.

"There can be no place for you in the House of Tz'Horzash," said the Guide.

A deep silence echoed in the room through the window. The only sound Mickie heard was a short intake of breath from Melkana. He watched the young X'Kasxi sitting on the cushion and could detect no sign of shock or other emotion.

"I read this in you at your birth," continued the Guide. "I read then that you were a Young Soul, just second stage, far too immature to follow any of the professions that we of this House must follow. You have suspected this yourself the last two years, we know, because you have had increasing difficulties with your studies here."

"The poor kid," Melkana whispered. "How terrible to sit there in front of your parents and hear yourself be ejected from your family. What happens to him now?"

Her question was answered immediately.

"You must not take this as failure," the old Guide continued. "Because it is not your failing that you were born with a soul too immature for the rigours of the great Houses of the Kindred. It is only that a different path opens up for you and this may yet be a more satisfying and rewarding path. You will go to the spaceport this afternoon and you will lift to the Kaloti ship in orbit above us. We have arranged with the captain that you will join as a crewman and learn how to be part of that life travelling the Universe of the One."

"He's coming with us!" Melkana seemed delighted. "Oh, he'll have a lot more fun on the ship than in this stuffy place!"

She received a warning glance from her parents and subsided with a small smile still on her face. "We'll look after him!" she whispered softly to Mickie and he grinned back at her with a pleasant sense of a shared conspiracy.

The ceremony had concluded and the child was left alone as the adults left. He sat still for another minute as if frozen, then slowly climbed to his feet and left the room also.

"That was pretty shattering," Allie commented. "Poor little chap. As Melkana said, that must be a distressing experience. He's been kicked out of his own family unit because he's too immature."

"But we heard more about this soul maturity concept," Grant said. "A Young Soul, the Guide said, a second stage Young Soul. This is all very weird. So we know that they believe there are young souls and old souls. I wonder if they have other ages?"

"And what was that stuff about 'The Universe of The One?'" Selvana, Fencris' mother asked. "That term, 'The One' has risen before, also."

"All in all, this has been a stunningly informative trip," Allie said. "But it's raised an awful lot more questions than we have answered."

"We've certainly had more insight into the religion of the X'Kasxi than ever before," Selvana added.

The discussion ended as the Principal entered.

"Your transport is ready," she said, and Mickie thought he detected a note of relief in her tones, even through the interpreter device. They followed her out and were back at the house within an hour.

Two days later, the transport holds laden with mineral ores, the ship left orbit with one more visit to make before returning to the home world of Kalamos for a much-needed vacation for the crew.

Chapter 20 – The Old Times of Merrison

"I'm really sorry you two can't come down with us on this trip," Mickie said as they worked on breakfast in their favourite coffee lounge.

"Can you imagine the mess I'd cause if I came along?" Fencris chuckled at the thought. "A primitive society like that where everyone looks like you lot, and they suddenly see a kid with a blue face, red eyes and no nose? We'd be lucky if we got out alive!"

"That's the problem," Melkana said. "They're really primitive. They still believe in witchcraft, so they'd really think you were the devil."

"Sounds like fun! I could go down there and yell curses at people or use a couple of my little anti-gravity machines to float around and I'd bet I could rule the world!"

"Just imagine what the Captain would say if you did!" Melkana looked half amused and half horrified. "The rules are so strict about letting primitive people know about off-world life. You'd spend the next century in the brig!"

"But just think about the legends he'd create!" Mickie was laughing at the idea. "I wonder if all those stories of demons and witches back on Earth all resulted from some crazy Cassolean kids borrowing a shuttle and looking in on Earth?"

"Probably my great granddad!" laughed Fencris. "He was nuts and he was a security agent on a ship for most of his life."

"I can believe it, if he was anything like you!" Melkana said, and the rest of the breakfast passed in great good spirits before Melkana and Mickie had to go and be measured up for local clothing for the visit to Merrison.

The group in the shuttle was the smallest Mickie had known since his first trip, his departure from Earth and the arrival on the ship. Just his parents, Melkana's parents, Melkana and he sat in the comfortable seats as the shuttle descended softly through the atmosphere, deliberately flying slowly as so as to make as little noise as possible and cloaked to avoid visual detection. He decided that he thoroughly enjoyed having that precise group. They had become the closest people in his whole life, just missing Drellion and Fencris to make it complete.

They all looked quite different from their normal appearances, he saw with amusement. The three women were dressed alike. They had long dresses in a dull brown colour, long sleeves that ended in flowing lace that covered the hands. Straw hats sat atop their heads from which the hair flowed freely, the only colour allowed to mediate the dullness of the garb being the red rose on the side of the straw hats.

"Both our planets have a time period of a culture similar to the one you will encounter," Allie said as part of a general briefing. "Neither of you two children has been here before, so it's vital that you know how to behave. If referring to your parents, each of you should use the terms 'Mother' and 'Father' and you should refer to the other parents as 'Squire' and 'Mistress.' Mickie, you must use our Kalamosian names here, so I will be known as Mistress Alliandra and your father as Squire Grantorel. So Melkana's parents are Squire Harrokarn and Mistress Mendorina. These name types fit within the Merrison structures, and you should give your name as the formal 'Michael,' which is near enough to the local name "Mikeel" to pass without question. You will be referred to as Master Michael. Our translators will interpret these titles to the precise equivalent in the Merrison dialect. And remember to keep your face covered below the eyes, both for courtesy and to hide the fact that your lip movements won't match the sounds made by your translators."

She looked round at the panels on the sides of the shuttle and nodded. "It's late evening in the town of Jelderan where we'll be touching down in fifteen minutes. Remember that we are all traders from the region of Krayandort, which is on a distant continent and so it is most unlikely that we will encounter anyone else from that region. If we do, do not get engaged in conversation about your home, make some excuse and curtail the discussion. The language of that region is one of the two from this planet that are programmed into the translators, so you'll be able to converse successfully. We're here to meet with our agents and obtain a close-up of how things are developing. And we *are* trading, for real. This planet produces some wonderful spices and we will truly buy a few hundred kilos. We'll store them in a warehouse outside the town and load them to the shuttle at night."

The briefing had been given before, but Mickie was happy to get a repeat. He felt a little nervous on this visit, worried that he might give the game away by some inadvertent word or action.

"Both our agents are waiting for us," Grant said, emerging from the concentrated silence of communication with the two men on the planet's surface. "They have horses and a passenger cart for the ladies and the two kids."

Melkana's father had also been silent, concentrating on piloting the shuttle through the control devices that were implanted in his body. "Planet-fall in two minutes," he murmured. "We'll in the woods about ten kilometres out of town as our men suggested."

"Speaker 356 confirms that there is nobody within two kilometres," Grant added. "Our guys want to come in and have a drink before we move to the city," he continued.

"I'm not surprised," Mendorina, Melkana's mother chuckled. "This continent has some puritanical influences and a ban on liquor has been in force for decades. I believe Baldorest has picked up your taste for scotch whiskey."

"That comes from being our neighbour at home," Allie said with a laugh.

"He's our neighbour?" Mickie was surprised.

"When he's home, sure. He and I were at University together."

Grant let out a loud laugh. "I've already told Mickie that! And that he was Alliandra's boyfriend at the time!"

The chuckles ran round the shuttlecraft's cabin and Allie tried to hide a small blush. "Well, you soon put a stop to that!" she said. "Luckily, Baldorest doesn't seem to hold it against you."

"Okay, people, business!" Harrokarn cut through the merriment. "We're down."

The door opened and Mickie saw the strange green light that came from the cloaking device reflecting off the trees near their landing spot. Two men walked in and the door closed again. Both were dressed in the same manner as the men in the shuttlecraft and they brought in with them the smell of old clothes, soil and wet leaves.

"Alliandra!" The larger of the two men emitted a bellow of delight and strode up to Allie, lifted her from her seat and swung her round, depositing her back on the ground with a kiss on her cheek. "My favourite woman in the whole universe!" He towered a good head over her and his bulk made the shuttle cabin seem a lot smaller. His face radiated friendliness, with a huge smile. He advanced on Grant and took his hand with an enthusiastic grip.

"And Grantorel, you old reprobate! It's great to see you and why haven't you poured the scotch yet?"

"Baldorest, you haven't changed! Sit down and I'll get to the drinks!"

Amid laughter and the welcome of old friends, introductions were made. The second newcomer, Candrost was a lot quieter and smaller, with a sharp, intelligent face and eyes that sparkled with humour. Mickie decided he liked both of them a lot.

With scotch glasses in the hands of the adults and sparkling helpings of *Sle'Ach* being sipped by the two youngsters, the group got down to business.

"As you know, we've been providing daily news briefings through the Speakers to you about what's going on here, and it's not good news," Baldorest started. "From what was just a straight-forward society of the time, behaving as we expected, it's become a strictly Puritanical world with some startling manifestations of religious fanaticism that have developed in just the last year."

"Have you been able to identify what's causing this?" Allie was looking worried.

"It seems to be a movement that started in the southern parts of the continent," Candrost said. "We can't identify any specific person who is behind this, so it looks like a social development that we never anticipated and for which we must have missed the earlier signs."

"It's very weird." Mendorina clearly shared Allie's worries. "This has all grown in such a short time, and when that happens, there's usually some charismatic leader behind it."

"Agreed," said Baldorest with a nod. "If there is one, we can't locate him."

"Have the Speakers been able to help?" asked Mendorina.

Baldorest grimaced. "That's what worries me most. They haven't. They can detect the emotions and unrest, but they've been unable to pinpoint a specific individual causing it."

"Then I agree, that is definitely a cause for concern," Allie replied.

"So how does that affect our visit this time?" Grant asked.

"Not a lot. Just be a little more careful about the face coverings, because if anyone got offended, that could cause some unpleasantness, never mind the possibility of them seeing the lack of synchronisation between lip movements and speech. That could brand you as a witch and then all hell would break loose. But the growing religious intensity is also causing suspicions and some paranoia, so we must be triply careful to do nothing that could raise any doubts about our identities."

"This is very worrying," Harrokarn said. "I wonder if we should leave the kids behind?"

Before either Mickie or Melkana could raise an objection, the agents did it for them.

"No, I think it would make things easier if the kids come with us," Candrost said. "It will emphasise the family picture, make you a lot easier to accept as travellers and traders. But kids, I must emphasise, you'll have to restrain the energy a bit. That means no running around on your own and you'll have to keep the noise level down. Treat any adults you talk to with great respect, call them Squire or Mistress, always give way to them if necessary, and all that traditional behaviour. Will you be okay?"

The two youngsters nodded, and Candrost gave them a warm smile. "You'll be fine." He stood up. "Time we should be going," he said. "We have a carriage and horses outside, and it's about five kilometres to the town. We reserved rooms for you at a small hotel, nothing too obvious. You have local currency?"

Grant nodded. "We'd better do an external scan before we leave. Mickie, why don't you scan the area and see if you see anything the shuttle's scanner doesn't?"

Mickie applied his new powers and stretched his mind outside the ship for as far as he could. "Nobody I can see," he said. "But you'd better have a second opinion, I can't always be sure this thing is working."

"Agreed," Grant said with a smile. "Speaker 356, any signs of humanoid presence outside?" He listened to a voice focused only at him, nodded and looked round the cabin. "Let's go," he commanded. "Grownups, make sure you take a breath cleaner before we reach town to hide the smell of the alcohol."

The rest of the group rose to their feet, gathered their bags and walked through the door to the outside. A warm summer's darkness greeted them, insects reverberated from the trees, and occasional bird noises added a counterpoint. It felt like a summer's night on Earth to Mickie and for a few seconds he felt deeply nostalgic.

An open carriage was parked a few metres away, two horses were attached to it, and four more horses waited patiently.

"Ladies and kids in the carriage," Grant commanded, and waited while the two adults climbed aboard, followed by Melkana.

"That's quite a trick you have there, Michael." Mickie realised that Baldorest was standing behind him. He turned and looked up at the huge man.

"I can't always do it," he said.

"It's astounding you can do it even some of the time. I didn't know anyone but the Speakers had that power."

"Mickie, come aboard," Allie said from the carriage. "Baldorest, ask my husband about our new son as you ride. He'll brief you on the rather unusual skills he seems to be developing."

Baldorest grinned a huge white smile. "I surely will," he said, and closed the small door behind Mickie as he climbed in and took a seat next to Melkana. With the four men on their horses, the party set off toward the town. At the front, Candrost was carrying a storm lamp within which a small flame flickered, and two more such lamps were suspended from the front of the carriage.

"An interesting parallel development, those horses," Allie murmured softly. "It's very rare that almost identical creatures should develop on planets such vast distances apart. So far, that's only one of just a tiny number we've found on our travels. Of course, Earth humans and Kalamosians are the biggest example and it opens some interesting questions about the origins of life forms around the universe."

The party pulled out of the woods and onto an open road that was more of a track. But it gave the moon a chance to illuminate the scenery. Mickie studied the satellite. It seemed to be about the same size as Earth's moon, but he could see no distinct features on it the way he could on Earth. He settled back and enjoyed the silent countryside and the warm darkness in the company of the people he loved most in the whole universe.

About forty minutes later they arrived in the town. The only light came from the moon and their own lamps, but as they rattled down a street that seemed as wide as a city street, a single flame burned outside a building on a corner. The party came to a halt outside the building and the men tethered their horses to a rail.

"This seems to be home for a few days," Allie said, gathering her bag. "Everyone, pull your veils across your faces and make sure they're fastened."

Once that was done, they left the carriage and entered the hotel. Inside, the gloom was heavy, alleviated only by a few candles at various parts of the lobby. A huge man was standing by the counter, the only person in the entire lobby. Allie and Mendorina moved to stand by the doorway and gently touched their children on the shoulders to stand with them.

"Men do the commercial transactions," Allie whispered softly. "We wait until all that is finished."

The two agents held a short discussion with the large man, a number of notes changed hands and the conversation was too soft for Mickie to hear. But keys were handed over, the guardian gave the two women and the children an intense stare then retreated into a room off the lobby. They were safely booked into their rooms, it appeared.

"Mickie, your father wishes me to advise you of the security arrangements." The quiet voice of Albert, the ship's computer broke into Mickie's thoughts. The computer was communicating through the device implanted in Mickie's shoulder and although it sounded to him as if the voice came from a few inches from his right ear, Mickie knew that it could not be heard outside his head.

"Yes, Albert, what is it?" Mickie silently formed the words and they were transmitted to the computer in the orbiting spaceship. Albert was undoubtedly giving the same details to the others in the same way.

"All of us will meet in your parents' room when you have unpacked. You will be discussing the arrangements for the next two days, the visits to be made and the social engagements that have been set up. You will be able to discuss these, but no other subject must be raised that could cause suspicion. Your communication devices have been programmed so that as you speak, they will emit the language of Krayandort, so that anyone listening in will hear that language spoken. That means you will have to concentrate hard on the translation directed straight to your hearing centres and ignore the audible speech. This is to ensure that nobody hears any other language but that one, or, as required, the local language of this region. Should you wish to communicate privately, make your comments or questions through me and I will transmit back and forth between you."

"Thanks, Albert." Mickie understood the requirement. There must be no suspicion raised at any time that the party was anything but what they claimed to be, traders from Krayandort.

The room he entered with his parents was large, plain, but warm. Candles provided the scant illumination and the smell of wax was the first thing he encountered as he walked in after his parents. One large bed stood against one wall, and a much smaller, single cot was against the other. That would be his, he realised. A well-cushioned sofa stood against the window across which dull brown curtains had been drawn, and four dining chairs surrounded a small circular table.

Simultaneously, he heard Allie's voice in his head and her voice also speaking a quite alien language that was being emitted by her translator in her shoulder. It was a little weird.

"Michael, unpack your clothes and then we will all meet to discuss tomorrow's program."

"Yes, Mother," he said, remembering to be very formal in his mode of address. Allie smiled and blew a kiss in his direction and he grinned happily back at her. He saw Grant smothering a laugh. He unpacked the few clothes he had with him and sat on his bed waiting for everyone to be ready.

Fifteen minutes later, a knock on the door announced the arrival of the two agents and a few seconds later Melkana arrived with her parents. Melkana chose to sit next to Mickie on his bed, and that delighted him. "Hello there, Master Michael," she said with an impish grin.

He struggled to keep a straight face. "Good evening, Miss Melkana, I trust you are well after our long trip?"

"Well enough, Master Michael. I thank you." Both of them had to struggle to stop from laughing and held hands over their mouths, not helped by the fact that the adults in the room were also grinning widely at the by-play. But a signal from Grant stopped the amusement and they concentrated on the meeting. To start, they pretended to hold a formal meeting aloud, to cater for any possible eavesdroppers who might choose to check out the new guests. At first it was dreadfully difficult to concentrate on the internal voices in his head while ignoring the audible and incomprehensible sounds coming from the various translator devices, but after a few minutes he got his mind wrapped round the problem and it became easier from then on.

"What have you set up for us, Squire Baldorest?" Grant asked of his agent.

"This should be a good business trip, Squire Grantorel," Baldorest replied. "Tomorrow morning, we will meet with a group of traders who will offer us several different spices. The season has been best for these..." He handed over a piece of paper. "And the prices requested seem reasonable. I have deposited funds in the local bank and they will accept a draft in full payment."

Grant studied the list and nodded. "Excellent, Squire Baldorest," he said. "What else?"

"Assuming the trades have been agreed, we will spend the afternoon examining the produce in their warehouse and make the arrangements to transfer our purchases to our company warehouse further out of town."

"That sounds good," Grant said.

"And in the evening, we are all invited to an outdoor dinner in the town square and I understand there will be dancing and other entertainment."

"Wonderful." Grant seemed genuinely pleased. "So I think it would be appropriate if we now bowed our heads and prayed silently for a few minutes."

He winked at the room, and silence fell.

"Okay everyone, that gives us a chance to chat without the audible stuff," Grant's voice sounded in Mickie's ear. "If we speak mentally, no sounds will be emitted by our translators and any eavesdropper will think we are praying silently. Is everyone okay with tomorrow's arrangements?"

"It sounds awfully boring," Melkana said.

"Ah, but the ladies are not expected to take part in the manly business of trading," Candrost said with a smile at her. "And that's only a cover, anyway. You two will accompany your mothers on what will appear to be a sightseeing expedition, but it will give the two social scientists a chance to meet people and evaluate what is happening here and perhaps get some insights into what's causing these ugly changes."

"That sounds a lot better," Melkana said. "And the evening sounds fun!"

"It should be," Candrost agreed. "The local dancing can be spectacular and the food is excellent, if rather primitive."

"How do people eat if they have to keep their faces covered?" Melkana seemed amused by the problem.

"Local public eating styles are designed to overcome that," Candrost said. "All food is served in small pieces and eaten with the fingers of one hand, leaving the other to raise the veil enough to slip the piece into the mouth. Be careful not to lift the veil very far, just forward a bit and lean forward to let the veil open enough to slip a hand to the lips. The same with drinks – just small sips. And of course, no talking with the mouth full and be extremely careful when taking something. Be sure you stop talking long enough to put the item to your mouth. Never let anyone see your lips move or they might detect the discrepancy between the movements and the words coming from your translators."

"And now it is time for bed for the children," Allie spoke aloud, and the adults rose to their feet. Melkana touched Mickie's hand and smiled. "See you on the sightseeing tour, Master Michael."

"It will be my pleasure, Mistress Melkana," he replied and both were immediately hit with an attack of suppressed giggles.

At a signal from Baldorest, those who were leaving replaced the veils across their faces and left the room, uttering formal goodnights to all. Mickie found a curtain could be drawn across his cot, and with a sudden attack of fatigue climbed into bed and was asleep within seconds.

Chapter 21 – A Day in the Past

Breakfast was served in their room. Baldorest had explained this was standard practice in hotels to avoid the problem of revealing faces in public, and Mickie was happy with the arrangement.

They ate in apparent silence, but the conversation was carried out through direct transmission to their hearing centres.

"Mickie," said Grant. "While you and the ladies are out, Allie and Mendorina will be observing what they can of the society, looking for signs of this new wave of religious extremism that the agents reported. You can play a very useful role here by using the new talents you've acquired. See what you can sense, try and identify anything that doesn't fit this age of technology and thinking. Are you okay with that?"

"Sure, dad!" Mickie was delighted to have his parents' trust and be able to help them in what was obviously a tricky task.

"So remember, if you talk to Allie or the others openly, do so in the very formal manner you've learned and try not to laugh!"

"Yes, dad!"

"And if you sense anything unusual, go to sub-vocal communications."

"No problems."

"Okay, go and have fun. See you all back at the hotel before tonight's festivities."

With that, Allie and Mickie went downstairs to meet Mendorina and Melkana to explore the town.

The smell hit them as they walked outside.

"Phew! What's the stink?" Melkana couldn't help herself and spoke the words openly. Luckily, there was nobody nearby.

"Careful, Melkana!" Her mother spoke sharply using sub-vocal speech. "It's horse droppings. When you have horses pulling carts and being used for personal transport, that's what you get all over the street. It's something we're all supposed to know, so make sure you don't reveal that sort of ignorance."

"Oops, sorry mother," said Melkana, also using the silent speech through the translator. Mickie was a little shaky, having been about to make the same mistake.

"Can I suggest you all request the computer to extend the sensitivity of your translators?" Allie said in Mickie's head. "That way, we can pick up other peoples' conversations from a greater distance and not appear to be eavesdropping."

Instructing Albert accordingly, Mickie followed the other women to what looked like a marketplace in the town square. He almost felt as if he were in a movie scene of Victorian England. All around him were people in long dresses or formal frock coats. The working people were dressed in heavy woollen clothing that looked most uncomfortable for manual labour on a hot day. Horses and carriages rattled all over the place and the smell of horses and horse dung was all-powerful. He realised he would have to tread very carefully as he narrowly avoided stepping in a very fresh pile. But he also realised he was enjoying himself enormously, being involved in his parents' work and taking part in a project that was highly important to them and to the Ship's crew. He just wished his other two friends could be with them, even though he knew how impossible that was.

As he followed along, he saw many children playing in the crowds and was struck by the fact that many did not cover their faces. After looking at as many as he could, he decided that the oldest was probably about ten. Although he saw others who were obviously children also, up to and including his own age of thirteen and possibly in their mid-teens, their faces were covered. He decided that the social rules made it okay for the younger ones to show their faces, but at some age, the custom of face veils took over. He checked his own and made sure it was secure.

He could hear numerous snippets of conversations around him, all sounding pretty well what he'd expect in a market scene and astonishingly similar to the conversations he could recall hearing in the supermarkets in his old home town in England.

"Poor old Margenta, her husband's sick and she's got those noisy kids to worry about, and one of them's missing school..."

"Did you see the way she had dressed those girls? I thought it was terrible..."

"Yes, he's doing well at school, though he finds geography a bit difficult..."

"I heard the Protector's coming to the dinner tonight. I hope we'll be alright..."

Whoops! What was that? Mickie woke up from his partial daydream and flickered his extended senses round the people nearby to catch that conversation. The word "Protector" was not anything that had arisen during his briefings on this world and something about it sounded like trouble. But after a few minutes he had failed to rediscover that conversation.

Something else happened instead. A shiver of anxiety ran through him. There was a presence... something or someone was watching him, he knew. He concentrated and sent his mind out into the crowd, checking each individual mind as he passed it. But he could identify nothing that was focused on him. And yet the sensation of being watched persisted.

"Allie, someone's watching us."

The reply was immediate, sent direct to his hearing centres and even though he knew nobody else could hear her voice, it seemed that Allie was standing by his right shoulder. "I'm quite certain we're being watched, Mickie. It's normal in a closed and rather primitive society that strangers would be watched."

"This is different, Allie. I can't find the mind that's doing it. And I heard someone talk about a Protector coming to the dinner tonight."

"A Protector? That's new. Baldorest, have you heard the term "Protector" before on this world?"

"Not to my knowledge, Alliandra. Who heard it?"

"Mickie did, but he can't catch the conversation again. And he's certain somebody is watching him."

"It would be natural to be watched. Stay calm, keep acting normally."

"Okay. Mickie, come and join the rest of us."

Mickie saw the other three women examining tapestries at a table a few metres away and casually moved back to them. The sense of being watched remained strong, but he could not reach out and identify the mind that was doing it.

He continued following the others as they examined market products and made the odd purchase and he kept listening in to conversations around him, but nothing else gave him any cause for concern and slowly his anxiety declined.

Three hours later, Baldorest contacted them through the computer.

"Hey, I've just picked up a reference to this Protector thing. It seems to be a new development and apparently this is a new position and there's one in every town. His role is to seek out unnatural conduct that may be deemed wicked and heretical. It sounds like the old witch hunters that several planets have experienced in their histories. We'd better all be extremely careful, even more so than we thought."

"Perhaps we should cancel the public dinner tonight?" Mendorina's tones radiated anxiety.

"That would only cause suspicion," replied Baldorest. "No, we have to be there, but we must be strict and watch out for everything we say. Have you detected any changes from your last visit, Alliandra?"

"There's no doubt that people are a lot more subdued," Allie said. "Much of the sense of fun has gone and they are far more reserved in their dealings with us. I've not encountered any hostility to strangers, but I think it's just below the surface."

"Okay, we'll all meet back at the hotel in two hours then go to the dinner which is being held where you are now, in the market square."

The next two hours passed for Mickie in a fairly boring manner as he tried to hear anything suspicious in nearby conversations, but nothing happened to cause further worries.

As they entered the town square again later that evening, it had changed a lot. Gone were the market stalls to be replaced by lines of tables and chairs, enough to seat several hundred. Lining the sides of the square were individual cooking stations from which wondrous aromas rose to fill the warm summer air. Mickie remembered the tales his friend's father had told him one day of his travels to Singapore and Malaysia and how this scene was common. Parking lots were transformed, the man said, into vast outdoor restaurants where you could take your pick of the foods on offer, then sit wherever you could, meeting many new people this way. Mickie had wistfully wondered if he would ever see such an exotic sight. He grinned happily to himself that tonight he was seeing such a sight, but his friend's father could never have envisaged how much further away from Singapore this scene was.

It reminded him, he had no idea where in the Universe, literally, he was, having forgotten to get his usual pre planet-fall briefing from Albert. He focused his mind and asked.

"Merrison is the third planet out from an "M"-type sun in the Greater Magellanic Cloud, the nearest galaxy to the one containing your old planet Earth," said Albert. "You are approximately 275,000 light years from Earth."

Mickie had become accustomed to the vast distances the Kaloti ships travelled, but he was still impressed.

As the group reached the square they were greeted by several people who obviously knew the two agents, Baldorest and Candrost and soon they were in the middle of introductions to a whole host of new people. When they sat down at a long table with several of the locals, Mickie was separated from immediate contact with any of his own people and found himself in a group of kids, mostly his own age, but some obviously younger, for they wore no face covering. The tables were already covered with plates of food, some looking familiar, but some not, and the flavours were intriguing.   Carefully, Mickie imitated his neighbours, taking one bite-sized portion at a time as the plates were passed around, slipping the item under his facemask and into his mouth. The conversations were easy, being mainly about the food, and any questions Mickie was asked he was able to handle well enough, telling the others about his parents' trading business and a little about the region that was supposed to be his home, getting silent prompts from Albert as he needed.

Now and again, he got a small probe from his parents or Melkana.

"Looks like you're enjoying yourself, youngster," Grant said at one point. "You're doing well!"

"Yes, this food is just great!" Mickie replied.

"You are just oinking out totally, Master Michael," came the teasing words from Melkana and Mickie was glad about the noise and his facemask as he laughed out loud at her comment.

And the dancing started. From nowhere it seemed, a squad of men and women filed out to the front of the square, perhaps twenty men and as many women. The women were dressed in long gowns quite different from the dull and dowdy style that Mickie had seen so far. They were multicoloured ball gowns, lots of frills and much gold and silver embroidery. The women had make-up on, also something new to Mickie on this planet. The men were dressed almost Spanish bullfighter style, jackets of many colours with sequins flashing in the mix of the bonfires around the square and the torches at all the tables. An orchestra struck up a pounding, exhilarating melody and Mickie looked round to see them on one side, almost hidden by the crowd standing there.

The dancing was wonderful. It was a group display, not individual couples dancing together, this was a well-drilled troupe where couples met and parted, where lines wove complex patterns, where some solo artistes performed for anything from a few seconds to several minutes. Mickie was quite entranced.

The first number ended to stamps and yells of approval from the diners. The subdued, sober and restrained atmosphere of the day had quite gone, replaced by an atmosphere of great enjoyment and relaxation.

The dancers took a break and a group of some thirty of so men and women formed into a semi-circle. Mickie saw no signal, but the group launched with perfect timing into a choral work that reminded him of the great Welsh choirs he had heard back on Earth. The harmony was beautiful and the melody was a haunting, lovely song that brought tears to his eyes. It ended, to be immediately replaced by a bouncing, lilting song in which the melody was woven through complex threads. Mickie tried to catch the number of parts, but gave up at nine and instead, he settled back in enormous enjoyment of the music, the colour, and the air of celebration that filled the town square.

But it all came to a crashing halt. From the darkness beyond the flame-lit square, a line of men appeared. All wore black robes with hoods over their heads. They strode through the crowd in an apparent rage, yelling incoherent shouts as they approached the orchestra. All the men carried heavy sticks and they proceeded to lash out at the players, hitting several of them with heavy blows, shattering some instruments. As the music stopped, so did the dancers who stood motionless.

"Oh God help us," a mutter came from Mickie's left. An elderly woman was standing in shock, tears running down her cheeks. "The Protector is here," she said. From points around the crowd, Mickie heard the same words.

"Mickie, Melkana! Gather round us," he heard in the direct transmission from Allie, and he quickly moved to join the adults, Melkana reaching them at the same time.

The black-robed men had advanced on the dancers, screaming with rage and lashing out with their heavy sticks. Several of the colourfully dressed men and women fell beneath the thumps of the clubs and Mickie saw blood on the faces of some of them.

"We have warned you!" bellowed one of the men. "We have told you this ungodly behaviour will not be tolerated! This music and dancing, this is evil before the sight of God!"

The rage in the voice was appalling. Mickie tried sensing the mind behind the voice but could detect nothing. Worried, he directed a query at his mother.

"Allie, I can't sense him, or any of the men in the robes. What's going on?"

"We don't know." Allie's voice echoed his anxiety. "This is obviously the Protector we heard about earlier, but we had no idea what to expect. Let's just all stay close and quiet and do nothing to attract attention."

The black-hooded speaker was still haranguing the crowd.

"There will be no more!" he raged. "We will not allow you to damn yourselves in God's eyes by this licence and debauchery. These evils come from outside and must be stopped. Tonight we come to stop it. Are you on God's side or that of the Devil? Answer me!"

"On God's side!" a few people shouted, rather timidly and it obviously irritated the speaker.

"There must be no doubts!" he screeched. "If I suspect doubts, then we will start to come among you with the rope and send the unbelievers to hell to rot with their Master, Satan. So, are you with Satan or with God?"

This time, the response was louder, the people around Mickie and his group shouting louder and the fervour in their voices was intense. Mickie began to feel a dreadful fear. Something horrible was happening and his fears were increased by the fact that he was unable to reach the minds of these frightening men in black robes.

The leader walked back to the frightened group of musicians who fell back as he approached. He seized one of the instruments, something a lot like a violin and strode to the nearest bonfire a few yards away.

"First the music must cease!" he roared and flung the violin into the flames. "All of them, to the fire!" he commanded and people followed with increasing eagerness, taking all the instruments and throwing them into the bonfires. The crowd was rapidly becoming a mob, and Mickie was not the only one to realise it.

"This is getting out of hand," Baldorest's voice sounded in his ears. "We're getting into a very dangerous situation. All of you, move as softly as you can, start heading to the nearest exit from the square. Walk backwards, keep your faces directed at those men, don't make it obvious you're moving."

There was a long way to go, at least fifty metres, Mickie estimated, but he moved close to his parents and slowly backed away from the table where they had been eating. Back at the centre, the rioting and destruction was getting worse. The mob turned on the dancers and Mickie heard dreadful screams as irrationally raging men and women turned on their fellow citizens whose dancing they had been enjoying just minutes before and began beating and kicking them viciously.

But worse was to come. The Protector's voice was heard again above the roars and the screams.

"The strangers bring these evils! They must pay for their heresy. Where are the strangers? Bring them to me!"

Mickie's group had moved about half way to the street leading out of the square, but they still had many people around them. The mob now encompassed the entire crowd and fury and hysteria could be felt in the air. Mickie's terror increased and he began to sense a build up within his body of the same dreadful rage and fear that he had experienced on the planet Kamotar when the terrorist group of Smegandri had advanced on him and his friends with obvious murder as their intention. Quite consciously he let it build, deciding that this might be the only way to save the people around him.

The mob turned in their direction and fingers pointed at them.

"The strangers! They are here! They are here!"

Mickie turned his eyes and focused on the man in the black robe who was the obvious leader and released his rage. It was almost like a sneeze, a violent paroxysm of fury that shot from him and went like a thunderbolt to the target. The man staggered, fell, but to Mickie's horror climbed back to his feet and raised his club at the sky.

"See the evil of Satan! They attack a man of God! Destroy the strangers!"

The crowd took up the chant. "Kill the strangers! Kill the strangers!"

Above the roar of the crowd, the Protector changed his shout and if Mickie had not been frightened before, he was doubly terrified now, because with the new call, a new and more deadly element affected the situation.

"Kill the Pfafth!" shrieked the Protector. "Kill the Pfafth!"

Mickie's mind reeled and a dreadful faintness seeped through his body. *"How do they know about the Pfafth?"* his mind kept echoing. And then he saw dark shadows that flickered in and out of the crowd, pools of blackness that absorbed the light of the torches. And as the mob became even louder with its screams of rage, he saw a tall black pillar of smoke that writhed furiously at the back of the crowd. He nearly fell, but was held up by his father. Vaguely, he heard several soft explosions behind him and sensed the movement of large shapes, but the fear was so overwhelming he couldn't identify the cause.

The crowd was advancing, bloodlust evident in the wide-eyed, raging faces of the people just a few yards away. The call of the Protectors had been taken up by the mob, and the loud chant of "Kill the Pfafth" was sounding from every area of the crowd. The madness in the eyes of the people who had been their companions just a few minutes earlier glared at Mickie like a searchlight.

And they stopped. The staring faces seemed to look behind Mickie and his party and the bloodlust changed to fear, such fear as it was almost impossible to imagine. Screams sounded from all around, and the people turned and began a panic-stricken scramble to move away as fast as they could.

"What the hell...?" Grant's voice was heavy with his own fear. Mickie turned and saw a most unbelievable sight. Just a few metres behind him were six of the massive Spiders. They moved toward the crowd and split up to pass Mickie's group, advancing further on the fleeing mob. People were falling and being trampled as others fought to escape. Mickie could see no sign of the Protector and his black-robed followers and the pillar of darkness had vanished.

"Now! Get away from here!" The familiar, icy, emotionless voice sounded in Mickie's mind.

"Straight to the horses!" Grant's command rang out firmly and the six adults and two children raced the two hundred metres to the hotel, into the stables and found their horses.

"There's no time to rig up the carriage," Grant snapped. "Just saddle up horses for the adults and we carry the kids. Go! I think those horrors will keep the mob at bay for a while."

A few minutes later, six horses raced out of the stables and onto the road leading to the shuttle. Mickie sat behind his father, clinging on for all he was worth, the first time he had ever sat on a horse, and the experience was not pleasant. Half an hour later, they stopped in the woods and Grant triggered the door opening in the cloaked shuttle. They trooped in, closed the door behind them and for the first time felt safe.

"I think we lift off now," said Grant with a surprising grin, and took a seat, closing his eyes in concentration.

"And you two had better come along," Allie said to the two agents. "This planet will be declared off limits for decades."

"Heaven knows what happened down there," Harrokarn said. "I'm not sure which baffles me most, the sudden riot brought on by those maniacs in black robes, or the appearance of the Spiders."

"And what the devil is a Pfafth?" Candrost asked. His question silenced the group.

"Who mentioned that word?" Allie asked, her face a little pale.

"The Protector," Candrost replied. "Suddenly he switched from calling for the crowd to kill the strangers to a demand to kill the Pfafth."

"Mickie, did you hear that?" Allie turned to Mickie.

"Yes, Candrost is right."

"So Pfafth means something?"

"We'll explain later, Candrost. But it makes this situation worse by the second. I think the most astounding thing though is that the Spiders appeared. And it's the second time. One appeared when Mickie was being attacked by a mob on Earth."

"But why? Apart from the mind-boggling aspect of *how*, why did they do it?" Baldorest was looking distressed. The after-shock of the terrible experience and the closeness with which they had all come to death was starting to work on them. Allie advanced to the food section and brought back a bottle of scotch and glasses for all. She poured out two large helping of the sparkling *Sle'Ach* drink for the kids who gulped them down fast and the six adults helped themselves to large slugs of the Earth liquor.

"We asked exactly the same questions when we realised that's what happened," Allie said. "But they came to save Mickie," she said.

The two agents stared at Mickie who tried to smile back.

"He's Pfafth," she added. "We'll explain all this after we've got back to the ship. How long, Grantorel?"

"Twelve minutes," Grant replied.

"Mickie, when the Protector stumbled and fell, was that you?" Allie continued, turning to Mickie.

"Yes. I couldn't help it."

"But it didn't do the sort of damage that it caused the Smegandri," she said thoughtfully. "And you couldn't sense the minds of any of those men." She was silent for a moment. "There was one thing that was really bothering me," she said eventually. "We all know that we're absolutely forbidden from revealing the presence of alien technology or concepts to pre-technological worlds and certainly from letting them know about life on other worlds. We caused a major calamity down there when the Spiders appeared. That legend will last for centuries, possibly millennia."

"You think the Protector and his crowd are off-worlders?" Harrokarn asked.

Allie nodded. "Without a doubt. Very evil, very powerful and quite alien to anything we have encountered before. And I think their presence has something to do with our son."

Mickie felt cold and began to tremble. "That black thing was there," he said. "It seemed to be driving the mob."

Allie quickly moved over and sat next to him, putting her arms round his shoulders. "Don't worry, Mickie. There are a lot of very powerful forces on our side too. You've already seen a few of them. They're just a start."

He felt Melkana's hand slip into his and he gripped it tight.

"Hey, with Drellion, Fencris and me around, there's *nothing* can hurt you," she said.

Mickie cheered up a little, despite the shock and poured refills of *Sle'Ach* for Melkana and himself.

Chapter 22 – The Council of the Zlan

"And now we return home to Kalamos," Allie told him as they breakfasted together in their quarters the morning after the escape from Merrison. "It's time you saw your new home world and learned to be part of it."

"How long is the trip?" Mickie asked.

"About two weeks," Grant answered. "We'll be taking a slow route as the Captain wants to make a couple of diversions for scientific research. He says there's a new sun forming and we'll stop and have a look at that from a safe distance and we have some supplies to drop off to an outpost watching a supernova develop."

"Anything I need to do in that time?" Mickie was hopeful that he could relax a bit from his brain-bending training sessions with the Speaker and spend more time with his friends.

Allie seemed to understand, and smiled. "Consider it school vacation," she said. "But some homework still! You should have just two more practice sessions with the Speaker and you should swot up a little on Kalamos, its history and its people."

"Okay! Can I go now? Melkana said we're all meeting in the hangar."

"Loopies calls, huh?" said Grant with an understanding grin. "Okay, kid, shove off!"

* * *

"Young Pfafth, it is time we talked."

The cold, emotionless voice entered Mickie's mind without warning as he prepared for sleep. For a second or two, he froze, his old reaction coming to the fore as he pictured the monstrous image of the creature speaking to him. He fought for control, telling himself that these nightmares were his allies and had saved his life twice.

"What is the problem that needs discussion?" he asked. "And if we are to talk, should I not have a name for you?" He felt proud of his self-composure.

"We are Zlan. Within our language, that is the name of the planet and of our species. You do not require individual names, as several of us are your contacts."

"Then I thank you, Zlan. You have saved my life on three occasions now."

"That is what we must discuss."

"Why?"

"Because we do not know why we did it."

The answer rocked Mickie back on his mental heels. "But you said that you had been ordered to protect me by the Pfafth!"

"That is true."

"Then how can you not know *why* you saved me?"

"Because we do not know who or where the Pfafth are. Not one of us has ever received a direct order, not one of us knows anything about the Pfafth."

Mickie felt disconnected from the world. The Zlan's words made no sense at all.

"But you called me Pfafth when you first trapped me," Mickie protested. "How did you know what I was?"

"We don't know. But the two who found you knew your nature. The survivor of that episode is unable to tell how."

Mickie remembered with sadness and embarrassment that one of the two spiders had been killed by his rescuers on that fearful moment that seemed to start his voyage of self-discovery.

"There is a second problem," the Zlan continued. *"Until that moment when we hit the Gelkka and let you escape, we did not know we had that ability. Nor did we know that we could monitor your activities across inter-galactic distances. And when one of us jumped to Earth, that was the first time we had ever made such a leap. We have always had that ability around our home world, but we had no idea that we could do it across hyperspace. We are baffled by these developments."*

Mickie's confusion grew even worse. "But what can I do to help you solve this mystery?"

"We want you to come here. We believe that if we can see you close up, talk to you again and examine you, we might be able to understand what is happening to us. On very rare occasions we hold a council of our greatest minds. We want you to come and talk to the Council of the Zlan."

Mickie got to his feet. He sensed the strength of the appeal and realised that he was being asked to help an entire species solve perhaps the biggest puzzle of its origins it had ever faced, as well as his own.

"I will be there," he said with pride.

The shuttle descended under the control of the Ship's computer, with Mickie the lone, silent occupant. The Zlan had given the designated landing spot to the computer, though nobody, not even Albert could explain just how they had done so.

"I have the coordinates," Albert had said. "But I don't know where they came from."

Mickie was disinclined to worry about that. He was about to step alone onto a planet that had frightened him more than any other place so far and he would encounter not just two, but possibly hundreds of the nightmare beasts called the Zlan. He rose to his feet and moved to the doorway as it slid open.

"I'm leaving the shuttle," he said aloud.

"Good luck, son," replied Grant from high in orbit in the Ship. "You know you'll be perfectly safe. Somehow, the Zlan are committed to protecting you."

Mickie walked outside, realizing he was in the middle of a huge natural auditorium perhaps fifty metres across, surrounded by a low ring of rising ground just a few metres high. At first sight, the ground of the hill looked black. But with a jolt of primitive terror, Mickie saw that the blackness was a solid crowd of the great Spiders. There were hundreds of them. Almost, he succumbed to the urge to race back inside the shuttle, but he forced himself to be calm and walk away from the shelter. He took a deep breath.

"Albert, return the shuttle," he said, and watched as the small craft lifted silently and raced upward to disappear in the pure blue sky. He was alone, surrounded by a mass of Humanity's worst nightmare.

"I have come," he said, realizing how inane his words must sound.

A small stir of movement ran round the mass of Spiders.

"And we understand how difficult this is for you, young Pfafth."

Mickie could have sworn he detected the tiniest trace of friendliness in the silent voice in his head. "Which of you is speaking?" he asked.

Off to his right, one of the monsters rose high on its rear legs and Mickie turned to face it. "It is easier for me to talk directly to one of you," he said.

"We understand."

"Then how do you think we can comprehend these weird events of recent months?" Mickie asked, starting to feel easier with each passing second. He sensed no hostility from the crowd of appalling creatures, possibly even the opposite.

Another spider rose up on its rear legs then returned. *"I was the one that first encountered you when you became caught in my web,"* it said.

Mickie turned to face the monster. "Then I owe you my gratitude," he said. "And also my deepest sorrow that we killed your mate in that episode. I was very young and we had no way of understanding what was going on."

"We understand that, also. But the fact is that until that moment, none of us had ever encountered the word "Pfafth." But I knew what you were, just as every one of us knows the same thing."

"That is certainly strange," said Mickie. "But why didn't you kill me, anyway? Merely knowing my species wasn't enough."

"I was about to," the Zlan replied, and Mickie felt a shudder run through his body. How close had he come to death?

"Every impulse was set," continued the Spider. *"But I froze, unable to make that jump and inject you. I knew*

as clearly as I know that we hunt for food, that you were a young Pfafth and our role was to protect you."

"I talked with people on my Ship and they say such a reflex can only result from deep psychological conditioning," Mickie said. He had spent hours discussing this situation with several experts on board in preparation for the meeting.

"This is our opinion, too. But you have seen our brain structure. Who could apply such conditioning to us?"

"Nobody that we know of," Mickie answered. "But you believe it was the Pfafth?"

"We know it absolutely. But it is beyond our comprehension how or when this occurred."

"How did you know about me on Earth?"

"Again, we have no idea. Just a few of us sensed your fear, and one of us jumped to Earth without having any comprehension of how he did it. After that, more of us discovered the ability."

"Tell me about the way you saved us on Mayoowani."

"All of us felt that tremor of your fear." The first Spider was speaking and Mickie turned back to face it. *"It shook every one of us over the whole planet. In just a few seconds, this Council decided to act and we directed energy at the Gelkka who were about to shoot you. But we had no prior knowledge that we could."*

"So how did you know where to aim your thoughts?"

"Again, we have no knowledge. The ability surfaced as we called for it."

"But you did not intervene on Kamotar when the Smegandri appeared."

"We were about to leap. But we saw the power building in you to unleash a mind bolt and we knew we could stay away."

"And on Merrison?" Mickie was becoming caught up in the whole question and the mystery of the Spiders and their astounding capabilities. He was rapidly losing all fear and discomfort in being surrounded by them.

"We suspect that the latent abilities were honed by the first episode," the Zlan replied. *"This time, a few of us teleported."*

"And saved us."

"Yes. It gave us great fulfillment."

Mickie began walking round the circle of the centre of the auditorium. He was now passing within just a few metres of the Spiders and he could see the multiple eyes staring at him. And he felt something else... slowly his empathic senses were starting to read the mind waves of these creatures... he could not identify just what the sensation was.

"And what did you do when you had completed these rescues? Did you try and work out what had happened?"

"Of course. With these brains, do you doubt that we exerted some very powerful attention to the problem?"

With a huge shock, Mickie realised the speaker was being sardonic. A sense of humour in a nightmarish monster like a Spider the size of a bus? He suppressed the laugh bubbling up inside him. This was just too serious for levity.

"And what did you discover?" he asked.

"That every one of us has this ability to teleport across intergalactic distances. We have always been able to jump like that around short distances on our own planet, but we had no idea of that scope."

"But yet, why did you leap to protect me?"

"*Because you are Pfafth.*"

"But *why?* And how did you recognize me?"

"*We think we have been developed for that purpose. This is a massive shock to us, because we are aware that our brain structure makes us perhaps the most intelligent species in the known universe.*"

"That is what we concluded when we did the...." Mickie stopped. It could not be courteous to talk about the autopsy done on the body of an individual whose partner was present. "It was the Pfafth who conditioned you in this way?"

"*We know it to be so, but that is disturbing, because the Pfafth vanished over a million years ago. And yet since that first encounter with you, each and every one of us knows with absolute certainty that we owe our abilities and powers to the Pfafth.*"

"And yet I am here. If I am truly Pfafth, and I was born just over twelve years ago, the Pfafth must be *somewhere.*"

"*You are truly Pfafth. We could not have known you otherwise. But as to the means of recognition of you, we still do not understand. So we have a request of you.*"

"What is that?"

"*We need a few of us to examine you.*"

This is what Mickie had been expecting and dreading after the small exchange with the Zlan a few nights before.

"I understand," he said, and stripped off his ship's tunic, standing only in his underwear. Immediately, three of the Zlan moved out of the crowd and approached him until they were just two metres away. They towered over him, so close he could smell the slightly acidic odour and clearly see the multiple eyes focused on him and the individual hairs on the beasts' legs. His breath came faster and he knew that the fear was about to overwhelm him again as trembles began all over his body.

"We understand your fear, young Pfafth," said the silent tones in his head. *"But you must realise this. We are here to protect you because you are Pfafth. If it is truly the Pfafth who have implanted this conditioning, do you not realise that you are the sole member of the race we still must hold as the Lords of the Universe, possibly even our Creators?"*

Mickie suddenly understood the nature of the emotions he was reading from the Zlan. It was awe. These frightful creatures regarded him almost with worship. And with that, the trembles vanished and he stood calmly as two Zlan extended limbs and gently touched his chest and shoulders and arms. A few seconds later, they withdrew.

"Now we understand," said one. *"There are minute but obvious patterns in your cell structure, your blood odour and your mental waves that to us identify you as Pfafth. And we must accept that our entire species is dedicated to just one cause, to protect Pfafth children all over the Universe. And you are the only one."*

Mickie slowly climbed back into his tunic as he let these words sink into him.

"It must be strange to have to accept this," he said. "You are an immensely powerful species, far more powerful than any we know of."

"And yet we must." Mickie was sure he detected a sombre note in the Zlan's words. *"Even if the Pfafth no longer existed, we must obey their orders. And we must*

also accept that those orders were placed so long ago that we have no recollection in our collective history of ever encountering those who gave them."

"Then when I have reached adulthood, you will be free of this commitment, unless my species appears again in the Universe," Mickie replied.

"It is possible. But as you said, you are a child. Somewhere the Pfafth must exist to have produced you."

"So you think they must be hidden so deeply that not even the Speakers can find a trace of them?"

"We do. Possibly in another Time or another Space."

"I don't understand how that could be."

"Nor do we, but if they could create us, they have powers beyond imagining. We have one last request of you."

"What is that?"

"Now that you understand that the Zlan exist to protect the Pfafth, you will see that for almost all of us, we can do nothing to fulfill our destiny and that is painful. So we ask you to stay here tonight before returning to your ship. At least that way, we can all play a part in protecting you, if only for a short period."

All of Mickie's remaining fears vanished at that point. For another few hours he wandered freely among the crowd of massive spiders, feeling no terror or discomfort, realizing he was among possibly his greatest allies. And as night fell, he settled comfortably on the soft ground and slept peacefully, closely surrounded by the hundreds of creatures who would normally be the most terrifying nightmare for any human being.

Chapter 23. Echoes of an Ancient War

Mickie spent the morning in a spirited session of Loopies with his three friends, followed by a rare classroom meeting of some twenty other children of his own age group. All three species represented in the crew were present, except for the Kaloti who had no children with them, and the class was a group discussion about life on all three home planets. Mickie found it absorbing, but so much of the topic was completely unknown to him that he felt overwhelmed by how much he still had to learn about his fellow citizens of this Universe he had joined.

By late afternoon, he was three hours into an intensive learning session on the subject with Albert, looking at many aspects of life on the home planets of the crew members.

"When will we get to Kalamos?" Mickie felt a strong feeling of wishing to see his parents' home world and learn to be part of it.

"Planet-fall is scheduled in 156 hours" Albert replied.

Mickie decided that the best part of his trip was still to come, and reaching a home he had never seen was the greatest idea of all time.

"And what about Cassolea?"

The computer projected a holographic image of the planet of Cassolea and began to describe the major cities.

"The world capital is Semandor," Albert intoned. "It was built for that purpose, as a government city when all nations of Cassolea joined as a unified planet over four hundred..."

Albert's voice ceased. Astonished, Mickie sat up from his comfortable position in his armchair.

"Albert? What's happened?"

There was no reply.

Puzzled but not yet worried, Mickie tried to call his parents. When silence greeted his call, he decided it was time to worry. He rose to his feet and walked out of his cabin to enter his parents' room, but as his door opened, he learned that the situation was about as bad as it could be.

A voice rang through the corridor. It echoed back in his cabin and Mickie realised it must be audible throughout the Ship. Somehow, the lights in the corridor had dimmed significantly as if drained by some unknown force.

"All life is mine!" The voice was a hiss of appalling fury and hatred and Mickie knew he had heard it before.

The pillar of smoke had returned.

"I will find the Pfafth in time, but I can start with the one on this vessel. You will regret saving it."

The door to his parents' cabin opened and Allie and Grant appeared. Their faces displayed the same shock and worry that Mickie was feeling. Mickie ran to them, feeling better for their closeness.

"This is the thing that appeared in your cabin?" Grant asked.

Mickie nodded, needing to swallow before he could speak. "And that's what it said the last time," he whispered.

"It seems to have suppressed all communications," Allie said. "I've tried contacting people on the ship, but internal radio is blocked and the computers aren't responding. And I tried calling the Speaker, but that doesn't work either."

"We'd better get to the observation lounge and meet everyone else," Grant said. "But if the computers are blocked, the translation devices won't be working. This is going to be tricky."

Mickie realised what he meant as they reached the huge observation lounge where a large proportion of the crew had gathered. He saw Melkana and Drellion standing with their parents and walked up to them.

"This is bad news," he said softly and then realised the magnitude of the problem. They shook their heads and said something completely unintelligible. Without the communication devices in their shoulders, they had no common language at all. He took one hand of each of them. "I'm sorry to be the cause of this," he said. "We'll work something out." He saw tears in Melkana's eyes and knew she understood what he had been trying to express. A few metres away he saw Fencris watching the scene and they expressed shrugs of helplessness, knowing there was no point in trying to exchange words.

He went back to his parents. As far as he knew, they were the only people on the ship who spoke an Earth language and the only ones he could talk to. They were deep in conversation with another Kalamosian couple, but they turned to him as he reached them.

"Each species can only talk with others of the same species," Allie said. "Remember what I told you before you got here the first time, it's almost impossible for one species to learn the language of another and now we're stuck with the problem. It means we can't join forces and share ideas of how to tackle this thing. I imagine the Kaloti are staying on the flight deck to see what they can do, so we won't see them here."

Mickie looked around and sensed the fear that was almost palpable throughout the lounge. It grew far worse as a pool of blackness materialised in the middle of the area. The blackness swirled and began to grow into the same black pillar that he had seen in his cabin and on the planet of Merrison. Throughout the lounge, people backed away from the evil shape until everyone was against the walls, their faces reflecting the same fear that Mickie held inside him.

"I have been away too long," the awful voice hissed. *"But now it is time for me to reclaim what is mine. Your lives are mine and you have served me by finding this Pfafth who hides among you."*

The pillar swept away from the middle of the lounge and moved to where Mickie and his parents were standing. It loomed over all of them then seemed to bend over Mickie's head and the white face with huge oval eyes appeared fleetingly, the laugh of triumph flashing before vanishing behind the black smoke again.

"You, Pfafth child, I will keep until you have led me to the rest of your kind so I can feast at will. But now I will eat."

The shape moved away and rapidly circled the room, seeming to examine every individual in turn before stopping before a trio of X'Kasxi crewmen. The pillar of black smoke started to rotate, occasional wisps of blackness flying off the main body and vanishing a short distance away from it. The white face flickered in and out of sight, the eyes seeming to grow with each appearance, and then the base of the pillar started to expand while the whole shape moved closer to the three X'Kasxi who seemed frozen and incapable of movement. The base expanded even further until it reached the legs of the three men and enveloped them up to the waist. The effect was horrible to see. All three let out a simultaneous hiss of pain and went rigid, their eyes widening to their full extent. Then they collapsed into the blackness and for a moment, disappeared. The smoke pillar slowed its rotation and the enlarged base returned to the same width as the rest of the shape. As it did, the bodies of the X'Kasxi appeared. But they had shrunken, as if all the material inside the leathery skin had been depleted and the skin itself had turned a light grey colour.

A wave of horror swept through the lounge and Mickie felt sick to his stomach. The black shape returned to the centre of the lounge.

"That is what lies ahead for all the Pfafth," came the monstrous hiss. *"But I can eat the souls of any of you."*

With a flicker of movement, it suddenly shot across to the group of Kalamosians where Melkana and Drellion were standing with their parents. The pillar rotated faster and it towered over the two children who shrank against their parents, trembling. For a second or two the white face appeared, the glee evident in the laughing mouth then it vanished again behind the curtain of smoke. Mickie felt a shriek of fear that the thing was about to eat his friends, but it withdrew back to the centre, leaving him sweaty with hatred for this awful being.

Somehow, the black pillar seemed to withdraw into itself and Mickie sensed that the thing had turned its attention away from the people. His mind started to clear and he began to think fast.

"Allie, Grant, when that thing spoke, did you understand it?"

His parents looked down at him, puzzlement in their faces. "Yes, of course we did," Grant replied for both of them.

"And did all the other Kalamosians?"

"Ah, I see," Allie said, realisation of the point coming to her. "And as the Cassoleans and X'Kasxi also understood, it means it was speaking telepathically."

"So not all telepathic bands are blocked," Grant added. "Does that mean...?"

"I don't know," Mickie said. "I'll try."

He took a seat, closed his eyes and concentrated hard to make contact with the Zlan. But nothing worked. Despite all his efforts, he still sensed the blanket effect over the room that blocked all communications. After ten minutes, a sick sense of defeat enveloping him, he had to give up and he shook his head at his parents.

Slowly, people began to move as they all sensed that the smoke pillar had withdrawn its attention for now, at least. Somebody draped covers over the bodies of the X'Kasxi and carried them from the room and people began to move away back to their own cabins, but the sense of fear remained tangible in the air.

Grant and Allie stayed in the lounge, talking softly with a group of other Kalamosians. It frustrated and alarmed Mickie to hear the conversation without being able to understand a single word. He resolved that if he ever got out of this situation, he would learn the language of his adopted world, for Allie had said that the similarities between humans and Kalamosians were so great that language development had followed similar paths and one race could learn to speak the language of both, just as Allie and Grant spoke English with no obvious difficulties, though they had not been able to master the tongues of Cassolea or any other alien race.

He watched the group and realised something was being developed. At one stage, four of the group left the lounge and two of the women walked across the room and approached a group of Cassoleans holding similar discussions. Pens and paper were produced and they seemed to hold a debate using sign language to understand each other. . Several Cassoleans left the lounge.

He moved to his parents. "What's going on?" he asked.

"That thing seems able to read your mind," Allie replied. "We don't know if it can read other people, but we have to take that chance. So we're keeping you out of the loop in case it decides to look into you and learn what's happening. Go away and keep trying to contact the Zlan."

Understanding the problem, Mickie walked away to sit in isolation by one window. Feeling loneliness and fear, he forced his mind to keep working on the problem of making contact with the outside and somehow summoning help.

Nothing worked.

Some hours passed. Not all the Ship's computer functions had been suppressed, it appeared, for food production continued and the crewmembers were able to get an evening meal, but when that was over, some gathered back in the observation lounge, seeking comfort from the community, even with the grim, black presence of the smoky entity.

As people entered, Mickie noted that several exchanged glances with Allie and Grant, seeming to confirm some secret process.

An hour after the meal, the lights in the lounge dimmed as if drained by some power source and the black pillar of smoke stirred. A current of fear ran through the room and all faces turned to the fearsome shadow. The pillar began to rotate and smoke rose from the base, spiralled up the pillar and was sucked down again at the top. Of all the strange life forms Mickie had encountered in his travels, he decided this thing was the weirdest and least pleasant of all.

The pillar did not speak. It remained in the centre of the room, the rate of rotation occasionally increasing and then falling back, and the white face did not appear. Few people spoke around the room, most just stayed close within their groups.

"*I have allowed the Ship to resume its voyage.*" The ugly voice suddenly sounded from the centre of the room. Faces turned to it, and then to the windows as the sounds of the engines began to increase in power. The Ship was in motion again and for the next few moments, most people watched the process of the Universe gather itself and vanish in a pinpoint of light as the Ship reached light speed and entered hyperspace.

"*I shall take control of all life on the planet when we arrive.*"

That's Kalamos, Mickie realised. The idea was too

horrible for words. Out of the corner of his eye, he saw Grant nod a signal. From within groups of both Kalamosians and Cassoleans, several people reached inside their tunics and brought forth musical instruments. All of them were small, Mickie saw, most seemed to be flutes or similar instruments, but at a second nod from Grant, they began playing in unison. After an astonished few seconds, Mickie realised they weren't really in unison at all. Some were even playing a different melody from the main group and the sound was pretty terrible. It had some effect but not the desired one.

From the black pillar of smoke, a scream of rage arose.

"You think I will succumb to that trick again?"

The pillar spun fast and faster and the base began to expand as it had when the three X'Kasxi crewmen had died. A stream of blackness suddenly shot out of the broadened base and snatched a single one of the Cassolean players. He had no time for anything but a short cry of fear before he vanished into the smoke.

From the crowd in the area, sounds of weeping broke out in several areas and people moved against the walls of the lounge as if to try and escape from the awful sight. A few moments later, the shrunken body of the Cassolean was flung out and lay motionless on the floor. Mickie saw that the man's face had been drained of its normal blue colour and was now an ugly, faded grey, like ancient parchment.

After a few minutes, a few courageous people advanced on the body with a blanket, covered it up and pulled it away, taking it out of the lounge.

"Do not believe that I can be caught that way again," the awful hiss spoke again. *"Do you think I am so stupid that I cannot protect myself?"*

"That seems to have removed our last weapon," Allie murmured. "I hope the Captain decides not to let the Ship reach Kalamos."

"I'm sure he'll make the obvious choice," Grant said and took her hand. "We've had a pretty good time these last few years, my love."

"We have." Tears were running down her face and she moved to rest her head on his shoulder

Mickie didn't have to think hard to understand what they were saying.

"He can destroy the Ship?" he asked, a deep sense of horror running through his body. "Even with the communications suppressed like this?"

But Grant didn't reply. He seemed to have retreated from the conversation and was lost in thought. His isolation reminded Mickie of the first time had seen Grant do this as he piloted the shuttle away from Earth. He could do nothing but try and hide his fear and just sat silently with his parents, taking comfort from their presence.

In the centre of the lounge, the black pillar seemed to have done the same as Grant. It was rotating slowly, no sign of the white face and it appeared to be paying no attention to any movements or conversations.

All around the lounge, people were slowly rising to their feet and moving out, most of them to resume whatever duties they had, perhaps hoping to take their minds away from what was happening.

Mickie decided to stand also, and cautiously advanced on the ugly black shape. It ignored him as he carefully walked around it, studying the pillar from all directions. He learned nothing.

A small rattle sounded from the walls of the lounge. He looked around but saw nothing moving and decided it must just be the sound of ventilation or circulation machinery.

"Go back!"

The shout came from the pillar of smoke and Mickie jumped. He took a deep breath and moved back to where Allie and Grant were sitting. Allie had sat up and was studying her husband curiously. Grant was still in his isolated, silent trance. Mickie looked at Allie, raised his eyebrows in a silent question, but she just shook her head, as puzzled as Mickie was.

The rattle came once more from the walls, but again, Mickie could not identify the source or identity of the sounds. He resumed his seat beside the distant Grant and tried to cover his fear of what might happen. Could the Captain cause the Ship to destroy itself and everything within it? Grant seemed sure he could, even with all the computer functions suppressed by the entity. If so, when would he do it? Mickie tried to steel himself to the possibility that at any moment, the entire ship and its crew could be blasted into atoms.

For two hours he sat still, his body aching. Now and again, he heard the mysterious rattle in the walls and after a while gave up trying to understand what the sound could be.

Next time, Grant stirred, stretched and sat up straight. He put one arm round Allie's shoulders and kissed her forehead. Then his other arm went round Mickie.

"One more try," he said softly. "This one should work."

Puzzled, but hearted by Grant's words, Mickie sat up straight and looked around, but nothing new was happening. Then he heard a soft, musical warbling that seemed familiar but he could not immediately identify.

Around the lounge, people were stirring, looking equally puzzled as the warbling increased in volume.

"Everybody, stay down!" Grant shouted, showing a sudden authority that he had never displayed before and it worked, for nobody in the area stood up.

Around the tops of the walls of the lounge, dark patches appeared at several locations as if something was burning through from the other side. And that was exactly what was happening. The patches opened up and small metallic nozzles appeared as the warbling sound became louder. Mickie remembered what the sound was. He had heard it as the laser vibrators shook the mountain of rocks into almost liquid form. How they had appeared in the lounge was beyond him, but here they were, all pointing at the dreadful black pillar in the middle.

"Stop that! You must not..."

The words were garbled into a terrifying howl of agony and the pillar stretched to the ceiling, bending over at the middle just as a man would double up in severe pain. It began to spin violently, small puffs rapidly being blown away and vanishing, and the top half the pillar bent even further over, the white face flashing in and out of cover, the mouth open in a continual howl of pure agony. Suddenly, the smoke gathered itself and sank into the floor. The pool of blackness span rapidly like water going down a drain and it vanished within another second or two.

In dead silence, Grant rose to his feet and walked over to where the creature had been. He bet over and touched the carpet, rubbing gently and stood up again, examining his fingers. There seemed to be a pale, grey powder on them. Carefully, he wiped his fingers on his handkerchief.

"Let's get this analysed, eh?" he said. He looked up at the silent faces staring at him. "It was obvious this thing had a problem with vibration and musical pitch, because on a previous occasion, music had driven it away. Clearly, it had learned to insulate itself against musical sounds, but I was pretty certain it couldn't cope with the lasers."

"But how did you...." Although deep in shock, one of the people nearby worked up the composure to ask the obvious question.

"I found a gap in the suppressor," Grant said. "The devices we have inside our bodies for piloting the shuttles were operating on a wave length that seemed immune. Because of my job, I have some basic control of the lasers, just enough to switch them on and off. I started doing that, very quickly, and the engineers in the mineral processing bay soon caught on to what I was trying to tell them. They started slowly moving them up here through the ventilation shafts. They're pretty small and it wasn't hard."

Mickie realised he had heard and understood what the questioner had said, as well as Grant's response, both spoken in Kalamosian. The computers were back on line.

"That is one terrifying entity," Allie said as Grant walked back to her. "The fact that it can suppress telepathic communications as well as the Ship's radio and other functions is pretty scary. I've just talked to the Speakers and they have no idea what that thing was."

"Whatever it was, it seems dedicated to killing me," Mickie said, realising that his whole body was shaking with the relief of the disappearance of the murderous black pillar.

"It's obviously something connected to the Pfafth history and disappearance," Allie said in agreement. "All in all, we've learned a great deal about your history and origins, Mickie. And whatever that thing is…"

"It said it was seeking Mickie's people." Grant said.

"So the Pfafth do exist somewhere," Allie mused. "That seems to prove it."

A small silence hung over the group as each of them absorbed the thought in their own way.

Allie suddenly moved back to where the entity had been. She stooped and picked up something from the carpet. She examined it as she walked back to Grant and Mickie.

"What do you suppose this is?" she asked.

Grant took it and held it in his open palm. It was about the size of his thumbnail, shaped like a small pear drop and deep blue with fine golden lines on the surface.

"Looks like some sort of earring perhaps?" Grant suggested.

"I doubt it," Allie replied. "There's no sign of any connection to hang it with and it's heavy, too heavy for an earring."

"Could it be something that thing was carrying?" Mickie asked, staring with fascination at the mysterious but beautiful object.

"Possibly," Grant murmured, also fascinated by it. "I'll pass it to the laboratory, see if they can make anything of it." He put the small object away and seemed to shake off the terror of the last few hours.

"Mickie," he said. "There's little we can do about it now. That thing has gone and now we know we have a weapon against it, it's unlikely to come back. But we have learned a lot about you and we have a long time to find out the rest. We've got years, in fact." He nodded in the direction behind Mickie. "And I think you've got much better things to occupy you in the couple of days before we get home."

Mickie turned to see Melkana, Drellion and Fencris approaching.

"That thing has really gone?" Melkana asked, her face pale.

"It has," Grant said. "I suppose we have to worry about if there are more of them, but least we can do something about them if another one appears."

"Hey, I'm glad we can talk to each other again, Mickie," Fencris said with a wide grin. "You don't make a lot of sense most of the time anyway, but making no sense at all was pretty uncool!" He seemed unaffected by the horrors.

The relief of the moment and the return to normality hit Mickie like a heavy surf, and he collapsed into a convenient armchair, laughing uncontrollably. With understanding smiles, the adults left, leaving the four children to resume their friendship.

* * *

He sat in the observation lounge with his friends and once more watched the Universe explode into being around the ship. Yet again, it left him feeling breathless.

"Albert, how long to Kalamos?"

"The Captain has timed it beautifully. We will be in orbit in under thirty minutes."

"Don't you mean *you* timed it beautifully?" said Melkana with a gurgle of amusement.

"I am a very modest computer, Melkana," replied Albert, and Mickie stared in astonishment. This was the first real sign of humour he had seen in Albert and he wondered if Albert and Melkana had established a different style of relationship from his own.

But the excitement of arriving at his new home planet over-rode any puzzlement he might be feeling and he stood by the huge windows with the others waiting for Kalamos to grow in the distance.

Smoothly, the tiny spark in the dark space ahead grew into a planet and Mickie could soon identify the continents that he had first seen on the holographic image in his cabin. Exactly thirty minutes after re-entering normal space, they were orbiting the planet and Mickie finally looked down on the continent of Benarth.

"Where's home?" he asked.

Melkana pointed to the south-eastern corner where a city could be seen under clear skies, coming closer to them as their orbit took them overhead.

"Molenstrom," she said, her eyes bright and the eagerness obvious in her voice.

Mickie looked down intently and saw a city that looked like concentric circles, a lake in the center and a huge river winding its way from the lake to the coast.

"It's all circles," he said.

"Yes, it is. It's a lovely city. We can take boats out on the lake and swim and all sorts of stuff!" Mickie looked sideways at her and saw how happy she seemed to be at going home.

"Where do you live?" he asked.

"Up there in the north-east quadrant," she said. "See those hills..." she pointed at a green line that cut across some of the rings in one quarter. "We live just near those. And your parents are only two kilometres away."

"It's beautiful, Mickie. You're going to love it!" Drellion was like his sister, animatedly staring down at the city.

"I know I am," said Mickie. "A month with you guys is going to be the best time ever. I wish you were coming with us, Fencris."

"I'd like that, too," Fencris replied. "But I haven't seen Cassolea for a year and a man needs to get home now and again. We'll all catch up when this leave is over."

"And heaven knows what trouble this young Pfafth is going to get us into on the next voyage," Melkana said with a straight face.

They all laughed and Mickie turned back to study his new home. For now, learning about himself and his origins could wait, he decided.

www.ingramcontent.com/pod-product-compliance
Lightning Source LLC
Chambersburg PA
CBHW060153260626
47160CB00001B/251